152

Nightmare and Dawn

Novels by Mark Aldanov

THE NINTH THERMIDOR

THE DEVIL'S BRIDGE

ST. HELENA, LITTLE ISLAND

FOR THEE THE BEST

THE FIFTH SEAL

THE ESCAPE

TO LIVE AS WE WISH

BEFORE THE DELUGE

NIGHTMARE AND DAWN

Nightmare and Dawn

by MARK ALDANOV

Translated by JOEL CARMICHAEL

DUELL, SLOAN AND PEARCE

New York

MANUFACTURED IN THE UNITED STATES OF AMERICA

VAN REES PRESS • NEW YORK

Nightmare and Dawn

1

THE house was one of those new ones that had just been built in a western sector of Berlin with the assistance of various profusely initialed organizations, such as DGB or BauGeMa, and with Marshall Plan funds. Schell's flat was small, just two rooms. A Venetian chandelier lighted the study, which had a great many books in it and two pictures—not bad, in a way, thought the colonel, arranging his cards, though without the signatures you couldn't tell what they were; an old-fashioned clock with little figures on it—something mythological?—and a little sideboard of carved wood with china in it. Not in the least like the study of a famous spy; on the other hand, he's just as he should be. A good player, but not unusual; for that matter I'm playing just as well myself.

"I've got three of a kind, kings," said Schell, showing his cards.

"Four jacks," replied the colonel. "You're out of luck. I've heard that during the past month you've lost practically forty thousand marks in the Berlin gambling houses."

"Your friends are well informed," said Schell, looking as though he were stifling a yawn. "But for today we've really had enough."

He took out his wallet and counted out some bills. "I think that's right, but please count it. I may have made a mistake."

The colonel put the money in his pocket without counting it. "That last hand did you in."

"The same thing once happened to Louis the Fourteenth. His Majesty didn't like losing; he often cheated, and when he lost would get out of paying by some joke. At that time they used to play a game something like our poker. The stakes were huge and the king lost. He didn't feel much like paying and said to the winner, 'I have three kings, but if you include myself that makes four. I win.' 'Your Majesty has lost,' replied the courtier with *sang-froid*. 'I have four courtiers.' You know, jacks," explained Schell, " 'but if you include me that makes five.' "

"I should think that at that time practically everyone cheated."

"It happens now, too. It's not hard. If you like, I'll show you how simple it is," said Schell. He gathered the cards together, shuffled them for a long time, and dealt. This time the colonel got the three kings and Schell the four jacks.

"I never knew you had that talent, too," said the colonel, laughing, but a little annoyed nevertheless. "You might put it to good use."

"Not for anything. All my life I've played cards honestly.... Would you like a snack? I've got something here."

"That depends a little on just what you have. On the other hand, I don't need much. Just give me lobster thermidor, pheasant, *crêpes Suzette*, a bottle of champagne, and I'll be satisfied."

"That, unfortunately, I can't offer you, but I have got some beer, cheese, and some of those countless German sausages:

4

weisswurst, bockwurst, knockwurst, leberwurst, and rothwurst. Only a little while ago I still had an old Johannisberger, to my mind the best white wine in the world. In 1948, when Germany was down and out, I got hold of two dozen bottles for ten packages of Chesterfields. It was sold either by Prince Metternich, the owner of the Johannisberg vineyards, or someone who had stolen the bottles from the prince: at that time it was hard to pick and choose. Now don't say, 'Aren't you ashamed of yourself, buying something like that!' I'm not particularly squeamish," said Schell.

He was lolling about in the easy chair with one leg flung over the other. There was an expression on his face of thorough-going satisfaction with life. The personification of idleness— and as though you couldn't see through it! He's probably lost the last of his money and is desperate, thought the colonel, who never played Sherlock Holmes but was always extremely observant, especially when hiring new and important agents; he tried to draw conclusions about them, though in contrast to Sherlock Holmes he never had the slightest confidence in their accuracy: he had been mistaken too often. He's very well dressed, the colonel went on musing to himself, though only a man some ten years younger should dress that way. As I recall he's forty-two. He's probably one of those people who say that a man should get his clothes either from two or three of the finest tailors in the world or else from an old-clothesman. His suit looks English, but it couldn't have been made in England, they haven't got such good cloth now. And not in the United States. . . . His shoes have built-up heels—very strange with his gigantic size. Can he want to hypnotize people with his height? If so, he's a *poseur:* not so good.

The colonel himself was dressed in expensive mufti, which he wore carelessly; the trousers weren't pressed. The colonel's young nephew, Jim, said that his uncle's carelessness was intentional and highly personal. "You're following Churchill's example, Uncle. His hat is as calculated as his politics."

"But what am I supposed to be calculating for?"

5

"And what is Winnie calculating for? Both of you are old-fashioned. But don't be upset," Jim went on. "As an old soldier not much is demanded of you. Eisenhower thinks he can wear civilian clothes, and Eden must get a big laugh out of looking at him, just as Ike would laugh at Eden if he saw him in a uniform. I'm really the only one around who's equally elegant both in uniform and in mufti."

"You really are a damned fool, Jimmie," said the colonel.

That was how their conversations generally ended.

"Just let me have whatever there is. When there's no Johannisberger, beer must be drunk; when there's no lobster thermidor, sausages must be eaten. That's my philosophy of life."

"Not a blaze of originality," said Schell, "but absolutely right." He was also "observing." What a lot of them I've seen! And it's time to get down to business. . . . Some of them do a Napoleon act, as though they never had a second free, and talk in Napoleonic tones—clipped, staccato. This one isn't like that. Schell liked the colonel, both because he was very simple and polite, even affable, and because he had come to visit him at home, eating and playing cards with him without behaving like a future commanding officer. His looks are skillfully deceptive, Schell thought. He looks like an old country doctor who treats poor patients and goes on bringing them medicines. Kindness, benevolence, and imperturbable tranquillity: everything in the world is going along splendidly. "Take it easy, don't worry. . . ." That's the great strength of the Americans, that's why they're the most powerful people in the world. . . . Gray hair, youthful-looking face, but the cheeks a little flabby already, with red veins. He may easily be the greatest expert in espionage I've ever known. What dramas must have passed through his hands!

"I'll bring along whatever I find right away," Schell said, and got up. He exits like Errol Flynn, thought the colonel.

There was a cello in one corner of the room. The colonel got up and walked over to the bookshelves. So he's one of the intelligentsia, after all! The colonel rather disliked the word, which

6

had started in Russia somehow or other and been taken up by English-speaking countries with scarcely any change in meaning. Freud ... Jung ... They say he once had a nervous breakdown for a while; that leaves some effect even after you recover. Is it still worth getting tied up with him? I'll have to wait and see.

There were some classics on the shelves, but also cheap detective stories. Hmm. Judge a man by his books. . . . I've seen agents like that, too, who weren't such great shakes either, for that matter. . . . The china is very good, tricolored Ming! But it's obvious there was a lot of money around, or else, of course, that he bought it here right after the war.

The colonel knew something about china. As a young man he himself had collected china, principally old American. He had bought a little property in Connecticut, a country house, out of his savings, and almost never lived there: he intended to move into it after his retirement. Although he liked country life, the idea of retiring after he reached the age was a nightmare to him anyhow; he couldn't see what he would do out of service and how he would occupy the twenty-four hours of the day. He was unusually attached to his work and never went in for the conventional groaning about it.

Aside from the china the room was full of a great many other small, contrived, and mostly exotic objects—on the bookcases, on the little table, and on the desk: little boxes, caskets, tower clocks, snuffboxes, little bottles, candlesticks. Several were beautiful and all of them were decidedly useless—the sort of thing bought by nervous travelers, not too well-to-do but openhanded, thought the colonel. In the other corner of the study, opposite the cello, stood a cabinet containing dumbbells. The colonel tried one of them and could scarcely lift it, although he was very powerful himself and in his youth had been something of an athlete. From what one hears he was a real Hercules; for that matter, you can see it now, too. . . . I can see my collection of human specimens is going to be increased by one more curiosity. He's probably going to ask for a lot of money. On the

7

other hand, that last affair of his in Belgium didn't come off; after that he ought to lower his rates somewhat.

"I see you've got a lot of books in foreign languages," he said when Schell returned with the tray.

"I used to like reading; now I'm slowly learning to forget it. It's no satisfaction any longer."

"Really? I said 'foreign languages,' but actually which languages are foreign to you? I suppose you're Russian by origin?"

"No."

"No?" The colonel lingered over the word unbelievingly. "Well, if you say so. You talk English almost like an American."

"I talk French almost like a Frenchman and German almost like a German. But that 'almost' is a dangerous business; a great many foreign spies in Russia must have come to a bad end because they spoke Russian 'almost' like Russians. I've turned up another bottle of vodka. Would you like some?"

"And why not? You may not be Russian but your tastes are."

"Vodka is drunk all over the world. There's nothing better, unless you count champagne."

Schell took off a ring with some sort of rare greenish stone, gave the bottom of the bottle a sharp blow, and the cork flew off. The colonel had never seen this done before and smiled. The ring must be some sort of good-luck piece, they're nearly all superstitious. And what strangler's hands! And those eyebrows joined together. . . .

They started drinking and eating. Schell took a small cylinder out of his waistcoat pocket, poured some powder into a glass of beer, and drank it down.

"Have you stomach trouble? Or a cold?"

"That's it. A slight fever."

"Have you had it long? When I have a cold I just take some good old aspirin."

"No, this is an exotic drug."

"Exotic?"

"Mexican. Mexico has wonderful medicines, still there since the days of the Aztecs."

8

"I heard you went to Mexico a little while ago. On business?"

"Yes, business, too. The principal ingredient is *ololiukvi*, called *La Señorita* colloquially, and scientifically, I think, *Turbina corymbosa*. But various other things go into it, too. It's also a soporific or something like it. It brings you sleep, together with visions. It's not really even a sleep, but a sort of *real* trance or delirium. You can hardly distinguish it from actuality. Sometimes, when in this trance, I see a man as though he were alive; I imagine his past, his character, habits, and thoughts. The secret as well as the open ones. It's sometimes been useful to me in my work. After all, I'm a psychologist spy. For that matter, what is delirium? In our world everything is delirium."

"I doubt it very much. And I can't quite imagine what a 'real' delirium is. My own dreams are always completely nonsensical. Last week I dreamed that Wild Bill took two million marks away from the Prophet Jeremiah at poker and brought the money to the Deutsche Bank, where it was immediately confiscated as non-Aryan property."

"Well, of course that's not the sort of dream I would call realistic. But who is Wild Bill?"

"Don't tell me you don't know? That was the nickname of General William Donovan, who was in charge of our counterespionage during the last war. Didn't you ever meet him? A very able fellow, even though a dilettante. He would have accomplished a lot more if he hadn't been detested by the army, navy, air force, and police unanimously. . . . So there's such a thing as a realistic delirium?"

"I myself never believed it before. Now I not only believe it, I know it. More correctly it's not realistic through and through, but alternating. The real turns imperceptibly into the fantastic, and the fantastic into something completely real. That's the special characteristic of *ololiukvi*. I've read about it in medical journals, but also know it from experience. I've given it a thorough tryout."

"But why do you do it? It's very harmful," said the colonel,

9

perplexed, actually almost disturbed. "What's the good of it?"

"What d'you mean, 'What's the good?' *You* have only one life, but aside from real life I have a dozen imaginary ones. After all, imagination makes the world go round."

"In our business it's impossible to use things like that," said the colonel severely. "The stuff may be just the same as opium or hashish. . . . So you were in Mexico on business, too? . . . What passport do you have, by the way?"

"As though you didn't know! Argentinian."

"You made a very good choice of name. Anyone at all can be named Schell: a German, Englishman, Frenchman, Hungarian, or Russian."

"I didn't 'choose' my name. It actually is my family name."

"In our little world you're quite a famous man."

"My name is known to fifty men, yours is known to a hundred."

"Wasn't your last nickname Count Saint-Germain, after the celebrated eighteenth-century adventurer?" asked the colonel, laughing. "They say you've had just as many adventures as he."

"Probably just like most old spies."

"To be sure that's the kind of trade it is," said the colonel. Perhaps at heart he does think of himself as a new Count Saint-Germain. "I think it's still not really known for certain just who he was."

"He's thought most likely to have been the son of a Portuguese Jew, from southern France, and some French princess."

"You've probably read a great deal about him?"

"Of course, if only because I was given such a nickname."

"You've been an aviator and aren't a bad parachutist. Is it true that physically you're practically as strong as Joe Louis?"

"Highly exaggerated. But there's still something left."

Schell strode over to the cabinet with the dumbbells and went through a few movements with the biggest ones. He did it as though it were extremely easy. He wants to show he's not getting weaker—a bad sign, thought the colonel.

"What have your agents told you about me?" asked Schell,

sitting down in the easy chair. "Tell me whatever you can. I don't think it's necessary in our business to hide everything and try to deceive whomever you're speaking to about everything. Especially someone hard to deceive."

"I don't think so either. Only *bad* spies think that. . . . What have they told me? A lot. Various things. In old-fashioned novels they would probably have called you a 'man with a broken heart,'" the colonel replied, also gaily. He handed an old-fashioned silver cigarette case over to Schell, who took a cigarette and ostentatiously pressed his fingers on the smooth surface with some force.

"Perhaps you need my fingerprints? Here they are."

"You've probably picked that up from your detective stories, aside from which I already have them."

"Is my dossier a big one?"

"Fairly. It's not short."

"Perhaps there's even more on me at Colonel Number Two's."

"Who?"

"That's my name for the Soviet officer who's your opposite number in Berlin, on the other side of the Iron Curtain. The odd thing is that you resemble each other not only in your jobs but also in your positions. You're only a colonel, but I know very well indeed that in your Berlin headquarters you're practically the head. The same thing goes for him. However, among them a man with the rank of major in the Ministry of Internal Affairs, the MVD, I think goes into the army with the rank of major general. Nor is secrecy much use there either. You know perfectly well who he is, and he knows perfectly well who you are. . . . You must agree that there's no other city in the world now which is more interesting than Berlin. It really is the show window of the world. It is the center of international espionage. In a free moment I once tried to count up how many foreign agencies there are in Berlin; I got up to thirty and stopped counting. And it's inevitable. Berlin, and Vienna, too, are the only cities in the world where it's possible to pass with every convenience from one world to

11

another in a few minutes by subway. . . . Well, is the world situation hopeless?"

"Difficult, but not hopeless. There are no hopeless situations."

"There are, there are. D'you want to listen to the radio? The news will be on now."

"Well, why not? Let's listen to it."

"We'll probably hear a great many nice things."

"Of course you understand," said the colonel, glancing at Schell, "that in talking to any candidate for our service we must ask ourselves the question: can he be a double agent? But in my experience, in the real sense of the word, there are hardly any double agents; every one of them always prefers one of the two sides and in reality serves only that one. Personally, I have nothing against such agents."

"Perhaps you even give them higher wages, which would be natural."

"I, for instance, would have nothing in principle against our agents sometimes, in a case of extreme emergency, maintaining relations even with 'Colonel Number Two.' It goes without saying only on condition that *in reality* they work for us. We pay more, too."

"Don't say that. I think they sometimes pay very well."

"We'll be able to come to an understanding on the money side. . . . You are quite free to cross into the Eastern Zone?"

"A simple enough matter."

"Have you connections over there?"

"No."

"Do you work only for the money?"

"You speak as though other people work out of conviction."

"A great many. Out of conviction and patriotism."

"Unpaid?"

"Of course not. People must eat and drink."

"I think that in your department, with the exception of its heads, foreigners predominate. They may also be patriots, but of what country?"

12

"Some of them work for revenge, out of hatred for the government of their own country."

"For such feelings they get very good wages indeed. But you don't expect *your* patriotism from me, I hope. And don't expect any firm principles from me either. I have an allergy against principles, and perhaps against good in general." (A typical phrase maker, thought the colonel, frowning.) "But even if we were to start talking about such subjects I should tell you what conclusions I've come to after many years of fairly diversified work in espionage. There are some distinguished people among real spies. They usually combine in themselves the good qualities of officers with the good qualities of—what should I say?— with the good qualities, for instance, of writers: penetration, observation, knowledge of people, imagination, the ability to project themselves into another person. Those of them who serve their own country are even respectable people. Judging by what I've heard about you, and from my own observation, too, you, for instance, are a perfectly respectable man."

"Thank you very much," said the colonel. Though, he thought, you may not be such an authority on the matter. "You speak of *our* trade. My trade is not quite identical with yours. I work behind a desk, and the main thing with me is system— the comparison and analysis of the reports I receive. Everything lies in being conscientious, attentive, and patient. Pure prose."

"That was your old school of thought. And you actually belong to it, even though together with General Bolling you've renovated it and made a great career in the last few years. But that's another question that doesn't concern me."

"Exactly."

"Would you be surprised if I told you that Colonel Number Two is also an honorable man, though with qualities of all kinds, to be sure, like all of them, and surrounded by scoundrels? He's in a difficult position. Generally speaking, Stalin must be told what he wants to hear. He can't endure disagreeable reports— a great shortcoming in the head of a government."

13

"What a commonplace."

"I didn't guarantee to make any revelations."

"But hardly an accurate commonplace. In any case, the heads of the Russian secret service, as well as of all secret services in general, require the truth to be reported to them. Whether or not they report it to Stalin unembellished, of course, I don't know."

"They embellish it. But for other reasons as well the colonel is not going to be able to hang on to his post. After all, with them it's like a crowded bus—everyone standing in the aisle hates everyone sitting down."

"He's not a bad specialist and is a former combat officer. At the end of the war he was in command of a regiment and was wounded in the leg. That's why he was transferred to the secret service. I think that's also why he's called something we might translate as 'gimpy'—*khromoy*," said the colonel, stumbling over the *kh* and pronouncing the Russian word carefully, as though it were unfamiliar. Actually he knew Russian but concealed it. "Is he a Party member?"

"Probably. Otherwise, he wouldn't have been appointed to such a post. But you know among the officers the Party insignia don't mean a thing; Tukhachevsky was also a Communist. So you know Russian?"

"Only a few words, unfortunately. 'The devil'—*chort*"—said the colonel, laughing. Though the Russian *ch* is pronounced as in English he made it sound like *t-sh*. " 'Son of a bitch'—*sukin syn*."

"Nice to hear," said Schell. "Colonel Number Two is not a son of a bitch. They say he's getting tired of the job he has now. I admit that decent people can be found everywhere, but . . ."

"Not everywhere. In the Gestapo there were no decent people and in the GPU there aren't any either."

"But the chemical formula for a spy would be something approximately like this: 50 per cent love of money, 20 per cent sporting instinct, 10 per cent stupidity, 10 per cent intellectual

14

considerations, 10 per cent boredom with an empty or unsuccessful life."

"Add a certain percentage of psychic instability."

"Yes, of course, the morphine and cocaine addicts."

"Those, too. Or, more exactly, many turn into morphine addicts; the work is difficult. And when they turn into morphine addicts they usually become worthless. It always amused me that Conan Doyle made Sherlock Holmes a cocaine—or was it morphine?—addict. That proves that with all his talent he knew nothing about police business. Holmes's deductions, for that matter, are usually not particularly convincing, but if he had been a cocaine addict he would soon have become a total wreck and in a year would have been even less gifted than Dr. Watson. . . . So you only work for the money," he said with some disappointment. "And I thought you would be just the one to have a very large percentage of 'sporting instinct.' I suppose Count Saint-Germain was primarily on the search for strong sensations. Is that true?"

"Money most likely entered into that, too. There was love, hate, jealousy, envy, wine, politics, sport, lofty and non-lofty ideas, while somewhere in all of that gold popped up, too. As with most people. Just why do they hide it or deny it?"

What a shallow view, thought the colonel. In his own life money did not take up much room. He had only one expensive passion: horses. As a young man he had served in a cavalry regiment, and had even taken part in one of the last cavalry engagements in history. He was sorry that the role of the cavalry was finished forever. For him an army without cavalry was not quite a real army.

"I won't ask you how much the English have offered you. We'll give you more. Does all this mean it's really just the same to you *whom* you work for?"

"Not quite the same. Circumstances vary. For instance, it's more dangerous to work for the Western world than for the Eastern. In case of a fiasco you people have a trial, but they

15

just shoot you, and what's much worse they torture you before-hand."

"Well, there you are, you do admit some difference between the Western and Eastern worlds: we give people trials and don't torture them. In our business we sometimes have to do things that don't correspond to the Ten Commandments, other-wise we can't operate. After all, we are protecting ourselves! I hope there's a difference, by and large, between a society based on freedom and one based on slavery. You don't see that?"

"Only snobs wouldn't see that."

"I heard you hate the Soviet regime for personal reasons, too. When all is said and done that actually isn't so important to us. In our business, as in the French Legion, you don't ask a man about his past. As long as he works for *us* honestly," the colonel repeated, still more insistently.

"You probably want to send me into Russia by parachute?"

"We never send anyone into Russia by parachute," said the colonel very coldly. "And we have no dramatic, hair-raising projects."

"It's a pity you don't. If your agents had killed Hitler fifteen years ago tens of millions of people would have been saved."

"Nevertheless, we've never gone in for anything like that," said the colonel still more coldly. "And I don't want to send you into Russia necessarily either. You would be able to act as you saw fit. We want to get one helpless man out of Moscow. He's a scientist and has nothing to do with politics. The only thing we want is his discovery."

"Not so simple."

"I shouldn't have come to you for something *simple*."

"But this is especially difficult. People don't come back from Russia."

"That's a great exaggeration."

"You're most likely surrounded by Soviet agents."

"Possibly, though I don't think so. I've had extraordinarily

16

few failures, aside from which I'm not going to say anything about you to any of my subordinates."

"And to your superiors?"

"They can keep that and other secrets, too."

" 'And other secrets, too!' Do admit that for me this secret has a certain significance."

"The pay is very high. Well, what about it?"

"I'll give you an answer in two or three weeks. I have to take a trip to Italy. Not 'on business,' just to take a rest."

"A delay is a little inconvenient. . . . Of course, if you have a fever . . . That's not a long-drawn-out business, I hope?"

"No, it's nothing serious. My health is all right. I simply need a rest in Italy. I'd like to bask in the sun."

"Like a serpent," said the colonel jocularly. "Where will you be going?"

"I don't know yet, probably Florence," replied Schell carelessly. He actually intended to go to Capri. "I'll make a decision there."

"What, in particular, makes you hesitate?"

"I'm simply sick of our trade."

"So that's it! Then you'll give me a reply not later than two weeks from now?"

"If I refuse I'll send you a telegram. In any case, I shall be seeing you before I leave. On some other business."

"Not about yourself?" asked the colonel, pricking up his ears.

"No, about a certain woman. There's no point talking about it now. . . . And does this Soviet inventor *want* to leave the USSR?"

"He hates the Soviet regime."

"And won't he report me first?"

"You can take precautions. I know it's a difficult assignment, otherwise I wouldn't have set aside so much money for it," said the colonel, with significant emphasis. "You will persuade him to leave."

"Of course it's very tempting. What's this scientist's name?"

The colonel lit another cigarette. There's no guarantee that

17

he's not *their* double agent, he said to himself. But no matter whom I found there wouldn't be any guarantee. Nevertheless, it's *almost* a certainty that he won't report it. It would be bad for him, too; then he would be done for! And according to everything known about him he's not an informer.

"How can I risk someone else's life when you still haven't given me an answer?"

"You know perfectly well that such a risk is inevitable. No matter whom you turned to, after all, you would have to give the name, and you couldn't be sure the man wouldn't report it. And I won't report it. Whatever I may be I have my own code of honor. The *Bushido,* so to speak, of the Japanese samurai," said Schell gloomily.

Something glinted in his eye. On occasion he might be frightening—a samurai himself, the colonel noted.

"Or, to put it less pompously," Schell went on, "you know there are chambermaids who will give notice if they see that money is being hidden from them. In just the same way I won't work unless I'm believed. And really I must know everything about him. I always begin by thinking often and at length about a mission that's coming up, and about the people I'll have to deal with. It's essential that I know everything about this scientist."

"But I myself know hardly anything about him. . . . His name is Nikolai Maikov," said the colonel after a short pause. "Am I pronouncing it correctly? I can add that his discovery is not of the slightest military significance. It has to do with lengthening human life or something like that."

"Then why are *you* getting him out?"

"Don't tell me *you* don't want to live longer?" asked the colonel with a laugh. "We want to, too. If you get him out, and if his discovery is a serious one, then it will be published in the scientific journals in complete detail. In that way it will be just as useful to the Russians as to ourselves and everyone else. And there'll be absolutely no chance of its harming anyone."

18

"Then why doesn't the Soviet government itself publish this discovery by one of its scientists?"

The colonel shrugged his shoulders.

"For various reasons, I've been told. First of all, this scientist is under a considerable cloud; he's been in prison there several times. Second, in a general way his views seem to contradict their philosophy, either Marx, or Michurin, or the scientific notions of Uncle Joe himself. Third, they think he's a lunatic and don't give him any money, nor does he ask them for any. However, I know even less about his discovery than about himself. For that matter even if I did know I probably wouldn't understand it. But a very well-known and influential biologist of our own told Washington that according to his information this Russian scientist's discovery was enormously important and under the right conditions might produce staggering results. I've been commissioned to try to help him. This really isn't part of my usual activities."

"There's nothing new under the sun. There was a lengthy competition between the Western countries and Russia for German scientists: who was going to get out how many and how important they would be. Probably the espionage services were necessary there, too. And perhaps you would all be delighted in general at an incident that would baffle the Soviets? I understand perfectly."

"There's nothing you have to understand. And I've already told you that we're simply protecting ourselves. We're never the first to start something disagreeable. . . . When I get your answer I'll tell you everything I know. Things will be clear as soon as we try working together. I know very well you won't report back concerning this Maikov. You're not capable of it, it would be a very dirty business, and no use at all to yourself: we would immediately inform every possible employer. I'm speaking simply and to the point. I know perfectly well you can be relied on. . . . And what are you going to do if you leave espionage?" he asked, though it was of no interest to him.

"I'm beginning to come around to the idea that I could earn

19

just as much and even more by working at something rather less dangerous."

"Don't tell me you're going to turn into a stockbroker or shopkeeper?"

"Hardly. In my youth I wanted to become a writer."

"That's obvious. You talk in a very literary way."

"It's not writers who talk in a literary way but lawyers. And now it's required of spies, too. In the opinion of the new school a good spy ought to be a brilliant conversationalist, talk about anything he likes, and not slip up on a single word. I'm just trying to fit in. But I didn't become a writer because I lacked the talent."

"Then why not finish your career as a spy by a brilliant mission? Then you'd have the money, too. . . . I heard you had a fiasco recently," said the colonel, half questioningly.

"If it was, it wasn't my fault," retorted Schell angrily. "For that matter, it wasn't a fiasco."

"And what if it was? Who hasn't had one? There's no need to look back: remember Lot's wife," said the colonel in a particularly velvety tone. "The future's another matter. Now, the sum we would pay you if you succeed would launch you on a safer life. Though I don't believe in it too much. People don't get out of espionage. . . . However, you can write your memoirs or a novel. All spies want to write their memoirs or a novel."

"I even know a few who went into espionage just for that reason."

"So have I. And what bad books they wrote! Good spies don't write books. You can be the first."

"Do you know Colonel Number Two?"

"No, that wouldn't be suitable for me, and especially not for him."

"Why not, actually? After all, the commanders of armies fighting each other exchange pleasantries. During the First Crimean War the English and French generals sent the Russians gifts of cheese and game, and the Russians sent back gifts of their own."

20

"Those times are finished forever. Keitel and Jodl were hanged in Nuremberg."

"By civilians. The victorious generals were extremely dissatisfied about it. Such a finale really does spoil the trade," said Schell. "Then you're willing to agree to wait two or three weeks?"

"What can I do about it? *T-short*," said the colonel.

2

AT the club, Schell played bridge, not poker, and again he lost. The last rubber was especially disastrous; his partner, after making an unjustifiable counterbid, was put out and, though it was no more than ten in the evening, refused to play any longer. He didn't even think up a polite pretext. According to club etiquette such behavior was inadmissible, but no one objected; it was easy to get up a new game, which is what happened.

Schell wasn't in it. Out of politeness, he was invited, with some apprehension, but not urged. He was considered a great master, and in the club very strong and very weak players alike were avoided. Schell always played calmly, never got excited, and did not even take part in the post-mortems of the bids and plays of hand that had proved sensational. The club didn't like that any better. Occasionally, before beginning a game, some peace-loving soul would propose: "Gentlemen, what about

22

playing today without any bickering or arguments, in the English way?" Everyone happily agreed at once, although the experienced ones knew that not only did the English not play that way but probably no one in the world did, thank God. After the game you were not supposed to quarrel or express— at least openly—any doubt about the intellectual abilities of your partner, but you were also not supposed to shut up like a clam; a certain proportion of high words and hubbub was part of the gratification provided by the club.

In addition an unpleasant feeling was aroused in nervous people by this gigantic man, with an impassive face of stone and the unhurried and important movements of a good actor. No one knew what his profession was. Some said he had inherited means and had no professional occupation; others claimed that he was engaged in the most sinister affairs; this was said without either proof or indignation; after all, why not mention it? At the club, especially during the first few years after the war, you could buy and sell anything you pleased, from gold and dollars to a shipment of Chilean nitrates and villas in Italy. Between rubbers people would draw each other off to the side and whisper to each other excitedly and violently. Schell didn't whisper about anything with anyone; this was regarded as suspicious. No one joked with him, either; on the rare occasions he lost no one made the gay remarks that had a sure success on the theme of "Unlucky at cards, lucky at love."

Standing away from the table, Schell thoughtfully calculated that his entire fortune now consisted of eighteen hundred dollars. Not so long ago it had been six times as much. Well, I'll leave Edda six hundred dollars. In all fairness she's not so greedy. When she haggles, it's more out of a sense of duty. And if I manage to unload her on to Colonel Number Two I'll be able to give her only four hundred dollars. Payment for a month in advance—rather gentlemanly.

He had scarcely settled himself at a small table, after looking at his watch, when a flunky came up to him and said respectfully that a lady was asking for him in the anteroom. Damn her!

23

thought Schell with irritation. The club was old-fashioned enough not to allow women inside.

"I'll be right down."

Unhurriedly he examined himself in the huge mirror on the wall. His tie was impeccably tied, not a single hair fell across his parting, artfully arranged so that the beginning of a bald spot was almost unnoticeable. The gray in his hair did not upset him—far better than baldness.

Schell walked out through the other two rooms. The building the club was located in had been lucky; by some miracle it had survived the bombings almost intact. It was not in Unter den Linden, and not in the Jägerstrasse or the Königgrätzerstrasse, like the other clubs, but near the Kurfürstendamm in the Western Zone. It had been built at the beginning of the century, in the best of the Wilhelmine era, when there were no visas anywhere, no unemployment, and no ration cards; when no one but economists had ever heard of, or probably would have understood, words like "valuta" or "inflation"; when one would have been taken for a madman out of hand at the mere mention of an aerial bombardment of Berlin; when at every corner, at an Aschinger's, with the blue-white façade, for fifteen pfennigs you could buy little sausages with a mountain of potatoes dipped in vinegar and a gigantic mug of beer; when two thousand people at once ate at Rheingold's under the stern gaze of Barbarossa; when in various *Amorsäle* waiters in green livery and gilt buttons doggedly kept struggling to seat guests at tables marked *"Reserviert für Champagner."*

There was an immense marble staircase in the building, covered with soft carpeting; there were little gilded balconies with flowers, and even a summer terrace for relaxation and sun baths. The club had been located here since even before the first war; it had been frequented by Staatsraths, Kommerzienraths, Gerichtsraths, Bauraths, Schulraths, Medizinalraths, Hoflieferants, prominent journalists, and lawyers. At one time it had also been adorned by the names of five or six liberal generals and barons, and even boasted a count or two as members.

24

The building had not been damaged by the bombings; only the sculpturing on the façade had been hit and the geranium pots smashed to smithereens. After the war the club had started functioning again, but the former members had died out and now the most varied kinds of people frequented it—foreigners of all nationalities, functionaries, *nouveaux-riches*, spies; there were even former Gestapo officers who had long since changed their appearance, names, and papers, and now held the most advanced views, although they were always glancing about to see whether some miraculously surviving prisoner with the concentration-camp sign burned into his hand might not still recognize them; although even then probably nothing too terrible would have happened, since they were shielded by time, the amnesty, a general mood of "What the devil!" Even now the club had a restaurant that was not too bad, which did not copy Paris, as in former days, but New York: on the menu the names of the dishes were translated into English, and you could always find not only "Goose with apples" but "Pot Roast Sandwich with Brown Gravy," and "Spiced Peach and Fresh Spinach," and on the wine list "Mt. Vernon, 10-year-old Bonded Rye," and "Old Grand-Dad, 8-year-old Bourbon." The police showed no special interest in the heavy gambling at the club, since sometimes there were also important people among the guests.

Edda was sitting in a corner of the huge, empty lobby, in a Gothic armchair near the gilt statue of Brunhilde holding a spear. And just as bloodthirsty as Brunhilde, too, thought Schell. Obviously there was going to be another scene, full of her usual "horrible nightmares." What was it today?

She wore a mink cape, and a light violet dress, and was made up "challengingly." Everything was painted—face, cheeks, eyelashes, feet, the hair a light gold color. And Natasha doesn't even know where to buy women's make-up! This one will have to be got rid of, no matter how disagreeable the method. . . . Because of that mass of gold her face looks twice as broad. She can't manage even that. She should have painted over the little mustache on her upper lip, it really disfigures her. Pouches

25

under her eyes already. She drinks too much; she'll soon lose her looks.

He composed his face to an adequate, though not extreme, degree of enthusiasm.

"How happy I am to see you!" he said, kissing her hand.

"I don't know. Are you happy or not? I have the feeling what you wanted to say was, 'And what is it this time?'" she began. Hoppla, he thought, off to the races! Smiling joyously, as though expecting a very gay chat, he pulled a Gothic chair up to Brunhilde's spear and sat down. From a distance the hall porter glanced at this disapprovingly, although Schell was a favorite of his.

"Nothing of the sort, and luckily you don't think so either. How are you?" asked Schell. An elegant guest passing through the lobby shot Edda a warm look. As a matter of fact, she's still very attractive, but Natasha's a hundred times better.

"How am I? Splendid. Wonderful. How should a woman be whose lover wants to get rid of her? But I haven't come here to make a scene."

"That's very nice to hear. There's really no point in making a scene."

"I'm sick of it myself and, as for you, you only find my scenes entertaining."

"Not in the least. I'm not a masochist. But to what do I really owe the pleasure and privilege of your visit?" he asked. For some time past they usually addressed each other in this tone, which both of them liked.

"You owe the pleasure and privilege of my visit to my having to know once and for all whether you've seen him," said Edda, dropping her voice sharply and looking around uneasily.

"Whom, my little sweetie pie?" he asked, in one of the American phrases he affected with her.

"First of all, stop calling me your 'little sweetie pie.' You're not American and neither am I."

"Is it my fault your name is Edda? Outside of Mussolini's daughter no one else is called that. And secondly?"

26

"Secondly, you know perfectly well 'who.' The Soviet colonel."

"I expect to see him today."

"So late?"

"He's given me an appointment for half-past eleven. . . . But have you made up your mind?"

"Surely I don't have to give a final answer today?" she asked. Her face had changed a little. He began to feel sorry for her. I shouldn't behave this way with her, after all, he thought.

"As you like. . . . Just remember that I'm not trying to talk you into it."

"You're lying; you did talk me into it."

"The last thing I was thinking of. I'll tell you once more: use your own judgment. It's a difficult and dangerous business, and not the least bit romantic. You've got a Mata Hari complex and a Nero complex as well. But you'll live for eighty years, and in your old age you'll be able to invest your money in second mortgages at 12 per cent."

"You've gone wild about these complexes! You've got a Churchill complex."

"Why do you want to do it? Write poetry. You're a first-rate poetess."

"You can't live on poetry—especially Russian poetry."

"But I've told you that you ought to write in French. And write prose. No, don't write prose. Some writers have been permanently ruined by Dostoevski and some have been permanently ruined by Kafka, although Kafka's talent was very slight. You've been ruined by both."

"As though you knew anything! And you know very well I am writing prose," said Edda, offended. She really did write, just anything, from incomprehensible novels to comic stories where Jews said "Vell, vell," and "Nu, nu," and Caucasians "My leetle darrrrling." Newspapers and magazines stubbornly failed to print her.

"Write French verse."

27

"No one reads poetry now. The bourgeois world is undergoing an unprecedented decline of cultural standards. A conspiracy of silence has been formed against me, just because I'm not just any Russian *émigrée*."

"Yes, that's true. Then don't write verse," he said. He knew it annoyed Edda to be agreed with immediately: agreement had to follow arguing and shouting. "In any case, you're not Russian either by origin or, for that matter, by education."

He actually did not know just what her nationality was, just as no one at the club knew his. Edda spoke Russian with an indefinite, scarcely noticeable accent, and spoke of her past rarely, obscurely, and always differently. They talked Russian, French, German, or English together: they had an unusual gift for languages.

Their affair had been going on for less than six months. They had come together accidentally, and with no great love for or interest in each other. Edda quickly found out that he was an agent. Schell himself had told her, over champagne, chiefly out of curiosity as to what effect it would have. Also, she was capable of not gossiping about whatever shouldn't be gossiped about; for that matter, no one would believe anything she said. After his nervous breakdown—and before Natasha—he had grown less cautious in general. It had an enormous effect. Edda was startled, rather agreeably: there had been no agents in her life before. For a long time she kept babbling nonsense about her enigmatic soul, about Dostoevski, and about Sartre. "If you like the idea so much why don't you take it up yourself?" he had asked, still almost without any ulterior thoughts. "D'you think I might be able to make a career in the field?" she asked, looking at him avidly. The word "field" annoyed him immediately. "It's a most suitable 'field' for you. And by no means worse than what you were doing under Hitler."

"What was I doing?" she asked indignantly.

"Oh well, one hears a lot about your various 'fields.'"

"You're lying, and even if people say it, it's vile slander!"

"Perhaps it is at that. People lie a great deal," he agreed. He actually didn't have too much confidence in the dark rumors about her.

"There's no 'maybe' about it! It's a vile slander! And I'm not going over to the Bolsheviks either. I don't like them."

"For this no liking is required."

"Though I consider that they have some intellectual justification."

"It's possible to find some intellectual justification. For that matter, it's very easy."

"But I'll never be a spy!"

"Not a spy and not even an agent, but a counteragent. We don't use the word 'spy,' it has a bad sound."

"What a book I might write about it! Why don't you write a book about espionage?"

"Because I know too much about it."

"There you are! That's just why you must write it!"

"I have no imagination. Dostoevski never killed an old woman moneylender and didn't have the slightest idea about how an investigation is conducted. Yet he didn't write too badly about it. If he had known more he would not have written so well."

"I'm not Russian, but you're not very Russian either. Altogether nationality is *vieux jeu.*"

"But why do you want to do it? I give you enough money."

"I believe I've never complained."

"That's true, but there's never been anything for you to complain about," he said more precisely. He liked having the last word and what he called the strategic initiative of the conversation. With Edda this was usually not so easy.

"You know perfectly well that if I go over to them it won't be for the money, but because . . ."

"Because you have a demonic soul. I can penetrate into its depths, I have a bathyscafe for women. That's the machine in which Professor Picard lowered himself to the bottom of the

ocean. And I into the depths of the female soul," he said, repeating what he told all his mistresses. In the more stupid ones
it created panic.

"If I go over to them it's because of my hatred for bourgeois
society! What they're doing now in America is a horrible
nightmare!"

"Yes, yes, I know, my cherry blossom."

"You always say, 'Yes, yes, I know,' and then to annoy me you
put on a look of boredom. No one is ever bored with me! . . . Do
I have circles under my eyes today?"

"Not the slightest. On the contrary, you're getting more and
more ornamental. Made to order for a *Life* cover."

"I've decided to follow a strict diet. I want to lose ten
pounds."

"Very simple—cut off a leg."

"Your jokes have been unusually dull lately. In general
you're not funny in the least, even though you keep cracking
jokes. Dancing keeps you thin. Are we going to dance tonight
till dawn?"

"No, we're not going to dance tonight till dawn."

"I'm getting fat on champagne. At dinner tonight I drank a
whole bottle," said Edda, and paused, waiting to be asked
"With whom?" Schell purposely did not ask her. "My life is all
in champagne and in love."

"In love and in champagne."

"And I hate the capitalist system because . . ."

"Because you have no capital."

"No, not because of that!"

"Very well, very well," he said. "I know you hate everything
that's *vieux jeu* and that everything in America is a horrible
nightmare. I know there's real freedom only in Russia. I know
you're a super-existentialist and that *l'existence précède l'essence*. I know you worship Sartre and the music of the concretists. I know all that." (Especially that you're a super-nitwit,
he wanted to add.) "But we have no time now for philosophico-

30

political arguments. Tell me plainly: should I talk to the colonel or not? There's a chance of it today and it's a good time: it's not Monday, it's not Friday, and it's not the thirteenth."

"Where would he send me to?" she asked, lowering her voice still more. "I won't go behind the Iron Curtain."

"They'd hardly send you to do some spying on themselves."

"Then where?"

"How can I tell? Perhaps Paris."

"I'd go anywhere if it were with you," she said shyly. "I want to be doing the same thing as you."

"It's obvious you imagine it all to be like a bank or a department store: you at one desk and me next to you at another."

"But I would go alone to Paris. Of course, only if they pay well. I must live."

"I give you four hundred dollars a month."

"You've been giving me that, but I know you've lost everything you had. And as you can imagine, it's not very pleasant for me to live on your money," she said sincerely. "I admit you're not stingy. But before you used to love me."

"I love you now, too. Even more than before."

"You're lying!" she said, gratified nevertheless. "You never tell the truth."

"Sometimes I do. I've loved you now for five months. Probably no one else ever loved you that long."

"No one before you has ever thrown me over, and I've really thrown everyone over very quickly. And how do you show that you love me?"

"An answer to that wouldn't be proper. . . . In any case, not by singing love songs together with you. For that matter, that wouldn't prove anything either. I think in one of Shostakovich's operas the hero and heroine sing a love duet but it turns out that they unite in love for Stalin."

"What a boor you are! . . . When are you leaving?"

"The day after tomorrow."

"For Madrid?"

31

"Yes, Madrid. I've told you that a dozen times. Not Honolulu—Madrid."

"You really have told me that a dozen times. That's just why I don't believe you. Why can't you take me with you?"

"I'll be busy there the whole day. It's expensive, too. And it's not so easy to get a visa for Spain."

"If it's not easy, you can make an effort. What am I going to do here by myself?"

"You've got a lot of friends."

"What a boor you are!" said Edda. She constantly kept saying, "What a boor you are," "What a boor he is." It meant almost nothing, simply that she didn't like the person. And not always even that.

"If you're bored, I repeat, write poetry."

"I write every day anyhow."

"I'm asking for the second time, should I talk to the colonel? Remember once and for all that I haven't given you any advice and I'm not giving you any."

"D'you think it's very dangerous?"

"I don't know about the 'very.' It depends on the assignment. But of course espionage is a risky business. I know you like to gamble with life, that's your most basic trait." A nibble, he thought. "Just the same, I'm not giving any advice. You look too nervous for such a profession. They'll probably just send you to Paris."

"Perhaps I'll agree just for the experience. One must experience everything!"

"I appreciate the aphorism."

"And if I get sick of it I'll drop it. But if I go over to them and they don't let me return? What will you do then?"

"I'll drop a hydrogen bomb on them."

"Fool! I'm looking for something to apply myself to and can't find it. That's my tragedy. Would you like me to read some French verse?"

"No, but go ahead."

"It's not long. Listen:

> *"'Nous avons perdu la route et la trace des hommes*
> *Parmi les méandres du ténébreux vallon*
> *Et oublié le nom de la ville d'où nous sommes*
> *Sans savoir celui de la ville où nous allons.'*

"Good?"

"Not bad at all," said Schell. She really does have something, after all. And her face suddenly looks inspired. Stupid, but inspired. Though for that matter the verses may not be hers. "Not bad at all."

"Just so. If I accept their proposal, will they send me off immediately?"

"Don't accept their proposal. Sit at home and drink champagne. . . . No, they won't send you off at once. First of all, the colonel will make some inquiries about you. He has a secret department of his own. Then that will all be transmitted to the administration of the MVD. You'll be interrogated by a commissioner—people who do that are called commissioners—he will send you to the *Glavrazvedupr*, that is, Central Military Intelligence. If you seem all right to the commissioner, then he may send you over there, but if you seem unacceptable to him, then it's practically certain that he'll send you there. Like everywhere in the world, but more so than in other countries, in their country the police and the military detest each other, and probably nothing would give the MVD headquarters more pleasure than a serious fiasco at the Central Military Intelligence. The reverse is equally true. So you'll have some time even if I speak to the colonel today. Now remember, I'm not giving you advice."

"You keep on insisting that you're not giving me advice. You have a dark soul. That's why I love you. Will you be back in two weeks? Word of honor?"

"And wherefore, my darling little dumpling, when you don't believe a single word I say?"

33

"If you have another woman in Madrid I'll drown her in vitriol!"

"Poor señorita. That might hurt her eyesight."

"And then I'll finish myself off!"

"The Anna Karenina complex? You can't have that together with the Mata Hari complex."

"Really, how you bore me! D'you want me to tell you a wonderful pun I just thought of today?"

"No, I don't," he said. Her puns had seemed to him unusually silly, even during the two weeks he had been in love with her. "It's too late now."

"Then tomorrow morning, remind me. . . . And what am I going to live on in the meantime? I've got a hundred marks left."

"I have a thousand dollars. I'll leave you half."

"I know you're not stingy. You gave me that mink cape. It's true I wanted a mink coat, but they're asking nine thousand marks for the cheapest ones here, and you've gambled away everything. With the money you've lost gambling I could buy two wonderful mink coats. They have one now for twenty-two thousand. Oh, what a coat. It's simply to die!"

"For the time being the cape is quite enough. With you it's a question of rank: the cape is a lieutenant and the coat is a major. Just hang on a bit longer. You'll still be a major."

"Everyone has a mink coat now. They don't even look at my silver fox any more."

Three young men were coming down the staircase. They glanced over at Edda. One of them smiled at her playfully and when he saw Schell turned away instantly. The hall porter gave them hats and coats.

"There are so many men here! And not one is like any of the others. And each one makes love in his own way. And each one of them might be my lover!" she said.

"And every one of them is richer than I," he replied. "Or perhaps not every one. That one just going out has the side pocket of his jacket on the right. That means the suit's been repaired."

34

"Oh, money isn't everything anyhow!"

"Of course, just the same it's nice. Naturally as a supplement to other things."

"The main thing is for a man to be a real man. The main thing is—character. A man's character must be like Shakespeare's. I cannot endure people with petty passions and self-analysis, people who say, 'Oh, I want that, but perhaps, on the other hand, I don't really.' A man ought to be *tout d'une pièce*. Probably you were that way *once*. Now you're old."

"Thank you," he said, irritated. "I'm not so much older than you. Now don't burst with rage! I take everything back, you're not even twenty yet. Under Hitler you were obviously no more than ten. Now, for the third and last time, I ask you, should I speak about you to the colonel or shouldn't I?"

"I've been hesitating myself for a long time."

"Then, damn it, stop!"

"I've been thinking it over a great deal. You know the last thing anyone could call me is stupid," she said. How amusing, thought Schell, she thinks she's very clever and very wicked, and what she is really is very stupid and rather kind; she would do everything for a man, as long as it didn't cost her a penny—after all, just like many other kindhearted people.

"But here there's no other way out for me. First of all, I'm fed up with Berlin. Why should everyone else live in Paris and New York? And how they live! Secondly, you've lost everything and soon there'll be nothing for me to live on. Thirdly, it happens that I want to gamble with life, get excited, triumph over people. The whole point of life is conquering, surely you feel that?"

"Of course I do. For some time now, as a matter of fact, you haven't conquered anybody."

"Except you! But there's one thing that stops me. I still think spying isn't a very noble business!"

"But how can you say such a thing!"

"I absolutely do not sympathize with the Communists! Suppose I look as though I were going to work for them, they give

35

me a visa and send me to France or the United States, and then I go over to the Allies, what then?"

"That's what a lot of people do. Actually that isn't so noble either. But if you seduce some American officer there that would be at least a little nobler. That's quite possible; you have terrific sex appeal."

"You think they would give me just that as an assignment? I adore the Americans, and that I can do. Talk to this terrible colonel, but I'll still have to think it over."

"In my opinion it would be better to think it over first and then talk to the terrible colonel."

"It would have to depend on a great many things. On the pay, on just what he proposes, what sort of work. If it's very dangerous, I'll have to think it over some more."

"If the worst comes to the worst they'll give you twenty years in prison. There you'll be able to seduce the guard, escape together with him, and write another poem: 'The sensitive soul of the poet revels in freedom after the dungeon.'"

"What a boor you are! Can I spend the night with you?"

"You can," said Schell, to his own surprise. She beamed. He looked at his watch. "Time to go. I know you adore making an exit by slamming the door. Here that's impossible: they have a revolving door."

"Fool."

The hall porter called a car. Schell was about to hand the driver some money but didn't. Let her pay, she dislikes that.

He went back up to the bar and ordered half a bottle of champagne. "My own brand. You've got it in half bottles. I'm in no hurry."

Yes, a horrible nightmare, he thought. But what can I do? Still, the colonel may not take her, he'll see through her immediately. But then he may, in order to get hold of me. . . . Oh well, they'll simply kick her out of France. There's not much risk in it for her. . . . Still, it's not so good. . . .

Some cards were lying on the little table. One deck was lying stacked in a corner. He made a bet with himself: if red comes

36

up I'll do it; if black, I won't. Mechanically he cut the cards, mechanically noticing the ace of hearts, picked up the cards, and the ace came out. Then he couldn't recall whether he had dropped it himself. That's settled. He went to a telephone booth.

"Natasha?" he asked. His voice and expression changed. "Hello, my darling. Is it all right my calling so late? Weren't you asleep? No, nothing has happened, everything is fine, don't be upset. I'll come see you tomorrow at noon. I've looked up everything, you'll be traveling without inconveniences, as they say. You'll be in Capri Thursday morning. And I'll arrive Sunday. . . . Yes. We won't see each other for three days. But to make up for it we'll be there the whole time together. . . . I'm very happy! Did you cough today? Thank God! On the way back I'll show you Italy. After all, you've never been anywhere, poor thing. . . . I adore you! And do you love me? Thank you, though I'm not worthy of it. . . . Thank you. . . . I embrace you. Till morning then, good night, my child."

He went back to his table. Two women, and on top of that now two agencies, my God! I've never been a double agent, and I never will be. It's disgusting! Schell drank his wine, looked at his watch again, and left the club.

3

IN appearance and manners he doesn't resemble the other one; each one of them has his own "style." Nevertheless, they have something in common. . . . This one doesn't get down to business at once either, he also demonstrates the "level of his intelligence." But he prattles on quite a lot; he gets off his commonplaces not badly, perhaps he says "conjuncture" too often. Somehow he speaks oddly, unnaturally. There's something uneasy, tense, and a little provocative about him. *He* wouldn't visit me at home, nor would he play cards and eat with me. He must make appointments only in his office, or possibly in special cases in some deserted spot. He's probably very fond of "plotting" and codes. His office here is the most ordinary kind, but with something military added. There's a coffee machine on the table over there. If he doesn't drink wine, he must be stimulated by coffee. In our business nothing else is possible. Could there be a microphone here? Who listens in on him? The GPU? Oh, what a bore he is, death and damnation!

Schell was thinking his own thoughts, without missing a word of what Colonel Number Two was saying. In his time Schell had done everything indicated: he could listen to two or even three conversations at the same time, pick a man he had seen once in his life out of a hundred photos, go in a flash from a dark room into a brightly lighted one and in that flash recognize with precision everything in it. In front of him at a large table sat a thin man of middle height with a long, sick, somewhat lopsided face, with small, yellowish, smoldering eyes. On his left cheek, just below a dark ring underneath his eye, there was a wart, which made his dry face seem even more lopsided. The colonel didn't get up when Schell came in, just barely looking as though he were raising himself in his chair, stretched his hand across the table as though he were reluctant to, and with a fatigued if not disdainful gesture pointed to a chair on the other side of the table. The other is far more affable.... When the colonel was sitting you couldn't see he was lame, but he did not sit quite normally. When he leaned across the table, a slight grimace of pain flitted across his face. They say he works fifteen hours a day. A lie, of course: no one works fifteen hours a day. But he may be overworked at that.... His eyes look intelligent. The cliché for them would be "cruel." No, probably not more than mean. His hands tremble a little, his face looks earthen. Is he affected, or just self-taught? And of course there he is, "casting a penetrating glance." Very well, go on casting it: anything you penetrate is all yours. Probably he also considers himself a connoisseur of the human soul. Another characteristic of the profession, sometimes ridiculous, too. But we are really professionals, he's more of a newcomer.

Nevertheless, Schell's ironic disposition and self-confidence diminished considerably in the Eastern Zone of Berlin. The transition was always too swift. At times he had the same feeling an experienced flier might have in suddenly passing into a "supersonic zone." No, I couldn't endure their arbitrariness, I should simply suffocate. I couldn't live with them, just as a fish can't live in the Dead Sea, he said to himself. Just the same he was in the eastern sector of the city often. He knew that in espionage circles he was considered fearless, and in fact he had often subjected himself to very great danger without losing his head; but he also knew that people who didn't know what fear was didn't exist.

". . . Churchill will disappear and England will be completely done for as a great power," said the colonel. He pronounced Churchill's name with the accent on the second syllable. "An able head, whatever you say. Doesn't believe in fate, isn't frightened by disaster, just as it should be. A massive historical figure!" (No microphone, thought Schell.) "The ablest of our enemies!" (No, there is one.) "Now, if he had been running America, with her gigantic potentialities. Suppose he is clever, what of it, if there's no money? It used to be a great power, but now it's just been washed away. It's simply laughable: England recognizes China, but China doesn't recognize England! The bones of Churchill's ancestors must be turning over in their graves. If you have a population of some forty or fifty million people you've got to cut your jib to suit the wind."

"But then the two greatest powers in the world would be China and India," said Schell, in order not to be too acquiescent. He had a professional principle: always maintain your independence and never look too respectful; this rule, of course, could sometimes be modified. He must have been able to arrange things here better, Schell thought, but probably the more uncomfortable it is the better he likes it. The room really was uncomfortable, regardless of the bright ceiling light. But it's a good thing he hasn't got that old trick: I stay in the dark and you're in a bright light. There was nothing on the table except a telephone (one instrument, not three, as they usually have) and an unlit lamp with a milk-colored shade; there were neither papers, an inkwell, nor an ash tray. Along the walls, bare of hangings, there was a mountain range of metal cabinets. All of them, of course, with a secret lock. There was only one small wall cupboard, of wood, without a lock. There was a

40

leather divan beneath it with a bump and a depression in the middle.

"They probably will be when China and India create a real industry. Then a new conjuncture will take shape in the world. But in the present epoch there are only two military-political colossi: the United States and Russia. Unfortunately, in all the statistical indices America is in the first place," said the colonel, with irritation. "For the time being we're only in second. But very soon it is we who will be first."

"Yes, for the time being you're only in second," agreed Schell. According to what one hears he's not very much attracted by women. Perhaps he likes redheads? Odd that Edda isn't a redhead naturally, it would have been so indicated for her. And if she charms him?

"You say 'you'; surely you're a Russian?"

"I'm Argentinian. Would you like to see my passport?"

"What for? What does a passport prove? I could give you a passport for any country you liked. However, why not see it? Show it to me."

Schell took a little booklet out of his pocket and handed it to the colonel, who leafed through it, as though negligently, and returned it. Of course he's noted both number and date.

"A nice little booklet," said the colonel with a sneer. "It opens the door to any country you like and doesn't arouse suspicions anywhere. Argentina is neutral by nature, by profession, by conjuncture, and for a thousand reasons. I see you don't trust much to luck. So you're not a Russian, though you were born in Leningrad. There've always been very few Argentinians there, by the way."

"Yes, a nice little booklet," agreed Schell.

"I know all about you, of course," said the colonel, emphasizing the "all." "I've heard a great deal, Count Saint-Germain. I've heard of your feats and I admire them." Schell nodded silently. "It's true you've done a great deal of work for small countries. . . . I've never been able to understand, by the way, what small countries have a counterintelligence for. In any

41

case, after all, they can't do any fighting and they won't. Just let a few weeks go by and there'll be a "government in exile' formed with American funds. The Americans have a lot, a lot of loose money. Basically they must despise all their allies in their hearts because they live off their money. But an intelligence service is doubtless needed by small countries in order 'to be like the big one.' Russia has it, so let us have it, too, eh? Well, how about it then? Have you made up your mind?"

"I'll give you an answer in three weeks."

"I don't understand. Why the delay? Just what is it that's holding you back?"

"It's just that it's time to get out of this business."

"Don't tell me your nerve is failing?" asked the colonel, with unconcealed satisfaction.

"No, my nerve isn't failing," answered Schell hastily. "I'm tired of the work."

The colonel looked at him with astonishment. "Tired of it?"

"It's become repellent."

"I never thought you were particularly idealistic?"

"No. Wasn't it the Russian writer Pisemsky who said that in his own and in everyone else's soul he never saw anything but filth?"

The astonishment on the colonel's face grew still more marked. He couldn't understand why a man who evidently wished to work for him should say that. Schell didn't understand why he said it either. I've actually started making superfluous remarks; before I never did.

"Pisemsky must have had a very bad time of it. . . . So he never saw anything but filth? But perhaps his nerves were in disorder, just like yours? It would be a little early for you, nevertheless, though you're not so young. A boxer or dancer can only work until thirty, and many of them not even that long. People who work with their heads keep much better. Emanuel Lasker was world champion until he was almost sixty. Do you play chess?"

42

"I play, but I've never learned the theory; I've never had the patience."

"Yes, but how can a game exist without theory?" said the colonel with a slight sigh. "But the pity is that there's so much theory. That's how it is with war, too. Suvorov was no theoretician, but how do all the Rundstedts and Guderians compare with him? In Russia even our chess players are the best in the world."

"Lasker and Capablanca were not Russians. Alekhine was a Russian, but a White Guard."

"Our music is the best in the world. Our literature, too."

"As far as your literature is concerned I'm doubtful. I have only one fixed requirement of literature: it mustn't be boring. It's a waste of time for you to export literature like yours. It might be just possible in Persia or India, but in the Western countries it's out of the question."

"Because according to you they know what's what over there?"

"This literature is what you're judged by there. Have you read George Orwell's book *1984?*"

"I haven't and I don't intend to."

"It's a parody on the USSR. In spite of the general opinion I consider it also rather boring. It's rather forced, and unlike either Bolshevik ideas or Bolshevik practice. But your literature was what gave Orwell some invaluable material." Now I've shown how intellectual I am and it's quite enough, too, for the new school.

The colonel did not, however, even attempt to look as though Schell's remarks seemed interesting or noteworthy. He was not very much interested in literature, nor did he read much, and then it was primarily Russian classics.

"Just so. Let's get down to business."

"You expressed a wish to speak to me tonight."

"I don't recall that I expressed such a wish," said the colonel, emphasizing the "I." "Is it only the money side of the work that interests you?"

43

"I take various circumstances into account: who pays more, where there is less risk, where it is more agreeable to work, where the superiors are more polite."

"If I were to take you on it would only be for a long time and only for very dangerous assignments. I would send you to America."

"In peacetime there are no such dangerous assignments anywhere."

"You think so? You're used to working with democratic windbags. But you know we don't stand on ceremony."

"In peacetime even you don't plan on blowing up American factories, and in all probability there's not going to be any war," said Schell at random.

The coffee has suddenly gone to his head, he's going to start babbling. Stronger men than he have done the same. Napoleons and Bismarcks have blurted out secrets too! . . . No, now he's just become the incarnation of the noncommittal. . . . I suppose he wanted to propose that I become a double agent, thought Schell. But he wasn't very much interested in any proposition the colonel might have for him: he had definitely made up his mind not to work for *them*.

"We don't want war at all. According to Marx, capitalism is doomed in any case. There is no point at all in *our* fighting."

"I quite agree with you."

"As for what we *pay* our agents," said the colonel, "we also take into account various circumstances, aside from experience and ability. You are a very expensive agent, you're not Russian, you have no principles." (He wanted to say, "You have no honor.") "You're a gambler, you're too well known in intelligence circles, your height and looks attract too much attention. . . . If you still can't give me any answer, then it's obvious that your wanting to see me was a misunderstanding."

"I wanted to talk about a certain woman, not about myself."

"The one you dined with last night in a Kurfürstendamm restaurant?" asked the colonel. "A very beautiful woman."

"That's the one. You didn't see her?"

44

"We're bound to know everything," said the colonel, not answering. He had not seen Edda. "Isn't her name Edda? Well, in principle I don't object, but I'm not going to talk to her for the fun of it. Haven't I heard she's a poetess? We don't need poetesses. Nor do we need fools."

"She's not a fool. And as you very rightly observed she's extremely beautiful."

"Of course that's important."

"Aside from which she speaks excellent French, German, and English."

"Also very important. But you yourself understand that you are one thing and this lady is another. I believe she has no experience?"

"None."

"Is she your mistress?"

"My private life concerns no one but myself."

"It doesn't concern us *now*. But as you must understand if you or she starts working for us then everything that concerns you will concern us, or at least everything that might be of interest to us. We're not going to pay *her* a lot. In Berlin she's of no use to us."

"She can go anywhere you please. To New York, for instance, or even better to Paris."

"All our agents want to go to Paris."

"In Paris you're sure to have some work for her. That's where the Western headquarters are."

"Thanks for this priceless piece of information."

"Basically there are only two places where there are any military secrets: in Washington and in Rocquencourt, that is, in the Pentagon and in SHAPE. In my opinion it's easier to find them out in the latter. After all, there are people of fourteen nationalities there."

"Thanks for this invaluable advice, too. They say that Saker . . ."

"Sakeur. The Americans pronounce it 'Sakeur.'"

"I don't like to be interrupted! And I'm not familiar with

45

their abbreviations. They say that this Sakeur is a first-rate general. Not our Zhukov, but first-rate, one of the best in the world, eh?"

"I've heard that, too. First-rate, but without an army. . . . Of course you have agents everywhere. Nevertheless, a beautiful woman, with an excellent command of foreign languages, may be useful."

He's ready to betray his own mistress, thought the colonel. A fine fellow! "And you wouldn't be too upset if she were to trip up?"

"That's a risk of our trade."

"Of course, if she's caught, then the French, in order not to start a fuss with us, will probably simply deport her. Maybe that's just why it's 'better in Paris,' eh? But you know we have a rule—them or us. What guarantee is there that she's not a double agent?"

"There's never a guarantee. That's a risk of *your* trade," Schell replied dryly.

"I hope you realize we don't beat around the bush with double agents."

"Really, everyone knows that," said Schell. He made a bet with himself (which he often did in a risky situation): heads I'll do it. "So there's no point repeating it. Why frighten people? Isn't that the method of the political police?"

The colonel frowned. "The political *police* have absolutely nothing to do with it! I'm a Russian officer, in the service of Russia and the Russian Army!"

Aha, so *that's* what his fixed idea is. Obviously there's no microphone, after all. "That's exactly what I was trying to say. *You* doubtless don't use this business of scaring people. I know that you're a former combat officer." Schell indicated with a glance the little ribbon pinned on the left of the colonel's uniform. "I did not mean to say anything offensive."

For a moment they looked at each other in silence.

"Nor would I advise you to say anything 'offensive' to me!"

"Of course I'm here on your territory. But I'm a citizen of

Argentina. Even the police wouldn't go looking for a diplomatic incident without any reason or point."

The colonel laughed sarcastically. "That, of course, is a very frightening business—a diplomatic incident with Argentina! Just think, she would move her troops on to Moscow. But I do like your not being someone who scares easily. Let me add that I had no desire to say anything offensive either. And I was not speaking of you but of this Edda."

"She's a beginner. How could she be a double agent?"

"You mean she'd be suitable only as a plain agent? Very well, we can take her on trial. . . . And as a supplement to yourself I should even take her on very willingly. Aren't you going to ask me about conditions?"

"That's premature. After all, I still haven't given you an answer in principle."

In principle! thought the colonel. Fine principles he must have!

Occasionally the colonel would ask himself what personal objective one or the other of the people surrounding him had set for himself, and almost always the answer was identical: first of all, to make as much money as possible; second, to please his superiors as much as possible; after that there might be variants, but these were of no consequence. In contrast to most people and to nearly all his colleagues, the colonel had the capacity to see himself from outside, and sometimes he would tacitly acknowledge that for the past few years he had had nothing to be proud of. He would appear almost loathsome to himself whenever he had to listen respectfully and submissively to the police heads. He considered nearly all of them the dregs of humanity. Nor were many agents any better than they. When first meeting an agent the colonel *tried* to feel as though he were a taster of sorts: he would try to taste the wine, ascertain its character and quality, and spit it out. But he could never manage it, and he usually limited himself to being correctly chilly, attempting to speak in a staccato manner, in just this Napoleonic tone of his.

47

Schell annoyed him too. Moreover, during the past few years all strong, healthy people aroused the colonel's ill-will, especially very tall people. From early youth his ugliness had been the cross of his life. He would have liked to be externally just such a man as Schell; he respected physical strength, and strength in general. Now on top of all this he was half an invalid. This specimen, of course, is a traitor on "principle." The colonel would have *liked* to feel revulsion toward him, but he did not. He would have *liked* Schell to have, for instance, a thin, piping voice, like that of some other giants, Bismarck or Turgeniev; but Schell's voice was perfectly ordinary, though not very pleasing.

"There'll be no trouble about money. We won't pay less than the *others*, but even more if there's something to pay for. Good-by. I'll wait three weeks. Three weeks and no more," said the colonel, and again pretended to raise himself in his chair.

The colonel had a private apartment of two rooms well furnished with requisitioned furniture. Overlooking the altered premises of a German functionary there had hung in succession portraits of Wilhelm II, Hindenburg, Hitler, and, from 1945 on, Goethe. The colonel also had had a choice between the prescribed four photographs—Marx, Engels, Lenin, and Stalin. He had no desire to have the portraits of any Germans hanging in his flat. His attitude toward Marx was indefinite, confused, and complicated. He knew he had to admire him, and when necessary—only, to be sure, in extreme cases—he called himself a Marxist. But this old man swamped by a beard had always aroused his antipathy and put him in a bad mood. He hung up Lenin's portrait—the only Russian of the four. To Lenin, moreover, the colonel had always had a feeling of personal thankfulness. He had come from the bottom, was the son of a peasant, had gone into the civil war as a volunteer, been promoted, had then studied at the Academy of Military Science, and had now gotten into if not the topmost social stratum then

48

at least into the one next to the top. For this he considered himself indebted to Lenin. But on the opposite wall of his study office there hung Suvorov, quite out of place among the four. Sometimes it seemed to the colonel that these two men were gazing at each other with astonishment: how had they wound up together? And people who rarely came into the colonel's private quarters looked at the tsarist field marshal in perplexed alarm: surely he had no business hanging there.

The colonel usually went out to spend the night at home, but today he stayed late; there was an early business meeting scheduled for the following morning and he had decided to stay on overnight. In his working quarters the colonel could not venture what he called a "domestic atmosphere"; the more austere and businesslike the better. Nevertheless, in his wall closet he had a blanket, a pillow, and ham sandwiches. He was not yet in the mood for sleeping.

He was a bachelor; he had no close friends either in Berlin or in Russia. He almost never gave any receptions or drinking parties; he would have had to invite people from the political police as well. Since the time of his severe wound women scarcely occupied a place in his life. How could they like a man who was lame, crippled, and on top of that ugly? In his time he had drunk more than a little; at the beginning of his new assignment he even drank a good deal. He had begun not to feel well, and had consulted the best doctor in the army of occupation. The doctor had shaken his head, found very high blood pressure, strictly forbade any alcohol, advised as much walking as possible, and no meat. The colonel considered Russian medicine the best in the world, but although it was not very appropriate and he couldn't speak German fluently he also visited a well-known Berlin physician. The latter also shook his head, also found very high (even though different) blood pressure, and said that drinking wine sometimes would not hurt—it helped distend the blood vessels—ordered him to walk as little as possible in order not to fatigue himself, and to avoid floury and sweet things. "As for meat, you can eat as much as your means permit."

One physician had ascribed great significance to the higher point of the blood-pressure reading, and the other to the lower point. Both agreed that he had to eat a great deal of vegetables without butter. "But I can't stand them!" the colonel had angrily told the army doctor. "On the contrary, they're delicious," replied the army doctor, who, however, didn't eat them himself. "They say vegetables make you stupid," said the colonel still more gloomily to the civilian doctor. "That has not been proved by science," answered the German, who also may not have had anything against a Soviet officer's becoming more stupid. The colonel continued to eat steaks, since they had not been forbidden him by the second doctor; he also ate sandwiches and cake, since they had not been forbidden him by the first. By accident both physicians had forgotten to forbid him coffee—he had purposely avoided asking them about it. He drank strong coffee in great quantities and thought it was the only thing that really sustained him in his work.

In theory he, like so many other Soviet people, unhesitatingly maintained that life was made for pleasure (the thing to say was "pleasure in work," or something like that). In fact, his life had never been pleasurable, not even in youth: at that time because of being poor and overburdened with work. Nor had he married, primarily because there had never been time, a flat, or money. Now he was living "ascetically" (the word pleased him), and consoled himself with the thought that he was living for his country. But that was what many people said, though he knew that most of them were deceiving themselves or simply lying: they were of no use whatever to their country. He himself had thought during the past years that he was undoing the intrigues of Russia's enemies; now, however, he realized that incomparably more intrigues were being woven against others by the Soviet government. In principle he saw nothing inadmissible in this: hadn't the world always been that way? Nevertheless, a great many things displeased him, and especially the people who dealt with all that sort of thing. He knew scarcely any members of the government and his feelings for them were extremely mixed. What he appreciated in Stalin and respected was strength, energy, and contempt for drivelers, but even if Stalin had been Russian by nationality he would not have been his hero. In his time he had had an extravagant admiration for Tukhachevsky, and if his plot had succeeded would have served him with utter devotion. But the other marshals seemed to him drivelers, however painful he found it to think so.

He had been ambitious, especially before: rank and decorations, especially for combat, gave him a great deal of pleasure. Now both the decorations and his pleasure from them were very slight. In his new post he might have had a distinguished career if he had crawled like the others. The colonel realized that he would soon have to retire—they'll refer to my wounds, to fatigue, or, for that matter, not refer to anything at all—"You're getting a pension, aren't you, well?"—and some scoundrel would be put in. He had attained neither glory nor a high position, in fact nothing he had ever dreamed about. Suvorov had, although his looks hadn't been heroic either. . . . So now getting out of harness wasn't far off. . . . Who was it who had called death "getting out of harness"? He had no religious feeling of any kind. He had never read the Bible, had scarcely ever even looked at it, although probably even in Soviet Russia there were few people who had never even looked at it. He didn't believe in an after life and did not even understand how it could seriously be believed in. He thought extremely rarely about what he was living for—there was no time for it. But when he did, he could console himself by replying that neither did the majority of people in the world.

In his new job nearly everything was vile, or at best involved something vile, but every now and then interesting problems would crop up. Some of these problems, those he had managed to solve, ended up with death sentences. But that was no concern of his, and he never thought about it.

51

Thus only one thing remained satisfying—chess. He had been passionately attracted to it when young. He had never had time for a real study of chess theory: he did not even know all the openings. As for the literature, he scarcely knew it at all, only the most celebrated historical matches.

He took a miniature chessboard out of its box (his other, larger, one was at home), turned on the table lamp, and started examining a problem he had composed not long before. He did not compose problems at all badly; two of his had even been published. This particular problem was especially interesting, even unique. Both White and Black had a strong game and were both on the brink of disaster. White could mate in three moves, Black in three also, and everything depended on who moved first. The colonel was suddenly startled by the symbolism of the position on the board.

The words "We don't want war at all" were common parlance. Like everyone else, he spoke this way constantly. For two hundred million people they expressed the plain truth. As for the members of the Politburo, the colonel did not know what they thought: who could make them out? He himself sometimes wanted war, sometimes didn't. One of the reasons why he did not lay in his not being able to take part in military action in any case: everything would be up to the young and healthy. It was painful and strange to think of this, and quite impossible to speak of it, even if he had had close friends who might deserve complete confidence. There were no completely reliable people, or at least he did not know them; his new job had given him too much experience.

The colonel took a long drink of coffee and began to consider whether there might not be a variant. He failed to find one.

4

IN spite of all Natasha's fears her trip went off very well. She had scarcely ever traveled, knew no Italian, and even spoke French badly, but Schell had given her a precise itinerary, explained everything in detail, taken her to the station, and given her a bouquet which was quite out of place in the third class. They embraced. "So I'll be in Capri Sunday," he said. "Don't wind your watch any more. In the French Chamber of Deputies on New Year's Eve they usually stop the clocks in order to vote the budget on time." This remark annoyed her a little. She got into the carriage, barely holding back her tears, and when the train was already chugging out from under the glass roof he was still looking after her, holding his hat high over his head in his left hand and blowing her kisses.

All the places in her compartment were taken. She didn't want to relinquish the bouquet, but it was awkward holding it on her knees the whole trip; she put it on the rack above her small, threadbare valise. Now we must be bridegroom and bride, she repeated to herself. After all, if he came to the station, and we kissed again. . . . Still, he didn't propose. . . .

She didn't go to the dining car, which seemed to her like the last word in luxury; she had never even seen such a car from the inside. For that matter, maybe they don't let people in from the third class, or else I might make things even more mixed up there! She didn't feel like reading, and her books were in the valise. How could I get them out in front of everybody? And they'll see that the book is in Russian! Well, at least I'm sitting here, thank God! But she didn't like sitting down without doing anything. Probably they don't let you knit in the cars. The opposite row of seats was taken up by a German family with a very sweet little girl. Natasha adored children and would have started talking to the little girl if the father hadn't been sitting there: she was afraid of people, especially of men, and especially of Germans. "You have a real inferiority complex," Schell had told her more than once, with tenderness and indignation. "What can I do about it?" Natasha had answered with a sigh. "It all comes from the German underground factory. They had specialists there in driving that complex into you. With lashes." "Even your being clever upsets you! Yes, yes, you take great pains to hide it." "I never knew it myself. I probably manage to hide it so well no one notices it."

She took off her cheap gloves, which, like everything artificial, gave her a disagreeable feeling. The threads at the fingertips were worn out so completely they weren't worth mending, and real chamois ones were impossibly expensive. During the preceding few months she had been saving every mark and putting it aside for the trip to Italy. Her stipendium was very small; she had also been making some scarves for a Berlin department store, and could also make hats; she sewed her own dresses. She had hands of gold. "I can't do water colors or practice wood burning, that's for old-fashioned young ladies of quality," she said to Schell with a laugh. "But as for mending, I can do anything, I wash linen excellently, as well as my own

54

head, and I never make a—what d'you call it?—a 'permanent.' "
Schell listened with mixed feelings. He loved elegant women
and couldn't understand why he had fallen in love with
Natasha. A fateful passion! he explained it to himself. He liked
words like that; he almost felt sorry that in this case they didn't
fit at all; there was nothing "fateful" in this new passion of his.

At the Italian border a customs official, after a swift glance
at Natasha and at her valise, did not examine her things. Another official scrutinized her Soviet passport with curiosity and
showed it to his colleague. Natasha had been about to give
an explanation in German, which she spoke fluently: she had
not been in Russia since 1941, ought to get an *émigré* passport
very soon, it had already been promised to her. But no explanation was required. She was asked further about money, and she
pulled her twenty-five thousand lire out of her bag and said she
was going to Italy for no more than two weeks, just as a tourist.
The official nodded with a smile. And there she was, over the
border, without the slightest unpleasantness! Suddenly she was
overcome by an extraordinary joy, of the kind she used to call
"attacks of baseless happiness." Lately, ever since she had come
to know Schell, these attacks had become quite frequent, even
though her life was still extremely oppressive (or just because
of it). Nothing worse than the past can happen; God won't
forget me and will compensate me for everything!
Her neighbors looked at her with interest. Her eyes kept
shining more and more; she felt this and covered them, as
though she were ashamed. Very pretty, very pretty, indeed!
thought a young writer, who was going to Italy to write the
thousand and first book about Renaissance art. He had been
looking at Natasha since Berlin until the lights were put on, and
he couldn't make up his mind what sort of ruddiness she had,
whether it was healthy and normal or morbid and tubercular.
Both one and the other had its own kind of poetic charm. Her
eyes, he decided, were of a dark gray Lyon velvet, but he
wasn't satisfied with this description; he perseveringly kept

working up his imaginative powers. Her eyelashes are simply too improbably long. What are they like? Like Lorenzo Lotto's women, he decided with satisfaction, although he was doubtful whether his readers would understand: they might never have heard of Lorenzo Lotto.

Just as in the theater after an intermission, the curtain now rose on a far brighter setting. Everything became different, and the people were different. New passengers opened up food parcels and Natasha, after some hesitation, did the same. They affably started talking with her, and she answered in broken French. They were all extremely amiable. An Italian woman, very modestly dressed, offered her an orange; an old man, apparently a simple worker, asked her whether she would not like some wine. Oh, how nice they are! In general people are nice. . . . Of course there are nasty ones, she thought, recalling the underground factory, but they're the exceptions. And that's not going to happen any more. And I'm not going to have tuberculosis either; after all, the infection has begun in only one lung. . . . And he's going to propose! What a stupid word— propose—stupid, but so sweet! He won't be able not to! Little glints kept flashing through her eyes. He probably doesn't understand himself. To listen to him, he's such a pessimist and man-hater, but really when he smiles it's a pleasure to look at him. And what's more, people always look at him, at the station they were all looking at him. He must be a head taller than all of them, she thought. He's happy at the idea that he's *discovered* something in me! Cleverness? Why does he like cleverness so much? I like it, too, but only if there's not too much of it, and it's not too wicked. Last Monday I told him, "Don't crack all your jokes today, leave some for tomorrow." He didn't like it. He said: "My darling sweet, if a man isn't afraid of anything in life, doesn't expect anything, and doesn't believe in anything, then he *must* joke."

A Berlin physician had told her about the infection that was beginning in her lung; Schell had forced her almost by violence to go to him. She was afraid of doctors. They never tell you

56

anything good, and if you don't go to them then you won't hear anything bad either. The words "the beginning of an infection in the left lung" sounded much better than the terrible, repugnant word "tuberculosis." Nevertheless, they alarmed her. But Schell, who questioned the doctor about her on the telephone, explained to her that it was all absolute nonsense and she calmed down at once. Later, to be sure, *that Thursday in Grunewald,* he said that it would be good for her to take a trip to Italy anyhow, best of all to the mountains, where even the "beginning of an infection" would vanish at once.

"What are you talking about? Do you think I'm a Wall Street agent living here incognito? You don't imagine my allowance is going to be enough?"

"Have no fears about money, my dear little Wall Street agent, I'll get you as much as you want," he had replied. Natasha appreciated his delicacy: "I'll get you"—that is, he was going to give her his own. To be sure, he was rich, he had a big commission business. "What is a commission business, Eugene Karlovitch?" she had asked. What she didn't like in Schell was his drinking wine, his eternal jokes, and even his patronymic. There's nothing German about him, and there are all kinds of Karls. Perhaps his father's name was Charles? She tried out "Zhenya." No, it doesn't suit him at all. Though it would be stupid to call him by his patronymic now. She tried not to call him by name at all, but when she quickly hurried over "Eugene" she blushed painfully.

He hadn't given a clear answer to her question, *that time in Grunewald,* about his business. Lying when talking to her, to his own astonishment, did not prove very easy, even though it was quite feasible. He no longer insisted on a trip to the mountains; the physician had told him that Natasha was still in no danger.

"Though I myself don't really have too much faith in them either," he told her. "Before they used to send people who were sick in the lungs to Menton; later it was acknowledged that this killed them off, but they still went on looking just as puffed up. Today it's the mountains, Davos, but tomorrow it may be they will admit that you have to send them to the North Pole. But you haven't got anything anyhow. Just don't catch cold."

"Well, there you are," said Natasha, delighted. "But I should go to Italy anyhow, though not for a long time and only to Capri. I'm saving up money. I need it for a second dissertation."

When he learned that she was writing a dissertation for some Yugoslav university on "Lenin During the Period of Recallism and Liquidationism" Schell roared with laughter. "What was that? Repeat it: 'During the Period of Recallism and Liquidationism?' But surely in Yugoslavia they can't endure Moscow?"

"Not Moscow at all, just Stalin! And they've always looked up to Lenin."

"Let them go on looking up, too. Then what's the point of Capri?"

"The Bolsheviks years ago used to have a school in Capri."

"There you are! It shows you how useful a higher education can be! Capri is a marvelous island anyway, I've been there. Would you like to go there with me?"

She burst with joy. It was during this December evening that they abandoned formality; he had kissed her. "Aren't you afraid? What if my illness is catching?" she asked him in some confusion. As though on purpose—on such a day!—she had coughed. "No, no, I can't go off on a trip *that way,*" she said, and it sounded even more stupid. He said nothing in reply. Then she had become sad. He was apprehensive of the too rapid changes in her moods, and linked them to her illness.

They were going to Italy separately. Schell referred to business affairs that could not be put off and promised to come to Capri in three days at the latest. Natasha sadly told herself that this was because he did not want to travel third class.

". . . I'll find myself some very cheap little pension and you live wherever you like, but not with me. Even then people there may think God knows what about us!"

58

He agreed with a smile. Even after their embraces, Natasha still refused to accept his money. It was only in the restaurants that she consented to his paying. She had heard that in restaurants it was always the gentlemen who paid for the ladies, even for the rich ones.

Until Naples Natasha saw almost nothing in Italy but railway stations. In Rome she had to wait an hour and a half for a train, but she couldn't make up her mind to go out even into the square. What if I get lost, or come too late, or get into the wrong train!

In Naples, too, she saw very little. She found she had to hire a car; she explained to the driver as best she could that she was going to Capri and had to get to the harbor. The driver nodded, and on the way said something to her and kept pointing. There was one place he called Santa Lucia, and there Natasha nodded her head happily: she herself had sung the little song by this name even as a child in Russia and recalled that the song had something or other to do with Naples. The driver also showed her Vesuvius, but Natasha was disappointed: there were no flames, and not even smoke. The driver said that Vesuvius no longer smoked. He was a little embarrassed about it himself, like all Neapolitans.

At the harbor she gave him a huge tip, without knowing just how much; she was still strange to Italian money although in Berlin she had made a careful study of the crumpled banknotes, of huge dimensions, which Schell had bought for her (she gave it all back to him in German money to the last mark). The driver was obviously satisfied, and was going to call a porter, but when Natasha, alarmed, shook her head—a sheer waste—he himself carried her valise to the pay booth. She got a ticket and took up the valise (she was quite strong physically in spite of her lung infection). It was snatched at once by a sailor, who looked at her with a tender smile. Natasha, hesitating a little, gave him a tip, too; he was about to refuse, but finally took it. There was nothing saved in this way, but

59

Natasha was delighted by the sweet, kindly human relations. What a wonderful people!

She drew a calm breath only after sitting down on the bench of the little steamer. She sighed when she saw the sea for the first time: she had never seen it before. Such beauty! And it'll be calm, I think! A German guidebook had said that the sea between Naples and Capri is sometimes stormy, and gave various practical pieces of advice. Because of this Natasha did not ask for coffee and sandwiches, although she felt like eating and the prices at the buffet were low (she had already learned to translate marks into lire in her head quite rapidly). But the boat didn't rock. I don't feel a thing, I'm a real sea wolf!

Two hours went by splendidly. Castellammare, Sorrento—the names were so musical. She recalled "See Naples and die!" Who could ever have said something so stupid? On the contrary, see it—and live! Live here, or somewhere else, the whole world is wonderful and life is wonderful, and the longer you live the better.... He said to me, "You're alone the whole time and I'm busy all day." (What is he busy with?) "Have you very few friends, you unlikely Soviet infant?" "I'm not an infant at all, I'm an overgrown twenty-five-year-old camel. And why 'unlikely'?"

"Because throughout Russia there's doubtless no one else like you. There everyone, under the construction of socialism, has such monstrous egotism, such careerist elbows made of steel the like of which has never been seen in the world, not only not in bourgeois society but in Papua, too. And you haven't got even a trace of any of that. You haven't told me whether you have many friends."

"Almost none."

"Young women or young men?"

"But I tell you there's none. And I've never been friendly with a young woman in my life."

"I'll come more often. O eighth wonder of the world."

"Come every day!" she had blurted out. *Tu sei l'embleme— di l'harmonia, Santa Lucia—Santa Lucia!"*

60

She quickly tired of admiring the sea, got her knitting out of her valise, which she kept close to her, and busied herself.

She stopped at an extremely cheap pension. On the way from the "funicula" station she visited two—French was more or less understood everywhere—and chose a third, the cheapest. They gave her a tiny sunlit room with whitewashed walls, a majolica floor with white squares bordered in black which always seemed moist, a very clean bed, and a chair at the window looking out into a garden. There was even a small writing desk. The first thing Natasha did was to put the withered bouquet into water. On the way to her room she had seen a bathtub; she would have gone in for this expense, but the proprietress, a handsome woman no longer young, said that although the bathtub had unfortunately been damaged it would be mended very quickly.

Natasha washed, took out of her valise one dress of the three, not the best—I'll wear the better ones when he's here. Downstairs the proprietress again gave her a welcoming smile and told her what time they had lunch and dinner; she asked how long the signorina intended to stay in Capri. When she learned that it was not less than ten days, and more likely to be two weeks, she smiled still more tenderly and said it would not be a tragedy if the signorina was sometimes late for dinner, they would leave everything for her. And on the days she made an excursion to Anacapri, to Mount Tiberius, or to Sorrento, they would give her sandwiches instead of lunch. She also said something amiable about her dress and coat. Natasha understood everything and felt as though she were at home, though where is home for me?

In the dining room (the pension had no living room) there was a miniature piano. This delighted Natasha. She played badly; during the years in the underground factory she had forgotten, but Schell liked her singing. Suppose no one was around, could I sing to him here, too? She sang different things, from "Bublichki" to the romantic songs of Glinka and Tchaikovsky. Schell particularly liked "Bublichki," that anguished

61

little ditty of the bourgeois woman ruined by the Revolution and later allowed to peddle for a living. What had he said? "In this stupid little song there is something symbolical and terrifying." Why symbolic? And why is it stupid? On the contrary, all of us felt that way there, it was so disagreeable, and that calmed us. But in Berlin she had seldom sung for Schell. He used to come to see her in the evening, and from nine o'clock on the mistress of the pension, a large, stocky old woman with a stern face—who told everyone she was the widow of a functionary of the imperial epoch—kept dropping into the clean little salon, nearly half of which was taken up by a Bechstein; and at ten she declared decisively that it was impossible to play any more (on top of everything else she didn't like either "Bublichki" or the tall gentleman's visits).

Everything in the street was drenched in a warm, already almost hot light, everything was delightful. On the road from the station to the pension she had looked at practically nothing, she was so excited the whole time: Would the boy steal her valise? Would she find a room she could afford? Would they understand what she said? Now everything was settled. There were three days left to wait for Schell. The weather was paradise, although spring was only just beginning. In Berlin there was still a real and very nasty winter, which scarcely resembled a Russian winter; it was a winter without the charms of winter. She was amazed by the crooked, asymmetrical, narrow little streets, the unfamiliar almost tropical vegetation, the white, cream, and red houses, each one more picturesque than the other, and more than anything the hills, often completely bare with terrifying vertical cliffs. Even looking at them from below was awe-inspiring.

She strolled about until evening, sometimes stopping in front of shopwindows. The shops, of course, were smaller and poorer than the ones in Berlin, but in Berlin she had never had time to look into the shopwindows. In one shop not far from the square there was a sale of women's dresses. Natasha looked at the dresses, at the prices, translated them into marks—cheap!

One dress, lilac-colored, she liked enormously; it looked like a winter dress—it was, after all, the winter dresses that were now being sold out—but it was completely springlike. You could actually wear it both summer and autumn. Lilac is his favorite color, that's what he said *that day in Grunewald*.... She thoughtfully calculated: if I save on absolutely everything would there be enough for me to buy this dress and go back to Berlin? Sadly she told herself there wouldn't be. God grant she would have enough even without the dress. Especially if we stay more than ten days. She left the shop and her disappointment vanished at once. I can get along splendidly without a dress! For that matter I don't even need one, I have three.

The stars came out—they were different, too. Still with an engaging glint in her eyes she thought of Schell, how strange he was, almost even ridiculous with his mysteries, how his eyes, which at first seemed to her cold and frightening, were actually good and even tender—at least sometimes—and not in the least "steely," but blue. What a pity, what a pity, that it was impossible to stay there longer! But if he actually does propose here? she thought, melting away. Then we could stay on, and perhaps, after all, I could take some money from him as a loan. Even though I wouldn't hang around his neck even after the wedding: I'll go on working, suppose he is rich. I'll persuade him to stay on here longer, it will be our honeymoon. He said he's never been married. How amusing *that time in Grunewald* that I still thought he was frightening! I told him that his looks aroused an unaccountable fear in me. Then he laughed and said, "Don't talk in such a literary way." But I was telling the truth.... And now I have no fear at all, neither accountable nor unaccountable. Natasha constantly said to herself and to him "that time in Grunewald," as Napoleon might have said "that time in Toulon." Nor did Schell always realize all at once just what she meant.

There were not many people in the cozily lighted dining room: there was a large family at the principal table, and an

63

old man and woman, none of them the least frightening, though foreign. A sweet-looking servant girl, very like the proprietress, seated Natasha at a separate table and changed the paper table cover, smiling amiably. When she trotted with a bowl past the old buffet the dishes in it clattered; there was something cozy in the sound. The waitress brought in spaghetti, fish, and meat, all delicious. She asked what the signorina had had time to see, and when she heard everything was *"Très beau,"* *"Bellissimo,"* and that the signorina had never seen anything more beautiful than Capri, she set down a second portion of spaghetti. There was a decanter full of wine on the table. This disturbed Natasha a little. Wouldn't it cost too much? In Russia she had never drunk wine; in the underground factory she was happy when she got water that wasn't too filthy. During the past few months Schell had accustomed her to champagne and to expensive Rhine wines. At first they had seemed to her insipid—just what did people see in them?—but she soon liked them; what she liked was not the taste but the agreeable little dizziness in her head. At their last lunch together in Berlin, Schell told her that *real* Capri wine was among the best in the world and that it was almost impossible to get it in restaurants, you had to look for it among the old inhabitants rather than the wine dealers. Natasha tasted the wine from the decanter. I suppose it's good. After all, they're old inhabitants. Can it be the *real* wine? Couldn't I treat him, if he came to lunch?

The old couple got up. Perhaps I ought to bow to them, Natasha thought. They nodded affably to her first. I suppose now it's already time to go, I mustn't take advantage. They didn't pay, probably everything here is put on the account. Will they put it on my account, too? She got up and went over to the exit. Something in the buffet rattled again. It's simply heaven!

It was cold in her room. There had been a stove in the dining room, and the other rooms in the pension were warmed by the sun. Natasha was about to unpack her things and put them

64

away but she felt too exhausted. That's not from the beginning of the infection but from all the walking I've done here, and from the trip. Going to sleep at nine o'clock both shamed and tempted her. Natasha lifted the cover of the valise anyhow.

She subjected herself to what she called her Turkish atrocities: she washed from head to foot with cold water. "Are there such happy people who always have rooms everywhere with their own bathtubs, with running hot water?" she had once asked Schell. "There are, Natasha, there are," he had replied, "and you'll have it, too." (He said "you will"—isn't that a sign that he's going to marry me?) "But why do you call this self-torture Turkish atrocities? The Turks are a very good-natured people. It would be more natural to say: Nazi atrocities." Natasha said nothing in reply to this: she could joke about the atrocities of the Turks in remote times but she had seen the atrocities of the National Socialists at firsthand, and it was impossible for her to be reminded of them in jest. I think there'll be a puddle! I can't help it, she thought, bristling with the cold. But this floor might let water through! Won't they complain down below? But now she no longer believed anything unpleasant was going to happen, or that anyone was going to complain about her.

Then she got into bed and wrapped herself up according to her own system. With some difficulty she pulled out the ends of the pink blanket, tightly fitted in between the mattress and the wooden bed, and bunched them up underneath her from all sides, so that something rather like a sack took shape; the sheet also got a little warmer.

Her eyes began to cling together, but she knew from experience that even so she might not fall asleep. As a rule it's like a sudden electrical discharge, and then there's nothing left of sleep. You have to pick the moment you *can* sleep, but if you let it escape—good-by, sleep. That's like life: there's just one moment, if you let it pass—that's the end of it. . . . And where else could a proposal be made if not on this enchanted Capri?

65

In Berlin he simply had no time: surely not over dinner between two courses? Why does he drink so much? And can men be in love when they have this—what is it?—inferiority? she asked herself apprehensively. She was completely—almost completely—convinced that there was no reason in the world for anyone to love her.

5

NATASHA slept like a corpse and woke up toward seven o'clock. The room was flooded with light. She extricated herself at once from the sack. The evening before she had not let down the blinds; now she opened the window. Oh, what air! You couldn't catch cold here even in nothing but a blouse. . . . A cold in the head would be awful, if it doesn't go away before he gets here! In the garden she was enchanted by flowers and trees she had never seen before. Here's where we'll sit together when he comes to see me. The stillness was extraordinary. Nowhere before had it ever been like that. She decided not to ring at once; it was too early. She determined to wait until eight. But from the kitchen side a woman's gay voice was heard, someone answered just as gayly, and Natasha felt even more gay. She rang, timidly, scarcely pressing on the button.

The same sweet-faced waitress wished her good morning, asked how the signorina had slept, and what she could give her for breakfast. Very quickly coffee was brought, butter, two white rolls, and a glass of cold water. Schell had told Natasha that on Capri drinking water was a rarity: it had to be brought from Naples. It must mean they like me! She's probably the daughter of the proprietress, or a niece. She would have been glad to start talking with the maid, too—she especially loved conversations with simple people—but since she didn't know the language, that was impossible, and for that matter the coffee would have grown cold. She felt very hungry. Again everything was splendidly served and tasted delicious. A little less coffee than milk was served. Natasha liked it strong and sweet. She poured almost the whole coffeepot into the cup at once, drank it down with pleasure, then poured into the cup everything left of the milk as well, just trickling into it what was left of the coffee. Nothing was left either of the butter or of the crisp little rolls. It's just a shame! In Berlin restaurants she had always been ashamed or conscience-stricken about something or other in front of waiters; this amused Schell enormously. He took her to restaurants far away from the center, sometimes outside the city, although in winter there were not many people there—this seemed to be one of his countless caprices; he also disliked walking and would immediately get into a car as soon as possible.

She went over to the window again and began inhaling the air. How ravishing! Perhaps in even ten days here I'll be completely healed! Some wash was hanging out on a line near the fence. This also seemed to her extraordinarily picturesque. Then with regret she shut the window and started working. There were three drawers in the bureau. The dresses and underclothes fitted, but there was no place to put the two hats she had brought. All her things were very cheap. Only the French scents were extremely expensive: they were Schell's presents. Natasha was not in the least ashamed of her poverty, but also did not glory in it, which is rarer.

She did not make her bed—something had to be left for the maid to do, too, or else she would be hurt. But she cleaned up the room probably better than it had ever been cleaned before. She even took out the drawer of the table and shook the dust out into the basket. She laid her books out on the table with precision. She had the strangest assembly of books. There were histories of the Russian church by the Metropolitan Makarios and Golubinsky—with great joy she had found these rare editions in Belgrade and had even bought them fairly cheap: the secondhand bookdealer had not known what Russian books were worth. There was the *Account of a New Heresy*, very useful for her first dissertation. There were also Soviet books, pamphlets, and historical reviews; the secondhand dealer had looked at her with some surprise when she picked out all of these. She had even thought it necessary to explain to him what it was all about. Her basic dissertation was "On the First Manifestations of Russian Socialism in the Writings of the Sect of the Unworldly." She had chosen the subject herself; the professor had agreed to it, although somewhat reluctantly. But her second work, supplementary and obligatory, on Lenin, had been proposed to her by the faculty. She had accepted this subject rather reluctantly in her turn. Like practically everything in Yugoslavia the university was in some strange way both Communist and anti-Communist. People would explain this away not very lucidly by speaking very quickly.

At ten o'clock there was a knock at the door and the proprietor of the pension himself came in. Natasha got up—she had got used to this in the underground factory and was still unable to divest herself of fear of men with some kind of title. It turned out that the proprietor had come to inquire whether the signorina was satisfied with everything and whether she would have both lunch and dinner there. It was cheaper that way, and he would very much advise her to, but they also had half-pension; his wife had not quite understood the signorina and he would like to know the signorina's final decision. Natasha answered with fervor that she would, of course, have both lunch and dinner.

"Everything tastes so good here! And what wonderful wine!

69

I suppose it's real Capri wine? But I don't have to have so much, I hardly drink at all."

The proprietor explained that the wine was real Tiberian wine and that her decanter was included in the price of the pension. That was also pleasant. Natasha gathered up her courage and mentioned something else. She was afraid that her Soviet books would be found in her valise or on the table after she went out and she would be considered a Bolshevik, and in addition the police would be informed—then she wouldn't be able to avoid unpleasantnesses. In German, supplemented somehow by French, she explained that she was busy with Russian history, was writing a book, and that for her scholarly, purely scholarly, researches it was very necessary for her to find out where Lenin had lived on Capri many years before and where there had been a Bolshevik school at the time. The proprietor listened to her with an affable smile, but as though he were somewhat astonished. However, he didn't seem to find anything terrible in the question. He said that the great Russian writer Maxim Gorky had lived not far off, in the big red house on the hill, which was now a hotel, he would give the signorina the address; about Lenin and the school he didn't know anything.

"Most probably our famous Capri boatman, old man Antonio, will be able to tell you that. He knew Lenin personally and took him and Gorky to the Blue Grotto. You can find him at three o'clock at the entrance to the funicula, he waits for the tourists there. But Axel Munthe also lived here on the island— another great writer. All the writers and scholars have come to Capri."

Natasha thanked him effusively in German, French, and even Italian.

"... Extremely charming! A professor! Studies history," said the proprietor to his wife when he got downstairs.

"She's not going to be studying history long," answered his wife disapprovingly. But she herself liked this Russian girl very much.

70

Natasha didn't sit down to work straight off. She studied the guidebook all morning, looking up the gardens of Capri, the Castiglione castle, the Church of San Stefano, the cliffs of Maraglioni, where the pirates, after luring sailors ashore by fires, killed and buried them on the spot. But Natasha left Anacapri, the Palace of Tiberius, and the Blue Grotto for Schell: let him take her there. After lunching in the pension she didn't rest—there was no point in being lazy—but went off to the station. There the old man Antonio was pointed out to her. Although Natasha didn't order a boat he gladly gave her all his information: yes, he had been a friend of the great writer Gorky, had taken both him and Lenin to the Blue Grotto; he had also visited their school which had been located in the Villa Pierina, on the road to the Piccola Marina, it had been left just as it was, and by accident there was no one living in it now. Other boatmen and porters listened to the old man with curiosity. They had heard of Lenin and the school, and were evidently proud of its having been on Capri.

Once again Natasha was in luck: she learned the address easily. Bubbling with excitement, she started off for the Piccola Marina, asking the passers-by, not the tourists, but the real Capresi. Everyone answered her affably, sometimes even interrupting their business and conversations. She had never received so much attention anywhere; she had never been spoiled by kindness.

The villa, which was on one side of a broad road, was white with two stories, with columns on the first story, and it stood in the depths of a lush garden filled with stone pines, palms, and rosebushes. Wherever did they get the money from, then, to rent such a villa? thought Natasha, perplexed. "Well, they killed someone, that's what life is like," as Maikov would have said. That's what he said about every sort of vile thing, "Life is like that!" and he said it with satisfaction!

Serious historians always test everything carefully, and in order not to be dependent on Antonio alone she walked farther on down the road, bought a bar of chocolate at a shop, and

71

asked about the villa: was it true that at some time there had been a Russian Communist school there? The old shopkeeper and his wife, who by some miracle understood her, said with pride: Yes, there was a Communist school in the Villa Pierina, the great writer Maxim Gorky came there by cab because of his poor health while Lenin went on foot, and they themselves had seen them with their own eyes; the tsarist police were always tagging after them. Natasha managed to understand them, too.

She returned to the villa, stood in front of the entrance for a long time, and, timidly looking around her, tried the gate. It was unlocked. Probably there really isn't anyone there, after all. Should I go in? Why, of course! Natasha went into the garden, and once again gathering up her courage—mightn't they take her for a robber?—looked in through a window: she saw a large empty room like a study. Of course, that's where they gave lectures! And then here on this terrace is where they discussed Recallism. Natasha was firmly convinced that it was up to historians to judge and describe everything "objectively." Nonetheless, the villa inspired her with disagreeable feelings. This is where everything started, in this gay little white villa! We used to be told that the Bolsheviks had shaken the world, and that's actually so. This and the Hitler shake-up shook me up, too. Papa would be in Russia, life would have taken a completely different course, and there would have been no war, they say. . . . But then, after all, *he* wouldn't be here either!

The Villa Pierina was her discovery—in the historical literature it had never been mentioned. Natasha, to be sure, still had some doubts: such as that Lenin had been on Capri for a very short time. But didn't he dislike this school? She also had some chronological difficulties with the Recallists and the Liquidators. But all that was just what might make a subject for discussion in her second dissertation. It'll take up at least ten pages, she thought happily. Best to write it all down as quickly as possible. I'll bring him here without fail; it will interest him, he's so educated. She made a mental calculation: there were

72

still forty-six hours before Schell's arrival, perhaps only forty-five.

Enough had been done that day for her second dissertation. Sitting down on a rock, she wrote everything down in a notebook with a little pencil attached which she had bought for the purpose in Berlin; she described the villa, the garden, the room, and jotted down brief entries on "the testimony of the local inhabitants." All that might be appropriate. From a historical point of view, of course, it's not so valuable, but it has human interest. It was annoying that the little pencil was hard and wrote unclearly. There was no ink in her fountain pen. I might ask the proprietress or else, not to be a bother, I'll buy a bottle tomorrow at the same time as the paper. The lack of ink was a legitimate reason for not thinking about the Recallists that evening. When he's here it'll be harder to work, and also, he'll keep laughing at my work. . . . Well, I'll have to get up early, I'll start writing at seven, and we probably won't meet much earlier than eleven. She went up to her room. By now she was already beginning to be bored, too. "Death and damnation!" she happily recalled his favorite exclamation, and started laughing with joy. No, I'm not bored, death can stay damned.

That evening, with a pencil in her hand, not the hard little one but an excellent one, she read a compendium about fifteenth, sixteenth, and seventeenth century sects in Muscovy: the Tonsurers, the Judaizers, the Unworldly, and the Josephites. Zacharias the Jew, who came to Novgorod in the suite of the new prince, Michael Alexandrovich, who had been invited by the Boyars, was learned in every device of evil-doing, sorcery, and necromancy, moreover, of astronomy and astrology, and with his disciples perverted many Russian saints, the archbishop, and the Metropolitan Zosima himself, and very nearly corrupted the Grand Duke of Moscow, Ivan Vasilevich. These ill-taught heretics propounded the astronomic book of Shestikryl and the metaphysics of Moses the Egyptian or Maimonides, but most of all the doctrine of Aristotle, the chief of all philosophers.

73

They said: "Nay, there be no Kingdom of Heaven, for those who die, die in the place of their sojourn. . . ."

Natasha herself had often thought about whether there was life after death, especially since she had begun coughing. She had no sympathy for what historians called the rationalism of the Tonsurers and Judaizers. She could not understand just *what* these people offered, what consolation, and why write such hopeless, depressing books; and what did they need their Aristotle for, and all their astrology? On the other hand, she had a tender affection for the Unworldly, especially Nil Sorsky, who had gone off to the Sora River away from the abuses of the world. She also liked Nil Sorsky's having listed woefulness and melancholy among the eight cardinal human vices. She had heard this before the war from Nikolai Maikov. After all, he's a descendant of Nil and knows all that. She had often repeated his remarks to herself while she was working in the underground factory. Sometimes they failed to help—what was being done at the factory was too terrible. But sometimes they did help.

Now Natasha read a few pages from the book, and she was happier than ever. Where will he stay? She had seen a large hotel in town, the Quisisana. The guidebook said that this was the best hotel in Capri, although even without the guidebook that was obvious just by looking at the people walking out, by the crowd of guides, and by the little donkeys standing around waiting for tourists. When Natasha walked past a haughty woman talking German was riding up to the porch on a little donkey.

Her sleep was cheerful, without reflection, a little uneasy. And suddenly the Emperor Tiberius burst through into the other nonsense. This time he was the teacher in her school in Kiev. He was reading about the Recallists and took an intimate interest in her. "Don't marry him!" said the emperor. "Surely you see he's a deceiver? You yourself thought so at first; it's no use trying to hide it from yourself. Run away from him as far and as fast as you can."

74

Natasha awoke in horror and sat up hugging her knees. Her eyes were wide, and her heart was pounding heavily. A deceiver in what? But in the beginning I actually did think so! How does he know that? Who knows it? Tiberius! What nonsense! She woke up completely. Nonsense, absurd nonsense! she cried out to herself, and even tried to smile. Why should he have started to deceive me? It's only that he never talks about himself. I'll ask him. Just like that, I'll ask him. . . . Oh, what nonsense people dream! I won't ask him about it for anything! I won't say a word. . . . And I won't say anything about my dream! she thought, calming down little by little. She was agonizingly ashamed of herself.

6

AFTER another interview with Schell, Colonel Number One decided to go to Paris. The trip had no connection with the Maikov affair, which had been imposed on him and didn't interest him very much. This time he had another scheme, of his own, which was rather more important. He had to talk it over with a general who occupied a high position in Rocquencourt. This general was a school comrade of his and in spite of the difference that had formed with the years in their ranks and reputations they were still friends.

The colonel could leave Berlin whenever and for wherever he liked, without asking anyone's permission. His superiors had an unusually high opinion of him and allowed him complete independence. He did not "demand more of himself than of others," as the obituaries say so often, but he really was very conscientious. He was particularly punctilious in matters where official and personal interests imperceptibly merged. That was

76

what this affair was about. The woman recommended to him by Schell was supposed to play a role in it, but his nephew, a young officer attached to SHAPE in the Public Information Division, was also supposed to participate. He had to put in a request for his nephew in Rocquencourt and the colonel did not find this altogether agreeable.

Before his departure the usual reports came in from the other side of the Iron Curtain. His papers were divided into Restricted, Confidential, Secret, and Top Secret. He referred these reports to Secret, but without exaggerating their significance. There was one valuable report; all the others seemed to him nonsense and not very honest. The colonel did not get angry; he had long since grown accustomed to it. He told his superiors just this: the agents may be telling the truth, or they may be embroidering—not with anything evil in view (which happened rarely)—but simply in order to puff themselves up or justify their salaries; they may not know anything for certain and so pass off rumors as facts; the worst ones, generally foreigners, simply make things up. For the most part he relied on his close assistants and on his old agents. His attitude toward Gelen's West German organization was mistrustful: he found a great deal in its struggle against Wollweber's East German organization at once disagreeable and amusing. After long experience, however, he knew that it was impossible in his profession to work only with honest people. While on duty he was polite, even affable, with almost all spies, but with a few he could not ultimately overcome his disgust. In his work he himself liked precision, facts, figures, and preferred methods as simple as possible, on the view that in most cases it was the most complicated combinations that failed.

Nevertheless, during the war there had been one intelligence project (since become famous) that was extremely complicated and difficult, and that had had enormous historical consequences. The Allies had thrown into the sea near Spanish shores a corpse that seemed to be that of an officer who had died with papers containing misinformation about their landings in

77

Europe. As had been expected, the corpse drifted ashore, the Spanish authorities passed the documents to the Germans and they got to Hitler himself, who was taken in by the misinformation. This was one of the causes of the German catastrophe. For imagination, for boldness of conception, for dramatic effect, for the technical perfection of execution, and most of all for the results, the colonel considered this enterprise an unprecedented masterpiece in the history of intelligence. He knew about it in great detail, but had had nothing to do with it. He would have liked to conclude his career with some such undertaking. In peacetime, to be sure, a similar intrigue was impossible; but the colonel's misinformation project might be enormously important if it came off. And there was a good chance of success. Gimpy is bound to swallow it. In spite of his ability he's a dilettante, after all, in our business. He very much wanted to make a fool of Gimpy. Their never-ending contest had long since generated a feeling of professional rivalry in both of them.

Breakfast was served: the sort always served in airplanes and dining cars—not very bad and not very good. The colonel ate heartily and kept on thinking about his scheme. It stands a chance. It's a pity that from what he says she's stupid, but he did say he's got complete control over her.

At first the colonel had not liked Schell. At their first meeting he had almost thought the agent was one of those people who like the reputation of good-for-nothings and boast of it. The colonel had also met a great many like that; he found the species particularly repulsive. Afterward his opinion of Schell improved. He saw so much evil in life that with the years he had become more and more indulgent. There's no doubt he's an extremely valuable agent. That Mexican drug of his may not be a calamity. . . . Strange that he plays the cello. A little unusual for an agent to have such an ethereal soul. He must have soaked himself in Dostoevski—an absolute social calamity. But he'd be very useful anyhow, no matter how this Maikov business ends up, all those scientific discoveries. . . . And does Jim have

78

to be brought into it? A light-minded kid. But it's time to get him out among people, he's going to turn into a worthless playboy. We'll try it out and see. For the time being there's nothing to worry about.

The colonel was a man of practically imperturbable calm—in this respect like one of Jules Verne's Englishmen. Friends jokingly compared him with Marshal Joffre. He also had the gift of relaxation, not, after all, so commonly met with. In the airplane he mechanically made his "observations," which bored him exceedingly. His neighbors' faces were already filed away in his memory forever. This memory of his was of various kinds and degrees: unerring for faces, almost infallible; for everything else mediocre or even bad. But these neighbors happened to be uninteresting. A man and a woman were discussing breakfast; the woman was saying she could never sleep after coffee. And how would she have slept, for instance, after that run-in I had last year with Hauser? I slept very well after that, too, the colonel thought, a little vexed at his own MacNabblike imperturbability.

After breakfast he started smoking with enjoyment—his style actually demanded that he smoke either a pipe or a cigar, but he didn't like them, he smoked only cigarettes, and cheap ones at that. He got out a French detective story he had bought at the airport; he had long since read practically all the English and American ones sold at airports and railway stations. For the hundredth time he deplored the French habit of publishing books with uncut pages; he used a piece of square cardboard advertising something to cut open the book and started reading. The novel turned out to be quite enjoyable. A disagreeable man was killed, the murder took place without any atrocities, the death penalty was unexpected, the official detective was not too stupid, and the private investigator was not too clever. Of course both of them were startlingly unlike any real detectives; but no resemblance to real life was demanded of detective stories. Naturally it was clear from the beginning that the one who had done the killing was not the chief suspect. You had to look around only among those on whom suspicion had not fallen. As a rule the colonel guessed at the very first pages who the killer was, and he guessed this time, too. Just why pay them money for it? he thought, smiling. Compared with what he himself had seen in his own day the author's imagination seemed to him rather pedestrian.

He thought of his imminent retirement. He intended to settle in the country. Thoughts about his house in Connecticut and about his training stables were pleasant, but he was afraid he was going to be bored. I'll go to the office now and then to find out what the news is. . . . But that won't be the same thing. He remembered an old man who had become a little senile, a former colleague, who kept telephoning friends who had died: he could remember their telephone numbers but had forgotten that they were long since dead.

In Paris the colonel put up at a good hotel in the center of the city. It was not one of the most expensive ones, and he always stayed there even though he usually traveled at government expense. Aside from that he liked this part of the city. Remote and very agreeable memories of his first trip to Paris were bound up with it. The Palais Royal was there and the old Régence Café, with Napoleon's table and with the best coffee in France, a bookshop with various complete collected works in gilt bindings. Fauré Lepage, the celebrated gunsmiths, were there, too.

He was in a very good mood. He was not in the least depressed by the airplane trip and felt very well. In the mirror he noticed, not for the first time, that his jowls were somewhat pendulous, that his chin might already be considered to be double, and that his round, brownish eyes had somewhat faded. He noted this almost without vexation; he never thought about death or illness. Why get upset prematurely? He lived just as though he thought he was going to live forever. The weather was fine, unusual for a Paris winter. And though he was by no means a sensitive man, this helped his good mood.

He divided up his time at once. It was easy to get a car to

drive out to Rocquencourt, he simply had to check in by phone. But he didn't; he did not feel like seeing any of the other officers. He decided to go out to Marly unobtrusively, by rail. There was no need to hurry, his nephew was not free until evening. Even though my playboy doesn't do anything, I won't disturb him at work, I'll dine with him later, the colonel decided.

He walked to the Gare St. Lazare. As usual he stopped in front of the windows of Fauré Lepage; he examined everything attentively and read out the various inscriptions: *Finement poli en long . . . Choke et demi-choke perfectionnés. . . . Quadruple verrou . . . Finissage irréprochable. . . .*

He was very much interested in one rifle. It was expensive. After a moment's hesitation he walked into the shop. He was recognized at once; he was a good and old client. He examined the rifle at length with love, couldn't resist it, bought it, and ordered it sent to his hotel. Then he went into the bookshop. Having splurged on the gun he didn't buy anything for himself, but seeing a finely bound edition of the *Mémorial de Sainte Hélène,* he bought it and arranged for it to be sent to his nephew. He'll find it useful. It's bad for a man to be too ambitious, but if he's totally devoid of ambition it's simply a catastrophe. He should read about Napoleon.

The second-class car was empty; the French went to the suburbs third class. The colonel put on his glasses (he was a little proud of using them only to read with) and opened the Paris American newspaper he had bought at the station. There was nothing very important on the first page. He turned to the sports section on the fifth page and saw with joy that "G. R. Peterson" had won first prize in the steeplechase. A terrific horse! Terrific! I always knew it.

Then he turned back to the first page. The colonel was far more at home with political affairs than most officers. Germany was reviving by leaps and bounds. Before she rearms by leaps and bounds, he thought. He had no particular opinion about the rearmament of Germany. Everything its partisans said was

81

completely true, but everything its opponents said was also completely true.

The suburbs looked rather miserable. Old, dilapidated and crookedly standing houses were visible everywhere, their walls sometimes without windows. A vast cemetery stretched out near Puteaux, with some little huts standing between it and the railroad. A lovely life, no doubt, between two such landscapes, the colonel thought.

At the tiny little Marly station he was told that a cab could be gotten by telephone, that the trip to Rocquencourt would cost five hundred francs, and that he would have to wait five minutes. The colonel strolled through the station. He came across some inscriptions on a wall, tattered and rubbed out. "Yanks, go home," *"Ridgway—la peste."* He was completely indifferent. He considered freedom of speech an unavoidable evil. In his experience it had occasionally had disagreeable consequences: eminent members of various parliaments sometimes blurted out facts which were far from suitable for broadcasting. This evidently was done in order to "enlighten the public." The colonel failed to understand why it was up to the public to be acquainted, for instance, with figures having to do directly or indirectly with rearmament; it forgot them the following day, whereas the military departments of enemy countries snapped them up like manna from heaven. But he knew that in the United States it was useless to argue about words like "public opinion," and "public vigilance" (the latter seemed to the colonel downright comic). He would have been sternly informed that the *real* secrets were never blurted out—public opinion was carefully watching out for that, too. The colonel thought the public should simply be told about the strength of the enemy and the necessity of spending twice as much on armament as was being spent. The colonel thought the earlier publication of the Smyth Report on atomic energy a lamentable mistake. And it was completely pointless for the civilian inventors of the atomic bomb to have printed articles and given interviews. A few such facts, however brief and peripheral, might—he had no doubt of it—suit the Bolsheviks very well indeed.

Nevertheless, he had almost no contempt for civilians. He knew from his experience in the service that the best secret agents in wartime had come from among the drafted civilians. But other civilians had very nearly destroyed his entire department in 1945 by sharply cutting down on its allocation. That was when he had wanted to become a military attaché—there was an opening in one of the major countries in Europe; that was also a form of intelligence service. But it turned out that his personal circumstances were not comfortable enough. It never failed to irritate him that the richest country in the world did not wish to pay properly for work that was most indispensable for it. Nevertheless, the intelligence services were created thanks to the energy and talents of a few well-known authoritative intelligence officers, of whom he was one. Now Congress was handing out money lavishly and the department had rapidly become, in his opinion, the best in the world, absolutely on a par with the Soviets. The colonel's attitude toward Congress and "public opinion" had grown softer; after all, they were also a part of the "American way of life" which he firmly believed in and was devoted to.

The old taxi driver drove him through the woods to Rocquencourt. The colonel was in mufti, but before he had said a word the taxi driver recognized him as an American officer. On the way he showed the colonel *Le trou d'Enfer*, the hunting preserve of the President of the Republic, and told him some historical anecdotes.

"All this once belonged to the Montmorency family, the most illustrious in the world," said the taxi driver, as though proud of it, "but there are no more left; the Montmorencys nowadays aren't the real ones."

"But where do you know all this from?"

"What d'you mean, 'where from'? From books. I've lived here all my life. How could I not know it?" said the old man. A thing like this is possible only in France; an amazingly intelligent people, thought the colonel, who liked the French but had the same attitude toward them he might have had toward the ancient Greeks. To be sure he considered all Europeans people of the past.

"But is it true you dislike the Americans so?" he asked good-naturedly. "There are all those inscriptions—'*Ridgway—la peste.*'"

"*Tout ça, c'est de la blague,*" said the taxi driver, shrugging his shoulders. "The parties have to have something to do. Why shouldn't I like you? It's more of a question of your not liking me. Right now I'll have to halt some way off from the entrance; they won't let me into the courtyard, since you regard all taxi drivers as Communists. And I'm about as much of a Communist as you are," the old man said just as good-humoredly.

The colonel gave him six hundred instead of five hundred francs.

He went over to the flat, long bright building with the green flag; this was where, if the destinies of the world were not decided, at least their decision was being prepared. On the extremely tall very slender flagpoles were fluttering the flags of the fourteen states which had signed the North Atlantic Treaty four years before. He was respectfully greeted in the vestibule by an officer he knew, who accompanied him through the long gray corridors overlaid with something greenish. They passed officers in uniforms of various armies. Then he turned off into another corridor marked "4-A," incomprehensible to outsiders. He hardly had to wait at all. In the large, well-furnished office, behind a desk with a telephone on it, the general stood up, a youthful-looking man with a very intelligent, forbidding face alive with will power.

Then there took place what always took place in this office whenever the colonel came on a visit: terse, comradely greetings from the general, followed immediately by an energetic monologue. He violently cursed everyone—the Pentagon people, government people, Allied parliaments, Allied generals. He said he had no real army, nor, with all these characters,

84

would he have; he cursed the day and the hour when he was transferred from his combat post to this tragicomic institution. The Allied ministers were only thinking of how they could keep themselves in power one more month. One out of every three Allied soldiers was a Communist—how could they be depended on? The only real money was given by the United States and there was very little of that. And there was only one real army, the American, which numerically was laughably inadequate. Then he calmed down a little and listened to the colonel's report very attentively, making intelligent comments, and asked businesslike questions from which it was clear that he understood everything from the first word on; he jotted down something on some pages of a notebook, authorized something, turned down something else. He approved highly of the colonel's scheme.

". . . Yes, that would be splendid. Let's try it. They may go for something new. I don't think they've shown any interest in the furnace yet. And if this young charmer is attractive, the youngster can amuse himself at the same time. I have nothing against it. Tomorrow I'll make arrangements for his transfer. In any case he won't be any more useless than in what he's working at now."

The phone rang. A very important personage was telling him something from Paris. The general's face grew still less amiable by far.

". . . That's what we have the Public Information for," he said testily.

But it was apparent that the important person was asking something very convincingly; the general, scarcely covering the receiver with his hand, cursed under his breath, fiddled about with his table calendar, and set an appointment.

"I won't give them more than ten minutes, and I can't have lunch with them, someone else will have to. . . . You're quite welcome. Good-by," said the general, hung up, and turned back to the smiling colonel. "That's what time is wasted on!

85

Some important persons or other from Reykjavik want to see me! What the devil is Reykjavik?"

"The capital of Iceland," said the colonel, though he knew his answer wasn't of the least use to the general, who knew very well where Reykjavik was and even what was going on there.

"If you mobilized the entire population of Iceland it would be impossible to form a single division," said the general angrily.

As always the colonel left this office somewhat reassured. Occasionally, at bad moments, it occurred to him that the world situation was essentially hopeless—oddly enough for both sides. Now he told himself that very important matters were in the hands of a very able man who knew his trade brilliantly well (the colonel had long since lost faith in the military *genius* of any generals at all, especially because he knew them all personally). What was also engaging about this general was that he didn't make the slightest effort to belong to the intelligentsia or to please it.

As a man whom the general had talked to for almost an hour, he was conducted out very respectfully and promised that his nephew would be called immediately. The working day was already ending. The ceremony of changing the flags was just taking place on the square: they changed places every day in a fixed order; the only flag that did not move was the French flag, which always occupied the same place, that of host. The colonel was fond of military ceremonial and liked this one, too. Our soldiers are certainly the best in the world, he thought.

His nephew Jim, a handsome young lieutenant, appeared at once. He had not been expecting his uncle and was delighted to see him. The colonel was fond of Jim, who had been left in his charge as a child. Toward his uncle Jim preserved the amiable condescension of a young man beginning life toward an old man finishing his career. He appreciated his solicitude and generosity, knew he could depend on him utterly, and listened respectfully to his constant admonitions. All this might be

86

stretched to mean that he loved him, but the colonel did not delude himself. After my death he'll be a little sad; it may even take him a little while to be consoled by his inheritance of thirty thousand dollars, not counting the house in Connecticut, which in any case he'll soon sell, he thought with a sigh.

"Will you be staying long?"

"I'm leaving the day after tomorrow. I'd like to invite you to a good dinner tonight. I hope you're free? We have to have a very serious talk."

"Actually I'm not," Jim replied, hesitating slightly, "but for you and for a good dinner, of course, I'll free myself, in spite of your very serious talk. I was supposed to dine with friends. I'll ring them at once."

"Yes, ring her. Where can we get a good dinner?"

"Well, Uncle, that depends on how much you're willing to spend."

"Let's say twenty dollars, that's seven thousand francs."

"Even eight. I exchange dollars on the black market. I hope you do, too."

"Don't hope," said the colonel severely, "and I forbid you to."

"I'll never do it again!"

"Have you heard the news? G. R. Peterson won yesterday."

"No!" exclaimed Jim excitedly. He followed the horses, too; it was one of the few traits he had in common with his uncle.

"Don't you read the papers! You probably don't know the alarming rumors about the health of Native Dancer, then!"

"You don't say!"

"I hope it's nothing serious!"

"We haven't had a horse like that since Man o'War! He must have made Vanderbilt more than seven hundred thousand dollars. How does your G. R. Peterson compare with that?"

"Well, of course, Native Dancer..." said the colonel, as though he were hearing a talented young poet compared with Shakespeare. "It's six o'clock already. What's the best restaurant here?"

"Here? You're not thinking of treating me to one of the local

87

restaurants! If you had called me for lunch we would still have been able to go to the Pavillon Henri IV in Saint-Germain. Louis XIV was born there. You may say that doesn't make the cooking any better; nevertheless, Louis XIV wasn't born in Lindy's on Broadway. But evenings in Saint-Germain are just as dreary as they are in this hole in the wall. I'll take you to Paris."

"Take me in what?"

"Since you still haven't given me a car I'll take you in a cab at your expense."

"Fine. And what do you do in the evenings generally?"

"I read Spinoza in Latin with a pencil in my hand, correct the latest version of the Einstein theory, and meditate on the Vedic period in the history of the Punjab Aryans. . . ."

The colonel waved a hand. "Show me your furnace before dinner."

"What furnace?"

"The one where they burn the documents. Surely it's close by?"

"Why do you want to look at the furnace?"

"None of your business. Out of curiosity."

There was nothing interesting about the square, rather low brick furnace. A reddish flame was shooting up in it as though something were just being burned.

"There's something symbolic in this," said Jim, raising a finger with a triumphant look. "Here the world's evil is being burnt!"

"Just a little less nonsense from you," said the colonel, but very amiably. He forgave his nephew even the fact that he was evidently slipping over into the intelligentsia.

7

"I HOPE you're going to let me pick the food, Uncle?" Jim asked, when they had sat down at a small table in a corner of the restaurant. "I'll order you a dinner the like of which you've never had in your life!"

"I haven't the slightest doubt of it."

"I don't deny that you yourself have rather good taste in food and especially in wines. But your doubts would be devoid of any justification whatever if you allowed me to go beyond the limits of twenty dollars. Would that be a catastrophe?"

"Order whatever you please. I'm delighted to give you the satisfaction, even though you don't deserve it."

"I quite agree, I don't," retored Jim with complete readiness. "It's true I still don't know just what you're going to scold me for today, but I have no doubt you're going to scold me, that's your business. And in any case you'll be absolutely right. . . . What would you say to lobster? Just don't call it *Homard à l'Américaine,* you'll disgrace me. You have to say *Homard à l'Armoricaine.*"

"That's a very thorny question. It's been debated for some time."

"There's nothing to debate about there. As though Frenchmen would name a dish in our honor! They have the greatest contempt for our gastronomical ideas."

"All perfectly pointless."

"I thought so myself before I started living in Paris. And what, Uncle, about some fresh caviar?"

"Order some fresh caviar, too," said the colonel, waving his hand.

"Then I'll ask for some vodka. It will be a Russian approach to a French meal by two Americans."

The maître d'hôtel and the sommelier respectfully wrote down the order; they saw that these clients, although foreigners, understood food, and could even make their way around the wine years.

"Now, first of all, tell me how you're living. You look healthy, cheerful, and happy. And so you should."

"Of course I should. The world is permeated by the cosmic rays of happiness. All we have to do is find them!" said Jim. He talks like an intellectual, very proud of his phrase; it probably comes from his diary, thought the colonel, with a smile.

"Go get a Geiger counter. . . . We're supposed to have a serious talk today."

"Let's work it this way, Uncle: you begin eating me out only from the dessert on. Why ruin my appetite?"

"I'll start eating you out immediately after the vodka. I'm not apprehensive about your appetite. But today you're going to listen to me very attentively, I insist on it."

"Very well. But before the vodka tell me about your audience. I have no doubt you're going to tell me everything the general said to you, you know what a clam I am."

"You have no doubt I'm not going to tell you a thing. But

there's one thing you can hear: the world situation is very serious."

"I've heard that, even without the general. Don't you know anything more interesting?"

"If I did it wouldn't be to pass it on to you."

"The newspapers write every day that war is definitely possible. I absolutely don't believe it. There's not going to be any war."

"Of course you know best. In case of war Russia will put together two hundred divisions, then very quickly afterward another hundred, and later on will bring its army up to five hundred divisions."

"I've read that in the papers, too. But all those divisions are coming over on our side. In Russia they hate Uncle Joe."

"Actually that's what the Soviet refugees who come over to us say. Then they invariably add that the only thing needed in case of war is to get the Russian people on our side and tell them over and over that under no circumstances do we intend to dismember Russia. Of course we're very grateful to them for such useful advice but we qualify it by the fact of their being refugees."

"As far as I can judge, Uncle, all your work is based on the refugees. What would you do without them?"

"That's just it, 'as far as you can judge.' But you cannot judge and don't have the right to. What do you know about my work?"

"Very little, but I don't think it's up to you to criticize the *émigrés*. Aside from which our Western ideas aren't applicable to Russia. I'm very fond of everything Russian."

"Caviar?"

"Caviar, *War and Peace*, Russian women."

"Do you know any?"

"I've met some. Aside from which you've evidently forgotten that my grandmother, your mother, was a Russian."

"She was the niece of a Russian *émigré* but was born in New Jersey and didn't know a word of Russian. All our other ancestors were dyed-in-the-wool Americans."

91

"Nevertheless, you don't go around harping on your Russian mother. Senator McCarthy might not like it. If he were an Englishman he would probably kick Churchill out for having a foreign mother. But I know you don't like to talk about McCarthy."

"It's true, I really don't. And I never do in front of foreigners; let them mind their own business, which I never remind them of. I have nothing whatever against the Russians as a people. Nevertheless, I dislike the *émigré* officers. It goes without saying that all of them, also invariably, refer to the Hitler experience; at first the Russian divisions surrendered one after the other into German captivity, and only began really fighting when they saw what the Nazis were. Beforehand, you see, they had no idea. I have my own opinion about that. It was the divisions that surrendered, as divisions, and not individual soldiers. The soldiers had no chance to discuss surrender. Aside from that a soldier who surrenders thinks about how he's going to be treated, or whether he'll be given something to eat; he thinks about anything at all, but not about political questions. There's a good deal of truth in what the *émigrés* say, but nevertheless it's impossible to depend on their assurances. The inertia of military discipline, especially a really tough kind like that of the Soviet, may have quite a far-reaching effect."

"What about the Soviet Army's pushing as far as the Pyrenees and the Atlantic Ocean?"

"That will never happen. But you must always proceed on the basis of the worst possibilities."

"On the contrary, you must always proceed on the basis of the best possibilities. That's what all the great military leaders have thought. Napoleon laughed at some of his generals: 'They think you can fight without any risk!' But let's consider your point of view for a moment. If the Russian troops are not going to come over on our side, then the entire army of the fourteen powers will be inevitably defeated, since the Russians are three times as strong on the ground. And if they get as far as the

Pyrenees and the ocean, their military potential, with the industrial riches of Europe, will be greater than ours."

"You're mistaken," said the colonel, with a disagreeable feeling; he thought so occasionally himself. "Our army will put up a desperate resistance. A military promenade to Paris is no longer possible."

"Not so long ago Marshal Juin said they would be in Paris in twenty-one days!"

"A lot has changed since then. Besides, marshals sometimes exaggerate very much in order to influence public opinion, governments, parliaments, and so on."

"Unfortunately they don't understand that remarks like that influence their own soldiers. My position is clear: we must find an ally in the Russian people. As for your position, I simply don't understand it. Let's wait for a little boy who will cry out that the emperor is naked. Surely the general doesn't think as you do? Does he say everything he thinks?"

"He doesn't tell the journalists everything he thinks. I daresay the general knows everything you do, and beyond that a great deal you don't. He's intelligent and one of the most active people I've ever seen. A man who's that lively is simply incapable of sitting in his room doing nothing. He doesn't play solitaire and doesn't collect postage stamps," said the colonel, who thought both things were the unmistakable signs of a man's limitations. "Napoleon was that way, too. I'll tell you one thing: the general spoke at some length about our difficult position and ended with the words: 'But of course there cannot be the slightest doubt of our winning in the long run! We, the world, and freedom will be saved by two things: firmness of spirit and the existence of the atom bomb.' D'you understand? Not its exploding, but merely its existence."

"Does he really think that?" asked Jim. His face brightened. "Of course, as an American he can't have any doubt of that!"

"Well said. When you get right down to it, we've never lost a single war in history. That psychological attitude may be something of a misfortune for us. We—and in the whole world

93

we alone—cannot imagine that it's even possible to lose a war. Nevertheless, it's extremely simple: people have won victory after victory, and finally been defeated. France was also at one time the strongest military power in the world. But I'm also convinced that if Russia decides to fight she'll be defeated."

"Uncle, you're contradicting yourself," said Jim, laughing. "And I am, too. That often happens; I've noticed more than once in arguments, especially in political ones, that a man suddenly begins to argue with himself and not with his opponent. Maybe it's because no one in the world is firmly convinced of anything, so everyone pretends he is. Isn't that a most profound thought? I'm one of the deepest thinkers of our age. And you, Uncle, I always thought you were surprisingly untypical for a spy. They must be totally different. I don't wish to speak about your colleagues. . . . And on top of it you're a man from the bronze age! A very fine bronze-age man."

"And what are you being now?"

"I read somewhere that the coat of arms of some French aristocrat is just one word: 'Fac.' That's my motto now, too!"

"Is that why you don't do anything?"

"That's why. Well, let's suppose that I had conquered the whole world, like Alexander the Great. That's probably not so hard, don't you think? But just what for? Alexander, after conquering the whole world, died of boredom and melancholy," said Jim, looking over the menu. Although everything had already been ordered, reading the menu gave him a great deal of satisfaction. "Such abundance now, Uncle, and so many things! Just to think that ten years ago there was hardly anything to eat in France and we had ration cards. D'you remember how they looked? Yes, as you were saying, we're going to win. Of course!"

"In any case we'll win in the air. It will be decided by the atom bombs. But what does that mean? That means that we shall wipe out, let's say, fifty million Russians, while they'll wipe out only ten million Americans. Delightful, what? One other thing should be remembered. It goes without saying that on the very first day of the war the Soviet government will propose that both sides renounce atomic arms. This will be very helpful to them, since they'll never have as many atom bombs as ourselves; our industry is much stronger, our scientists are better, we have more so-called know-how. Nevertheless, I repeat, they, too, will be able to wipe out several millions of our civilian population and we know it. What will happen if the pressure of public opinion forces us to agree to their proposal? In that case, how can we win? To be sure ways and means will be found. Nevertheless, it'll be extraordinarily difficult."

"For that reason, and for a thousand others, everything possible must be done to avoid war. Everything compatible with our honor and our interests."

"I'm in complete agreement with you. But try to convince Uncle Joe of that."

"Then if war begins we'll have to devote all our energies to getting the Russian people on our side."

"That is one of the ways and means I mentioned."

"Excuse me, Uncle, that's not a means, it's an end!"

"If the Russian people are on our side that means the marshals will take power. Who else is there? All the other leaders there are despised by the majority of the population, we know that very well. But only a victorious marshal will be able to stay in power. Otherwise, he'd be a Pétain. The marshals will have to win military victories, and as the French say the appetite grows with eating. Marshals dislike renouncing territorial acquisitions."

"But generally speaking no one can predict anything. I was reading that old novel by Edward Bellamy, *Looking Backward*. Bellamy prophesied radio sets but didn't foresee a few bagatelles like two world wars and two decades of revolutions. Probably that's the way prophets are. By the way, according to his novel, in the future society a man will retire at the age of forty. Just think, Uncle, I have fourteen years of work ahead of me at most, so is it worth struggling? And you should have retired twenty years ago."

"Not twenty, only eighteen," the colonel corrected him with irritation. "But let's leave politics. Nothing but commonplaces are said and written about it. Here comes your caviar."

"I'll drink the first drink to the one I owe it to," said Jim.

"Thank you, my boy."

"That would be G. R. Peterson, of course. It's true, Uncle, isn't it, that you had some money on him?"

"Jackanapes," said the colonel. He expected his nephew to be respectful; Jim knew it and never exceeded the due limits, but had thought up a form for respectful impertinences. "By the way, as a gourmet of the old school, I should never have ordered both caviar and lobster. Either one or the other," he said, twitting his nephew.

"I'm taking advantage of the opportunity. Without you, I shouldn't have ordered them for myself, I'm too broke. They're the most delicious things in the world. If according to the eternal silly question I were sent to a desert island and told I could have only *one* thing to eat the whole time, I would take these *two*. And you?"

"Let's have a second vodka and talk sense."

"Okay. You can now chew me out if there's no help for it."

"There isn't. When are you finally going to grow up? You're twenty-six years old now and you have the character of a six-teen-year-old. . . . How are all your love affairs? You wrote me you had broken up with her," said the colonel. Jim told him the truth about his intimate relations; at least the colonel thought so, and it made him happy.

"We got tired of each other. She got angry about something or other. I daresay she was right. Oh well, it doesn't matter; there will soon be another. I already have one in mind."

The colonel shook his head and assumed an expression of disappointment. At heart he was rather proud of his nephew's conquests. "Women are going to be your finish, my boy. I can scarcely believe you're going to find a suitable wife for yourself. A real woman would take you down a peg or two."

"Just to spite you, at the moment I'm running away from a 'real' woman. . . . But why don't you marry yourself, Uncle?" asked Jim, although he knew very well he would get no reply. He had heard long ago that in his youth his uncle had been in love with some beauty who had preferred a rich businessman. That might have generated contempt for women, hatred for rich businessmen, or a decision to get rich himself in one way or another, but it hadn't done any of these things to Uncle, Jim always thought, with some perplexity. To be sure he later consoled himself rather often with women. It's only me he insists on lecturing. At one time he must have been pretty hot stuff, too. His uncle seemed to him to be on the threshold of old age.

"That's none of your business. You're always going to go on having affairs lasting two months on an average."

"That's not so bad at that."

"Then some cook will grab you. You've read too much Dostoevski," said the colonel, who ascribed the most baneful influence to Russian novelists, especially Dostoevski, although he was rather vague about him; he had once begun *The Insulted and Injured* and hadn't been able to finish it for boredom.

"You've told me that more than once already."

"But just now you're not really in love with anybody?"

"No. But I don't know just what you mean by 'really.'"

"In any case, you're not engaged? You're not getting ready to get married?"

"Oh no! What d'you take me for, Uncle?" asked Jim indignantly.

8

"VERY well now, let's get down to business," said the colonel after a moment's silence. "Are you still as bored with your work as ever?"

"Of course I am. Infernally bored! Why, actually, did you ever have me assigned to it?"

"My dear boy, it was not easy to get you assigned even here. Don't forget you got out of the Point next to the bottom of the list."

"It's true I was next to last but only because of mathematics and conduct. Of course it would have been better to graduate last: that would have had at least some effect—last in the class!"

"Are you suited at all for a military career? And if not, then just what are you fit for? It wasn't so long ago that you wanted to make music your career, you really had some talent for it...."

98

"Genius! But you would have thought it a family scandal if your nephew had turned into some wretched composer like Wagner."

"You're really becoming a blowhard!" said the colonel. He knew that Jim did not suffer from megalomania, but, on the contrary, was not completely sure of himself; he had simply taken up this odd way of talking.

"No, I'm no blowhard. With me everything depends on mood. Sometimes I feel like a conqueror, even arrogant, like a young woman who's put herself up as candidate for Miss America. And once when I was on a steamer and saw the word Gentlemen on the men's room I almost had to ask myself whether I had a right to go in."

"How you do go on!" said the colonel, laughing. "As to your being a gentleman, there can be no doubt of it, but that's not what we were talking about. There are a great many young people who can play a grand piano."

"But *how* I play! I'm a matchless expert! I even have Riemann's musical lexicon, although, like most pianists, I never look at it."

"Stop joking, I'm speaking very seriously. If I thought you might become a Wagner I should be the first to wish you luck on a musical career," said the colonel, not quite sincerely. "But you're simply an aesthete—rather an empty species of humanity. You've also shown a talent for literature. When a man has too many different talents..." The colonel, seeing his nephew's vexation, didn't finish the sentence. "In any case, you enlisted in the army voluntarily and did extremely well. It was just your bad luck that the war ended just as your military training was ending. But if you had happened to be in the war you would have been very disappointed. War might have been poetic in the old days, today there's nothing poetic about it. And a new war would simply be a slaughter. There would be nothing romantic in it if only because for the first time in history the civilian population would be subjected to even greater danger than the army. You wouldn't have a chance to show off in front

99

of young women in New York, there would be more young women killed than officers."

"Especially than staff officers. Ever since airplanes came into existence there has been a tacit agreement between the staffs: Foch didn't drop bombs on Hindenburg, or Hindenburg on Foch; the Germans in Africa didn't try to kill Montgomery, and the English didn't try to kill Rommel. It would have been inelegant."

"Practically the only kind of military service that still retains some romance is my own—intelligence."

"Then why didn't you have me appointed to it?"

"I won't deny that I hesitated. You're actually not very suitable. So you're dissatisfied with your work in Public Information? Just what are you doing there now?"

"I have a great deal of work. First of all, I have to learn just how many governments there are in the North Atlantic Pact."

"But everyone knows that."

"Scarcely a hundred people in the world know it. Try counting them yourself, Uncle."

"The United States, Great Britain, France, Italy, Greece, Turkey, Belgium, Holland, Denmark, Canada . . . Norway . . . Iceland . . ."

"Bravo! But that's only twelve," said Jim, who had been ticking them off on his fingers. "And now the other two?"

"Odd, I can't recall them at the moment."

"You've forgotten Portugal!"

"That's right."

"And Luxembourg! You've left out Luxembourg, with her powerful army!"

"And what else have you learned?"

"But the names, of course! And what names! Did you know the name of the Dutch representative? His name is Alidius Warmoldus Lambertus Tjarda Van Starkenborgh Stachouwer! Try to repeat that! To say nothing of pronouncing it correctly!"

"I can see you're not overburdened. I also think your promotion is going to take a long time. Does that upset you too much?"

"It upsets me, but not too much."

"I know you're not ambitious. Or, rather, you yourself don't know whether you're ambitious or not. Do you ever think of your future at all, not about today or tomorrow, but the future?"

"I do," replied Jim. But there was no assurance in his tone.

"In my opinion you never even ask yourself: What do I want? What am I capable of doing? What am I going to do in life? You're intelligent. I shouldn't even have said you *couldn't* think; you've simply never tried."

"It would be very sad if that were so. But it's not. I think a great deal."

"Perhaps only when you're speaking. There are people like that. If I were to ask you what you're thinking *about*, you wouldn't be able to answer. My dear boy, you've unfortunately acquired a strange, sometimes jocular, sometimes ironic attitude toward life, as though it were a matter of leading it as merrily as possible and there were nothing serious in the world."

"You're exaggerating," said Jim. He may be talking sense, but it's strange he should be the one; a man who's spent his whole life in espionage shouldn't fall into the tone of Emerson, he thought. "You're exaggerating a great deal. I think a lot, and not just when I'm speaking, but much more at home, alone, at the piano or my desk. And if you had wanted me to become more serious, then why, I repeat, why did you assign me to the most futile section in Rocquencourt?"

"They didn't want to take you on in any other section. And I thought it would be useful for you to see Europe, polish up your French. . . ."

"I speak French a great deal better than Ike, or Winnie, or the Duke of Windsor. They can't even be understood on the radio when they pronounce a few supposedly French sentences. I also know argot like a Parisian."

101

"Just see to it that your bragging in jest doesn't turn into the real thing, that happens. In fact, you did receive a good education. You also know you're my only heir. Just don't wish me an early death," the colonel said jokingly. "What's more, if you needed money now I should be willing to give you an advance against your inheritance. Of course, on condition that the money would be used for something worth while. If so, write me."

"Thank you most sincerely, it's agreeable to hear that. You always have spoiled me, Uncle, and I don't deserve it. But what did you want to speak to me about?"

The colonel kept silent a moment. "Would you like to work in the same department as myself?"

"So that's it! You want me to work with you!"

"Not with me. I simply want to give you one assignment. You would stay on at your post."

"Surely that's not possible?"

"It's done. You would be temporarily detached from your work and assigned elsewhere. Then we'll see. Today I asked the general for his agreement. He doesn't know you."

"I've been introduced to him twice!"

"A lot of people are introduced to him, he can't know all of you. All he remembered was that I had a nephew here. Actually, the fact that I even brought you up with him was something of a breach of regulations. But we're old friends; I told him what I needed and he gave his agreement, or rather promised to shut his eyes."

"You don't want to assign me to something illegal?"

"A great many of our activities overlook the rules somewhat. Nevertheless, the general's attitude toward the project was favorable. He asked me whether you're good-looking."

"Uncle, for heaven's sake, tell me what it's all about! Are there women mixed up in it?"

"Your eyes are gleaming already. Not women, a woman."

"Beautiful?"

"Very. Don't be too happy too soon; she's a spy."

102

"Don't depress me, Uncle! What's Hecuba to me, especially a Hecuba who's a spy?"

"She's being sent here to find out some of our military secrets. Before continuing I want you to promise me faithfully: all this is to remain absolutely secret."

"I swear by my life!" said Jim solemnly, starting to raise his hand.

The colonel frowned. "You're a daredevil and don't have too much regard for your life. Instead of swearing simply give me your word of honor as an American officer that everything I tell you will remain an absolute secret."

"Of course I give you my word."

"In order to enter our department you'll have to undergo various formalities, there's no point talking about them now. Just now the question is about one trial project. If you fulfill my assignment well it will be possible to discuss your coming over to work for us. It's very hard work, but it's more interesting than what you're doing now."

"Uncle, how did you find out they're sending this beauty over here?"

"In our department it's not done to ask superiors whatever they don't tell you themselves.... They also send a great many of their agents to the United States secretly."

"Secretly! But they can't ask us for our permission. That would be as though in wartime one government were to ask another to give out visas for invading soldiers."

"You said yourself 'in wartime.' There really is such a thing as a cold war, and we can't use exclusively legal methods, either. It would be up to you to start a liaison with this woman," said the colonel finally.

Jim opened his eyes wide. "I never thought I would hear such words from you, Uncle! You were just asking me whether I intended to get married!"

"And that was why I asked. If you were in love, I should never have suggested this business to you."

"And what if I don't like your little spy? What then?"

103

"A stupid question. No, actually, maybe it's better for you to stick to your own department."

"Where is this Hecuba? How do I get acquainted with her?"

"I'll give you her description, tell you where she lives, and in what restaurant she eats. It would be best to get acquainted with her at the restaurant itself. The rest is your own affair. You'll have to take her to Rocquencourt and show her, as a journalist, that furnace. It is shown to journalists. The person in charge of the furnace will be you, at least in a few days from now. Then you will 'fall in love' and pass on to her a number of documents which we will prepare for you."

"I understand: misinformation!"

"That will be the end of your role."

"A dubious role. I never expected this of you!"

"What can one do? Things like this have to be done, too. If it's done for your country, there's nothing bad about it."

"Up to now I've even had affairs with beautiful women not for my country. And for my country I'm all the readier."

"*T-short,*" said the colonel.

9

THE moment the little steamship came to rest Natasha, who had already been walking up and down on the shore for an hour, saw Schell and ran toward him along the rampart, overtaking the porters with their barrows. He raised his hand, swiftly strode over to her, embraced and kissed her. He smelled of wine.

"You look wonderful. Is everything all right? Healthy? D'you like Capri?"

"It's just heaven!"

"Not always. Everything on the island depends on the weather. If the weather's bad, it's mortally depressing."

"The weather's been wonderful the whole time. And how are you?"

"You haven't been coughing?"

"I haven't coughed once," she replied gayly, although the

question upset her a little—it meant he wasn't sure it was all stuff and nonsense, after all.

"Thank God," he said, and started talking Italian to the porter who had brought his suitcases from the steamer. Natasha was surprised at how many there were: five or six, all of them magnificent. Surely he's not going to change his suits every day, as he did in Berlin! His dandyism was something from another, unknown world which she found incomprehensible, which may have been just why she liked it. But he looks worn out! she thought, as he arranged the suitcases in the red funicula car together with the porter. The other passengers looked at them curiously, which also gave Natasha satisfaction. The other small funicula passed them going the other way, filled with people who were leaving. It occurred to her that in not more than ten days they would also have to leave this marvelous island.

Schell didn't stop at the Quisisana; he said he might meet people he knew there.

"And I don't want to see anybody but you. There's a very good inn not far off, where I lived three years ago. We'll ask there."

He was known at the inn. There was a room free, which wasn't bad, but for the same money the innkeeper offered them a separate cottage, rather far off, at the bottom of a large, steeply sloping garden.

"I remember, I remember. It's very old, you were always rebuilding it. Well, perhaps," said Schell, after a moment's thought.

"I've put in two bathtubs; I'm giving it to you so cheap, signor, because it's you. And also, to tell the truth, because a lot of people don't like going that far several times a day. But Signor and Signora are young and strong."

"The signora is not my wife. She already has a room. Well, take us to this cottage."

He also spoke Italian fluently, even scattering about a number of "*Mamma mias.*" All three of them descended the steep old stone staircase into the garden. The cottage was also old;

106

it consisted of a very large room with three windows, two bedrooms, marble statues, and huge fireplaces.

When the innkeeper left, Schell took Natasha in his arms again. "D'you want to live here with me? I'll think up something to tell him, but for that matter they really don't care at all."

"Never. You know that . . ."

"Yes, I know, I know," he said impatiently. "Very well, let's not quarrel. It's all the same, we—"

"What's all the same?"

"Nothing. Dearest, I have to bathe, shave, and change. It'll take at least half an hour. Will you wait for me here, or over there in the hotel?"

"It's not quite convenient," said Natasha, blushing. Schell burst out laughing.

" 'What will they think,' is that it? O wonder of nature! Were you brought up in a boardinghouse for well-born maidens somewhere in Spain? Well, that's that. If it isn't proper for you to wait for me here, go to the Piazza Umberto and sit in a café on the terrace. I think there are only a few cafés and I'll find you. D'you know how to get to the Piazza Umberto? It's the only square here."

"I already know Capri like the palm of my hand."

"And it's not unseemly to sit alone at a table in a café? Thank God! But what do you do here all day long? D'you read the whole time? By the way, I've brought you a little present, an old edition of Turgeniev which I found at a secondhand bookshop."

"Oh, thank you! How wonderful! I love Turgeniev, *Spring Floods* and *First Love* are my favorite books! Wasn't it too expensive?"

"Not so very."

Whenever he tore himself away from his gloomy espionage world, Schell always felt great relief. Now he really did not want to see anyone but Natasha. People irritated him. In the

107

train the people in his compartment had aroused something in
him very close to repugnance. I feel as though I've fallen into
very advanced, enlightened company. They're probably going
to some advanced, enlightened convention. . . . He did not exchange a single word with anyone; he had opened a newspaper
immediately, to forestall conversation, but didn't read it. The
same thing all over again, he thought. This Indian opposite me
berates the United States for its "lack of spirituality," gets in-
dignant because it gives too little money to Asiatic countries.
To make up for that he doubtless is very enthusiastic about
the Soviet government, even though it sells them goods for
money, and at high prices at that. One of Nehru's men, of
course. . . . And this woman in a violet dress with long sleeves
and spectacles, also terrifically advanced, looking as intellectual
and disdainful as she can. All of them have obviously wangled
themselves into various government pies and are getting huge
salaries. They get married to rich people—not, of course, for the
money, the money is only incidental, but what they have, don't
you see, is ideas in common. . . . I'm the only one who hasn't
landed anything for myself, now getting on into my forties
without having got hold of anything, without owning anything,
wallowing in filth. . . . I feel more or less like a man who turns
up in a dirty jacket at an evening party where everyone is
dressed in dinner jackets or dress suits. . . . I was right! he
thought almost happily, recognizing from his neighbors' conversation which convention they were bound for. Everything
boils down to money, in spite of their unusually intellectual and
respectable appearance. Blast and rot them all! he thought, con-
soling himself, as usual, with the consciousness of his enormous
physical superiority over these people. I could strangle every
one of them like a chicken.

He thought about Natasha again. It's as though my heart
were lit up from within! What a banal business! But isn't love
always banal, both in life and in art? And happiness is also banal,
for which thank God! Aside from her I have nothing and never
will have. I'm like those pious Muslims who are supposed to

pluck out their eyes once they've seen Muhammad's grave. I'll never see anything on this earth loftier, purer than she, thought Schell, "literarily," as he usually did. I've got myself completely entangled! I've turned out to be not just a scoundrel but a damned fool, too. I don't know myself what I want. I'm madly in love! Oh no, in love, but not madly! We'll see what happens when we meet. Will I be disappointed, even a little?

He had been drinking in the dining car, at the station, and even on the little boat from Naples. The test had gone off splendidly; he wasn't disappointed in the least.

But nevertheless, in the bathtub now, he didn't know why, he sensed reviving in him a cast of emotion that tormented him. At the age of forty a man can't fall in love like Romeo. . . . Yes, I have to admit I thought up this whole trip to Capri in order to *make* her (what a vulgar, nasty expression, too!). Not too difficult: the usual tricks, lies, cunning, wine, and they almost always give in. But I cannot, I simply *cannot,* do that now. Does that mean I'll marry her? That's all she wants, only that, that's all she dreams about, and keeps trying not to show it, poor sweet. . . . Get married, with my past, in my profession, and having to hide everything from her?

Three months before the first notion of marrying Natasha had seemed grotesque. Then he kept trying out the idea, at first, by long habit, with a sneer at himself, in a cynical form: "Saved by the Love of a Maiden," "A Mysterious Affair, or the Love of a Spy, a Tragedy in Five Acts with a Prologue." For from its very inception he had been irritated by just this *banality:* a fallen man, desolate of soul, falls in love with a pure maiden. Like Lermontov's Daemon. At heart Schell had regarded himself ever since youth as a demonic spirit. What is the use? Life is just as vulgar as the movies, he thought.

Little by little his feelings passed into another channel; first cynical and mocking, they turned repentant. It's true, I was desolate, inwardly desolate. But generally speaking there are very few "fallen" people, people fall and rise. My path led from good to evil—could I be on the way back now? For twenty years

I've been oppressed by moral solitude—for that matter, just plain solitude; after all, it's as though we were living on some uninhabited island. . . . Sometimes on airplanes I've thought it might be a good thing for me to fling myself out, then everything would be done with. But I may have been pretending to myself: no, life is good, too, it's never too late to do away with yourself, various little pleasures are still left, there's still champagne. . . . Get married? By now that's almost impossible, even practically. How can I get married when I have no money and can get some only by staying a spy?

He had once found himself with no money whatsoever, but that had been a long time ago; he had grown unaccustomed to it. Before, a thousand dollars seemed almost wealth. Now it's a month of living, at best two months, if I deprive myself of everything. He had made a lot during the preceding few years. The demand for his services, as a result of the world situation, had grown very great. Aside from which he was usually lucky at cards. But in Berlin—like an idiot!—he had lost around forty thousand marks. Schell had long since made it a rule not to be upset by mistakes he had made and not to think about whatever could no longer be remedied. But you couldn't keep to all the rules; it was becoming more and more oppressive to recall the money he had lost.

The colonel had offered to give him an advance of two thousand dollars. Schell actually did set less value on his life than the great majority of people, and the assignment was an interesting one. And, most of all, if he was successful, a sum was assured him which might very well allow him to abandon his occupation, of which he had long since tired, and which was dangerous and exhausting. He had dreamed of this, although he was completely at a loss as to what other work he might be able to do. The job would take about three or four weeks, he thought. Let's say (I'm still thinking in terms of "let's say") I could think up some pretext for Natasha. I'll tell her I have to take a trip to liquidate my affairs. I'll leave her five hundred dollars. Like that blasted Edda, he thought with revulsion.

110

She'll go on working on her Recallism somewhere in Italy. What address could I give her for letters? And how could I write to her? To be sure I could leave letters with the colonel to be forwarded. Dearest, dearest Natasha, when you receive this letter . . . just remember that I . . . Ready-made touching phrases flashed through his head. But if the thing comes off, everything will be all right. Then it will be possible to go on hiding things from her. . . . Oh, I don't feel like going away. . . . And I'm afraid. . . . Of course I'm afraid. There's not much of a chance of coming back from there; after all, I'm not a kamikaze. But what else can I do? If only there were a little money, I could run off to South America. . . . Tell Natasha straight out that I'm ruined, that I haven't a thing left? She would probably fling herself around my neck and tell me in raptures that it's much better that way and that she was going to work. . . . He involuntarily laughed at the idea of his living on Recallism. Or else tell her the whole truth?

He had also thought about this more than once in Berlin, even imagining the whole thing in detail. Dinner, vodka, champagne. Word for word. "You're in love with a scoundrel!" I won't say the word "scoundrel" even after the champagne. "You're in love with a *fallen man!*" Impossible! had been his answer even then, and he had smiled in spite of himself, astonished at the histrionic trait in his own character. And how would she react? Would she leave me, "her eyes wide with horror and despair"? No, that would also be a movie, and she hasn't even a trace of vulgarity. I would give everything to be able to tell her about my past as honestly as possible, about why I embarked on such a career. I'd give her the "intellectual motivation" I gave Edda. But that wouldn't soften things any more either. "Spy!" Of course it's out of the question! And I'm not going to think about it any more here on Capri. I'm not going to spoil these two weeks for myself, these two weeks wrenched loose from my tormented life.

In spite of his moroseness he had an enormous natural store of good humor. After a hot bath he got into a shower, turned

111

on only the cold water, and came out a moment later, making
an effort not to be out of temper and not to shiver. As he nearly
always did, he admired his own torso in the mirror. Oh well,
I'll think of something or other. In any case, even if it's only a
day, it's mine! And not just a day but two or three weeks. Isn't
that the whole point of life? Only a day, but mine. . . .

10

JIM left Edda's hotel toward dawn. The night porter morosely accepted one hundred francs and opened the door for him. Should I send Uncle a telegram? For instance: I came, I saw, I conquered. But he didn't. In the street he quickly sobered up and no longer thought there was anything to joke about.

But he had done everything very well. At one in the afternoon he had gone into the restaurant indicated to him by his uncle and had recognized Edda immediately: the colonel had received her picture from Schell. Really beautiful! He was very agitated; he had never seen a spy before in his life. All the tables were taken. Jim walked down the long room, went back, put on an irritated look, then stopped, and in French asked the young woman for permission to sit down at her table. He sat down, overcoming his revulsion and fear, as though there were some serpent in front of him. After a moment's silence Jim asked whether he might look at the menu.

Edda, also agitated—it's come off!—answered in English that she didn't need the menu any longer, she had already ordered. Almost smiling, she nevertheless preserved her "inaccessible" expression. The colonel had not had a picture of Jim, but he had described him to Schell with great precision. Ninety chances to a hundred that he's the one! thought Edda. "Oh, how well it's worked out! Schell, to be sure, had told her that the American officer had lunch in this restaurant every day— but really it had come off: he had sat down all by himself! Such a lucky coincidence might have seemed suspicious, but with Edda suspicion didn't even raise its head. And actually Jim didn't in the least look like an agent. His face always radiated straightforwardness and honesty (particularly when he was lying to beautiful women). Really, by her looks, she's a fool, Jim thought happily. Really, by his looks, he's a fool, Edda thought happily. But what if he shouldn't be the one? I'll find out soon enough. But even if he isn't the one, it's not such a tragedy, it'll just be a pleasant acquaintance. Both of them hastily mapped out a plan of campaign.

"You speak English very well," Jim improvised.

"I've been taught languages ever since I was a child; my uncle owned a large hotel. I'm a Swiss journalist," Edda replied. That was what Schell had instructed her to say. Though perhaps I shouldn't tell him all this in the very first breath?

Jim explained immediately that his own aunt owned a hotel in Atlanta. He had no aunt, but in his opinion it was up to a spy to lie as often and as much as possible; you simply had to keep everything in mind.

"Her name is Mildred Russell. A wonderful woman."

"Isn't Atlanta in the United States? Are you an American?"

"I'm an American officer, on duty at SHAPE." Jim also thought that he shouldn't have told all this in the very first breath, but just the day before he had decided to carry out the affair at the pace of Julius Caesar.

So there's no doubt at all! thought Edda. "Have you been in Paris long?"

114

"I arrived the day before yesterday."

"For the first time?"

"Oh no, I know Paris very well."

"Me, too. I've been on duty here for two years already" (it had been only a year). "Let me introduce myself. . . ."

He gave his name. Edda gave the new name she had on her passport, which she had gotten through Schell. Her face kept growing more and more clever and wily and his kept growing more and more straightforward and honest.

". . . You resemble a celebrated portrait, but I can't recall at the moment just which one!" said Jim. He said this to all the women he courted; it was invariably successful.

"But which? Just don't say it's the Mona Lisa! In my opinion she's hideous."

"Oh no, a modern portrait. Van Dongen? Laszlo?" Jim mentioned the first names that occurred to him. "No, neither De Laszlo nor Van Dongen . . . I remember—Trevelyan! Gabriel Joshua Trevelyan!" Jim exclaimed joyfully. He had invented this painter, too, by some unconscious association of names: Gabriel was Rossetti, Joshua was Reynolds. "You're a Gabriel Joshua Trevelyan to the life! You probably know his portraits; they're sweeping America now. He's a personal friend of mine." (Remember: Gabriel Joshua Trevelyan.)

"Why yes, of course, I've heard of him. I'm very interested in American culture. So you're on duty at SHAPE? What's that?" asked Edda. Her question seemed to her very subtle. Mata Hari herself could hardly have done it more craftily. "I've never heard the word."

"Not really?" asked Jim, and explained to her what it meant.

"So that's it? Oh, I'm so remote from all that. And who is the American Supreme Commander?"

Either she's a complete idiot, or else she has a very cunning scheme, thought Jim, but what sort of scheme could it be? If all Soviet spies are like her, then the United States isn't threatened by any great danger. He explained that the Supreme

115

Commander was in fact an American but was not the American Supreme Commander.

"He's Saceur."

"Is that a name?"

"No, that's an abbreviation made up out of the first initials: Supreme Allied Commander Europe," he replied. A waiter came over. Jim ordered an expensive wine and the most recherché dishes this second-class restaurant had. He thought this useful for business; besides, he always felt like eating and drinking. Edda had only a tiny bottle of mineral water in front of her. He asked permission to pour her some wine. By the time lunch was over they were chattering merrily away. Complete frolicsomeness was not yet there, but it was swiftly approaching.

"Would you like to spend an evening with me? I implore you, don't say you're busy."

"And I won't. I'm not busy."

"Let's go to the theater. What would you like to see? The *Folies Bergères?*"

"Never! I don't acknowledge anything but serious theater."

"With you I'm ready to go wherever you like, even a play by Corneille at the Comédie Française! I can't imagine a foreigner, to say nothing of a fine healthy fellow like myself, getting any pleasure from these highbrow verses, but for you I'm prepared even for that sacrifice!"

"It's a great pity you don't like poetry. I'm a poetess myself."

"Forgive me, for the love of God! I adore modern poetry! Read me your verses!"

"After what you just said, not for anything in the world."

"It was a slip of the tongue. I said something stupid. Not for the first or last time, either. I implore you, forgive me!"

"No, you're not worth it. And I'm not in the mood."

"What do you need for your mood?"

"Love and wine."

"We'll have a wonderful evening together."

116

"Some other time."

"Never! Not for anything! This selfsame day! I insist! Come here for dinner. D'you live a long way off?"

"I live in this hotel."

"And I eat lunch and dinner here. You must see the hand of fate in that?"

"Oh, I've always believed in fate!"

"Me, too. We'll meet every day." He was about to add "and every night," but then the tempo would have been really unusually rapid. By now Jim had almost even forgotten that Edda was a spy. He talked with her as he always talked with attractive women. Over the liqueur, he recalled it, to his astonishment. I've drunk too much. But it's no tragedy. By today things will be triumphantly concluded. Or rather triumphantly begun. *Veni, vidi, vici,* he repeated to himself.

At the theater the set represented a hotel in the style of the Second Empire. A servant brought in a young man, and the two had a long and rather enigmatic chat. The mood was slowly established. In the hotel it was quite impossible to put out the electric light. Sometimes the bell worked, sometimes it didn't. There were no books in the room, but there was a paper cutter. There was a Barbedienne bronze; it turned out to be so heavy the young man could scarcely lift it. He wanted to get a toothbrush, but the servant said no toothbrush was needed there. Then the servant went out, and two women appeared. One of them was in a blue dress and so refused to sit on the green divan. She would sit only on the brown one; the young man gave it up to her at once. It also turned out that in the hotel in the Second Empire style it was very hot, and there was not a single mirror. This plunged all three of them into a depression. The first woman thought that the young man was an executioner, but he firmly denied it. Slowly it became clear that this hotel was Hell.

The young man was a Brazilian pacifist; he had been executed and had showed himself a coward. Both women

117

recounted what they had on their consciences. The first woman sang some Parisian couplets. The young man pensively listened, covering up his head with his hands. Since there were no mirrors, the first woman offered the second her eyes as a mirror. Then the second woman spat into the first one's face and kissed the young man, while the first woman enviously proved it was impossible to love a coward. The young man declared that both of them repelled him. In desperation he rang, but the bell didn't work. He tried to break down the door going out, begged to be released, and agreed to submit to the most terrible torments if only he didn't have to stay on in this hotel. Finally the door was opened wide. A long silence supervened. The young man reconsidered and decided not to leave the Second Empire hotel. The first woman laughed at him. The second woman flung herself on the first from behind and tried to push her out, begging the young man to help her, but he refused and told the second woman that he would stay in Hell because of the first woman. The first woman was delightedly surprised by this, but he called her a viper and resumed kissing the second woman. But the first cried out in torments of jealousy. The young man repulsed the second woman and explained that he could not associate with her in the presence of the first. Then the second woman seized a paper cutter and attempted to kill the first woman with it; the latter burst out laughing and declared that it was impossible to kill her since they were all of them dead anyhow. In desperation the second woman threw away the knife. The first woman snatched it up from the floor and tried to kill herself, but this was impossible for the same reason. Then they all sat down on the green and brown divans and roared with laughter.

On this the play ended. It had a great success. The audience applauded tempestuously, especially the numerous strangely dressed young people. But of the older people a number, as Jim thought, applauded undecidedly and as though perplexed. The author was very well known and very fashionable, in addi-

118

tion an innovator, who was blazing new trails in dramatic art. Edda was in raptures, and at the particularly priceless and profound remarks she groaned and nudged Jim. He also applauded. He thought to himself that throughout the play there was not one single clever or even simply witty word, but he acknowledged his own incompetence at literature. But he had not been listening too attentively. He was asking himself whether he wasn't making some mistake on the "job." We didn't have to stay in the restaurant until three, he thought; maybe she'll wonder what an American officer was doing sitting about in a restaurant while on duty. And didn't I drink too much? On the other hand, she drank just as much. And there's nothing in the least snakelike about her. What nonsense! It's just that. . . . He had prudently brought along a pocket flask of cognac. But where can I take her afterward?

After the show they sat in a café on the heated terrace.

"I'll order some champagne. Would you like some?" He asked her in French, in order to be able to say "*tu*" to her.

"Sartre is a very great writer. . . . What did you say? Champagne? All you Americans say 'champane,' " she mimicked him, although he had only a very slight accent. "But who drinks champagne, just like that, on a café terrace?"

"I feel like it!" he declared in the peremptory tone that had often been so successful with women. To the waiter's pleasant surprise he ordered champagne, with the air of a wealthy tourist, which became him very well and pleased Edda enormously.

"Your face looks ecstatic!" he said as the bottle neared its end. "I, of course, am accustomed to arousing such feelings in women, but do try not to show them, it's not proper."

"You're stupid, very stupid, remarkably stupid. . . . And what if I fell in love with you?"

"I should take it under advisement," Jim replied. His "technique" actually didn't change merely because he was dealing with a spy. He told a risqué anecdote. Edda countered with one that was quite improper. Then he asked her again to read him her verses.

119

"But of course not here!"

"Then let's go to my hotel."

"Is it possible at your place?"

"This is a free country," she replied, by now laughing half-drunkenly. Edda was convinced that all Americans spoke this way constantly, on any and all occasions.

She had a corner suite of two rooms. There were no neighbors, and in spite of how late it was they could be quite free and easy. And so they were. Over the cognac Edda read him her French verses. She read them sometimes stretching her hands out in front of her, sometimes raising them to the ceiling, gracefully leaning forward and then back. These gestures, especially the last one, had an effect on him. He was also affected by the verses.

She was sitting on her knees near him in a blouse and "worming secrets out of him." She smelled of cognac, cigarettes, and expensive scents. He considered whether he shouldn't worm some secret out of her, but recalled that that wasn't part of his assignment: his uncle had ordered him not to ask about anything; he was simply supposed—not, of course, instantly—to tell her his own secret.

Edda was in raptures. She was all Delilah. She had never looked into the Bible in her life, that was really completely *vieux jeu,* but she had seen the opera several times. She said she acknowledged only the music of the concretists, and in Berlin she used to treat her friends to records by Varese and Anton von Werner, but Saint-Saëns was the one whom she really adored. On this first night Edda made no attempt to obtain the secret documents. It would be incautious and, for that matter, she thought, he doesn't carry them around with him in his pocket. For the first night it was quite sufficient to learn "in what lay his great strength." In his drunken state Jim also felt himself something of a Samson. As a beginning he almost tried to think up something like the "seven green withes that were never dried," and then "to break the withes as a thread

120

of tow is broken when it toucheth the fire." But he couldn't think of anything. His assignment was a simple one: all he did was to "confide" to her that there was a furnace in Rocquencourt where the most important top-secret documents were burned.

II

"YOU ask why I keep being reminded of Tiberius here," said Schell. "But how can you not be reminded of him on Capri? He is the principal benefactor of the island. If he hadn't lived here two thousand years ago, if there weren't those dreadful legends, the island would lose half its interest, and there would be no tourists. His enormities feed the Capresi, who thrive on what their remote ancestors execrated. Thus at some time the Lubyanka will doubtless feed the Moscow hotel owners.... Aside from which I read some books here about Tiberius. Yes, and today I have a special reason for remembering him."

"What?" asked Natasha. "I think that's the eighth tangerine you're eating, and you're even swallowing the pits! That's dangerous. There was no point in your buying so many downstairs."

"No point at all," he replied distractedly, and thought that no one ever before had paid attention to his health. Yes, it will be a petty-bourgeois life, he thought.

Everything he had thought out en route to Capri had been realized with precision. Through the proprietor, and at great cost, he had hired a troupe of male and female dancers and three musicians. They were neighbors; they lived next door to the hotel and usually arranged a tarantella for tourists in their own small house, the music from which could often be heard in the hotel until the early hours. During the day Schell took Natasha to the Blue Grotto. In spite of the cold weather, he went for a swim there; he had put on a bathing costume at home under his jacket that he thought most suitable for showing off his gigantic figure. Then the boatman took them to a restaurant looking out on the sea, where they dined; he drank two bottles of wine and made Natasha drink a few glasses; she was soon quite dizzy. At dinner he talked about his surprise party, there was going to be a tarantella, the famous folk dance, a specialty of Naples and Capri, on the theme of which great composers had written masterpieces. He added that his own life was downright tarantella; he spoke more expansively and coarsely than usual because of the wine and his excitement: he was sure everything would be consummated that night.

At ten o'clock they went into the room of their little house, lit up by varicolored small lanterns. Near the lavishly laden table they were greeted with deferential dignity by the actors and actresses in motley. The tarantella began, which really did turn into a frenzy very rapidly. In a fit of jealousy a handsome dancer stabbed a beautiful girl with a dagger. Natasha cried aloud in fright. "It's a game, of course, she's alive and well," said Schell, leaning toward her. Hesitating for the last time, he asked, "Natasha, will you marry me? I've looked into everything, there won't be very many formalities, but I can't wait, I simply cannot wait any longer!"

Suddenly the sounds of the tarantella were interrupted, and the principal dancer, breathing heavily, went over to them and

123

asked for permission to kiss the signora's hand. The buffet keeper brought over a tray with goblets of champagne. Schell, without asking permission, kissed the girl who was the star dancer. Natasha, completely stunned by happiness, pretended not to notice. Then, accompanied by the troupe, which was delighted with them, they went into the little garden drenched in moonlight. The whole arsenal of poetry, thought Schell. He was still making an effort to think cynically, but was almost as happy as Natasha. She can hardly stand on her feet. Why not just carry her into the bedroom in my arms? he thought. No, that really would be a movie. But he carried her out in his arms.

"What a stunning sight!" said Natasha. "So this really is the ruin of Tiberius's palace?"

"Yes. Is it uncomfortable for you to sit on the stone? Aren't you very tired? It's a pity you didn't want to borrow a donkey from the old man. Everyone here rides on donkeys."

"A fine sight I should look on a little donkey! And under you the poor little donkey would most likely collapse immediately."

"Why? In Greece I often rode on donkeys, everyone rides them there, too."

So he's also lived in Greece, thought Natasha.

"And that unfortunate old man would have walked along-side us on foot?"

"He's used to it."

He misses something, thought Natasha, a little hurt. The poor little donkey. The unfortunate old man, the poor little pits, thought Schell.

He had been in a strange mood that day. Natasha saw this and felt sad. To his surprise she had been weeping the evening before and had tried not to let him notice it, and he pretended not to. She herself could not understand why she was crying. For happiness? I don't think you cry for happiness. At least not I....

"How heavy are you? D'you know, I've somehow lately thought that if you had been a head shorter your whole life

124

would probably have been different. . . . But of course I know so little about . . ."

"A woman once told me my height gives me a pseudo-important look," he said hastily, laughing, and reverted to what he had been talking about before. "You know it was from this cliff that Tiberius, after an orgy, ordered his girls and boys to be flung into the sea, with himself watching. They were smashed to death, and if anyone below was still breathing, having convulsively clutched at something on the precipice, then he was struck down by the oars or clubs of assassin boatmen provided expressly for it."

"I'll never be able to believe such a thing!"

"And I, on the contrary, always believe such things."

"Surely the people wouldn't have endured that!"

"The people endure everything, that's their specialty. Perhaps they consoled themselves with singing 'Bublichki' or something of the sort. Tiberius had an intelligence service and an all-powerful police."

"I simply cannot tell you how I hate all these police and intelligence services."

Go ahead, now, tell her the truth, he thought. Of course I never will.

Schell had already told the colonel that he was going to accept his proposition, and had asked him to send the two thousand dollars. Asking for an advance was always disagreeable; it lowered his standing. Now it was far more disagreeable still: he had definitely made up his mind not to go to Moscow under any circumstances. Even if I go broke, I'll get the money later, I'll give it back to him! But he had no idea at all of where he would get it; he did not even know where to begin looking.

"In his old age Tiberius began to be particularly afraid of attempts at assassination. D'you remember how he ended his days?"

"It's not that I don't remember, I never knew. I don't know anything about either ancient or medieval history. I only like history beginning with the sixteenth century. It seems to me

125

that before that there were no people in the world, but some sort of animals.... Though it's bad to talk that way."

"They're just as they used to be. Tiberius always had political favorites who together with him performed every conceivable kind of bestiality. Then, when they acquired too much power, or had aroused his suspicions for some reason, or he had simply stopped liking them, he ordered them to be killed. He was the most suspicious of the tyrants. His last favorite was Macro— *Macro intrepidus*, as Tacitus calls him."

"You know Latin, too!"

"Not at all. When I came to Capri I naturally brought along Tacitus and Suetonius in editions with a German translation printed opposite every page of the Latin text. I quote a few words of the original more for the effect. As you've probably noticed I'm fond of effects. I'm also fond of pretending to be an educated man."

"I've never noticed that. In the first place, you really are a very educated man, and secondly you never pretend to be anything."

"Tacitus says that in his old age Tiberius began to weaken rapidly. But his furtiveness, suspiciousness, and cunning remained as before. The obsequiousness around him was such as the world has never seen since ... until *he* appeared...."

"Which 'he'?"

"Bezoshvili. Chizbikov. David. Ivanovich. Koba. Nizheradze. Ryaboy. Soselo. Soso. Oganes. Vartanovich. Totomyaets. Vasiliev. Stalin-Djugashvili."

"There were some others, too, I don't remember them all.... And then Tiberius was finally overtaken by illness, a real illness, his last. He lost consciousness and lay in a coma. The well-known physician Hariclus, who was treating him, felt obliged to tell the chief functionaries that the emperor's hours were numbered. The joy was unprecedented; he had been loathsome even to those whose fortunes he had made and whom he had showered with favors. They all had grounds for trembling about their own skins—a favorite today, but what of tomorrow!

126

In the palace there appeared his triumphant heir, Caius Julius, who passed into history under the nickname of Caligula. Macro was radiant also; he was calculating that with the new emperor he would rule Rome, i.e., the world. And suddenly some people came running in from the sleeping chamber with the news that Tiberius had come to himself, said he was well, and was asking for dinner. Caligula was horrified; he had no doubt now that what was awaiting him in place of power was death. A panic began in the palace. In alarm many fled, others pretended not to know anything about anything, still others expressed hypocritical enthusiasm over the emperor's convalescence. The only one who was not disconcerted was the intrepid Macro. He plunged into the sleeping chamber and there smothered the aging Tiberius with a pillow. It may be that Stalin . . ."

"But what happened with Macro?"

"His hopes weren't borne out, Caligula quickly finished him off. Under Caligula people began to mourn Tiberius. And now it's an accepted thing in historical writing to defend Tiberius. It's true, he was a despot, they say, but he conducted victorious wars, was a remarkable administrator, and did a great deal for the majesty and glory of Rome. And that's how it always is. The historians earn their living by having original views. What value would they have if each one of them repeated the ideas of his predecessors? A few of them are even inclined to believe that no one killed Tiberius, that it was all invented by Tacitus and Suetonius."

"So that he may have died a natural death?"

"Everything is possible. It's sometimes seemed to me that if a countless multitude of people hate one single man fiercely, then that hatred in and of itself has a mortal power. Perhaps Macro just helped Tiberius's death along a little bit. It wasn't so difficult to connive at something, even with the physician, if the latter knew that in any case the emperor did not have long to live. Surely it can't always be unavoidable to *smother* someone? It's possible simply to *adjust* a dying man's pillow

127

or increase the dose of medicine a trifle. It's quite possible that Tiberius stifled in the hatred Rome felt for him, in the eternal fear that he would be killed by the Macros. . . . D'you know I dreamed of Tiberius here? . . . What's the matter? Your little face quivered. Are you cold? We'll go back at once."

"No, it's nothing at all. You dreamed of Tiberius?"

"I dreamed of him by a phonetic association between Tiberius and Beria. . . . I often have odd dreams, especially when I take a sleeping powder. Sometimes I have a choice: either not to sleep the whole night or to take a small dose of sleeping powders. Which, by the way, is agreeable, too: I swallow a powder, so then that's its own affair, let it get to work on me. My thoughts get a little mixed up, and unpleasantnesses and vexations disappear. You feel that you'll be falling asleep in an instant, and that repose is beginning. . . . From everything. . . . Have you never thought of the dynamics of dreams?"

"Now there's one thing I really have never thought of!"

"Don't tell me you've never dreamed of Russia? Perhaps I can see her better than the people living there. I see her with her monstrous yearning, her unendurable ennui, which makes sensitive people finish themselves off. . . ."

"I never felt such ennui," said Natasha sadly. "You left Russia too long ago. One can't judge from a distance."

"One can and one must. I'm not a writer, but don't the writers judge from a distance? From a distance both in space and in time. The greatest writers, Shakespeare, Goethe, Hugo, Balzac, Flaubert, and in Russia Pushkin, Gogol, Tolstoy, were historical novelists or playwrights, that is, they never saw half of what they wrote about."

"But I wasn't speaking about that. There you're absolutely right, and I should so like you to become a writer! You would probably write profound things, describe wonderful people."

"If that were so then I should be all the worse at literature. Describe wonderful people? That's just when everything would be most likely to come out dead. A novel must be written so

128

that from the very first chapter the reader feels, But these are all friends of mine, I've met them all! Though I have written about outstanding people. For instance, I've always been interested in Count Saint-Germain, the eighteenth-century French adventurer, and this spring I wrote a novella about him. . . . I like the word novella. . . . It's about one incident that really happened, it's described in the files of the French police. The count saved the life of some girl."

"Let me read it!"

"The manuscript's in Berlin. And it's not worth it; my little story is no good. It's rather a sketch for a short story. I have a great many such sketches, and they're none of them actually any good. I remember everything, my memory is excellent, and it always comes out badly: dry and disagreeable in tone. In other words, I have no talent. But sometimes I have dreams. . . . You remember I told you about that drug I brought back from America. It helps me even with the pangs of creation. Sometimes I write down my dreams. And sometimes I dream about what I've written down."

"For God's sake, stop taking that drug! Why do you do it?"

He was about to reply to her, too, in order to have ten lives instead of one, but he remembered he had already said that to the colonel. I've started repeating myself far too much, he thought with annoyance.

"It gives you a particularly agreeable sensation: what you dream seems thoroughly logical and authentic, even the first few seconds after waking up, when you can still hear the voices of the people you've been dreaming about. And later you simply don't understand how such nonsense could come to you at all."

"Yes, yes, I know all that, it must be so, but it's not right to take such drugs. And—forgive me—but you drink too much, too. That's also very bad for you."

"But one has to have a few pleasures in life," he said, irritated. Natasha turned white as a sheet. Instantly he raised her hand

129

to his lips. "My angel, with you, you must understand, it's not a question of pleasures, with you it's happiness!"

"Not very much happiness," she said, scarcely holding back her tears.

"I was speaking of the minor pleasures of life."

"I see you're fed up with Capri already."

"Without you I wouldn't have stayed here. And in addition I'm more and more afraid of being alone. Sometimes there's a *tramontana* wind that blows here. That's a frightful thing. At one time I had what the Americans call a nervous breakdown."

"What did you say? A nervous breakdown? What happened to you?"

"Don't get upset, it was nothing serious."

"But please be sensible—what was it?"

"A mere trifle. And you, could you live in Capri the whole time?"

"I? Probably I couldn't, either. But with you I could even go to the North Pole. So it was completely unimportant? What did you do about it?"

"The same as now. I often ask myself: when should such and such a man have been born? To my mind I should have been born at the beginning of the eighteenth century. There was more choice at that time, you could even choose your country. And *he* would have had to be born in the eleventh century."

"Who?"

"Stalin, of course . . . though not really. He was born just when he had to be: in an epoch of delirium. . . . Well, all right, let's stop talking about such things. Then we'll be married the day after tomorrow and leave. A Honeymoon in Venice—very banal."

"Why are you afraid of banality? You often talk about it, but . . ."

"It's wrong, I know. Because of it I've made more than a few

130

mistakes in my lifetime. . . . But you know whom I've been thinking about a great deal the last few days?" Schell asked suddenly. "About that Maikov of yours."

"*Mamma mia!* But why?"

"Out of envy. You described his looks to me, and I feel I can see him before me, as though he were alive. But I can't see him from within: something very pale. He's a 'meaningless wrack of ships victorious,' isn't he? They haven't been so victorious during the recent era, nevertheless he's old Russia— that is, something very great. You see, I'm talking literature."

"And wonderfully well, too. I only wanted to say that you didn't chase after effects, it's something else again. And today you're not in the least like yourself. Has anything happened?"

Schell took a newspaper out of his pocket. "Yes, something's happened. To me, to you, to the whole world. You see, I do chase after effects, and this one effect I've been saving till the last. This newspaper just arrived today from Naples. I had actually wanted to read it to you, when we go down to dinner, but I can translate it now, too. Listen:

" 'The Central Committee of the Communist Party of the Soviet Union and the Council of Ministers of the USSR report the great misfortune that has befallen our Party and our people, the grave illness of J. V. Stalin.

" 'During the night of March 1st Comrade Stalin had a cerebral haemorrhage in his Moscow flat that struck the conscious portion of his brain. Comrade Stalin lost consciousness.

" 'This was succeeded by a paralysis of the right arm and leg and by a loss of speech. Serious pulmonary complications took place.

" 'Medical specialists were rallied for Comrade Stalin's treatment: I. Kuperin, P. Y. Lukomsky, N. V. Konovalov, A. L. Myasnikov, Professor Y. M. Filimonov, Professor I. S. Glazunov, Professor P. A. Tkachev, Professor V. I. Ivanov-Neznamov, and Professor Y. M. Tareyev.

" 'Comrade Stalin is being treated under the guidance of

131

A. F. Tretyakov, the Minister of National Health of the USSR, and I. Kuperin, the head of the Medical and Hygienic Department of the Kremlin.

"'Comrade Stalin is being treated under the constant supervision of the Central Committee of the Communist Party of the Soviet Union and of the Soviet Government.'"

12

Delirium . . .

"BUT why don't you want to go to America, Citizen Maikov?
You would be made the director there of an enormous laboratory and get twenty thousand dollars a year salary, perhaps
even more, with a share of the profits. The laboratory you'd be
given would be first-rate, you would be in sole charge, with
about ten young scientists working under you. You'd have your
own house with a garden. You would be known to the whole
of the scientific and even the nonscientific world, the newspapers would send reporters to interview you—a great invention
like yours is no small thing.

"Here you live in this shabby little cubbyhole with a dilapidated sofa, an unpainted chest of drawers, three dirty chairs,
and a wobbly little desk from which everything probably keeps
falling off. Have you a bathtub? Not even a bathtub. A man
without a bathtub cannot even pretend to a claim on esteem.
And your neighbors? Aren't they making your life a misery?

It would be difficult even to conceive of a more ungifted existence for such a gifted man as yourself. In the West we've heard, from fools, that philistine prejudices are alien to your people. In your country no one would say that, of course. Like ourselves you would like a pleasant or at least a tolerable life. Naturally that includes freedom, especially in living conditions; doubtless you could get along without political freedom. You are a scientist, an inventor, independence is important for you, contact with other scientists is important. Here you work in a state laboratory, not a very bad one, but not a very good one, either, you have a great many superiors over you, and you must obey orders like a schoolboy. There are most likely good people among your colleagues, but because of the nature of Soviet service they are primarily competitors. Every success of yours represents a failure of theirs. Willy-nilly they follow you about, some of them intrigue against you, reports are circulated about you. Your invention is studied in a committee. Its leaders are Communists and as a general rule know nothing about science. The majority of the others have no desire for a new man to move up.

"And what does that mean, to move up? If your invention is considered valuable, you'll receive a promotion in scholarly rank, you'll have a two-room flat, just as dirty as this one, you may also receive some decoration or other. Your colleagues will sputter and jeer. And at the very first failure, however minor, you'll be devoured by jealous enemies. I know that in your time you were arrested, I don't know what for. Probably someone sent in an accusation against you, at best it would be a scientific one: a mistake, a miscalculation, a failure to achieve a promised result. It may all have been just nonsense. But let's grant that your rival told the truth: you did, in fact, make a mistake. That happens, indeed it's inevitable. In America private entrepreneurs discount possible errors in their own calculations. If it was a very big mistake, a scientist in the West might lose his position. But you were put in jail. And at worst you were charged with having been at one time a Cadet, or a Menshevik,

134

or a Socialist Populist. Surely it's impossible in such circumstances to work fruitfully? Or is what I'm saying incorrect?"

"I don't understand the point of your saying all this."

"I hope you don't think you're working for Russia? Only fools can think that, or people who clutch at a straw in order not to turn their life into a piece of utter futility. You are working for Stalin and for world revolution, that is, for an ignorant, obtuse, however cunning, evil-doer, and in order to transform another billion people into a stupid, rapidly degenerating herd of cattle. What is there for you to do here? Your discovery would interest them only if some high official sponsored you. And how could you get through to him? You wouldn't know how to crawl through the jungle to him.

"It's also rather dangerous. From the Kremlin to the Lubyanka is only a step or two both in the direct and figurative sense of the words. There's a logically composed novel here, the composition structure is first-rate, as with all mediocre novels: Chapter One: He's a Nobody. Chapter Five: He's a Very Important Person. Chapter Fifteen: In the Torture Chamber. But let us suppose, just suppose, that everything goes smoothly. Will the Bolsheviks let you go abroad for an exchange of views with Western scientists? Hardly. For that you have to sell yourself to them body and soul. Can you read the foreign books written by the best modern writers? You cannot; the High Command is in charge of your literary tastes, you read what you're permitted to. In America you would at once get together a large and wonderful library. What bliss it is to buy and read books! ... You remember Pushkin's address to them before dying? 'Farewell, my friends.' And here you have this wretched little shelf, and the only papers you read are the Soviet press, which is, quite apart from anything else, the most boring and talentless in the world. Isn't that so?"

"That's so. Nevertheless, take yourself off instantly. I cannot endure spies."

"What is a spy? Edith Cavell was a spy; one of the warring sides forty years ago had her shot, the other set up a monument

135

to her. In wartime thousands of Frenchmen died in the Resistance as spies, today all France considers them heroes. '*La trahison est une question de dates,*' said Talleyrand. It was not for the sake of money that they did what they did, but they were paid anyhow, which is perfectly natural. 'People have to eat and drink,' as the colonel says. And their motives? But why do you want to know mine? Whether I've sold myself or not is a personal, private, and quite uninteresting question. In general you mustn't judge too severely, or else far too large a bench will be needed for the accused later on.

"You have one alternative: you can become a martyr. That's not so good. Under the tsars you could be a martyr to a variety of resounding words. After all, there are such words, gems, all of them, though most often fake—'I die for freedom,' and so forth. But today that's impossible. No one will even learn of your martyrdom, or remember it in two weeks if they did. For that matter absolutely no one cares, there's just one more martyr. Better console yourself with pangs of conscience; for coquettish people they're invaluable. Or aren't you coquettish? Natasha never told me, I don't quite see you as that. The *ololiukvi,* after all, was also in order to be able to understand you. For heaven's sake, say something, don't talk in monosyllables, talk clearly. . . .

"Well, there it is, here you are one of the best of men, but you, too, signed various loyal telegrams to Tiberius: 'Executed such-and-such, heartiest thanks, O great Stalin!' It's true, isn't it, that you signed them? And in your place I would have, too, but 'would' is in the subjunctive, and in the declarative I never signed anything. Let's be off to America, and not sign anything else, eh? Even repentance here is inappropriate, after all; out of a dozen people you talk to at least one is surely a stool pigeon. A little vulgar that, eh? Perhaps, but it's the plain truth. Surely it's only through a deluge of truth that man can be healed, and even then it's not very likely. The Russian intelligentsia no longer exists. There was a Russian intelligentsia, there was! And there was a literature, and what a literature!

136

Noble, talented, at times the work of genius. We thought that Russian literature could not be sold, or bought, and that it could never be terrorized. And now just open any book at random—the author has sold himself; if not wholly, then he's sold himself 50 per cent, or 20 per cent, or 10 per cent. It's true that your government used to be haughty and dull-witted. Under Nicholas I it was forbidden not only to abuse the government, but also to praise it: 'We have no use for that.' The present-day rulers have thought it all out: 'How is it possible *not* to praise us? Let them wear their foreheads out groveling!' For thirty years now they've been corrupting people with enormous, stunning, astonishing success. The Russian people were one of the ablest, the most sensitive, the most 'spiritual' in the world. But they did not withstand the action of the most colossal corrupting force in history, nor could they have. The same thing happened with the Germans under Hitler; almost everyone joined up with him—writers, philosophers, scholars. You might still say that it had nothing to do with the individual, or even with the nation, but that a new historical epoch was beginning, and so on. Make sure you say it—it's a splendid consolation, a sociological one. . . .

"Nevertheless, I hope that at least some slight feeling of irony has remained to you from the past, eh? Natasha told me that before you used to execrate everyone and everything, and now you have some kind of panacea. It would seem you're coming out a little tarnished, Nikolai Arkadievich. I can't make you out, I don't understand. . . . But perhaps you feel you would like everyone in the West to sell himself, too, so that there would be nothing but crawlers everywhere. But that's not how it is. I have never been asked for welcoming telegrams, and if anyone were to ask me I'd tell him to go to hell. Yes, and the West has no purges, either. . . . Listen to me, what about the ennui, the monstrous, improbable, and unendurable ennui of Soviet Russia? Have you ever actually kept a record of your day? Bad work, bad dinner, this horrible room. And the same tomorrow, and day after day, and year after year. They say

137

Soviet youth has 'blazing eyes'; even without freedom, don't you see, it is 'joyously building a new life' in this monstrous ennui. Well, it's possible, may it go on building! But as for this kind of new life, it would be better if it weren't built at all. They are, after all, optimistic atheists—a rare and imbecilic species. What can their parrotlike Komsomol minds understand! And their eyes are not blazing in the least. There are some fanatics among them, to be sure—they are rewarded splendidly. There were doubtless blazing eyes among the Hitlerite fanatics, too.... No, let's be off for the West, let's be off, dear Citizen Maikov. I am not saying, of course, that all the evil is to be found on one side of the Iron Curtain, there's enough on the other side, too. And there are almost no statesmen in the West at all. Churchill is the only one, but he's something out of Walter Scott, he instead of Ivanhoe should be fighting in a jousting tournament at Ashby de la Zouch. Aside from him I don't think there's anyone else. Many people will describe Nehru to you as one. I detest that hypocrite who considers himself the savior of the world. But he does have one bright idea: he was the first one who understood that under the guise of an extremely new democracy it was possible to persuade people to acquire any broken-down old property at all, Kashmir or what have you. Nevertheless, in the free world our statesmen are men, while your statesmen are beasts."

"You're wasting your time. I'm not going abroad. And it was not worth your while to come here in order to talk to me about the comforts of life in America, or about the advantages of political liberty over slavery."

"I started off with practical conclusions. I understand very well that for you they have no meaning. Of course I was talking commonplaces, but after all your people have even forgotten the commonplaces, too. One moment: are you afraid the Russian émigrés will give you an unfriendly reception? I don't know very much about them and have less interest. I can't say anything bad about them, except, after all, the worst —they are a negligible quantity. Chiang Kai-sheks without a

138

Formosa. There are probably both very good and very bad people among them. You see I have no fear of commonplaces. And it would be strange if Russia had only bad ones left, while all the good ones were abroad, or the other way round. The fact of departure itself, after all, was determined by a myriad accidents, including people's opinions. At all times and everywhere in the world there has been one principle: *cujus regio ejus religio*. I recall Voltaire's telling me that. . . ."

"Who told you that?"

"Voltaire. In France under Louis XV I met the most famous people. How many times have I not spoken with the king himself! Frederick was also fond of me, he said Count Saint-Germain was the most remarkable man of his age and of course the best physician there was."

"Really? Is it simply that you're out of your mind? . . ."

"You're out of your mind," said the coachman. "Unheard of, to have a coachman go to Moscow from Berlin! Fly there by plane and descend by parachute. That's how Colonel Number One always does it with his agents. If they don't capture you, that's how you'll get that Maikov of yours over to the West."

"Nothing is easier than giving stupid advice, and I wasn't asking you for any. In Pompeii, too, I went by carriage and I drove Natasha all around Capri. I'll give you a thousand-lira tip. But I'm in a great hurry."

"Nonsense, there's nowhere to hurry."

"But tomorrow I have to take an examination in the history of religion, and I don't know Nil Sorsky's doctrine, I never had the time to read it."

"That's a common nightmare. You have no examination at all. I also dream sometimes that I haven't had time to learn the tarantella for an examination at the conservatoire."

"But how can you, an ordinary coachman, be studying at the conservatoire! You're a thoroughgoing liar. The tip will be two thousand lire."

"For two thousand lire I can take you to the lunatic asylum.

139

You're going to land up there anyhow, you probably have bad heredity."

"How dare you talk so insolently! I'll strangle you like that Arab in Santander. . . ."

"Only a madman can believe in panaceas. . . . Your colonels are light-minded fellows. . . ."

". . . Strange that I get the two colonels mixed up, they're really after all quite different people. But everyone is the equal of everyone else. . . . And Edda? What d'you think of her? I mentioned her in my sketch of Count Saint-Germain, but only just put in a mention without finishing it, actually like the whole sketch itself. . . . No, I haven't turned into a writer. That's my misfortune; after all I'm ambitious, verbose, and snobbish. A great pity. . . . Let me have some vodka."

"I have none."

"Scandalous! What have you over there in that cupboard reaching to the ceiling? It's locked with a special lock."

"That's my cello."

"You play the cello? What if you played a tarantella! Hearing that here would be like listening to the Zionist anthem in Hitler's house."

"What tarantella? What nonsense!"

"My life is a film set to tarantella music. I repeat, I express myself in an ugly way. Basically, I'm rather a vulgar fellow— demonic. I'm Count Saint-Germain. . . . And what is your discovery about?"

"You know perfectly well, that's why you came, isn't it? It's a way of prolonging human life. I've discovered a panacea."

"For a long time now humanity has been searching for a panacea. Liebig said there was no idea more refined, more exalted, with a more powerful effect on people's creative energies. And his contemporary, also a famous chemist, Raspail, was convinced he had discovered one. Didn't it turn out to be camphor?"

"Raspail made a mistake. I was the first to understand that

140

a panacea had to be a catalytic agent. I hope you know that catalyst is the name for those substances that accelerate chemical processes. Now, I've discovered a negative catalyst, that is, a substance that slows down chemical processes. That's how my panacea will lengthen life. I'm explaining this to you in an elementary way, in one or two words, since you're a layman."

"Of course your discovery is written down as it should be, with formulas, numbers, and so on, eh? Where do you keep the description? Also in that kitchen cupboard with the special lock?"

"You're probably very fond of the movies? That's straight out of a movie: a folder with secret documents, which the spy lays his hands on, thinking, meanwhile, And if he doesn't hand them over I'll kill him. . . . You've probably killed people? Perhaps you boast about it? Even though only to yourself?"

"No, I don't boast. I've sometimes had to kill, like so many others nowadays. After all, I've been in combat. When people burn before your eyes, set on fire by your flame-thrower, and you're rewarded for it, moral concepts become simplified in the extreme. Yes, I've killed people; it's very simple. Once I even strangled a man in Spain. D'you want me to tell you about it?"

"No, I don't."

"Don't be uneasy about my having an attack of delirium. My delirium is something special. Who else in Europe takes *ololiukvi?* It's a pity I didn't bring along the notebook with my sketches; it's still in Berlin, on the left shelf, where I have a few frivolous engravings. Edda once found them and was vastly entertained."

"This madman's delirium of yours is tiresome. And you'd never succeed in strangling me. I'd yell out and the neighbors would come running."

"But, please, it's never even occurred to me. Though a wee little idea may have crossed my mind just then."

"You have a strangler's hands."

"Colonel Number One also kept staring at my hands. And

141

I've only strangled one man all told: that Arab in Santander. . . ."

". . . Santander had only just been taken by General Franco's army. Spanish and Italian troops were moving up through the outskirts; there were also cars arriving with German officers, looking contemptuously fastidious, lorries with supplies were coming up, and returning refugees were dragging their carts back, with their heavily-burdened donkeys, mules, and even cows. On the sidewalks, in the empty lots, in the gateways to the houses damaged by bombs, at the windows with blown-out glass panes there were crowds of people. Many were weeping with joy. When the Spanish flags appeared there was great enthusiasm. The people stretched their arms out in the Fascist salute, but someone would occasionally make a crude mistake and raise his clenched fist in the ritual of the People's Front, instantly snatching it back when he noticed his mistake. The Italians, Germans, and especially the Moors were hardly applauded at all.

"The tall man in the blue suit had been sitting on the café terrace from the morning on. Tables and chairs were there, but no food, and not even drinks. He had been left by the Loyalist government, who had abandoned the city. He had been a pilot in their service. More than once he had jumped behind the front in a parachute; he would pass himself off sometimes as an American journalist, sometimes as a businessman, sometimes as a foreign actor who had found himself stranded in Spain.

"Now he had an assignment: to ascertain the numerical proportions between the various segments that constituted the enemy's army—by habit he actually spoke of the 'enemy' and even thought of them that way, even though he was not very much interested in who won. He realized that he could not learn anything with precision, but he did not wish to accept the large sums of money, which the Loyalists were paying him, for nothing. The victors were advancing into Santander

142

by two highways, and just the evening before he had made note of an observation post for each highway.

"For three hours he watched from the terrace, counting and trying to keep in mind the four numbers, which kept growing with each moment that passed. It was, of course, out of the question to jot anything down in full view of everyone. As it was, he attracted attention because of his great height and by being both smooth-shaven and much better dressed than the others. He calculated how many *Requetes* passed by in red berets, Falangists in blue uniforms, Legionnaires in green shirts, Moors in fezzes and turbans. For all three hours he kept an expression of joy on his face over the victory. He gave the Fascist salute carefully and correctly, but more seldom than the others. He was too indolent to get up; he was exhausted, he had scarcely slept for two nights. He very much wanted to eat and particularly to drink. In a large sack lying at his feet, which in normal times would not at all have gone with his looks or clothing, there was sugar, a box of preserves, and a bottle of wine, but he felt embarrassed at eating in front of so many hungry people. Behind the man in the blue suit there hung a poster with an enormous inscription: 'Remember, there are spies everywhere! Don't say anything superfluous! Report every suspicious-looking person to the authorities immediately!' The poster had been left by the Loyalists, but there was no emblem of any kind on it and the members of the *Guardia Civil*, who had passed through the suburb a few hours before, had left it on the wall after a short consultation.

"He ate somewhere in an empty lot. He avidly ate the little he had, but drank only half the bottle and put it back in the sack. He also had an ordinary workman's corduroy blouse, and some clothes, as well as a red necktie of the latest Madrid model. If he were detained and searched, that would have been enough to have him shot. But all the same he had nothing to lose, since in the back pocket of his trousers he also had a revolver, and he did not wish to and could not be separated from that.

"After he had eaten, the man in the blue suit set out for the southern highway, where only the day before bitter and bloody battles had taken place. His second observation post was a small, very old peasant's hut, of which there remained only the walls with shattered doors, part of the fireplace, part of the floor covered with rubble, and a bed that had somehow survived, with a filthy mattress and a pillow. He went into the little house from the back, and after looking around unobtrusively arranged himself near the window without panes. He took out a little notebook. He recalled the former four figures, though with annoyance that he was not sure which of the first two referred to the *Requetes* and which to the Falangists. . . . I think the Falangists . . . almost certainly . . . but what if they don't? He thought that his memory might have been getting weaker from his lengthy fasting, from the complete lack of meat, or from his having been drinking too much during the past months (there was not a serious shortage of wine in either camp).

"But it wasn't very important. The figures, in any case, were accidental, the proportion between them might have changed very much after he left the café, and for that matter these data were not very valuable in any case. It's simply that both sides have very active dilettantish intelligence services that have to demonstrate their abilities. The man in the blue suit used to read in the foreign newspapers that there were four times fewer Carlists in General Franco's camp than Fascists.

"The proportion he had calculated between the first two figures did not conform with that. He wrote down the numbers and began to jot down in little lines (one line for approximately every ten soldiers) the data on the southern highway along which the same thing was taking place as in the suburb. He kept doing this until it turned dark. . . . Still a different proportion came out. Take the average, he thought; in reports everything always comes out very well.

"It was plain that the owners had abandoned their little house only at the last minute, just before the actual battles
144

for the accesses to Santander. He knew that the populace everywhere, especially the peasants, agonizingly refused to abandon the scorched areas, but was just as agonizingly afraid of the Moors—dreadful rumors were circulating about the Moroccan cavalry just as there were about the Communists in the other camp; as it happened the Spaniards were also shooting each other, but between themselves it was possible to come to an understanding and even establish good relations; lootings were very rare. The splinters of some cheap, coarse earthenware were scattered on the floor, and a broken dish with the remnants of some beans. The man in the blue suit drank the wine, got some powder out of his sack, sprinkled it on the mattress and pillow, and stretched out with delight on the bed. He didn't take his revolver out of his trousers pocket. Now the troops were no longer of any consequence, and no one was going to be interested in a shattered peasant hut; the country was full of them.

"It turned quite dark. The hubbub on the road had died down, all the military units had already passed by. Exhausted, one ear cocked, he thought about his own affairs. It would be impossible to stay on any longer in Santander. Some people in the city knew he was a foreign journalist who had been in good odor with the Loyalists; there would be no end of trouble, and a search was highly likely. He thought that the hotel-keeper would not report him—he seemed to be a decent fellow —a hidalgo, though they were all hidalgos—and had no reason to be annoyed with him. Indeed it would be both troublesome, pointless, and dangerous; it wasn't sensible for hotelkeepers to get into arguments with Americans. But anyhow there's no point staying on. I'll slip round back, get my things, and say good-by. In Bilbao I'll remain an American journalist, and tell anyone I have to that I'm going to write about the Carlists and the Falangists. How they'll suck up to me then! For some reason he found the Carlists, with their antique opinions, much more agreeable than the Fascists. He thought that, though Spain was one of the most beautiful countries in the world and

145

the Spaniards one of the noblest peoples, it would be a good idea to leave as soon as possible for some country where there was no civil war, preferably France; he was thoroughly fed up with everything in Spain. With these thoughts he fell into the sensitive, uneasy sleep of a man who was always in mortal danger, especially at night.

"He had no idea why he woke up. It could hardly have been the increase of noise on the highway—a clatter of horses' hoofs was heard, a tardy cavalry unit was advancing into the city— his ear had already accustomed himself to this noise during the day. Then, as he woke up, in some incomprehensible way he sensed a human presence. In a flash he sprang soundlessly to his feet. . . . If I shoot it'll be heard on the highway, they'll burst in here; that'll be the end. From the same side as he himself had entered the hut he now heard a rustling. I think he's alone. . . . Some looter? An amateur murderer? He leaned forward slightly. Suddenly at the other end of the room a tiny light gleamed. A Moor appeared, with a flashlight in one hand and a dagger in the other. From where he stood the man in the blue suit bounded forward like a cat and seized the Moor by the throat. . . ."

"By the throat? Hardly. Some traces would have remained, and thousands of people would have been allowed in to see the body. It's more likely they poisoned him. Or 'treated' him by the methods of Heinrich Yagoda. But even that can't be said with certainty. It will probably remain one of the 'insoluble enigmas of history.'"

"I think so, too. Something like Timberius's assassination. On Capri they don't say 'Tiberius,' but 'Timberius.' They are all very fond of their Tiberius. Natasha never wanted to believe it. But didn't I tell you that I married Natasha? She was your favorite, wasn't she? Could you have been in love with her, too? It's just that the poor sweet doesn't know what sort of man I am. And what will happen if she finds out, eh? What should I do then: commit suicide? I thought of that once when

I was still young, and would probably have done it if I still hadn't had a slight hope of finding some peaceful haven. . . . So you think that Joseph Vissarionovich was assisted to his death? That would be very agreeable, very agreeable indeed. After all, a more terrible man never existed. How I regret never seeing him! Did you?"

"Yes. I went to see him with a report concerning my discovery."

"No! It's not possible! You saw Stalin?"

"Yes. A school comrade of mine who was an official at the time managed to arrange an audience for me with him, but unfortunately when Joseph Vissarionovich received me he was already thinking of having this official shot, and a little while later I was thrown into the Lubyanka. I escaped by the skin of my teeth."

"But give me some more details about the visit, if you really don't want to say any more about this panacea of yours. What was he like, Comrade Stalin? What kind man dat?"

"He also had a panacea. I have two, and he had a third. His panacea was—provocation. That's also a catalytic agent, though not for biological but for historical processes. He spent his whole life provoking something or someone, and nearly always successfully."

"Where did he receive you?"

"In his office. Where else?"

"Yes, yes, I've read some descriptions of it, I've read so much about him! On the table there were five telephones, the most important ones in Russia. Portraits of Marx and Lenin hung on the dark-green walls. That's also a symbol of his panacea: he never looked into Marx's books his whole life and he couldn't bear Lenin. What else?"

"But what d'you mean, what else? You're telling the whole thing, not me. . . ."

"That's because I embody everything in yourself. Or try to, though badly. On your way over you doubtless passed through a few rooms with people. The faces of all of them expressed

147

'worship.' Some of them doubtless 'worshiped' him like 'soldiers.' Thinking to themselves that the more brazen the flattery the better. They may sometimes have been right. And he was right, too; *cela fait partie du métier.* Sometimes he would pretend that this ocean of flattery was repugnant to him. Tiberius also pretended to dislike obsequiousness. After some meeting or other—was it the Senate, or what?—he said: 'O human vileness!' or something like that. After which people who knew him well flattered him still more. But Stalin, of course, acted as though he considered the torrents of flattery useful for the 'cause,' in view of the people's sheeplike stupidity. He didn't think that up either. And perhaps it is necessary; it's only people like him who do, in fact, have real prestige. In democratic countries prestige is created only after a man dies; in the slave countries, after a man's death, it vanishes. But like all of us, after all, he is not so interested in what happens after death. You think that time restores everything? But just what is time? One age will restore everything, and the next will change it about. It may be that immediate posterity will begin with a thoroughgoing hatred for him and his deeds: anything you like as long as it's not like him! But then there will be throwbacks to Stalinism. And what does posterity matter, anyhow? Posterity's a long way off! Now nothing matters to him but foreign policy, though before, to be sure, it never even interested him. Enemies at home are more or less annihilated. The temptation is enormous—in two or three months he might control the European continent. It's true that even as it is he's ruler of half the world, but he doesn't find the semi-civilized countries, from China to Albania, very interesting. The temptation is enormous, but so is the risk. Though with his chances Napoleon would long since have gone to war—a Communist Napoleon, naturally. Here, too, he's 'mediocre.' That's the sign of the epoch—it has been thrown into turmoil by a man who is terrifying and nevertheless mediocre. The enigma is that there's no enigma. There's nothing in him in the least dramatic, he doesn't resemble either Mephistopheles or Richard III; he

148

has an almost inconceivable absence of romance. For a historical personality that is, of course, a failing. But the biographers will think up something; in all ages there will be stupid and inventive biographers. Well, they'll discover historical merits, they'll even find a psychological merit—he constructed a vast edifice on nothing but evil and hatred, and opened up an enormous reservoir which will flow for centuries.

"Yes, our salvation is due to nothing but the enormity of the risk. In my day it was possible to begin wars with no risk. My friends Louis XV and Frederick II knew that a defeat would threaten neither them nor their thrones. But today there is a green room in Nuremberg, with a gallows and scaffolding, and a trapdoor. . . .

"So he turned down your discovery? Contradicts dialectical materialism, eh? Of course. But he died anyhow, eh? I myself read about it in a Neapolitan newspaper; even Natasha read it. She was startled, but 'not especially.' . . . Natasha always says 'not especially.' And don't tell me I was dreaming. . . . Colonel Number One dreamed that the Prophet Jeremiah had lost two million marks at poker, while I lost less than forty thousand. . . .

"D'you take *La Señorita?* In Mexico the people call *ololiukvi La Señorita,* I have no idea why. Perhaps because the delirium is so often bound up with women. I used to have visions like that, too. . . . Probably all these officials, especially those who drink a lot when they go to dine with him, must think, What if something horrible happens and over the wine I blurt out what I really think of him! He sometimes does invite the more important ones over for an informal dinner. A throwback to old-fashioned Caucasian hospitality? Does he like giving people hospitality, drinking with them? He's human, after all, eh? Or is that where his panacea is, too? 'I'll "blab" over the wine, then they'll blab, too.' After all, he quite often passed an evening with Bukharin, and he used to drink with Rykov. And doubtless felt no malice toward them. Perhaps he didn't feel any even when he sent them to the torture chambers; it was

149

simply that things would be better that way. But as for the small fry—that was a different matter. These were actually proud of seeing close up the most powerful, the most famous man in the world every day. Because of him they would go down in history, appear in novels and plays of the twenty-first century. Indeed, their raptures were also partly authentic. One way or another he had maintained himself in power for so many years, he had destroyed all his enemies, no one had ever been able to cope with him. The more intelligent ones probably had some doubts, too: what was all this anyhow? how could it have happened? We know, after all, that there is nothing special about him, even though he's intelligent and crafty; he never even learned to talk Russian properly, he's read nothing, he never in all his life wrote or said anything in the least bit interesting. But of course what predominated in them was horror. Like Hitler he, too, had complete control over that quality which is so precious to a political figure: he was capable of arousing fear in people. And those who trembled more than anyone else were the highly placed officials, that is, those to whom he showed favor; it was they, after all, who knew better than anyone that he was organically incapable of speaking the truth. The chief functionaries would sometimes still get into arguments with him, but they knew very precisely when it was necessary to stop arguing. Some of them may have considered him mad, and they weren't so far wrong. . . . Yes, yes, I'm saying everything instead of you, forgive me. Well, what happened?"

"Just as I was brought in to see him his secretary was serving him tea. . . ."

"He would have liked it better if his tea were given him by some minister or general, but he would not have entrusted it to every official. His secretary, of course, was an old woman, a veteran Communist, tried a hundred times over, 'with doglike devotion.' But of course he realized perfectly well that if things had turned out differently she would have gone into Trotsky's office with exactly the same look of solemn worship. And who

150

knows what she had in her mind, her tiny little mind? But, then, what did he say to her?"

"He said one word, 'matches.' I had the impression he was annoyed about something. But what is there for me to tell you about when you know better about everything?"

"Of course what he said was, 'My mother once had a goat; you look very much like her.' It's said a great many officials used to hear this witty joke from him often, and probably their faces, like hers, hastened to broaden into an enthusiastic smile. . . . A heap of papers lay in front of him. Rumors have it that he could grasp everything immediately and make an instantaneous decision. Sometimes he would write a few words in the margins, usually coarse and nearly always ungrammatical. Before he used still to be a little ashamed of his bad Russian. Trotsky's and Bukharin's literary abilities irritated him. But for a long time he hadn't paid any more attention to that. And in essence whatever he wrote on the papers probably seemed to him intelligent and purposeful, just the sort of thing that should be written by a dictator who knew his business and his subjects well. His decisions did not have a veneer for the ages, like the remarks the tsars used to make on state papers, but were read by his subjects with immeasurably greater trepidation; from almost every one of them one subject or another might foresee his own fate, more or less remote. Stalin seldom came to grips with people at once.

"There must have been excerpts from foreign newspapers, too. If they called him a devil he doubtless read them with gratification. But he flew into a frenzy when it was said that he was ignorant, or else that he was not all-powerful, that the power was in the hands of the Politburo. Nevertheless, in general this reading gave him pleasure. He would see, every day he would see, that the foreign powers not only did not want war but trembled at the very thought of it. While Russia declared the exact opposite; that's all part of the panacea. Now today the principal question is, Will there be war or not? The difference between him and the rest of mankind was that the answer to this question just happened to depend on him. What bliss!

"And Communist principles? It may be that at one time they occupied a place in his life, a tiny little place. Even at that time his intellectual life was homeopathic. But even of this nothing was left, nor could be left, in the blood bath he lived in for so many years. And when could he ever have been upset about the happiness of mankind? He could never, after all, endure people. The future society was not of the slightest interest to him. In that society he would have been unendurably bored, he simply would not have known what to do with himself. He never liked anything in this life except power. In his youth it might have been power over dozens of lost souls, now it was over hundreds of millions. Without it life would not only have lost all its charm for him, but also all its interest. In order to stay in power you have to kill people, which is just what he did. Perhaps at the beginning he was disturbed—naturally about his own skin: 'I may break my neck!' But later he did it calmly, without regrets and of course without any 'sadism.' It was doubtless only in exceptional cases that he felt any pleasure. The reports on the preparation of Trotsky's assassination, then on realization of this little project, were probably one of the greatest joys of his life. People may imagine naïvely that at night he was harassed by nightmares, as though endless ranks of executed people passed through his dreams, as described in various classical and nonclassical tragedies! In reality he probably never even thought about them, at most doubtless simply the way one might recall something through some accidental association, sometimes perhaps an entertaining one, too.

"It must have been awkward or even painful for his flunkies to talk with him about their tortured comrades: not everyone, after all, has nerves like his. Some of those executed not so long before had been drinking wine and joking with them. It was someone's turn last night, but whose will it be tomorrow? And what if a shadow suddenly flits across his face? And how they probably longed to find out the details of Trotsky's assassination! Perhaps they did find out, by hearsay. And what were the ideas behind it? In his own company they never even mentioned 'ideas': there was no time to, and what was the use? After all, there is that old philosophico-political syllogism, you can always recall it and rattle it off, like this: here we are, striving for the happiness of mankind, that is what our Party is leading the world toward, and consequently whatever is good for our Party is good and whatever is bad for it is bad. Nothing that helps the Party can be called criminal, not even the bloodiest crimes. Nor were they even the ones who had thought this up. But even to recall this and rattle it off there was neither the time, the necessity, nor the occasion.

"And of course it goes without saying that Joseph Vissarionovich would have begun a third war without the slightest hesitation and sent a hundred million people into a better world if there had only been some assurance of victory. But there wasn't! There were chances of it, great chances, but after all who knew *how* it might end, eh? Hitler was completely convinced he was going to win the world war, indeed he *almost* did. A great many officials were hoping to please him by valiant talk; excessive optimism might destroy them only later on, but excessive pessimism instantly. Who in Russia looks far into the future? Joseph Vissarionovich knew, very well indeed, that in case of disaster it would be the fanatics who would be the first to betray him. That was how it was with Hitler, too. Mankind's salvation was that he often thought of Hitler: he had also gone from strength to strength, he had also been 'worshiped.' If Stalin were loved in Russia, as the fools and hirelings say in the West, that would be the proof of the most monstrous decadence of the Russian people, both an intellectual and a moral decadence. But that's not so. And what does he care? Rulers like him do not maintain themselves through the love of the people. He is a man with a streak of madness in him. By now might he not even be altogether insane? But his nerves must be something like cables, a very rare event. Hitler lived in mortal danger

153

only twelve years, while this one lived much longer. . . . But I keep forgetting he's dead. He is dead, isn't he?"

"He is."

"He is Death-in-Life, like the old Russian saying: a manlike being completely devoid of soul. You are not surprised at my clothing everything in an ironic form. Natasha also says I joke too much: 'Don't make all your jokes today, save some for tomorrow.' She said this *'there in Grunewald.'* . . . In my time I had a nervous breakdown. Is it very obvious that I'm not quite in my right mind?"

"Very."

"You say that out of spite at my having instigated you to leave by mocking at the Russian intelligentsia. But what else can I do? Natasha can't endure it either. She is sweet, wonderful, but she doesn't understand anything about people. She hasn't even seen through me! . . . I've thought a great deal about you through what she told me. How could I approach you? I asked myself what thoughts, what feelings would an old Russian intellectual have, a man who has thought a great deal, who has lived through thirty-five years under the Bolshevik regime? I answered: there can be nothing there but an aversion to people, to himself, to everything. He will, I thought, snatch at escape. I will produce proofs, both rational, based on advantage, and irrational. . . . I was judging myself through you. And what emerged was that you, so to speak, are a spectral supplement to myself, which has completely annihilated me. Don't tell me everything is burned out in you? Did you never have passions, did you never fall in love, did you never lose everything you had on the turn of a card, were you never a hair's breadth from destruction? Or did you have merely intellectual passions, with never a tarantella among them? . . . Don't get angry either at yourself or at the Russian intelligentsia. I take everything back. I'll admit that it is in Russia and only in Russia that there are true lovers of righteousness. I say this in all sincerity. There are only a few of them, a handful, but there are some. But they are not what matters. The Macros would

154

be better. Yes, they might have, they might have helped him die! For them, you see, the question was just the same as it was for Caligula; it was plain, after all, that he had become senile. Has Timberius simply become a dotard, if only because he's preparing to croak such fine fellows as ourselves? Now it's either him or us. That is, either him or me; none of the Caligulas had anything more to do than the others with 'ideas.' Oh, what Shakespearean scenes those must have been! Nighttime, a sealed-off room, someone consulting someone in a whisper. . . . Are there two of them? Three? More? But then whom do they call in? What is said in such circumstances? How is it said? With lofty ideas? 'You must understand, Comrade Hariclovich: it is demanded by the highest interests of Communism. The Party is confronted by this horrible necessity. You must perform your painful duty.' Or, on the contrary, as routine, very simply, 'cynically,' to use a stupid word which has become unbearably vulgar. 'Well now, Hariclovsky, you yourself must realize, you're no fool, you have no choice. D'you remember Henry Yagoda and his physicians? They had no choice either. They did it, and you'll do it, too, or else of course you realize that. . . .' Of course Hariclovsky was pale as a ghost. But probably the Macros had trembling hands, too, oh, they must have trembled violently! Would he argue? Would he agree immediately? And the next chapter? Comrade Hariclovich stood at the bedside in a white dressing gown—'Here you are, Joseph Vissarionovich, take it. . . . This will help you a lot.' And that must be said robustly, firmly, with assurance. God help you if your voice trembles or your face changes expression. . . . Finished! He's swallowed it! Good God! . . . And then you have to go out just as though nothing had happened. Till tomorrow, Joseph Vissarionovich. . . . And not faint dead away on the floor. And pass through the corridors and staircases so calmly that not a single muscle in your face twitches. Oh, the Yagodas and their agents don't have an easy trade! If anything is to be forgiven people because of the *horror* they've gone through, these will be forgiven quite a good deal. . . . If only I could see

155

those dreadful places where all this happened! Those Kremlin walls have absorbed so much that it will be terrible to breathe there even a hundred years from now....A hundred years won't be much, Citizen Maikov, for you to draw out people's spirits. I know, I know, I've guessed what your second panacea, the ethical one, is; that's a Russian idea, too, and 'We're a nation of extremisms,' and Nil Sorsky and Dostoevski, and 'pan-humanity'—none of which matters. And it doesn't matter in the West either, even though there are things like that there, too, and even better. The Hellenic spirit, for instance. It's strange that all thinkers of dubious respectability are so fond of going on about the wisdom of Epicurus and the 'spirit of ancient Hellas.' "

"The train had just left the station. Policemen were walking up and down the platforms. The third-class car was filled with Greek refugees, fleeing from some military engagement. Someone was abusing the English, others were morosely glancing over at him. Just as the train started a beautiful, very pale woman sitting near the window, in a veil, leaped from her seat and rushed past the people standing in the corridor out on to the little platform. There was no one there. She crossed herself and opened the little doors of the carriage. A tall ragamuffin, in a shirt without sleeves or collar and a huge straw hat, ran out from behind the water tower, skillfully leaped into the train that was picking up speed, and slammed the doors shut. The pale woman tried to embrace him, but did not, she simply looked at him, scarcely breathing. She was incapable of saying a word. Inclining his head imperceptibly, he quickly passed to the other end of the carriage, frowning at the smell of garlic. There's Hellas for you! The meadows beyond the mountains are always greener....I barely escaped, or did I? Why did I choose this Saint-Germain kind of life? But what else could I have been? A people's tribune? Get off political vulgarities before the masses? Perhaps. Write a remarkable book? No. And that's the only thing that has value, the only thing that

156

lives—remarkable books. Well, to hell with them, I'm not going to live for the ages. Women? Now that Greek girl has gone away for good. *Mille e tre.* Louis had a thousand eight hundred of them. But I never had a Deer Park...."

... The Deer Park didn't resemble the numerous *maisons de plaisance* which the princes, dukes, tax farmers, and bankers had built for themselves in Paris during the eighteenth century. The demand created the supply. A school of talented architects, painters, sculptors, and decorators came into being which specialized in the construction, trimming, and decoration of such houses. Every rich man felt obliged to give his house originality and a *cachet personnel.* Nonetheless (or therefore) the houses usually resembled each other very much. There were small salons everywhere, boudoirs, hidden groves, secret little nooks. Everyone had painted ceilings, frescoes, and mythological or simply indecent paintings. Generally there were no dining rooms, but in some of the villas when one pressed a button the ceiling moved to one side and a luxuriously set table with crystal, Vincennes porcelain, dishes, and bottles was lowered on a platform by levers from the upper story to the lower; in others the same kind of table was lifted through a moving floor from a lower story to an upper. The presence of servants was considered inadmissible; the host and male guests served the ladies themselves. The *cachet personnel* was expressed primarily in the selection of the women, the dishes, and especially the wines; the guests of this old-fashioned school did not recognize champagne. And even in the building of the little houses a struggle went on between red wood and pink. The rich were advised by the celebrated Boucher, the constant companion of their diversions. Actually the debauchery in those times was only a little greater than at other times, but under Louis XV it was bolder, franker, and prouder.

State affairs no longer interested the king. Even before he had devoted about an hour a day to them, thinking that was more than enough. He saw no profound meaning in his own policies, for that matter they were constantly changing: sometimes he was with Frederick, sometimes against Frederick, now with Maria Theresa, then against her, now with the Protestant countries, then with the Catholic, now for war, then against war. He thought the policies of the other great powers had no more sense. If wars started it was primarily because some king or other needed martial glory very badly. In his time he himself had done a good deal of fighting. He had won a brilliant victory over the English at Fontenoy, that was enough for him. He didn't like war very much. Louis XV was rather kind-hearted, and the sight of the dead and maimed repelled him. Aside from that there were rather few joys of life in wartime, even for kings. He took his mistresses with him to the campaigns, and there was a great deal of good wine in his baggage train. But there were not many comforts, and really you had to do too much riding. It was far better to sit about at home. On his deathbed his aging ancestor Louis XIV had advised him, as a child, not to follow his example: fight less and build fewer palaces. He remembered this and thought that the old man, taught by lengthy experience, was absolutely right.

He did not like Paris, nor did he like Versailles very much. He kept moving from one palace to another. He was also fed up with etiquette. Indeed he was fed up with everything. No one was ever so bored with life as he was. Even the conversations he now carried on with ladies were most often funeral addresses: he would merrily tell his mistresses, if they were in ill-health, where and how he was going to bury them. Nonetheless, he valued his own life and, although he was not a coward, was very afraid of assassination. He told his intimates quite often that in all likelihood he was going to be murdered. He knew that the people who had idolized him before now hated him and called him Herod. There was not a sin, vice, or crime they did not ascribe to him. He thought all this highly exaggerated. Why Herod? When had he ever slaughtered infants? He was doing what everyone else was doing, not only the oriental sultans but also the French autocrats in their *maisons de plaisance*, it was just that he had far more possibilities and money. Why deny oneself pleasures? He was not very interested in "public opinion" and did not give writers any money, though he knew that some were being maintained by the Marquise de Pompadour. He regarded writers as rogues, scarcely different from courtiers. His domestic policy primarily consisted of getting more money. The king took as much as he wanted and could get out of the state treasury, but that was not always enough, and he sometimes had to speculate on bread, which he did with great success. His expenditures were vast; no one in the world had ever spent so much. He was not interested in bookkeeping, and did not know very well where the money was going. Everyone was stealing, of course, but that had always been so, nor could it be otherwise.

It was said about him that he had had more than eighteen hundred women. He thought that an exaggeration, too. Who had counted them? He was very open-handed with women, but he had furnished the Deer Park without any luxury. He had given it the character of an exclusive women's academy. Perhaps it would be less boring that way. By now he scarcely selected his women any longer. He was fed up with that, too. It was the marquise who did the selecting for him, she had grown old early, was ill, and had long since lost even traces of beauty. Later he entrusted the selection to his steward Lebel.

In a remote, scarcely populated part of Versailles an isolated country house and garden were bought, called Parc-aux-Cerfs. Louis XIII had once raised deer there. For a long time there had been none, but various buildings remained. It was not Boucher who was invited to decorate them; he had already turned senile with drink and debauchery. There were very few grown young women in the house. Girls between thirteen and sixteen predominated; there was also one nine-year-old. The house was bought openly; in the notarial documents the owner was actually designated: *le très haut, très puissant et très excellent prince Louis par la grâce de Dieu roi de France et de Navarre.* But in the house itself he was called "count." The girls

159

were supposed to have absolutely no idea who he was. Even the youngest of them knew very well, of course, and slyly told the count he greatly resembled the portrait on the coins for six livres; the count would smile benignly: he realized it was quite impossible to keep the secret. The locality was, to be sure, uninhabited; there was only a single neighboring house, and that, too, had a windowless wall facing the park. Nonetheless, the silent rumors about the house went through Versailles, Paris, and the whole world. The police knew absolutely everything about it and had even established a special detachment near by for the unobtrusive observation and protection of the king. In their reports the inhabitants of the Deer Park were usually referred to as "pupils"; a precise dossier was established for every one of them.

Lebel had limitless means and naturally preferred an amiable agreement with the parents; it was here, after all, that both the demand and the supply were equally high; the police read letters of the parents, who proffered their daughters and eulogized their beauty. The first thing every pupil did was to display herself to the king's physician. Some of them were displayed preliminarily by Lebel to the *très haute et très puissante dame, la duchesse marquise de Pompadour;* she took a great interest in the Parc-aux-Cerfs. It was only in the most exceptional circumstances that Lebel conducted them to their modest little quarters in the Versailles Palace, where the count himself looked in on them there for a moment; he usually confirmed his steward's choice. He was always extremely tender with the girl of the moment, made her presents of sweets, and sent her off to the Deer Park. Sometimes he would have a friendly business conference with the marquise. He never consulted his own daughters. The rumors had it that they, too, were his mistresses. They watched over appearances, though not very much. Among themselves they referred to the marquise as *"maman putain."*

In his early youth the king had been very handsome, but he had aged prematurely and put on weight. His face was now

160

leaden in color and almost terrifying. He was afraid of being murdered; he walked around the Deer Park in the evening, trying to slip stealthily through the gardens, and pulled his cap down over his forehead. The passers-by pretended not to recognize him. The pupils would meet the count gayly, they were on familiar terms with him. One of them, a spirited girl, once asked him whether he did not, ultimately, intend to throw over his old woman. For this quip about the Marquise de Pompadour the king affectionately pulled the girl's ear. He allowed severities in the Deer Park only on the rarest of occasions. Discipline was maintained by "Madame," a distinguished old aristocrat. She was aided by two other ladies whom the girls called *sousmadames*. One of them was a foreigner, a very beautiful, stupid, proud, and greedy woman. She bore an odd, short, and apparently Italian name, though she wasn't Italian. She had been taken into the house on the basis of a secret recommendation of the police. She had lovers everywhere. She spent all the money she had on clothes. In the house she was made fun of, but they couldn't do anything against her; she never intentionally did anything unpleasant to anybody.

None of these three women had very much to do in the way of work. They simply saw to order and to the manners of the pupils. There were no teachers, except the count himself. In the evenings he would lead away the current pupil into the schoolroom. The pupils shamelessly referred to this as "lessons in theology."

The Deer Park consisted of two sections, one for noble girls, the other for commoners; the difference between the sections was only that the pupils dined at different tables, and in the noble section the servants were in blue livery while in the other they wore gray. The pupils (or rather their parents) received ten thousand livres a year each. After a sojourn in the Deer Park husbands were sought for them, who received a substantial promotion as well as a large dowry. There was no equality here! No pupil was given less than two hundred thousand, but there were also those who received four times as much. After the French Revolution the pamphleteers with furious pleasure reckoned that according to the police documents the Deer Park had cost France nearly a billion livres. This, of course, was greatly exaggerated. The truth would have been quite sufficient. A hundred and fifty years later Clemenceau, reading memoirs about Louis XV, said, with impassioned invective, "It's simply impossible to understand how we French endured it all for so long!"

Like the marquise, the king was ill and loved to be treated. He had a great many physicians, who were conscientious and learned; they treated all debilitating illnesses with purgatives, irrigation of the stomach, and bloodletting. But there were also ignoramuses whom the learned physicians despised and called charlatans. The charlatans used elixirs of life, invocations, panaceas, and magic drugs. The more intelligent of them had some success even with followers of the Encyclopedists. It's possible that on occasion the Encyclopedists themselves turned to them. One of these magicians, a certain Count Saint-Germain, had become the mode a short while before the creation of the Deer Park.

This was his best-known name, but he had other ones, too, at different times: Marquis de Monterrat, Marquis de Belmar, Count Saltikov, Count Tsarogui, and so on. No one knew just what nationality he was; he spoke a number of languages equally well. The famous royal minister, Choiseul, maintained that the count's real name was Wolf and that he was a Jew; this was what was said by Jewish bankers, too, who claimed to have known his father, an able merchant. However, no one was particularly interested in the origin of the magician: count is as count does. He very soon found himself in the highest society. The Marquise de Pompadour was mad about him, and under her influence the king was favorably inclined toward him, too.

He looked to be about fifty, but at court it was said that he was five thousand years old: at one time he had been a Pharaoh of Egypt. The ladies reported other facts of his life, too: he

162

had lived for a long time in Jerusalem, had been intimate with Pilate's wife, and with her help had done everything he could to rescue Jesus Christ. He himself, to be sure, never said anything of the sort about himself, but he was a remarkable storyteller and in conversations gave brilliant descriptions of Socrates, Caesar, Francis I, Mary Stuart, and other celebrated people, spoke about their looks, their private lives, and the way they talked—even imitating it. With a smile he corrected Homer's mistakes: Penelope deceived poor Ulysses with anyone she could, and he ought to have thrown her out of the house after returning to Ithaca; at the time of the Trojan War Queen Helen would have been a hundred and sixty years old. The ladies enthusiastically agreed that there was at least one thing it was impossible to doubt, the count knew them all very well indeed.

Saint-Germain himself also had no doubt about one thing—people's extreme stupidity. He was versatile and knew something about various sciences, especially chemistry; he had had his fling in literature, and in music, he played various instruments, best of all the cello which had emerged not very long before, and could do an excellent tarantella, either of his own or someone else's composition. He was a physician by necessity. At that time it was the easiest way to acquire a sorcerer's reputation; it was so pleasant for rich people, especially with titles, to live that they disliked dying very much indeed. How could an elixir of life, or a panacea, which was so beneficial to one's health, be denied? Or the philosopher's stone? That would mean denying the power of science which, as everyone knew, was going ahead by gigantic leaps and bounds.

Count Saint-Germain took a luxurious flat in Versailles and installed an alchemical laboratory in it. He was visited by the most varied people. He showed them terrifying experiments with explosions of fire, and also displayed his collection of diamonds, which he had fabricated himself by his own alchemical methods. He gave precious stones to very influential ladies as souvenirs, affably remarking that they cost him nothing. The ladies showed them to their jewelers, who were simply dumfounded: they were absolutely authentic, splendid diamonds, we're ready to buy them on the spot! But it cost an enormous amount to produce the panacea; the count sold it for a great deal and warned people that its effects would not manifest themselves very quickly: only two years later, or even three. Saint-Germain did not live very long in any one country. He said that he had traveled through the whole world, and had been to India, China, and America. He was intending to leave for England, Holland, Prussia, or Muscovy very soon. But he would only travel abroad if he had some important secret mission from the king; the count was fond of politics, especially secret politics.

The sorcerer's gifts were able to gain him access to politics, too. It was only necessary to demonstrate them before the king's own eyes. Probably Louis XV knew what sort of man the count was. The king both believed in pedigree and didn't particularly: he thought the aristocracy a more reliable prop for his throne than the people; under him, in contrast to Louis XIV, access to military rank was open only to those who had been noble for more than three centuries. But the king's class attitudes ended there. Madame Pompadour, who became the premier personage in the state, was the daughter of a petty salesman—her family name, Poisson, which provoked endless quips at Versailles, was the cross of her life. With all his illiteracy the king was far from stupid. In women, for their beauty, and in men, for their intellect, talents, and especially their entertaining conversation, he forgave even origins which were thoroughly unacceptable.

Success was bestowed most often for intellect, but it might come to anyone from anywhere: from the *coulisses* of a theater, from a horse doctor's reception room, from a juggler's tent. It might also come from the Deer Park. Saint-Germain began frequenting it. Men were seldom allowed in, but an exception was made for physicians. Madame liked the sorcerer; he was always very well dressed, polite, and affable. The girls liked

him, too, he was tender with them, but did not find minors
attractive: that way you'd descend to the level of the debauched
canaille, he said to himself, thinking of the king, although he
was rather fond of him: Haven't we all got our failings?

He received reports about the new pupils from the police
and from Lebel. With the police he was generally on the very
best of terms always and everywhere. He received the royal
steward at home, when there were no other guests, and not
only gave him lavish tips, but also treated him informally to
expensive wines. In general he said that social prejudices had
outlived their time—in ancient Rome they had been simply
unbearable! He himself had nothing against people from a
plebeian milieu, he had nothing even against actors, and would
not refuse to sit down to dinner publicly, in full view of everyone, with Molière, who belonged to just this caste, *la sorte de
gens la plus méprisable du monde*. Poets he simply invited
home, and lavished food and gifts on them. One of them wrote
some verses in his honor:

> "*Ainsi que Prométhée, il déroba le feu*
> *Par qui le Monde existe et par qui tout respire;*
> *La nature à sa voix obéit et se meut*
> *S'il n'est pas Dieu lui-même, un Dieu puissant l'inspire.*"

The count gave him a large crystal bottle full of panacea, a
piece of gold-embroidered velvet bought by him once in Vera
Cruz at a sale of the ancient collection of the Aztec Monte-
zuma's things, also a portrait of the Muse Clio in a frame en-
crusted with pearls, very small, to be sure, but given him in
India by the Grand Mogul. Eminent police officials were also
his guests. These did not accept the panacea, but gladly accepted packets of gold coins as gifts, after counting them over.
From them and from Lebel he was very nearly the first in
Versailles society to learn in full detail that the new pupil,
Hélène de Palois, had been removed by force from her parents'
home to the Deer Park the day before, and that—an unheard-of

165

event—she had absolutely refused to give herself to the king. The girl was a great beauty and no longer so very young—she was sixteen years old.

Girls were taken to the house by force very rarely. Nevertheless, on occasion—what could one do?—it was necessary to resort to force, too. Lebel had a chat with the father of Mademoiselle de Palois. Unfortunately the girl was in love with an impoverished young nobleman, Rodes, who was in love with her, too, and it had been decided by them that in time they would marry. In case the father refused his consent Rodes had suggested taking her away secretly to the Compiègne where he owned a scrap of land. And it was just their misfortune that Hélène was seen in the street by the king, who was riding in his carriage! She curtsied. Louis XV doffed his cap and smiled at her, scrutinizing her attentively. Then he said something to the man standing behind him and the latter leaped from the coachman's seat. Hélène was extremely frightened and ran home. Lebel followed her.

The following morning the count, as usual, arose early and set to work at once in his laboratory. He had two tables there: one for alchemy, which he showed to visitors, the other very simple, where he worked preparing his pigments. His whole life, until his very last days, he dreamed of preparing some sort of dye which ought to bring him in far more than the panacea and the philosopher's stone.

He drank half a bottle of champagne. Before important enterprises he drank nothing; before the less important ones he drank a little. The enterprise for that day, which had already been carefully elaborated by him, was not a great one, but he was hoping to earn something by it, although it was not certain. He changed his clothes, poured out into a vial exactly twenty drops of a bluish liquid, corked it, and put it in his pocket. He ordered his horses to be brought up. He had excellent horses, Arabs, Mecklenburgs, and Andalusians. His saddle, caparison, and harness were also luxurious. The passers-by recognized him and gazed at him with curiosity, fear, and respect: "The

166

sorcerer! Count Saint-Germain! That's the one!" After going through the city to the less inhabited parts at a walk he broke into a gallop. He stopped at the back wicket gate of the Deer Park, dismounted, led the horses into the park, and tied them there to a tree. He was seen from the windows immediately, and as usual they were all delighted. He went into Madame's study, exchanging affectionate greetings with the girls on the way. They were all fond of this physician who never gave them nasty medicines when they were ill and as a treatment often prescribed sweets. That day everyone in the house was excited about the unusual event. The boldest of the pupils tried to interrogate him but he only waved a jocularly threatening finger at them.

". . . She hasn't slept the whole night and has been crying all day long. She won't eat or drink. What a goose! She's in love with some poor fellow," said Madame, in distressed puzzlement.

The old bitch, thought the count, and sighed portentously. "Yes, it's a very strange thing to happen."

"I simply don't know what to do with her! Shouldn't she be whipped? What d'you think?"

"Under no circumstances!" said the count. "Heaven forbid!"

"I was brought up at Saint-Cyr, founded by Madame de Maintenon, and there older and nobler girls than this little hussy were punished for misbehavior with birch rods. It helped wonderfully."

"That may be, but our present beloved monarch has forbidden it. And she's not to be put in a dungeon either. What is essential here is treatment, and especially suggestion. Where is she?"

"I've given her the best room."

"Allow me to go to her. I wish to speak with her alone."

Madame allowed him to do so, he was a physician, though not an official one, and she knew him to be correct. She led him along the corridor. He entered without knocking and locked the door behind him: he was afraid of eavesdropping, either by Madame herself or by the Cerberus, which was what they

167

called the steward, a giant with such a thick bull neck that an executioner would have found it difficult to strike his head off with one blow.

Hélène de Palois was sitting in a chair with drooping head. When he came in she looked at him horrified, with hunted eyes, leaped up, and then sat down again. Lovely! he thought, what a woman she's going to be in a year or two! Some covered dishes, bottles, and glasses were standing on a little table. She hadn't touched a thing! The count greeted the young girl very gently, moved a chair up for himself, and sat down opposite her, looking at her attentively.

"Don't be upset," he said in a soft, insinuating voice. "I'm not going to do you any harm. I'm your friend and want to help you. I can heal all illnesses. I am Count Saint-Germain."

She looked at him in timid astonishment. She had heard about him and also knew of him as a sorcerer. But his words, the tender intonation of his voice, and the kind and sympathetic expression of his face soothed her a little.

"I'm not ill," she whispered.

"I think so, too," said the count, and then said in a loud voice: "I can see you're not well at all. Allow me to feel your pulse."

He fell silent a moment, without touching her hand, then said still more loudly: "Aha! A hundred and ten. You are ill, just as I thought. I shall examine you at once."

He then spoke to her in a whisper, while asking her occasionally in a resounding voice questions about her heart, lungs, and stomach. She understood nothing. Suddenly he got up, walked over to the door swiftly, and opened it. There was no one behind it. He called the servants and ordered water to be brought. He took a decanter and a glass from one of the lackeys in blue livery, shut the door again, and sat down at the little table. Now he was at ease: no one was eavesdropping. He poured some wine into the goblet and drank it with satisfaction. I didn't believe they gave them such good wine, he thought.

168

"Please come here, Hélène," he said. She came over to the table and obediently sat down. "Would you like some wine? If you don't, there's no need to; for the time being perhaps it's better not to drink anything. . . . Calm yourself, the count is not going to do anything to you."

She quivered, and her face twisted. "I know what sort of a count he is!"

"I know, too. . . . Is your fiancé a kind man? Rodes? I see by your face he is."

"D'you know him? Who told you?"

"I know everything; I'm a sorcerer. If you obey me in everything they'll release you from here no later than tomorrow. And you'll get married to him."

"Are you telling me the truth? Tell me, for God's sake . . ."

"But if you don't obey me you will be destroyed!" said Saint-Germain in a low voice but very impressively, leaning toward her. "For the time being they're dealing with you nicely." He lifted a cover from one of the dishes. "You see, chicken. That's not going to last long; they're going to put you into a closet and starve you to death."

"Let them starve me!"

"They'll beat you."

"Let them beat me!"

He burst out laughing. "Well, you are a brave girl! Splendid . . . you're very sweet, but silly," he said paternally. "They're going to do with you whatever they please. You're not the first one. What can you do against them? They have the power. The only answer to force is craftiness. I'll teach you everything. . . . Have you ever been in the theaters?"

"In the theaters?"

"Yes, in the theaters. I'm speaking plainly. Don't ask me any questions, and answer sensibly."

"No, never, my father never let me, he said it was immoral."

"That's true. I'm glad your father is such an honest man. . . . It's a pity that young as you are you didn't see Adrienne Lecouvreur. She was a famous actress. How she portrayed hysteria!

169

And how she could die! No other actress ever died in such a lifelike way, so naturally as she did. Then she was poisoned."

"Poisoned!"

"I told you not to interrupt. Yes, she was poisoned. And now I'm going to poison you.... Don't look at me with horror. I'll poison you in such a way that a few hours later you'll be completely well, I give you my word of honor. You've probably never had an attack of hysteria? It's not difficult. You know how to weep, of course. All young girls know how to weep. Just think of your fiancé and it will come out splendidly." Saint-Germain poured another goblet of wine, then took a vial out of his pocket.

"What's that? What are you going to do?!"

"Listen carefully. This is a drug I've brought back from Mexico. That's a country in America. I've brought back a great many drugs from there. My 'curative salutary Mexican tea' is known everywhere in the world. It's saved thousands of people's lives. But that's something quite different. This drug will give you a fever. In two hours take everything in this little flask. Leave only two or three drops. Don't drink any water after it, just this wine. Drink two whole glasses of it. Then begin weeping and groaning as loud as possible. You can even fall to the floor and thrash about in convulsions. People will come running in. Tell them you've 'committed suicide.' For heaven's sake don't say it was I who brought you the poison, say you brought it from home, and show them the bottle. They'll send for the doctor. Say I'm the only one you have any confidence in. They'll send for me, too. Their doctor may come galloping here before I do. He'll see the drops, say they're a dreadful poison, and that he must stay near you constantly. They'll probably insist that your stomach be washed out. Try to fend them off, it's too unpoetic. But if that's impossible, well, what can be done? Then I'll come and cure you. The count himself may come...."

"I don't want to see him!"

"Don't dare speak that way about the good 'count.'" He

170

drank another glass of wine at one gulp. "The count is very kindhearted. In France they're continually breaking people on the wheel for stealing, but he is never present, and if he were he would probably lighten their sentences. In France hundreds of thousands of peasants die of hunger every year, although that scoundrel Voltaire assures the Marquise Poisson that the people are thriving. Voltaire wants to become a marquis himself. And for that matter why not? If the count were to see peasants starving he would give them some of the bread he's collected to speculate with. Not, of course, a great deal of it. . . . You see how frankly I'm speaking to you. I know you won't report me. But even if you did report me no one would believe you, and it's dangerous to get into a quarrel with me!" he said very impressively once again. "So there you are, the count will come, see you groaning and thrashing about in convulsions, and immediately order you to be released: he can't bear people who are ill. Aside from which he'll be overwhelmed by compassion for your sufferings, he'll think of all the torments of hell. The count doesn't have much faith in God, but he's terribly afraid. Suppose there is a hell, after all? You'll see, he'll give you some money."

"I don't want his money!"

"Your opinion has not been asked!" said Saint-Germain, angry for the first time. "You can give part of it away to charity. I'll even take that on myself, I'll take a tenth of what the count gives you and distribute it to the poor. The rest will go to you as a dowry from the count. After all, your fiancé is poor. It's impossible to be happy without money, at least it's a hundred times harder than with money. . . . I can see by your little face that you understand. Now repeat everything I've told you."

She repeated it. He nodded approvingly. Then he rinsed out his goblet with water, poured the water into her glass, and wiped the goblet off with a napkin.

"What are you doing?"

"Don't tell anyone I was drinking wine, it was you who were drinking. Well, then, everything's all right. So a very quick

171

good-by, my dear, for a very short time. Thrash about in your hysteria as much as possible and cry out as plaintively as you can," he said, and got up. He wanted to kiss her but just because he felt like it he didn't.

"Very bad indeed! She's in absolute despair!" he said to Madame in her study. "I've calmed her down a little and persuaded her to drink some wine. And now please leave her in peace, she may fall asleep. Tomorrow I'll come again, but if there's any sudden need today send for me. This evening I'll be at the palace ball. There are going to be figured dances. His Majesty is opening the ball with one of the princesses and I'm dancing in the eighth couple," he explained carelessly. Madame was stupefied with deference. "But of course I'll leave the ball in case of an emergency and come at once. It's a pity about the poor girl. She's a little silly; she doesn't understand her good luck."

Forgetting about his incognito the king came whirling down in his carriage to the Deer Park. Count Saint-Germain followed in a ball costume with huge diamonds on his coat and slippers. Louis XV was pale and distraught. Madame wept, and said she wasn't to blame for anything. Her beautiful assistant sighed and kept trying to capture the king's attention.

Hélène was thrashing about convulsively on the divan in her room. The doctor, who had only just arrived, was looking at Louis with bafflement and at the count with hatred. He muttered that this was a poison that was stronger than arsenic, that there was not much hope for her getting better, and that her stomach had to be irrigated at once.

Saint-Germain examined the sick girl. Adrienne or not, he thought, she's a crafty little wench. It's astonishing how they all love play-acting. "Yes, that's so," he agreed aloud. "It's a poison that's more dangerous than arsenic."

"Save her!" cried the king. "I cannot have her die!"

Saint-Germain pondered. "I'll try," he said, after a moment of reflection. "Have a crystal beaker brought in to me," he said,

172

turning to Madame. Perplexed, she asked whether crystal was absolutely vital.

"Absolutely, if I say so," he repeated sternly. Madame hurried out after a beaker. "Now I'll lay down a magic circle."

Saint-Germain leaned over and began making strange gestures above Hélène with both arms. They all gazed at him in astonishment. Now and then he would mutter some incomprehensible words. When the beaker was brought in he poured several drops of a green liquid from a new vial into it. "I'm never separated from this," he explained to the king in a whisper.

"Open your mouth," said Saint-Germain peremptorily to the sick girl, and poured the liquid into it, then, handing the beaker back to Madame, he raised both arms to the ceiling and again started muttering something or other.

"Did it work? Will she get well?"

"It has worked, Your Majesty," Saint-Germain answered, breathing heavily. His face looked distorted. "In four minutes she will be completely conscious."

The king glanced from him to the sick girl. The doctor was seething with fury, mingled with fear and envy. "Then there's no more danger?" asked the king, wiping his forehead with a handkerchief.

"Not the slightest, I swear it on my head. But for a month or two she'll have some vomiting and diarrhea. So by no later than tomorrow she'll have to be taken somewhere to the woods to convalesce. Compiègne would be best of all."

"Let her be taken away tomorrow morning!"

"Now undress her and put her to bed. Give her something to eat: bouillon, chicken, compote, and a little good wine. I'll see her once more in ten minutes."

"And what about irrigating her stomach? An irrigation is essential," said the doctor plaintively.

"Not just now. You'll be able to go to Compiègne, and then you'll see," replied the count, who realized that everyone had to live. The doctor subsided. The men left the room. The king

173

went to the schoolroom and sank heavily into an easy chair. Saint-Germain came in after him and glanced curiously around the room, which he had never been in before. There was not much furniture in it: two easy chairs and a bed with a low headboard, surrounded on three sides by tall upright mirrors.

A quarter of an hour later Saint-Germain, very gay and lively, returned to Hélène's room. She was lying in bed, pale and exhausted. He patted her cheek caressingly.

"The count has left already. You'll never see him again. You're going to be taken to Compiègne. I'll arrange things so that your fiancé visits you there. And tomorrow I'll come back with an official of the Treasury. The count has bestowed on you two hundred thousand livres! . . . Be quiet, little fool—though you're not a fool but a very clever girl. . . . I tried to get three hundred thousand out of the count, but he gave only two hundred. He said that was quite enough, too, for the gratification you gave him. I think he added, 'And may she go to the devil with her diarrhea!' I hope you're not offended?"

"I'm so happy! Thank you," she whispered. "Will I really have that?"

"Have what, my dear?"

"Diarrhea," Hélène barely whispered.

"You'll have nothing at all. . . . When the official leaves you'll give me twenty thousand for the poor. Don't give a sou of the rest to your papa. I'm even going to order that he not be allowed to see you. Don't give anything to your fiancé either for the time being, there are all kinds of fiancés. . . . Don't be angry. I was joking. Well, good-by, my child, I wish you luck. In two years I'll come to visit you. You'll introduce me to your husband."

"Come before that, I beg of you!"

He burst out laughing. "Perhaps I won't come in two years either. I'll probably be in Muscovy."

"In Muscovy? With the Turks? Why must you go to Muscovy? They may impale you on a stake there!"

"But perhaps they won't."

174

"But what will you do there?"

"Heal people. Panaceas. . . ."

". . . So you have two panaceas, is that it, Nikolai Arkadi-evich? You not only want to lengthen people's lives, but to teach them good? Very well, very well, in the West you'll be able to preach your moral panacea, too. You have to acquaint the world with it. But without your biological discovery no one will even listen to you. If Dostoevski's artistic genius wasn't there the West would hardly listen to some Myshkin, or Al-yosha Karamazov. What do *they* want? Who are they? One is an idiot, the other a boy. It's a completely different matter when the one speaking is a great scientist who has blazed new trails! Listen, I'll arrange articles in the newspapers for you, radio broadcasts, television, whatever you like, not for you, but for your idea.

"Let's leave, Nikolai Arkadievich! For you I've made use of Stalin's panacea. I won't go into details, but I gave him an idea for a new provocation. They've given us an airplane, it's waiting for us! Of course at the border they intend to kill us. You under-stand what a charming, what a divine provocation this is: the capitalists have been trying to get one of their agents out, that is, yourself, but this was prevented by the vigilance of the workers' and peasants' state! It was suggested that I drop by parachute, and various good things were promised. They often live up to the conditions they agree on with provocateurs, but I wasn't tempted. Of course I agreed to everything with com-plete readiness, but they have their plan and I have mine.

"I don't promise you a comfortable flight. If we get killed we'll get killed, you say yourself you have nothing to lose. It's all fifty-fifty, everything in the world today is fifty-fifty, even the existence of the earth. . . .

"Listen, if you die here, what will happen to both your panaceas? The papers in the green folder will be thrown into the wastebasket. Let's suppose you mark them as being very important, then the green folder will get to the Lubyanka. At

175

best the papers will be transmitted for review to one of the scientists, one of *his* pets, a trustworthy rascal. Either he'll claim that your discovery has no value at all, or else he'll pass it off as his own. He's more likely to do both: at first he'll say that the papers are nonsense, but after a little while he'll report *his* discovery. Perhaps the government will actually know the truth, too, but it will support the version of the favorite; it's much better for the author of a great discovery to be a Communist than a White Guard bandit who's been a jailbird. He'll say that he made his discovery under the guidance of Joseph Vissarionovich. And for the rest of eternity he will remain the discoverer....

"You see, now even your face has twisted.... Something else is possible, too: they won't show your papers to anyone, they'll simply draw no one's attention to them. After all, what sort of discovery could be made by a wretched laboratory technician, a failure, who was kept on at his job out of kindness! In the Lubyanka nothing is ever destroyed, anything can come in handy, so the papers will go on lying there.... Let's suppose the Bolsheviks fall in ten or twenty years. Before their destruction they'll probably burn everything, to the rapture of the countless GPU stool pigeons.

"And even if they don't, it'll take centuries to disentangle everything. Do you know that in France to this day only a part of the archives remaining from the Great Revolution has been put in order? Aside from which the people who disentangle the archives won't have any grasp of biology. Is it possible to imagine them stumbling across just your dossier out of the millions lying around there? Is it possible to imagine them taking an interest in the work of some laboratory technician no one knows, who died in prison of a cancer of the prostate? That they'll read and appreciate a half-decayed scientific memorandum?

"No, don't deceive yourself: your name will remain completely unknown. Any rewards, honors, and glory will be given to the thief. It's he who will become famous, and it's he, of

176

course, who will be spared on the day of retribution, if there ever is such a day. On that day he'll become a turncoat, like everyone else, and become 'our Russian pride'....

"Don't surrender the papers to Macro! Hand them to me, and you'll be a benefactor of mankind! ... I swear on my honor that we'll behave differently! Of course, you're entitled not to believe in the honor of a secret agent, but consider, just *why* should we deceive you? Even if there were a scientist among us who was such a scoundrel, wouldn't we know where the discovery came from? We'll give the papers to some competent commission to review; it will be convinced that the author is at liberty and is somewhere in a Western country; we won't name you by name until we know for certain that you're no longer alive.

"And then we will name you by name! We'll proclaim it throughout the world! That will also correspond to our own interests, it will be our revenge for Fuchs, for Pontecorvo, for so many others. It was we who obtained a discovery by a great Russian scientist! The Communists couldn't make use of it. The Americans were needed there, too.... After the war you'll go back.... Yes, there's going to be a war! Moscow will find an occasion. An occasion can always be found. You have no choice, Citizen Maikov: you are a doomed man, yours is the fate of three or four of the great men who may now be living in your unhappy, Godforsaken country! ...

"And if you don't want to fly away with me then kill yourself immediately! They're coming for you this very night. Away with you to a better world! Or else let's flee; the airplane is waiting in the street."

"The airplane is waiting in the street? ..."

"Yes, yes, without an airdrome. Listen to me, you'll be able to see Capri! The sun is shining on the green water of the sea. D'you remember that water? You'll see Venice, we'll spend the night in St. Mark's Square. You'll see Natasha—Natasha de Palois! ... Let's flee...."

"That's the Red Square underneath us! D'you hear the death

177

march? They're burying *him!* That's what the bells in the Kremlin tower are tolling for.... Sirens are screaming in all the factories, workshops, steamers, and locomotives. They're playing a dirge. The triumphant banners are dipping over the dust of the greatest warrior of all times and all nations. Marshals are carrying orders and medals on scarlet velvet cushions.... And how monstrously they're lying: the marshals and the locomotives! Who's that making a speech? That's the Dauphin, Beria, Berius-Tiberius ... he's in a jacket.... Dauphin! Dauphin! In this country you can't rule in civilian dress! Dauphin, Dauphin, there are other dauphins at your side, kill them off quickly, or they'll kill you! ... Farewell, Moscow! ... The chase has started.... Have no fear, Citizen Maikov, there's no better pilot in Europe than myself, they won't kill us.... They're playing a tarantella! My whole life, yes, one long tarantella...."

"... The airplane came down on Capri. And how well it passed down the stone staircases. Nothing happened.... How long was I flying? Why did the war begin? Because of me? So soon? No, it's too insignificant an occasion.... But where's the green folder? We must have a conference with the colonel at once.... It's too late, if the war's begun.... But pay he must!"

Schell, opening his eyes wide, trembled beneath the blanket. The delirium was already ending. So I saw the funeral ... it couldn't *all* have been delirium! It can't be ... but they're playing a tarantella, after all!

It was only after a moment or two that he came to his senses. They're playing it over at the neighbors'.... Could they have been dancing over there till morning? Yes, that's it, it was all nonsense! I didn't get anyone out.... And I'm not going, not for anything am I going to go to that terrible country.

178

13

TWO alternatives had been indicated to Edda. According to the first she was skillfully to abstract the secret documents from Jim, have them photographed (she had been told where), Jim was to be left pure, and everything would be in perfect order. The difficulty was in *how* to abstract them. For a long time Edda racked her brains but could think of nothing. Mustn't he take them directly to the furnace from his office? Doubtless Schell would be able to think of a plan. Should I ask the Soviet colonel? But he's such a boor, he spoke to me so dryly that time! And it would mean ruining my prestige: "You got acquainted with him and that's all you did do! You couldn't think up anything else!" She had already sent off to the colonel by indicated methods her first triumphant report. She painstakingly put it into code, for which a bulky lexicon had been given her: it was necessary to designate every word by the page and by the order of the word on the page. The encoding took her about two hours; she worked on it with a sort of horrified delight, after bolting the door to her room.

The second variant was far more dramatic: Jim was supposed to be *seduced*. She turned over the details in her mind. Wine, a great deal of wine. And then—an orgy? On the orgy theme she had already conceived a poem which spoke of passionate kisses and mad embraces—she crossed it out: passionate embraces and mad kisses. Then tell Jim *everything*: "I am a spy! I was assigned to track you down and through you find out all of Rocquencourt's secrets! But I never became a spy for the sake of money, but by conviction: the Communists are right, they're going to save the world from the horrors of another war, they must be helped! But now I've had a stroke of bad luck—I've suddenly fallen in love with you. Now you make all the decisions. If you wish to, slay me! If you wish to tell your superiors, let them punish me! But if you love me, break with your past, share my ideas, and we'll toil together...."

This variant moved Edda to tears. But it, too, had serious shortcomings. Jim said that he was madly in love with her, which, for that matter, was quite obvious. Nevertheless, she was not sure of how he would behave. Suppose he really does kill me then and there, though it's hardly likely. And how would he kill me? There's a bell over the bed. If he seizes me by the throat, I'll ring. I'll leave the door open. No, he'll get up from the bed—and leave. Then I'll fly back to Germany immediately, I have a visa and the money. If he's such a cad that he'll go off to report me at night—no, at night it's impossible, there's no one around, he'll wait until morning—in any case, I'll be able to escape in time. Then the colonel won't give me any more money, but I won't return what I have left. And if Jim agrees—he can't help but agree, he's so in love with me!—then everything will be wonderful. We'll get the documents, get the money, and go off to Italy. There, to be sure, there was another complication. She would be very glad to go off to Italy with Jim, but she didn't want to be separated from Schell for

180

too long a time. If I don't watch him he may simply evaporate. . . .

But no matter what happened there was no doubt that what was going on was the *play of life*—the same thing she liked better than anything else in literature and the movies. She decided to reflect a bit more. She marked a date for the orgy, in case the second variant turned up: March 13, which was a Friday—the coincidence of a fateful number with a fateful day—she was flinging a challenge at destiny. That's what I'll say to him, too—*"J'ai lancé un défi à la destinée."* In English it doesn't sound so good. . . . She spent some time visualizing it all, with enjoyment: first he sobbed, then he sank to his knees in front of her and swore to renounce his past, his people, his parents, his brothers—"Now all I have is you! and only you!" Then they drank champagne again and she read him her poetry. Then they set off for Venice and in the evening, under the moon, they embraced, floating in a gondola. . . . *"Gentille gondolière—dit le pêcheur épris—je cède à ta prière—mais quel en sera le prix?"*

It was this second variant that materialized, with a negligible deviation from the projected program. Edda didn't buy any champagne, it was too *gay* a wine, not suitable to such an occasion, and where could she get it chilled at night? She got a bottle of cognac instead. That also made it cheaper—the colonel hadn't given her much money. Meanwhile, there were a great many expenses. For the orgy she bought a nightgown of black crepe de chine with sleeves, very long and cut like a dress, *très travaillée,* from Lebigot; she had been dreaming of something like it for a long time, also, it was more suitable than pajamas; she paid ten thousand francs for it. Edda had thought spies could lay out money without thinking twice; it turned out not to be so.

Everything turned out brilliantly well. Jim took her to Rocquencourt and showed her the furnace, producing a thick packet which was burned before their eyes. She saw that he was in charge of it. Their fifth night together Edda—not, to be sure, very à propos—started speaking rapturously of the Russian music and ballet. Jim agreed with her in all sincerity: he loved Russian music and ballet. Then she said that contemporary Russia was being maligned. He did not dispute this, either; there was a good deal of maligning going on. She abused the United States government; he supported her. Ten minutes later Edda declared to him that she was serving the Soviet regime, which was bearing peace and happiness to all nations. Jim did not seize her by the throat. Another five minutes and he was on his knees in front of her crying that her people would be his people, that for him there was now neither father nor mother nor brothers (which, for that matter, he had really not had). Jim recalled all the Russian films he had ever seen. He knew he wasn't acting very well, and his astonishment kept growing. How can such a simpleton be a spy? Though Uncle had said that in his department there were even more fools than psychopaths.

"...I'll bring you one very important piece of information," he said, panting, "but it'll have to be thrown into the furnace the same day. Your people had better have it photographed very quickly."

"Not 'your' people, but ours! You're one of us now! We will toil together!"

"For you I'm betraying my country! Now I have no one but you! We'll run away together!"

Jim got a letter from his uncle. The colonel congratulated him on his success and told him there would be an important package for the goose and that it had to be handed over without fail on March 18. "I see you have pangs of conscience. But remember that you're not doing this for yourself but for your country," wrote the colonel, squeezing out the pompous words with difficulty. "Aside from which this fool is not in any danger. Let her leave France for wherever she likes. Judging by what you tell me about her she's of no further use to us. Try to get rid of her as quickly as possible. If necessary, you

182

can also leave with her for a short time. You'll be given a furlough and money. You'll be doing something extremely useful. To tell you the truth I should prefer that you broke up with her as quickly as possible, but if it's impossible *otherwise* (underlined twice) go to Italy with her and leave her there. Give her as much as you think necessary—though not *very* much: government money must be taken care of even more than one's own. At your leisure you can think over whether you want to work in our section in the future, too. I'll soon be in Italy also, by the way. We might meet in Venice."

The package really was very important. Locking himself in his office and seeing almost no one, the colonel worked for a whole day and part of the night, experiencing a feeling very close to what is called inspiration. In his profession there was a preponderance of somber base prose that often poisoned his life, but at times he also found an authentic poetry in his work, so extraordinary sometimes were the schemes, complications, combinations, and psychological play. The misinformation referred to atom bombs, to their number, strength, and distribution. Everything was put together extremely skillfully, especially the letter from the Pentagon to the Saceur. It was the *magnum opus* of the colonel's life.

14

THE colonel was given the address of the best hotel in Venice. The money was to be deposited at Schell's request in a Swiss bank where he had had an account for years. There were now nine hundred and five francs still in the account; for some reason it had come out as an uneven figure.

In Naples the evening before, just before they left, while Natasha was taking a bath, he took out a notebook and reckoned up everything he had. He wrote down the figures in a little book: in spite of his prodigality he used to write down the expenditures by the day; he tried to do this when Natasha wasn't present. But just then she came out of the bathroom in a peignoir.

"I forgot to take the soap," she said shyly, and when she saw him writing something down, she guessed at once. "Bills? I used to write everything down in Berlin, too. Tell me, aren't we spending too much? Now you have far more expenses than you had before, without me. I'm costing you a lot, aren't I? I still haven't got my own money."

He never discussed money matters with her; but each time after their marriage, whenever money came up, her face grew frightened. It was at these moments especially that he wanted to become rich. He smiled, set her down on his knees, and kissed her tenderly.

"Your hair isn't shining, that's how I like it. . . . You're ruining me, naturally. I've squandered thirty-six million gold francs on you, like Louis XV with the Marquise de Pompadour. Don't be upset, the bills don't mean a thing."

"There you are, you're always joking, and it upsets me. Nowadays every woman works, and I should earn something, too."

"And I would be upset if you earned anything. That's a man's business. I'm very old-fashioned."

"Prehistoric! But I adore you! . . . And do you love me? Really and truly? Like whom? Like Lavretsky and Liza? Like Romeo and Juliet? Like Paolo and Francesca? I know perfectly well that I'm as far from them as from a star in the skies! . . ."

"Like Schell and Natasha."

"Like Schell and Natasha! Yes, that's best of all! D'you know you look a little like an elephant?"

"I've been told I resemble a Chinese hangman."

"Heavens! Such nonsense! What people won't say! A Hinese changman. You see what stupid jokes I can make, too! . . . And you said I was intelligent, didn't you? I'm terribly stupid," she said, smothering him in kisses.

He often read in the bath; Natasha also started taking a book along, some cheap, unbound, shabby one, which when dozing off she would suddenly let fall into the water. But she didn't read, she kept on thinking. I adore him, of course! Perhaps now even more than before. . . . No, not more, only now in a different way. I suppose it's that way always? And he doesn't hide anything from me, he just doesn't speak, that's

185

not the same thing. But I would so much like to enter into his life, enter into it completely, know everything, share everything!

Natasha could not get used to doing nothing for her husband. Everything remained as it had been. They lived in hotels and ate at restaurants; she had no worries about managing, since there was nothing to manage. Nor could she help Schell in his business; she knew nothing about it; perhaps he had no business. If only he would dictate letters to me. He has a good handwriting, but strange: firm and at the same time changeable, as though different people were writing.... And after all how can a woman not know exactly what her husband's business is? It's simply unheard of! Of course he did tell me it was all "episodic middle-man deals," but he said it evasively, even dryly. And what can "episodic middle-man deals" be? Should I ask him? Yes, I will, but a little later.

Schell even unpacked by himself. She told him she was not bad at mending laundry, but he replied that he threw out everything that was the least bit torn; and in fact in front of her he gave a hotel servant several pairs of socks and a silk shirt the scarcely frayed collar of which it would have been very easy to mend. Such nonsense, of course! Why he loves me I simply cannot make out! He says I'm intelligent (she often tried to think up jokes for him, when her eyes would glint mischievously). I'm not intelligent at all. What would I do without him? Don't I know that no one ever fell in love with me before? I never had any "success" with men. It was a word she disliked. Before, not quite recently, the idea that men didn't like her much was one of the most painful in her life. Now she thought about it almost gayly. Yes, I'll work. And I won't buy any dresses for myself until I've put something aside from my wages. And what do I need any Diors for anyhow? Or whatever they're called there....

She thought wealth was a sin, and was convinced that living in poverty was *necessary*. But there were things now which she appreciated: first of all, her own bath with hot water all day

186

long—she had never had anything like it in her life. It would be good if *that* were left. And also traveling sometimes, to see Venice. It would be good if we were able to buy books. But I don't need anything else. What a pity he needs so much.... As long as he doesn't fall out of love with me!

Before also Natasha had always prayed, even in Soviet Russia, even in the German factory. Now she prayed more, and more fervently; she thanked God every single day for the unprecedented, unheard-of happiness she had been given. She concealed this from Schell, although it occurred to her that it would please him.

It was easy to say that expenses don't mean a thing. It was easy to tell oneself that, after that night of delirium, money in general oughtn't to mean anything. But, after all, it was simply delirium, senseless delirium, I didn't see any Maikov, he didn't tell me anything, the whole thing was nonsense, he thought. In his thoughts, however, he stubbornly kept returning to the same thing. And there's nothing new in this idea of a return to good from evil. I had thought of it myself even before that.... That is, that was just the reason I dreamed of Maikov, with his ideas, which were *my own* ideas, and not even the most interesting of my ideas at that. There's probably not a good-for-nothing or a criminal who, even though infrequently, even though only once in a lifetime, hasn't dreamed about a so-called honest life.... The words "so-called" he still put now as before into ironic quotation marks, but he knew that now the irony was getting to be more and more difficult. Yes, a banal story, Natasha's influence, a man's spiritual rebirth—it's all been heard before, Schell said to himself with vexation. But aside from that, is my story so banal? I'll have *les hauts et les bas*, and without the *bas* I couldn't extricate myself now, simply couldn't. All honest philosophy, whatever value it has, can be of no use whatever if I—now together with Natasha—have no money left to pay a hotel bill....

Actually, in spite of his own new feelings, he kept wondering in growing alarm: what if the colonel hasn't sent the money? He may have decided to pay it out only on the spot in Berlin. From his point of view he would be right; he doesn't know me personally, though of course he's heard that I'm accurate about money. If he hasn't sent the advance, the whole question is finished, I won't work with him. . . . That's also easy to say. But then what should I do? In accordance with a long-standing rule (but which allowed for exceptions) he never borrowed money from acquaintances. But he had met no one in Venice he knew. For that matter, people wouldn't have been overgenerous in other places, either, he thought.

However, even if he hadn't been expecting an advance from the colonel, Schell would have stayed in the best hotel anyhow. In his opinion there were two ways of life for people who weren't rich. One, which he couldn't stand and called petty bourgeois, consisted of living "modestly," or, even more —the ultimate in vulgarity—laying something away for a rainy day. The second, which he had adopted long since, was based on the conviction that for a real man money always, sooner or later, turns up, and for someone like that it was not only improper to save it but you had to fling it away, showing in every way that you had just as much as you wanted. A great deal depended here, to be sure, on just that "sooner or later": if the money appeared very tardily the second way might lead to a scandal or even, with bad luck, to jail. However, in his complicated, tangled, and adventurous life this had never happened; at the last moment money had always turned up.

Now the limit of "sooner or later" was precise: two weeks. Schell's showy looks, his expensive suits, the magnificent valises with labels of famous hotels and steamships ("First Class": the labels with "Cabin Class" and "Tourist Class"—there had been all kinds—had been scraped off) made an impression on hall porters and managers. After the bill for the first week you could say negligently, "I'm leaving next Friday, I'll settle everything at the same time." But after the second bill things became difficult.

188

Now, too, he told himself uncertainly that he was known in this hotel: he really had stayed there several times during the periods when he had had ample money. In anticipation he had even then paid somewhat carelessly, and when he settled his bills left enormous tips; this was how he established his credit. But it was difficult to rely on that; managers and hall porters changed, and even the old ones, in spite of their remarkable professional memory—like detectives—did not always recall his habits; there were also skeptics among them on whom the valises and labels had no effect, after two weeks they mournfully and respectfully requested his account be paid.

But that was not the main thing. He had definitely made up his mind not to go to Moscow. Consequently the colonel's advance had to be returned as quickly as possible. Not returning an advance, while rejecting the assignment, would have been much worse than an unpaid hotel bill: it would mean the inglorious conclusion of his career as an agent. It would also mean crossing that not very clear but unmistakable line that separates the adventurer from the cheat. Then you might as well pass out rubber checks! Like all "real" adventurers Schell had never given a check without funds.

As before, he had absolutely no idea of what to do, how to secure himself six or seven thousand dollars a year which was absolutely necessary for him and Natasha, even with a way of life that was threateningly close to the petty bourgeois. He bought the American newspaper published in Paris and attentively read the announcements: "Help wanted," "Situations wanted." There's something humiliating in this deferential braggadocio, in all these "dynamics," "reliables," "great experience," "fluent French," "good appearance," "first-class references. . . ." And the worst of it all is that Natasha thinks I'm a rich man! There would be nothing either odd or indelicate if after the wedding she were to ask me about my means. He himself was surprised at her not asking, and he had been thinking beforehand of something to say by way of reply.

189

He had accomplished the formalities about the wedding very quickly. He told Natasha about them on the morning after the tarantella. She was so agitated she almost failed to understand what he was saying. She was in a daze throughout the succeeding days, too.

They were married in Naples; Schell had conceived almost a horror of Capri after the night of his delirium. He told Natasha that they would be going to Venice—for a honeymoon. He smiled involuntarily; these words were so inept, especially after the wedding—their witness was the hall porter of the hotel. Natasha said she was in raptures, but at heart was not very happy. She would have liked it better if they settled down as soon as possible, settled down stably, it didn't matter where, as long as they settled down.

"Wonderful! Then where are we going to live? Berlin?" she finally decided to ask.

"We'll look around and think it over. I still don't know myself; it depends on business," he answered unwillingly, and, afraid that she would ask about it, hurriedly added, "And where would you like to live yourself?"

"As long as I'm with you it's all the same where. But I would like some kind of a permanent home by now. You'll see how well I'll manage, everything will sparkle like a monocle!"

He said nothing in reply, which hurt her a little. When she heard that in Venice they were going to stop in one of the most celebrated hotels in the world Natasha was alarmed. But how will I slip in there with my three dresses? On Capri, Schell had bought her a ring and said there was no point ordering dresses there, since there wasn't even time.

"But what dresses! Why? I've still got some things in Berlin," she answered timidly.

"We'll soon be in Paris, and then you'll get some dresses by Dior."

"Who's Dior? Is that some very expensive tailor? I don't need dresses like that. And I'd look ridiculous in them."

"You would be uniquely beautiful, both in dresses by Dior
190

and in rags," he said quite honestly. And thought, quite some Romeo!

His words wounded her. It's true he's talking figuratively, but since the factory I've never been in rags. I paid twenty-two marks at a sale for the dress I have now! As long as he's not ashamed of me, it doesn't matter to me at all.

They arrived in Venice late in the evening. The enchanted city stunned Natasha, she kept oh-ing and ah-ing the whole day along the Grand Canal. "I could never even have imagined such a thing!" she said, without entirely understanding herself whether she was talking about Venice or her own happiness.

The hotel manager proved to be the same as before. In the morning Schell got in touch with his Swiss bank by telephone and found out that two thousand dollars had been paid into his account; somehow he was not happy about it. All the same, I'll have to think up something very quickly.

They spent the whole day looking at the city. Natasha's enthusiasm made Schell happy. At dinner he told her about Venice and said that he knew "all two hundred palazzi." He could name about thirty or forty.

"This city was given absolutely nothing by nature. Everything has been created by human genius and labor. If I were capable of being proud of mankind this is just the place where I would be. . . . There was a time in my life when I used to come here every Easter. At that time there were still very few steamboats and motorboats on the canals, the stillness was absolute, just the thousand-year-old cries of the gondoliers, 'Eh-a!' which you heard today. Nothing was better for quieting the nerves than that stillness."

"For that our little countryside was even better. I adore nature, especially in Russia. Don't you?"

"Well, yes, even though I'm a city dweller. . . . Flaubert didn't like nature and said so openly."

"It's not possible! A writer!"

191

"He said art was much better. And would you like to move to the country?"

"Terribly, but where? We're not going back to Russia, after all?" Natasha said sadly.

"Who knows? You, perhaps, may live that long. But I have no hopes.... Don't protest, it's unnecessary; we can't deny that I'm considerably older than you. And what if we bought a villa in Italy, eh?"

He started talking about the surroundings of Venice and was again eloquent, although a little more diffuse than usual. After dinner he advised her to go upstairs to the room and take a rest: "With your poor health you have to lie down more."

"But my health isn't in the least poor! But all right, sit by yourself for a while in the lobby or take a walk, else you'll just get bored with me, death and damnation," she said as though joking, and got up. Actually, she felt a great fatigue.

He went out to the lobby, ordered a coffee, and started smoking. He was still thinking about the same thing, the same boring subject: money; he was ashamed of himself. Just that one worry—accursed money! Should I go back to Berlin next week? I'll tell the colonel I can't go to Moscow and ask him to give me another assignment. He'll tell me to go to hell. And for that matter that's not the way to behave. In any case, then, I'd have to have the two thousand in my pocket to give back to him if he doesn't agree. Where will I get it from? Part of it will disappear right here. Let's suppose that when we leave I would be able to give him back only a thousand five hundred and tell him I'll give him the other five hundred very soon. But he visualized the expression on the colonel's face and felt he couldn't say that either: it was impossible. And what would there be to live on then? The cards would be left.... Well, no, I'll never stop playing honestly, regardless! he answered his own undefined feelings. A fine beginning my regeneration would have! He recalled, almost with horror: when I was young sometimes, though rarely, to be sure, I admitted that

192

I would be capable of stealing money from rich people, if it could be done secretly and with impunity. I had an authentically criminal nature. But a regeneration can only take place by stages, any other kind can only be a fairy tale.... The only thing left is to sell the pictures and the furniture; when you're in a hurry you never get a thing. And then what?

In the lobby, accompanied by the manager, a short, dark-haired man of exotic aspect in a dinner jacket was coming down the staircase. He said something angrily to the manager in Spanish. The latter shook his head quickly, evidently not quite understanding, and replied in French. Really very deferential.... Who can it be? thought Schell. A pleasant and miserable face. There's something primitive about him, as though he were ready to snatch up a knife. Well dressed; hook-nosed; his mustaches are slightly lighter than his hair. Almost automatically Schell entered all this on some ribbon in his head. Puerto Rican, perhaps? ...

"I don't know French. You should have people here who understood Spanish," the man said angrily, and went into the bar.

"Who's that?" Schell asked a servant.

"A billionaire!" the flunky answered in a mysterious whisper. "A billionaire from the Philippine Islands! Just got here, took the best rooms."

"What's his name?"

"No idea. He can't speak any language. Are you having cognac or benedictine?"

"Cognac."

A few minutes later, after drinking his coffee, Schell got up and went over to the manager.

"I'm giving you a check tomorrow on a Swiss bank. I have no account in Venice. You can arrange it. Around three thousand Swiss francs; that will be enough for me for the time being.... And who is that gentleman?" he asked casually. "His face seems familiar; I think I've met him somewhere."

"You may have seen his picture in the papers. He's fabulously rich," said the manager with a smile, and pronounced a long triple-barreled name. "He wants to buy a palazzo here and arrange some sort of magnificent festival. A billionaire!"

"There are no more dollar billionaires around, while a billion lire is less than two million dollars," said Schell carelessly. Land, I think! he said to himself. In sight of land! and he went to the bar. The Filipino was stretched out in an easy chair smoking. He looked glum. Schell sat down at a neighboring table.

"What a splendid evening!" he said in Spanish. The man with the triple name cheered up a little.

"Are you Spanish?"

"Argentinian," answered Schell, and introduced himself. The swarthy Filipino mentioned his own name.

"At least with you it's possible to speak Spanish. At this hotel no one else understands it!"

"I noticed that the manager didn't understand it very well. If I can be of any use to you, I'm at your service."

"At home in the Philippines everyone tries to talk English now, but I'm glad I don't. I don't feel like playing second fiddle to the Yankees."

"Quite right. Then you don't like the hotel?"

The Filipino sighed. "Why shouldn't I like it? Probably it's very good. They say the building is historical. Doubtless the style is remarkable. I don't understand anything about styles, like everyone else, but they pretend they do and I don't. In Seville I have my own palace; everyone's mad about it but me. I dislike this European chasing after antiquities. You have to live in a modern way. I built myself a house in Manila with seventeen bedrooms, each one with a bath, not standing ones, either, but built right into the floor. And here I have a suite with four rooms but with only one bath. . . . I can see you've already decided I'm a parvenu? As a matter of fact, I am, but an honest one. I'm rich and I'm aware of my duty to society. Here the rich Europeans do nothing but imitate dukes and aren't of the slightest use to society. . . . But Venice is a beauti-

194

ful city. It's like absolutely nothing else. I like that. I'm planning to buy a palazzo on the Grand Canal."

"A very fine investment," said Schell. "Real estate is going up everywhere. I know that from my own experience. I bought myself a private house in Paris after the war for eight million francs, and now it's worth twenty-five or thirty."

"I don't need any capital investments. I simply want to have a palace in Venice. I'll be coming here sometimes. Aside from that I want to arrange a gigantic intellectual festival here and invite the most important people in the world. A rich man ought to be aware of his duty to society!"

"Of course. An extremely interesting idea."

"I've decided to call my festival the Festival of Beauty. Will that sound all right in other languages?"

"First-rate."

"In my opinion Venice is the right place for it. A palace is essential. But which one should I buy?"

Schell named several palaces at random. "Of course I don't know which ones are for sale, I'm not buying anything here. How many people are going to be at the festival?"

"Three thousand."

"Then the Desdemona Palazzo won't be large enough."

"Which Desdemona?"

"That's one of the local sights. The Vendramin Palazzo actually would be more suitable. That's where Richard Wagner died. You remember the famous German composer."

"Oh yes. But do you know all the palaces here?"

"In Venice I know every stone, I know the history of the city, its past, everything. This is the hundredth time I've been here. This time I've come to take a rest with my wife. I've just gotten married."

"Really? I'm not married. Do you intend to stay here long?"

"I don't know yet. I've been liquidating my affairs. I'm trying to live as pleasantly as possible. If my wife likes it here, then we'll try a month or even longer."

195

"That's very nice to hear. We might even ... so you also know Venetian history?"

Schell started talking about the Venice of the eighteenth century, about the festivals of the doges. The Filipino listened to him with interest.

When Natasha came into the bar at ten o'clock they were playing cards.

"I've met an old acquaintance," Schell told her cheerfully. "Unfortunately he speaks only Spanish. I'll be the interpreter."

He introduced the rich man to Natasha. The Filipino said something extremely flattering and flowery. Schell thought it possible to translate it condensed. Nevertheless, as it seemed to Schell, a somewhat wary look came over the Filipino's face, as though he were afraid that this new acquaintance might fling herself into his arms.

"I'm very ashamed of myself, I've just won three thousand lire from your husband. If he'll pardon me, he plays badly. In addition I always win at everything. Even gambling."

"A real man ought to win at love and at cards both. Otherwise he's not a real man. . . . My wife has grown accustomed to my constant losing."

"I've been looking for you everywhere," said Natasha. She was not very pleased about meeting someone new. Thank God, I don't speak Spanish, I don't have to make conversation, she thought. . . . She sat down for a moment and then excused herself, mentioning her fatigue. Schell kissed her hand affectionately but didn't express any desire to go upstairs with her.

"I'll be up very soon, my dear."

He did not rejoin her for an hour and a half. She was waiting for him, concealing her distress. So that's how it is, he's bored with me already! I mustn't show him I'm angry. . . . It's all nonsense; it doesn't mean anything at all.

Schell was very cheerful. "A very nice fellow, and amusing. I know him from Paris."

"What's his name? Who is he?"

196

"You wouldn't remember it anyhow, he has a triple family name and five or six Christian names. I don't know them myself: José? Rodriguez? Ramir?"

"What should I call him? Don José? Or Señor Rodriguez?"

"I've just remembered: it's Don Ramón. But you can also call him Don José. I'll tell him that it's from one of Beethoven's operas, *Carmen*, adapted from a novel by Dostoevski. He himself says he's a parvenu, and I've never met any parvenus like that. What they usually do is brag, dress tastelessly, and are supposed to have fingers 'bedecked with costly rings,' but he dresses very well indeed, only a little worse than myself...."

"There you are, bragging about yourself!"

"At certain moments it's allowable. And his manners are not in the least like those of one of those old-fashioned, bloated, boasting jumped-up tradesmen. It's true he boasts, but not much. There are naïvely vain people who are put into a frenzy by an article in the paper, by the publication of their picture. It's their chief joy in life, they instantly start thinking of how they can best exploit their success. He's not that way, he accepts everything as his natural due. In any case he's not a 'boor,' as a woman I know says. And it's amusing; he said himself that he doesn't understand anything about any art, nevertheless there's a strong aesthetic element in him. It's sometimes vulgar, but it's a powerful, alluring thing," said Schell, who was thinking of himself and even of Edda. "His soul 'seeks after beauty,' and beauty that is nothing if not 'magnificent.' Strange, all the aesthetes I ever knew were physically ugly. He, on the contrary, is quite personable, not at all bad-looking. He is, of course, a megalomaniac, not personally, so to speak, but by 'class.' He told me that only private wealth can save the world. Not private property, just all-powerful private wealth! I daresay it's supposed to abash the Bolsheviks with beauty. He talks nonsense with an unusually portentous look, death and damnation, but the strangest thing about him is his eyes: pensive, sad, even, if you like, beautiful. And they still say that the
197

eyes are the windows of the soul. And just imagine the intellectual scheme he's cooked up."

He told her about the festival, and how he had promised to give helpful advice. Natasha listened with a disagreeable feeling.

"Then that means we'll be kept here?"

"Where are we in a hurry to? Let's hang around Venice for a while."

"I wanted to tell you," said Natasha, overcoming her awkwardness. Her eyes began to look frightened. "I'm not paying board any more in the pension in Berlin, just for a room, which I paid for a month in advance. The landlady knows, of course, I'll give it back to her, but if we stay on here any longer I'll have to send her some money anyhow, or else she'll sell my things. And then it's embarrassing in front of her. I already owe her money!"

"How horrible! Don't get upset, I'll send it to her the first thing in the morning."

15

A PALAZZO on the Grand Canal was bought very quickly. It had everything it should have: an *atrio, cortile,* mosaic floors, ceilings painted by celebrated masters, chimneys of Greek marble, faded gilt, bronze, old-fashioned divans, easy chairs, and coffers. A great deal of it had to be mended, a great deal more bought in addition. In the Venetian shops furniture in a historical style was available in inconceivable quantities. Ramón was satisfied with the palazzo, though he would have preferred to buy the Ca' d'Oro. "I can't get you the Ca' d'Oro," said Schell; "try for yourself."

The interests of the sellers in no way differed from his own. However, he didn't forget himself; he protected his principal and bargained. He himself sometimes thought with a sneer of his own unusual code of honor. Ramón was almost thoroughly disinterested in prices, and if he sometimes requested and got reductions, then it was only, as he explained to Schell, in order not to be taken for a fool. Schell received no commission of any kind from him. And he had indeed agreed to deal with the purchases only at the insistent request of the Filipino.

". . . You've done me a service, and have spent a good deal of time and effort on the purchases, but every effort ought to be paid for, it's a matter of principle with me," said Don Ramón in the vigorous voice he used to express such thoughts. "I ask you to indicate a remuneration for yourself."

"That would be most strange," answered Schell with dignity. "I'm helping you because of my own interest in your idea of the Festival of Beauty. I consider it beneficial in the highest degree. While as for money, thank heavens I don't need any."

Ramón agreed to retreat from his principle. Like all rich people, he was instinctively suspicious in money matters and had obscurely guessed that Schell was getting a commission from the tradespeople. However, he had nothing against that: it was in the nature of things. He appreciated Schell's not accepting any remuneration from him; he felt a certain respect for people who rejected his money. I suppose he's guessed, Schell thought with a disagreeable feeling; well, so be it, I'm not obliged to work for him for nothing. They were both satisfied with each other. Friendly relations were soon established. By the second day the Filipino asked to be called by his first name. Natasha found this very amusing.

"Does that mean he's going to call you Eugenio or something like that? D'you know, I'll call you that, too: it sounds better in Italian! But good heavens, I'm incapable of calling a strange man by his first name."

"But what's the difference? You can't talk to each other anyhow. He clings to me just because I speak Spanish."

"I understand that, but why do you cling to him?" she asked, and was disconcerted to see a grimace of irritation flit across his face. "But I have absolutely nothing against him, I'm glad an acquaintance of yours has turned up."

"It's true I like this Filipino. He has some very attractive traits."

200

"What?"

"He's kind, likes to give people pleasure, and doesn't even require any gratitude for it."

"Then I forgive him everything. The main thing in a person is kindness."

"In addition he's not stupid. Or at least he's not invariably stupid. Sometimes it's interesting for me to talk to him. But he chatters too much."

"Please stay with him more and don't think about me. I want to study Venice properly, while you know it and there's no point in your constantly accompanying me."

"There's also no point in talking to him too much. In spite of everything he's a thoroughgoing ignoramus."

This was acknowledged quite readily by Ramón himself when he talked to Schell. They sat on the terrace of the hotel. Schell drank cognac and the Filipino only smoked one cigarette after the other. Tobacco had the same effect on him as wine on others. "... I never received any education at all. My father made his fortune when I was already a young man. He was a brilliant financier."

"There you are," said Schell, though he knew that everyone who's gotten very rich is invariably considered a brilliant financier. "But you're exaggerating somewhat."

"You know perfectly well I'm not. I'm an ignoramus. I know nothing. Remember that I notice everything. I also noticed that thing about Desdemona.... D'you remember, when we first met I asked you which Desdemona? And after that you explained to me who Wagner was. I notice everything, everything. I'm an ignoramus, but no fool. I notice a great deal without seeming to." (My commission, thought Schell, with a still more disagreeable feeling.) "I really had forgotten who Desdemona was. For that matter, I didn't even forget, I simply never knew. Is that shameful? Ridiculous? But others remember only the name, and nothing else. I know about Wagner, I've even heard *Tristan*. I was infernally bored, like nine tenths of the audience. And I can never distinguish Wagner from

201

someone like Brahms. I'd thank my stars if I could even distinguish him from the *Merry Widow*. Others distinguish him from the *Merry Widow* but not from Brahms. And the *Merry Widow* doubtless gives them greater pleasure than *Tristan*. They're all lying, and I'm sincere. And basically I'm better than a great many. I'm aware of my duty to society. I feed a great many people. I'm supporting people who are of absolutely no use to me. I'm quite used to it and have been for a long time. My principal shortcoming is that I'm obstinate. That's true. But as for Desdemona, that's all nonsense. As a matter of fact, I don't read much. Books don't give me any pleasure, I never got myself into the habit in childhood. And diplomas are of no use to me. At any moment I could become a doctor of . . . what's it called? *Honoris causa*. In return for a big donation any university would give me a degree. . . ."

"Surely not any," replied Schell. The rich man annoyed him in spite of everything.

"Offers have been made, offers have been made. But why should I be a doctor *honoris causa?* And why should I give money to universities when I don't understand anything about science and don't even have much respect for it? It's brought about a great deal of evil, especially during the last few years. Or let's say art. I have some pictures in Seville, but I know nothing about them. Here I was shown a picture . . . what's his name? Giorgione? The guide said, if I understood him, that this was the most expensive painting in the world. He was probably lying. Some kind of a special sky! And there's nothing special about his sky, the real sky is much more beautiful. But sometimes I do buy paintings. I myself don't know what for. . . ."

"You might buy some here at that. Some real masterpieces have been preserved by the local patricians, you can buy them very cheap," Schell put in.

Ramón smiled slightly. "I don't intend to at the moment."

"Then there's no need to. . . . A great many people probably hate you because you've been so lucky."

"I don't think so," said Ramón, surprised and hurt. It was plain that this idea had never entered his head. He was naïvely vexed. "I don't think I'm hated."

"I wasn't expressing a very original thought. I, too, hated rich people before I became rich myself." They were silent for a moment. "Nevertheless, I would like to grasp the aim of your festival as well as possible. In my opinion . . . "

"You just said you appreciated my idea!" said Ramón, annoyed. "I don't like repeating the same thing. There's a struggle going on now between two worlds. My idea is that it is only private wealth that can show mankind the significance of Western civilization. You cannot defeat the Communists with force, and not with science either. They figured out the atom bomb themselves. They must be dealt a blow by means of beauty!" he enunciated, with three exclamation points in his intonation. "I want my Festival of Beauty to surpass anything ever seen by the world! . . . I asked you to think of a theme and a program. I hope you've done so?"

"Yes, I agreed to think about it. I've done some reading about it," answered Schell. His tactic lay in keeping himself completely independent and occasionally underlining his independence. "Though to defeat the world by beauty is not so easy. But in any case with unlimited credit the sensation may be terrific."

"An uproar is really essential. I don't say that out of vanity. For myself, personally, an uproar is unnecessary." (Really, his vanity is only beaten by his thickheadedness, Schell thought to himself.) "The main thing is my idea!"

"I suggest the following: we'll reproduce, with complete precision and dazzling brilliance, the ceremony of electing a doge. This will also be the apotheosis of the idea of *elections*. Thus, by way of beauty, you will counterpose to the Communists the democratic idea, too."

"That might be a good idea. . . . Yes, yes . . . a wonderful idea. . . . Does that mean we'll have to rent the Doges' Palace?"

"No, they won't let us have it."

"They will! That's my affair. You'll just translate what I say."

203

"Money is a great force, nevertheless it's futile for you to imagine that everything can be bought," said Schell weightily. "You won't get the Doges' Palace, nor is it at all essential. As a rule this is how the affair went off. Guns were fired throughout the city, bells rung, and the people went into a frenzy. We'll do that, too. To the sounds of music the new doge left his private palace. Yours, as you know, at one time belonged to the family of one of the doges. Then he went through St. Mark's Square. A historical umbrella was carried over his head, the *umbrella Domini Ducis*. He was accompanied by patricians, senators, and all the estates, right down to the tailors and cobblers. In this way three ideas are realized: beauty, the electoral principle, and social equality. I'm expressing symbolically what you indicated to me. These ideas are yours, not mine."

"You flatter me. I didn't say all that, but I like your plan very well indeed. I thank you heartily."

"For nothing. We might even call your festival the Festival of Beauty and Freedom."

"No, I don't want to. Let it be called as I decided: the Festival of Beauty."

"That's all right, too. Now the intellectual side of the matter is quite clear to me. But there is, after all, the personal side, too, isn't there? It seems to me I understand you correctly as a man. You're fed up with everything, you're looking for, well, let's say new sensations, magnificence in beauty, isn't that it?"

"I don't deny it. Yes, new sensations. You're a clever fellow."

"You will play the role of the doge."

"I? The doge?"

"You even look the part. We'll simply paste a beard on. The doge wore a splendid gilt mantle. Looking like that, your photograph will appear in every newspaper. The most beautiful women in the world will be at your festival—perhaps you'll even find personal happiness, too, Ramón," said Schell, laughing.

"What will my part consist of?"

"The doge seated himself on the throne above the Scala dei Giganti. D'you remember that monumental staircase in the
204

Doges' Palace? And from there he threw the people gold coins by the handful. Silver coins will do just as well, but we'll say in the newspapers that you threw gold ones. I know that you're not a publicity seeker in the least, but who was it who said the Lord God himself needs the ringing of bells?"

Ramón laughed, though he was slightly embarrassed. He was getting to like Schell more and more: he made things gay. "I don't agree with you, but go on."

"You'll sit on the throne in your palace. Bodyguards will be standing behind you. They used to wear velvet robes and jackets of various colors, short trousers, and long hose, also velvet. The sabers were straight, thin, and long. For you we'll order a sword with a hilt studded with precious stones. That will cost a lot, but after all you'll be able to keep the sword. After your picture with it is taken for the newspapers and magazines you can hang it up on the wall of your study."

"But what will actually happen? I can't just sit on the throne."

"Of course not. We'll be true to history again. The new doge's lady, the dogaressa, came to join him. She was brought there in a gigantic gondola with a pavilion. The luxury of this gondola ought to be indescribable. Again, I warn you, this will cost a lot."

"You probably want your wife to play the dogaressa?" asked Ramón. "Of course she's very beautiful, but . . ."

"I never even thought of such an idea!" said Schell, suddenly getting angry. "Look for a dogaressa yourself."

"I didn't mean to say anything offensive."

"Nor would I permit you to say anything offensive. In fact, I'm ready to abandon the whole thing at any moment. I don't care a damn!"

"Please don't be angry, my dear friend. . . . And what happened with the dogaressa?"

"To the sound of an orchestra, accompanied by a resplendent entourage, she floated to your palace, towed by *bucentauri*."

"What are *bucentauri*?"

"That was a sort of mythological monster the doge's gondola

205

symbolized. He always rode on *bucentauri*. That is, not always, but at major ceremonies, for instance when he married the Adriatic Ocean."

"But where will we get the *bucentauri* from?"

"The same place the doges did: from a workshop."

"Then you also want to represent my wedding to the Adriatic Ocean?"

"Why the devil should you marry the Adriatic Ocean? What's the point of marrying the Adriatic Ocean? And after all we have to show off your palace. So the dogaressa comes out of the gondola, goes up to you, and sits on the throne next to you. The populace goes into a frenzy. Then we'll set up a show in the grand ballroom as it was during the Renaissance. At that time it was called *representazione di ciarlatani*. And in the audience there will be all the celebrities of the world, nobility, writers, movie stars. . . ."

"We'll explain to them the intellectual significance of the Festival of Beauty! They can't help understanding it!"

"Of course. Aside from which it's publicity for them. That, too, they can't help understanding. And just as soon as we publish the first list of those invited we'll be besieged by requests for invitations. The festival will end with a magnificent historical banquet. The menu will be the same as the doges had. First of all, hors-d'oeuvres. . . ."

"We'll order caviar straight from Moscow. Two hundred pounds of caviar."

"In those days caviar was unknown in Venice. But there we might depart a little from historic authenticity. The hors-d'oeuvres will be followed by three soups, including *zuppa dorata*. Not less than eleven kinds of fish have to be used."

"Eleven kinds of fish?"

"No less. *Chieppa, orada, anguilli, loto, corbetto, girolo, lucino, astesi, cevoli, bamboni, lampedi.*"

"What a memory you have! I don't even know what kinds of fish those are."

"Neither do I, but the chefs are bound to. After the fish the

206

doges had roasted peacocks. Here there will be some difficulty. It really isn't easy to get peacocks; they're not like writers."

Schell was growing more and more cheerful. He was no longer irritated by the sight of the fortune's favorites who crowded the luxury hotel. Now he himself was a success of equal status. Money was flowing into his pockets as never before; nor had he ever gotten it so easily, without the slightest danger, almost without effort. According to his rough estimate the festival might bring him in around twenty-five thousand dollars. He now had even less justification than before for any doubts about his star. He rapidly became popular with the tradespeople. They saw that he could be dealt with—live and let live. He told himself that what he was doing was customary and legal. He thought, to be sure, frowning, that he was returning to the path of good via a dubious though not actionable activity. Well, what of it, it's for the last time in my life. And for that matter nearly all private riches in the world have been acquired by the same methods. And I'm not struggling to get rich but only for material independence, that's all I require. Haven't I the right to a human life, too?

He had not yet returned the two thousand dollars he had received from the colonel, although now it would have been easy. He was trying to think up the best explanation. Of course he's going to decide I got cold feet, or "he's grown weak, he's finished." I needn't be afraid of being accused of cowardice. General Kornilov never exposed himself to fire unless it was necessary; he knew it would never enter anyone's head that he might be afraid, thought Schell. In spite of his decision to leave intelligence work for good it was unpleasant for him to have his former professional colleagues consider him a failure.

Once while riding in a gondola with Natasha he thought: but why don't I just tell the colonel the truth? I'll write that I fell in love unexpectedly, still more unexpectedly got married, that I can't leave my wife, am compelled to turn down the assignment, I earnestly beg his forgiveness, and am enclosing a check for the two thousand. The colonel would shrug his shoulders, curse up and down, and everything would be over with. He was amused that this idea—of telling the truth—was the last one to enter his head. "Agony of the *Former* Schell."

When he was alone he set about composing a letter to the colonel. Without a signature, and without the name of the sender on the envelope, it could not be compromising for anyone; for that matter it was not very likely to be intercepted. However, a rule was a rule: all letters were supposed to be coded. For less important communications the code was a simple one: a Russian-English dictionary, though not the same one Edda had been given. Schell wrote out a short text in Russian and started to encode it. The Russian word for "unexpectedly" was on page 320, the twenty-eighth word from the top. He wrote down 320.28. The Russian word, "to fall in love," was on page 56. Schell started to write down the corresponding figures but felt he couldn't; it would come out too stupidly. He imagined the colonel putting on his glasses at his desk, looking it up, and reading it. No, it's impossible! Say it in a different way. Why tell him I'm "in love"? It would be far easier to tell him face to face in Berlin. I'll say it with a little smile, making fun of myself, "Just imagine, in my old age something like this had to happen: I've gotten married!" At worst the colonel will say in an icy tone, "That is not how one behaves, Mr. Schell. Because of you I've lost a great deal of time for nothing, and your romances don't concern me in the least!" At best he'll shrug his shoulders, also laugh, and congratulate me on a legal marriage.

Instead of the letter he sent a telegram—"Arriving shortly." That wasn't very suitable; he'll feel still more certain I've agreed. But no harm done.

There was also some satisfaction to look forward to: everything was finally going to be thoroughly explained to Natasha. The poor darling simply doesn't know what to think: why Ramón? why do I spend so much time on this idiotic festival?

208

The following day he said to Natasha, "Well, have you decided where we should live? High time we made up our minds."

He spoke as though he had already put this question to her
many times and she still hadn't replied. Natasha was both embarrassed and overjoyed: a conversation at last, a real conversation! "I? It's all the same to me. It all depends on you. I
suppose you have business in Berlin?"

"I'm getting rid of my business. It was too boring, death and
damnation. And I don't like Berlin. Well, choose."

"But how can I? ... Surely you can't live wherever you
please?" she asked, frightened. But what if he thinks I'm interested in his money?

"We have enough for a simple life. And it's much the same
to me where we live. Like Louis XIV in his old age, *je ne suis
plus amusable*," he said, forgetting he had already told her
that once or twice.

"Louis XIV was in his eighties, and you're half that," she
answered, also not for the first time. "Your forty-second year
is scarcely the end of youth."

"Thanks for that, too," said Schell, a trifle more coldly. "I
prefer Paris to all the other capitals in the world. But it's impossible to find a flat there now. In my aging years—I beg your
pardon, at the end of my youth—I should very much like to
have a little house of my own with a garden. In Paris, under
the talented government of the Fourth Republic, prices are
such that only Ramón and his like can get a corner to themselves there. What if we settled in Italy? We both like it so
much here."

"I should adore it!"

"You've never asked me about anything. I know you're
tactful to the point of foolishness. And I didn't want to speak
to you before, since until now my business hadn't been cleared
up. Now I can tell you that I've sold it to Ramón. And that's
why I want to show him my thanks by helping him with his
idiotic festival."

"So that's it! I admit I never realized ... Oh, I'm so happy!"

"We now have a property approximating twenty-five thousand dollars."

"Heavens! But that's a fortune!"

"It's a very small amount, not even the outskirts of a fortune, but it will be enough for a certain time. I was asking the manager. We could buy a small villa with a garden here—not in Venice itself, of course, but very close by—for five or six thousand dollars. What would you say to that?"

"I simply couldn't even imagine anything better!"

"You won't be bored? You could go on keeping yourself busy with history here."

"Of course! Without fail! Of course I'll need a library."

"You'll buy books. And if they can't be bought, we'll take a trip to Paris sometimes. The Bibliothèque Nationale has everything. I think it's the best library in the world. There are no apartments in Paris, but there are hotels, thank God. You can make summaries there. Of course I don't give a damn either for the Recallists or for the university. After all, you don't seriously intend to become a teacher and live in Yugoslavia."

"But why not? You just said nothing matters to you, after all, you're like Louis XIV."

"Louis XIV would never have agreed to live in Yugoslavia either."

"I'm so happy! I love you so!"

"You can prove it to me at once." She flushed crimson. "Oh my shy darling child."

16

THE commissionaire of the hotel suggested a number of suitable villas on the Lido and on the outskirts of Venice, and Schell went off with Natasha to look at them. The first villa proved unsuitable, but they both liked the second enormously. It was not far from the Excelsior, a one-story cozy house in a little garden, with five rooms, very comfortable, clean, and pleasant. An old Italian woman was selling it; she wished to move to a different place after the death of her husband, who had built the villa before World War I.

"Did your husband also die here?" Schell asked uneasily.

"Oh no, he died in a hospital in Rome," said the owner, and continued explaining the various comforts of the villa. The bathtub was excellent, the kitchen very large, and there was a fountain in the garden.

"... Modern comfort has its advantages, nevertheless. If the villa were historic, we would be getting rats together with the history," Schell said to Natasha, though not quite sincerely; he would have preferred a villa built "after a sketch by Sansovino." "You'll see how happy we'll be there."

"I'm in raptures! But it costs more than you wanted to pay. Isn't it too expensive for you?"

"Not 'for you,' but for us. You know what our finances are now. And I won't go on without earning something."

He bargained adroitly. Natasha was astonished, although she didn't quite understand the conversation. He pointed out the house's shortcomings, insisted that the price was very high; contrary to his usual way he haggled, kindly, politely, and even jokingly. He got a slight reduction. Then he told Natasha it would be possible to get it down another thousand and fifty lire, but he didn't want to: why offend the old woman (in this, too, he was unconsciously atoning for his sins). When they had come to an agreement, Schell, without a notarized contract, offered the old lady a down payment of two hundred thousand lire, and gave her a check.

"And now would it be possible to sit in your garden for a little while?"

"But please, the house is yours! Stay as long as you like! I'll send you and the charming signora coffee or wine," said the owner, visibly charmed by him.

"Thank you. In that case wine. We shall drink it with delight."

"You didn't even get a receipt from her!" said Natasha, demonstrating her business sense. Schell smiled at her.

"*Il lui jeta sa bourse et la brave femme fondit en larmes.*"

"What? . . . Where is that from?"

"From all the best novels," answered Schell. It annoyed him a little that Natasha's French was so bad. "I should add that the check itself is a receipt. And in general it's not necessary to do everything literally and with too much formality. You know there's a kind of strike in which the workers purposely do everything with absolute precision according to the regulations. The social order is manifestly such that if everything is done accord-

212

ing to the regulations in a funny way what is achieved is chaos."

"You're a skeptic."

"No, I'm a pseudo-skeptic. And a pseudo-misanthrope. And a pseudo-pessimist."

"I know, everything is 'pseudo,' 'pseudo,'" she said, and kissed him quickly, glancing around at the door.

A table and some wicker chairs were in the little garden. The weather was magnificent. The owner brought them a carafe of wine and a plate of cakes. Schell moved up a chair for her and poured the wine into the glasses. I think she's looking at his hands, thought Natasha. She did not like Schell's hands either, and tried not to look at them.

"Vinci," said Schell. His instant recognition of this unfamiliar wine also impressed the owner, who said that they could move in by Friday, that everything would be ready.

"Not Friday, that's an unlucky day," Schell said, also to her thoroughgoing satisfaction. "We'll probably move in a little later."

"In that case I'll lock the house and bring you the key. Give me the address.... So you don't want to buy some of the furniture? I'd sell it cheaply."

He refused the furniture, saying (with a haughtiness that astounded himself) that they were young and wanted to have everything new.

"What a sweet thing!" said Natasha when they were left alone. "What was she saying? What a pity I don't know Italian! I'm going to learn it now, I'll buy a self-teacher. And how you charmed her, too!"

"Thanks for the 'too.' She was suggesting that I buy her furniture, but I refused. After all, I have the furniture of two rooms in Berlin, which isn't too bad at that. We'll go fetch it very soon. And the rest we'll buy. Old-fashioned or modern?"

"Whatever you like. I like old-fashioned things very much, especially Russian. But for the life of me I'm not going to sit in a narrow, old-fashioned chair with a straight back, and I'm not

213

going to put my linen in a 'moth-eaten coffer of the Renaissance' "—Natasha sometimes now unwittingly imitated his style.

"We'll buy modern. In the big room we'll set up a working
study. . . ."

"A working study? But that's splendid. Does that mean you're
going to work?"

"Nowhere is it so pleasant to do nothing as in a working
study. That will be our living room. It even has a *baie vitrée, en
pan coupé*, as in all the fashionable French plays. Next to it will
be your boudoir."

"A boudoir, too! What do I need a boudoir for?"

"As we are now middle class you simply must have a boudoir," he said gayly. "I'm not going to buy any more pictures.
Renoir's flowers or Cézanne's fish are arresting, but a mortal
ennui would seize me if they were hanging in the identical place
at home a whole day and a whole night. Moreover, I've burned
my fingers in buying art, like most amateurs. I thought I would
grow rich from the paintings I bought, but in fact I had bought
them terribly dear. I consoled myself with the reflection that
Cézanne's wife used to stuff pipes with her husband's water
colors. . . . And those two rooms next to each other that enter
on the garden will be the bedrooms. Don't be annoyed, I'm used
to sleeping alone."

"As you like," said Natasha, blushing.

"They often don't put dining rooms in new apartments nowadays, but there should be a dining room, too."

"The main thing is this study of yours. I haven't seen your
Berlin furniture, but you'll need a large desk, with shelves for
books, and they must have good bindings, then large easy
chairs. I'll also bring my own books here from Berlin. I haven't
very many, but we'll put them on shelves, too."

"We'll bring everything of yours here, everything down to
the last dress. As a souvenir."

"Really? And the little corner room will be a guestroom,
'for friends.' Have you any friends?"

214

"No, rot and blast 'em all."

As he said this, almost automatically, it also occurred to him that in the whole world the only thing that was close to him was this helpless creature, thanks to whom, however offensively banal it was, he really was beginning a "new life."

"So there! And you won't be bored, Eugenio?"

Instead of answering he embraced her. Again she glanced at the windows of the villa in embarrassment.

"I've lived all my life in big cities and, like the Berber nomads, always considered it shameful. Man is made for the country. It's a pity this villa doesn't have a few hundred acres of plowland. Then we might be able to carry out, let's say, a three-crop rotational tillage. D'you know what that is?"

"Not too clearly."

"And I even less so," he said, laughing. "Tolstoy mentions some kind of talisman, he calls it a sneezewort, I don't know just what a sneezewort is, I've never seen one. But in the classic landowners' novels all that is enticingly described, and the words are so agreeable and cozy: 'The fragrant ranks of the mown meadows under the slanting rays of the sun.' Your mouth simply waters. But to make up for that here in our garden we're going to put a fruit orchard. Can you plant trees? No? Scandalous! Neither can I."

She laughed merrily, too. "We'll learn. I'd like a lilac tree. They grow in Italy, don't they? For me it's much more enjoyable than any palms or cactuses."

"We'll put in a lilac tree, too."

"How wonderful it will be, especially in spring! I'm so happy, so happy! Our own niche, and what a niche! But nevertheless tell me honestly, are you quite sure you won't be bored? That's the only thing that troubles me," said Natasha. (This was an abbreviation of "Won't you be bored *with me?*") "Let me tell you once again, in your place I'd start writing a novel or a short story. What do you think?"

"For that I lack just one bagatelle: talent. And then it's so easy to say, Be a writer! Of course, I'm thinking of the *real* writers. You can frolic about as you please, there's no law against it. But to write, to teach people—what? And am I the one who's going to do the teaching? Buffon used to put on lace cuffs when he sat down to write: for solemnity. He was holding a divine service, he thought he was writing for eternity. Now no one reads him. Literary immortality—you're lucky if it lasts twenty years. . . . No, I won't be bored. The only thing I'm afraid of is whether the Venetian climate will be bad for your health. But for a month now you haven't coughed. And then we'll be living on the Lido, after all, and not along the canals. By the way, there's a magnificent library in Venice, with hundreds of thousands of books. We'll go to the city every day, it's no more than a stone's throw away. It's always seemed to me that that was the ideal thing: to live in this fabulous city, sit on the terrace at Florian's, feasting one's eyes on that unique square. I'll wait for you there after the library. If you write a book about Nil Sorsky we'll publish it at our own expense."

"Truly? Is that possible? I'll work for days on end!"

"Then begin writing books instantly. And buy everything you need, get our house ready. . . . She called you the charming signora. Did you understand that?"

"No. I'm going to write a book, but then what will you be doing?"

"I don't know yet."

"And we can live that way, without earning anything?"

"We'll see. Living doesn't cost much here, by the way. We'll just have a maid who cooks. D'you like Italian food? Yes, you said you did. I prefer French and Russian, but Italian is good, too. We'll drink this same Vinci we just had. That's the little place Leonardo came from. It's very strong, rather a good wine. We shall live wonderfully well. And how we'll be able to sleep in this stillness! . . . By nature I'm a very active man, nevertheless I say the greatest pleasure in life is to sleep, to sleep well. Without sleeping pills."

216

"No, that's not what the greatest pleasure in life is," said Natasha.

When they returned to the hotel the hall porter handed Schell a telegram. It was from the colonel. It said: "Nikolai dead coming Venice soon await arrival."

17

IN the morning Schell sat down in a corner of the terrace of the Café Florian. From long habit in cafés he always sat down near the wall or else facing a mirror—he had to see what took place behind him also. Natasha set out for the Santa Maria Mater Domini; she was studying all the churches, district by district, not omitting a single one. Schell drank coffee and lazily thought that things were not arranging themselves at all badly.

The colonel's telegram had startled him. The trip to Russia had fallen through, and not through his own fault in the least. What a stroke of luck, my not sending him that letter refusing! Now I would have the moral right not to return the advance. . . . Ever since becoming a man of property I've been using the words "moral" and "morality" more and more frequently. That's also one of the *former* Schell's ideas, blast him! . . . Of course I'll give back the advance. I won't have to refer to my getting married. "Please accept the money. Would

218

you like it in dollars or in Swiss francs?" "But after all, Mr. Schell, it wasn't your fault in the least." "Neither was it yours. I'm not accustomed to accepting money for nothing." He'll be stunned; in our milieu people seldom behave that way. That is, in my *former* milieu, which I'm definitely out of. . . . Nevertheless, this Maikov's death is surprising; it coincides so oddly with my own delirium. Could he have finished himself off? And what, actually, am I going to do from now on? . . . The orchestra on St. Mark's Square played something dashing. Tourists were fussing around with cameras. Suddenly Schell sat transfixed: not fifteen steps away from him Edda was feeding some pigeons.

He gazed at her as though he had seen a hippopotamus in the square. He was about to try to slip off unobserved, but just then their eyes met. Edda didn't look surprised, and after tossing away the little bag of bread crumbs she came over to him with a smile that seemed to bode nothing specially bad. As usual she was dressed neither well nor badly, but somewhat improbably.

"How are you, my dear? Have you been back from Spain long?" she asked sarcastically, sitting down at his table. Natasha! he thought. He had not told Natasha he would be at Florian's, they were supposed to meet at the hotel; nevertheless, she might come through the square, too.

"Hello, my little sweetie pie. How are you?" he said, kissing her hand. "You're looking wonderful; you've gotten still more beautiful. I thought you were in Paris?"

"I was. You probably know I carried everything off brilliantly well."

"I don't know a thing, but about that I never had the least doubt. But why have you dyed one strand of hair?"

"That's the latest Paris fashion."

"Not the latest. More than a few geese did that last year already."

"What do you know about anything? I've just arrived and found out to my joy that you were in Venice. I saw you from

219

the shore riding in a gondola with a little biddy *fichue comme l'as de pique,* and with a rather ugly little monsieur."

"Yes, I have some acquaintances here."

"Is she your mistress? I'll drown her in vitriol!" said Edda, though rather peaceably.

"*Cela fera très César Borgia.* Only she's not my mistress."

"I know you! But first let's talk business."

"Let's talk business, my own little cherry blossom."

She told him how she had picked up the lieutenant, very quickly—"in the twinkling of an eye"—seduced him, made him her accomplice, and gotten some extraordinarily valuable documents. She spoke in a half-whisper, though there was no one around them, and with a modestly triumphant look. Schell kept interpolating approving and even enthusiastic exclamations. The question is only, Is she lying, or not? He knew that Edda sometimes lied almost pathologically although such attacks happened to her rarely.

"... In the evenings we drank champagne, I read him my verses aloud, and he fell madly in love with me. *Coup de foudre!* He's a very sweet boy. You know I'm an international-ist, but I adore the Americans, they're so straightforward! You lied when you said I would manage it as an enchantress; with him I worked it by playing the fool!"

"I can imagine how worn out you are! But what you've accomplished is simply astounding," he said, when she stopped to wait for further raptures. "And where is this lieutenant now?"

"He's arriving tomorrow. For my sake he's broken with the Americans for good! But we couldn't leave together, that wouldn't have been conspiratorial. And just imagine, even be-fore he met me he was Left-wing! Jim is against the partition of Russia."

"So Jim is against the partition of Russia. Not really? Prob-ably you fell in love with him, too?" asked Schell hopefully.

"No, he's not intelligent enough for me. I like only intelligent people, even if they're boors like you. And I don't like the name

220

Jim! What could be more prosaic? People ought to be called Baldur von Schirach! Now there's a marvelous name!"

"Marvelous. Did he pay you well? Not Baldur von Schirach, but the American."

"Not a penny. It was all for love. I wouldn't even have taken any from him."

"Perhaps you have a Phèdre complex? No matter, my angel, the Soviet colonel will give you a great deal of money. Strike while the iron is hot! Leave for Berlin quickly, in fact today!"

"But why strike with the iron so quickly? No, I'll hang about here with Jim and you," she said mockingly. "And your Soviet colonel is not only a boor but a miser as well."

"Have you already given him the papers?"

"Of course. The same day Jim told me to," replied Edda. This wasn't entirely accurate: Jim had told her the packet was to be handed over on the eighteenth, but she had a number of fittings at her dressmaker's that day and she handed the packet over the day before. "And d'you know how much they paid me?" She mentioned an amount that actually was not very large. "Of course they explained that they had to determine the importance of the papers and for the time being were just giving me expense money. My expenses were enormous. I can't go around dressed like that biddy of yours! Is she your mistress already or just on the verge? You're a man with a double life in love, too."

"You're a fool, my little sweetie pie. You understand: fooool. 'F' as in fat-headed, 'o' as in obstreperous, 'l' as in laughable. Talk sense for a change. You recall that Balaam's ass one single time started talking in human speech. D'you need money?"

"I always need money! What d'you think? They gave me chicken feed and now you ask me!" she said with indignation, but a little vaguely: it was the Soviet intelligence that had given her the chicken feed and Schell had been generous as always, which she acknowledged.

221

"I could supplement it for you, my angel. Not by very much, of course."

"Is that so? Have you gotten rich?"

"I got hold of a thousand dollars. I can give you half."

"Delightful. But what can I do with five hundred dollars? You don't call five hundred dollars money?"

"I'll send you more later on."

"Later on? Send me? You mean you're not going back to Berlin for the time being?"

"I'm going back very soon. I don't know yet just when."

"You're a boor," she said, by now quite good-naturedly. When she was angry she always stuttered over the "b's": b-b-boor! Now there was only one "b." "And please don't think that I'm so much in love with you. Thanks for the five hundred dollars anyhow. They come in very handy. Isn't it inconvenient for you to give them to me?"

"It is, but I'll do it. So that means you weren't living on the young American?"

"I haven't taken any money from him for a thousand different reasons. First of all, he doesn't have any."

"In that case, honey, there's no point analyzing the other nine hundred and ninety-nine reasons."

"It's true that he has an uncle who's a millionaire, but he probably gives him very little."

"What a contemptible uncle! I take it the lieutenant is throwing you over, my little peach blossom?"

"No one ever throws me over! But I'm soon going to throw him over. I'm fed up with him."

"He's probably not demonic enough? Well, my love, are you satisfied with your new profession?"

"No. Completely dissatisfied! You're always making fun of me and talking to me as though I were a fool. D'you suppose I don't see that? 'Not demonic enough.' Oh, how stupid! I'm not an angel, but you yourself are no better than I. Have you ever tried, just once, to look into my soul? Would you like me to tell you the story of my childhood? . . ."

222

"No, I wouldn't. . . . That is, I would, but some other time."

"Have you any idea of how fed up I am with everything, with baseness, with filth? And all I want to do is live the way decent people do. D'you suppose I don't know what I am? I've have a great deal of bad luck all my life," said Edda, and suddenly, to Schell's astonishment, she burst into tears.

"I meant that to my mind you were trying to make your life as poetic as possible. There's nothing bad about that. . . . But, then, what do you want?" he asked in a different tone.

"I don't know myself what I want! One thing now, something else a moment later! I only know that I'm unhappy. In Berlin once you talked about a peaceful haven, that's what I need, too, a peaceful haven. And I can't stand your intelligence business any more!"

"But you can throw it over!"

"Then what will I live on? It's always this accursed money! And you still defend capitalism!"

"We have to think. Where are you stopping?"

She named a hotel, luckily not his own, but also a very good one.

"Aha! Probably expensive. And I live at the same place as that ugly little monsieur, as you call him. He's there with a girl, the one you saw. Would you believe it, I found some work with him and he's paying all my expenses."

Schell told her about the Festival of Beauty. Edda listened mistrustfully but attentively. She liked the name of the festival enormously.

"All that's very interesting if you're not lying. So that little biddy is his mistress? And does he pay well?"

"Tolerably," replied Schell. An idea had flashed through his mind. I must palm her off on Ramón, but in such a way that she doesn't stay here long, doesn't meet Natasha, and sees her as little as possible. "I suppose you speak Spanish?"

"So-so. Why do you ask?"

"He's a Filipino and can't speak anything but Spanish. Wait, I've got an ingenious idea. You must go to Berlin at once."

223

"'At once' is out of the question. They already have the documents."

"Aside from the documents you have to make a personal report. And right away at that. I know very well what I'm talking about."

"He can wait a little while. And if he pays less than a thousand dollars I'll stop working for him!"

Schell's face took on a sepulchral expression. "D'you think it's that simple? You just tell him, 'I don't want to work for you any more, good-by,' is that it? My dear, your inexperience is simply touching! I know you love gambling with life and aren't afraid of dying, but there's a limit to everything. You don't leave *them* that way! They may let you go if the business is handled with sense. But to leave of your own accord! ... I pity you. He's naturally going to think you've gone over to the Americans! I won't be surprised to hear you've been found at the bottom of the Grand Canal."

"What is this, is that a joke?"

"I'm speaking absolutely seriously! I warned you that working for the colonel is dangerous. He's a terrifying man. ... So the lieutenant is arriving tomorrow? You say he's broken with the Americans?"

"He's decided to break with them. Meanwhile, he's gotten a month's leave, he hasn't had one for two years."

Schell couldn't make out what the lieutenant was coming to Venice for. Or can he actually have fallen in love with her? But if not, does that mean the Americans have decided to use her for another job? That really would be dangerous for her.

"You must leave the colonel, but you must do it without fail on good terms."

"How can I do that? And what should I do in general? If you're telling the truth. ... Perhaps you simply want to get rid of me?"

"Why should I want to get rid of you? On the contrary, I missed you terribly. I'd like you to stay on here. Not only that, but I'd get you work here with my Filipino."

224

"Why did you ask me whether I spoke Spanish? D'you want to get me a job as his secretary? I won't be a secretary; it doesn't interest me."

"No, I want to get you a role in his festival—a very good role. You'll look more stunning than ever. We'll get you a dress and after the show you'll be able to keep it. A very expensive dress!"

"Now that's much more interesting!"

"The dress must be ordered in Berlin. It's impossible for you to return to Paris, and you won't get one here in Venice. He'll pay *you* well, not what he pays me."

"That's very important!"

"But for that it's absolutely essential to liquidate your relations with the colonel, if you've already decided to do so. There will be thousands of people at the festival, including, of course, Soviet agents. I don't want you to be stabbed to death in general, and not in the palace of my boss in particular. You have to leave for Berlin at once. I'll explain to you how the colonel must be talked to. Try to make him despise you."

"Thank you."

"You might tell him, for instance, that the American has fallen out of love with you."

"I would never tell him such a nonsensical thing! And he would never even believe it."

"It's going to be rather complicated," said Schell, without listening. "No, for the time being you explain to him that your lieutenant has gotten leave for a month. If he's surprised at their having given him such a long leave tell him he hasn't had one for two years. If he wants the lieutenant to return earlier, say that that might arouse the suspicions of his superiors: people don't cut short their leaves willingly. Then the colonel will give you a leave, too. The lieutenant will have to be ordered under no circumstances (God forbid!) to break off relations with his superiors. After that either your passionate love for the lieutenant will end—or his love for you," interpolated Schell, "or else they will transfer him somewhere else.

225

In either case the colonel will despise you. Q.E.D. The main thing is, what to do now? From long experience I never look further than a few weeks into the future. Now the point is for you to leave him on good terms. After that come back here for the festival itself, in order not to start any rumors. Your American can either hang around here or travel wherever he pleases. And my boss will give you money."

"Will he give me a lot? If he's so rich, why is that hussy dressed like a government instructor in Estonia?"

"I have no idea," answered Schell, with annoyance. As a matter of fact, it's time for Natasha to be dressed properly! he thought. "Now leave this business of yours to me. I'll get you a good role. That requires diplomatic preparations with my boss. But in principle you can count on there being a role for you. And the salary won't be less than two thousand dollars!"

"With an advance?" asked Edda, on whom this figure had produced a powerful impression.

"I'll also arrange for an advance, but on the fixed condition that you get a leave from the colonel."

"Let's be a little more precise. Does that mean I don't get the advance before the leave? Otherwise, I won't have anything to get to Berlin on. How much of an advance?"

"Not less than a thousand dollars."

"In addition to your five hundred?"

"All right. I strongly urge you to leave for Berlin at once. The talk with the colonel will take time, and it's not so simple to get an audience with him."

"What are you in such a hurry about? I can't leave at once. Jim's only arriving here tomorrow. And we have to rest up a little in Venice from everything that's happened."

"But then you won't have time to have yourself a dress made in Berlin."

"But how can I have a dress made before knowing what my role is going to be? And where is the money I'm going to have it made on?"

226

"I'll send you a design. We'll transfer the money to Berlin just as soon as you know exactly how much everything's going to cost. You're going to be a Venetian lady of rank, we won't pinch money on the dress, and, I repeat, you'll be able to keep it."

"What am I going to do afterward with the dress of a Venetian lady of rank?"

"You'll exchange it, light of my life, or sell it."

"No one'll buy it. Should I have it made with lace? I've seen some wonderful lace in one of the shops along the Kurfürstendamm. But that's very expensive."

"By all means have it made with lace."

"All this has to be thought over. Let's have dinner tomorrow together with Jim. I'll introduce you and we can all talk it over."

"Are you out of your mind? I'm even afraid of our being seen here together," said Schell. "We're lucky there seems to be no one suspicious looking around just now. But we can't possibly meet any more, to say nothing of Jim. That would be very dangerous both for you and for me."

"I don't understand. Why dangerous? Jim is now one of *our* people, all three of us are working for the same cause. So how can we compromise you or you us?"

"You're evidently forgetting that the Americans also have an intelligence service which isn't at all bad. They have agents everywhere; it's entirely possible that they're even having you followed here." Edda turned pale. "It's even highly likely that they're having you followed: it's no joke, an American officer in charge of the Rocquencourt furnace! You must get out of here at once and remove your traces as far as possible. And I have absolutely no desire for them to arrange to have me followed, too. No, we can't meet here any more, that's out of the question. Except that I'd like to show you to my boss. Without Jim."

"Then let's have dinner, all three of us, this evening."

"With you I have to spell everything out: I repeat, I *cannot*
227

show myself with you. But here's what. Tomorrow at eleven in the morning I'm coming here to Florian's with my boss," Schell improvised; Natasha was supposed to go to the Lido. "You walk slowly past us. I'll show you to him and say you're a famous actress. Naturally, I won't nod to you and you won't look as though you know me: we're not acquainted with each other, it's simply that I've seen you a great many times on the stage. Walk to the end of the square and then if you like come back the same way. Dress challengingly, it'll make an impression on him. I'm depending on you, I know what taste you have. You should resemble a bird of prey. Then I'll start telling him all sorts of things about you."

"Very well, I agree. In spite of everything you are a friend," said Edda. He looked at her and thought that she, too, even Edda, had some good qualities. Like everyone, like myself, even like the out-and-out scoundrels. And she's so stupid she has a right to all the extenuating circumstances available. And actually she is no worse than I. I really must arrange a peaceful haven for her, too. Everyone needs a peaceful haven.

"But don't forget for a second that we don't know each other. And mind you don't smile at me. You can even encompass us with a disdainful look; that's your crowning number."

"I'll encompass you with a disdainful look," said Edda, ready for anything.

18

A DAY later Colonel Number One arrived in Venice.

This trip was on business too, but he was also entitled to a leave. A number of people who were familiar with his latest enterprise were enthusiastic and had no doubt that in Moscow the documents were considered authentic; in a year or two they would, of course, catch on, but during this time how many useless measures would they not take, how many millions would they not spend for nothing? An old general clapped him on the shoulder and called him the "Shakespeare of Misinformation." The colonel modestly deprecated his achievement; nevertheless, though complacency was completely foreign to him, he did feel somewhat as Shakespeare might have after finishing *Macbeth*. In any case, he felt very sure that he had never done anything better than this in his work and never would. Now he could retire with honor.

En route he thought about Schell again, this time quite

benevolently: Schell had done him an enormous service. Of course he has some shortcomings: a poseur, drinks a lot, and has visibly weakened a little. The fraternity dislikes him, which is in the nature of things. Many of the colonel's secret agents kept reporting on each other, or else imperceptibly tried to undermine his faith in other agents. There were actually no reasons for this: he had enough work and money for all of them. The colonel was surprised at nothing, and didn't assign much importance to such accusations, all the more so since they canceled each other, but he stored it all away in his memory anyhow. Schell had never said anything about any of his colleagues in particular, though he had an ironical attitude toward agents in general. He's damned conceited; it doesn't go with his trade. You can make a long-term agreement with him, a man like that always comes in handy. I won't send him to Russia; I don't think he would have gone anyhow, thought the colonel, who generally had a negative attitude toward dropping spies by parachute, as essentially unfruitful schemes. I won't ask him to return the advance. In the first place, he wouldn't give it back; second, it's not his fault, and the main thing is that he deserves a reward for that nitwitted girl. Two thousand dollars was not too large a sum. In the colonel's department money was spent openhandedly, sometimes being thrown out with very small hope of any useful return.

The colonel knew that Edda was in Venice, too. He didn't want to meet her; he considered it inadmissible for him to meet Jim's mistresses. He could chat with Jim, sometimes sternly, sometimes with affectionate friendliness, but there was a limit to familiarity which it was improper to overstep. But the colonel would have liked to see Edda; he believed in his impressions of people, though he knew he had made mistakes more than once. "She's extremely stupid," Schell had told him at their last conversation. "I wouldn't tell this to any other employer, but I'm telling you. You're perfectly well aware that there are a great many idiots among woman spies." "We don't

230

have any complete idiots," the colonel had objected indecisively. "You do, you do," said Schell with assurance. "Moreover, she's not a *complete* idiot."

But it was necessary to have another very serious talk with Jim. He had coped brilliantly with the assignment, but he had written a rather strange letter, discontented, almost acid—he had never written his uncle that way. It seemed Jim no longer wanted to remain in the army. Disillusioned, I suppose. Already! Then I won't hold him back. Perhaps it was wrong for me to give him such an assignment. What can I do with him? Send him back to Public Information? No, that really is the most futile job. He won't find anything by himself; he's too proud, too light-minded, one of his superiors may speak to him in not quite the right tone and he'll walk out at once. It would be best if he went home and had a plain job in the army. But alas, it's clear that he's getting to be more and more a member of the intelligentsia. Anything can be expected of him. What else is he going to present me with in Venice? And why did he go there with this little charmer? Is it possible she wants to stay and work for me?

For the time being Jim couldn't be officially rewarded, although his work had been appreciated. The colonel decided to give him a present. A new Lincoln would cost too much. Jim might be able to buy a secondhand one in good condition for a thousand dollars. This was a considerable sum for the colonel, but he regarded all presents to his nephew as tax-exempt advances against his inheritance.

The colonel had been in Venice several times—always with the same joy as in Paris. Jim had once told him that among the connoisseurs of art a *renouveau* of Venice, only recently considered banal, was beginning. That was the word he had used: *renouveau*. At first the colonel had not even understood; the very word reeked of the intelligentsia. Here, too, he always stopped at the same hotel—a good one, not too expensive. His nephew was to visit him in the evening, but he had scarcely any doubt he would see him that same day: in Venice you couldn't help running into people.

Going out into St. Mark's Square, the colonel had the feeling that, *renouveau* or not, the city was unique, the loveliest in the world. Everything is as it was: the enchanted cathedral, the enchanted palace, the enchanted square! What luck that those two wonders—Paris and Venice—were not destroyed in the war! And Florian's was still the same, also almost timeless, the delight of a dozen generations. The orchestra on the square, as it had forty years before, played *Traviata*. The public itself might have been a trifle less elegant than before World War I, but the women were just as beautiful, or seemed so, as though ugly women would have been ashamed to spoil all this beauty. The colonel stopped in front of the display windows, although he had no intention of buying anything. A Communist poster was pasted on the walls: *"Compagni! Il Partito Communista vi invita ... "* he read with a sigh. When he got to the Piazzetta he feasted his eyes from there, too, on the palace, the cathedral, the library. Some policemen in triangular caps sauntered toward him. He looked at them benevolently. But physically they're no match for our own, he thought.

The colonel went back, sat on the terrace at Florian's, ordered something with a melodious name, and bought a newspaper from a little boy running by but didn't open it. Reading, after all, on St. Mark's Square! He was not actually thinking about anything—or, rather, he thought he would gladly live another sixty years considering that the slight ailments he had didn't have terrifying names and, most important, gave him no pain. His friends in America told him that at his age a man should go for a checkup at least once a year, as you went to the dentist. He agreed with them completely; he had long since learned that the best thing was to agree at once with people who gave you such advice: it disarmed them. But to himself he thought that, if a healthy man of his age went to a physician for a checkup, after a dozen examinations and analyses he would be found to have a dozen illnesses; it would be

232

impossible to cure them in any case and his state of mind would be ruined. He very rarely visited the dentist, either. All his teeth were there, sound, with hardly more than three or four fillings, and white, in spite of his smoking two packs of cigarettes a day and agreeing immediately with friends who spoke of the evils of chain smoking.

Florian's was wonderful, but he had a dual sensation, on the one hand that he could go on sitting there endlessly, but on the other that there was a special vigor and joy of life brought about by the miracle of Venice—you had to do something; even in your seventh decade life was not over with. The compromise was that after sitting there for half an hour he decided to telephone Schell. He got up and crossed the square. The orchestra was now playing "Flight of the Valkyries." I knew it, thought the colonel, there he is!

He had seen his nephew a few steps away. A happy smile flashed through the eyes of both of them, but neither one gave a sign that they knew each other. Jim was sitting on the terrace of the café with Edda. The colonel looked at her with the glance of a retired connoisseur. Very beautiful. I hope my playboy doesn't involve himself seriously, but he's well under control. *Bon chien chasse de race,* he thought. As he said this to himself he sat down "unscrupulously" two steps away from them so that he could listen to their conversation. "Yes, I'm sitting here and am going to go on sitting here, and there's nothing you can do about it," his smile seemed to say. "Sit there just as long as you please, you're not disturbing us; in any case I'm sitting here with a beautiful woman and you, Uncle, are alone, and old to boot," should have been Jim's reply. But it wasn't; his nephew looked gloomy. "Oh, what a fool, what a fool! What else d'you want? You've had some pleasure, nothing's happened to this damned fool of a girl, and now you've come to Venice at government expense. Or is the money gone?" asked his uncle's look. The Valkyries flew off with shrieks and squeals. "*Haia-ta-ha!*" the colonel's thoughts gayly accompanied the music. "*Haia-ta-ha!* Except there's nothing good about it," was

233

now the clear answer from Jim's face. They had once listened to Wagner together, the nephew in bliss, the uncle not without enjoyment. Edda said contemptuously that this music was *vieux jeu* and that only fools could enjoy Wagner, and old ones at that. "Is that so? Then tell her to go to hell right away. *Haia-ta-ha!*" advised the colonel. "*Haia-ta-ha,* but I have practically no money," was the explanation he gave himself of his nephew's look. "Oh, you fool, you fool, all gone already! Never mind, I'll give you some. . . . Well, that's that. I'll leave. But make sure you see me this evening. . . ." Without waiting for the waiter the colonel reluctantly got up. I won't go back to Florian's, there's a café on the Piazzetta, too, that's where I'll phone Schell from; he may be home. Once again the colonel scrutinized Edda from head to foot in an unobtrusively thoroughgoing way and walked on at his vigorous military pace.

19

SCHELL was at home; he invited the colonel to meet him at Quadri's at half-past six. He had wanted to invite him to dinner, but changed his mind: he usually dined with Natasha in a small restaurant which wasn't bad—not on St. Mark's Square and not on the Grand Canal. Natasha thought this restaurant very picturesque; in reality she could not get accustomed to their spending some seven or eight thousand lire on dinner in the hotel.

"Of course you know where Quadri's is?"

"I'm an old Venetian," replied the colonel with a smile. Anyone else would have made the meeting place somewhere on the top of the Campanile, he thought, going out of the telephone booth; they all adore conspiracy. He can't be being shadowed, I haven't noticed anyone after me either. I think he's glad to meet me. Perhaps he has far fewer offers of work than he used to, and feels like an aging woman at a charity bazaar who no longer attracts any customers.

That morning Edda was shown to Ramón. In the most unlikely costume she walked past Florian's very well, tossed them a haughty glance. Couldn't be better, thought Schell. He nudged the billionaire.

"Don't you know her?" he asked, when Edda had walked off. "That's the famous actress; you've probably seen her on the screen."

"I never have. Who is she?" asked Ramón, very much interested in such a beauty. Schell told him Edda's real name, or the one which she gave as her real name. There was no risk: Ramón didn't know anyone or anything.

"Have you invited her to my festival?"

"Not yet, but I can. A very good idea," said Schell. I believe he's taken the bait, he thought with satisfaction.

"Get hold of her today," said Ramón, but corrected himself, knowing that Schell disliked peremptoriness. "Please ask my secretary to find her. She's not at our hotel. I haven't seen her there, or else I would already have noticed her."

During the day Schell reported to Ramón that he hadn't succeeded in finding Edda, but had learned her Berlin address and would send the invitation there.

"What d'you mean, you haven't succeeded!" asked Ramón indignantly. "I want to see her!"

"You can't have every wish," answered Schell with the offended look of a man appealing an unfair decision. "She was probably here just for a few hours en route. But if you want to get acquainted with her so much she can be offered a part in the show. I understand you, she's very beautiful, just in your Rubens taste. . . . Listen," he said, striking his forehead (it came out quite well), "what if you offered her the role of the dogaressa! There's something Venetian about her looks."

"That's just what I had in mind."

236

"It'll cost quite a lot. I don't think she'd do it for less than three thousand dollars."

"Offer her five thousand; just make sure she's here!"

This time Schell didn't think it necessary to be offended. He had already displayed his independence, and it would be too risky to annoy Ramón too often. And the main thing was that the sum was a pleasant surprise. He didn't even consider taking a commission on it. But with pay like that it would be easy to free himself of Edda forever.

"It will be done," he said conciliatingly.

". . . So Maikov didn't finish by suicide?" asked Schell.

The colonel waved his hand. "I don't know. All I know is that he's dead. Why do you think so?"

"Simply an idea."

"It's very possible."

"But perhaps it was cancer of the prostate?"

"Why cancer of the prostate?"

"Or he simply suffocated in the Soviet atmosphere." Schell had been about to mention the fishes that suffocate in the Dead Sea, but remembered that he had already said that.

"But how can you have any ideas about it at all?"

"The *ololiukvi* helped."

The colonel looked at him in surprise. "I don't understand. That's that drug of yours, isn't it? The soporific?"

"Oh no, it's not a soporific. There's very little in common between sleep and delirium. And even the delirium that comes from this drug is peculiar. In the beginning it is almost reasonable and logical, everything is often illuminated in a new way, everything is clear, you can even penetrate into other people's minds. Then the swerves begin, which also come and go, progressively, with outbursts of irrationality. It usually ends up in complete nonsense, especially when you *want* to come to your senses. . . . You've probably never had such a feeling, that now you're going to see something others can't see!"

"Never," answered the colonel dryly. "I don't take such

237

drugs. . . . I wanted to discuss our future work together. First of all, let me thank you sincerely for that woman."

"Did she prove useful?"

"More or less."

"Her career is settled," Schell said cheerfully, and told him about the Festival of Beauty.

"If you were going to spend some time here I would send you an invitation. You've probably brought along a dress suit or a dinner jacket? I think you can go to see the Queen of England now in a flannel jacket, but not us. I'm going to go in costume, I'm representing one of the doge's bodyguards."

"One of the doge's bodyguards," repeated the colonel, listening attentively, as always, but with growing surprise. "Excuse me, but are you sure you're all right?"

"Quite sure. A masquerade is a very agreeable diversion. You would also see Edda there."

"She's of no use to me any more. But I'm soon going to have something for you to do."

"Thank you, but I can hardly be of any use to you, either," said Schell, and took out a checkbook, savoring the effect in advance. "Since our affair never came to anything, allow me to return your two thousand dollars. I received them in Swiss francs and so I'm returning them to you in Swiss francs: eight thousand five hundred and forty francs, isn't it?" he asked carelessly.

"Please; there's no hurry about it. You're not in the least to blame for the thing's falling through because of Maikov's death."

"Nor are you."

· "But I'm not refusing to do any work with you in future. Is it that *you* are refusing to? Or are you dissatisfied with us?"

"Not in the least. It's simply that I'm not in the habit of accepting money for nothing. I told you, if you recall, that I might be leaving intelligence work. At that time I didn't tell you everything. You see, I've got married," said Schell, although he had almost decided not to say this.

238

"Married?"

"Yes, I got married."

The colonel suddenly burst out laughing. That happened very rarely. "I congratulate you! I sincerely congratulate you. I wish you luck."

"Thank you. And what were you laughing about, if I may ask?"

"You must excuse me.... You see, I still haven't been able to grasp the sort of man you are.... After all, you also play the cello! ... Now it's more understandable. Perhaps you went into intelligence in order to have an extraordinary life, and now your life is becoming ordinary? If you've 'repented,' then perhaps the principle of the cello has, so to speak, repented in you."

"It's very possible," replied Schell coldly.

"Permit me to drink to your good fortune with this greenish-yellowish wine, for some reason called white."

They drank another glass apiece. Schell looked at his watch.

"Are you in a hurry?"

"I haven't much time.... You evidently used to consider me an adventurer by nature?"

"Not in a bad sense. But after all, you really have had more than a few adventures. If you will allow me to speak frankly, I thought that the only things in life that interested you were adventure, women, and money."

"But that's a great deal, after all. Nevertheless, it's possible to go through a large number of adventures without being an adventurer. People are seldom adventurers by nature, they are made so by circumstances. In the Soviet Union, for instance, only officials can be adventurers.... In former times I would have chosen a military career."

"But weren't you a pilot during the Spanish Civil War? I think on the side of the Loyalists."

"Quite so. They paid huge salaries to foreign pilots."

"Why wouldn't it have been better for you to serve in the

Russian Army? But I've forgotten you're not Russian but Argentinian."

"I am not Russian either by passport or by blood. But I had very serious reasons for not working for the Soviet government. Aside from that, when I was young the Soviet Army was still very weak, and I don't like the weak. . . . In the old days there was still one career for people who liked adventure, a swift career that demanded no merits or gifts from a man—revolution. But in our days that's been monopolized by the Communists and I hate them. Now there's nothing for me to do."

"But you *have* an interesting profession."

"You consider it interesting? Well, it's true that you are, so to speak, a poet in it. It's odd; it's hard not to become a cynic and misanthrope in espionage, but you're one only to a degree, to a very slight degree."

"Actually I'm not a cynic or misanthrope at all."

"Another surprising thing is that you're not a chatterbox. However strange it may seem, we have an enormous multitude of chatterboxes."

"That, unfortunately, is true," said the colonel. You, above all, he thought. "Well, well! I hope that in any case you're not going back to work for our opponents?"

"You can be absolutely assured of that. I think one of the English kings tried to blackmail Pope Alexander by threatening to turn Mohammedan. I'll not go over to the Bolshevik faith. If there is anything genuine in me, it's my hatred for that. . . . I still don't know what I shall do. Now the most dangerous profession is being a test pilot for new planes."

Oh, what endless posing! thought the colonel with annoyance, both bravery and quotations. "With the years the stronger passions disappear, or so to speak pass into a colloidal state," he said, mockery slipping into his tone.

"Quite right. I'm not so old as you, but I'm not young either, and I've gotten tired of risking my life. And as far as anything to do with politics is concerned, I'll steer completely clear of it. The present world situation reminds me of that senseless chaos they used to have in the old comic films when everyone was running off somewhere, pushing someone and upsetting something. The public laughs, though there's nothing the least bit funny about it. That's how the world is now."

"I don't see that. But there really is very little to laugh about. . . . So you're retiring? Actually marriage is no reason for retirement."

"I've married a girl who has no relatives, and I can't leave her for long periods. Of course you imagine she's rich. She hasn't a penny."

"But if you're not rich, all the more reason why you shouldn't leave the service and return me an advance. I thought you were fond of our trade, in spite of everything."

"I can't bear it."

"Yes, you told me that. But everybody speaks that way. Ask any famous writer, journalist, or political figure. They'll tell you that they curse the day and the hour they chose their occupation."

"Not all of them. Louis XIV said, *'Mon délicieux métier de Roy.'* . . . You've served your country, but I've served those who paid the most."

"You say things like that too often for them to be true, altogether true. . . . I've known disinterested people even in intelligence."

"You must have been lucky, I've never known people like that in any profession. In any case I myself am far from disinterested. I like what money can give: a 'beautiful life,' as they say sometimes with irony. To my mind you should have spent billions on purchasing government people in the hostile states, that would have been far from the most unproductive of your expenditures."

"It would be easy to fight in that way as well: if you've bought up the enemy commander, victory is assured, wouldn't that be so? But I can't recall any such instances in military history,"

241

answered the colonel. "You're not a man I can understand very well."

"There's nothing hard to understand about me. I'm a man of no birth or family, an eternal and ubiquitous *sale étranger*. And a supreme egotist on top of that, 'surrounded by himself on all sides,' as Turgeniev said. Or, more exactly, I *was* that. And after all the choice is limited for almost all of us. When a man is young, his life is most often poisoned by poverty. When he's old, there's no more pleasure left even in money. And my tastes have changed. As a child I dreamed of becoming a salesman in a sweetshop, then I wanted to be a chauffeur, and still later a soldier. Now I dream of a quiet, tranquil life."

"But can it really be that you don't want to return to our trade? The French say, *Qui a bu boira*."

"No, I'm not going to backslide. I'm like a heavyweight boxer who's reached retirement age."

"But probably he dreams of the ring at night until he dies."

"Possibly, but they don't go back to it."

"But what are you thinking of taking up?"

"Idleness. It's the best occupation."

"Not a bad one," said the colonel uncertainly, recalling his own house in Connecticut. "Where are you thinking of going now with your wife?"

"We're going to settle somewhere in Italy," answered Schell. He didn't feel like saying anything about buying the villa.

"On the sea near here there are wonderful little corners, and not expensive."

"Perhaps here at that. Although I don't like the sea. In spite of my love of adventure I've never been able to finish reading a single novel of Conrad's. I'll read books, memoirs, biographies, that's my favorite reading. I still have a little curiosity left, in spite of everything. When I was a boy I very nearly wept that I hadn't seen and never would see Napoleon," he said, laughing. "So take the money."

"Thank you," said the colonel, glancing fleetingly at the check. I just hope it won't bounce, he thought. "I'm very sorry

242

indeed. Let me add that in similar circumstances not everyone would return an advance. I appreciate it very much."

They fell silent, looking at each other curiously. The colonel's glance once again paused at Schell's hands: they *are* a killer's hands, he thought. Probably I'll never see him again in my life, Schell thought, with unexpected regret. And our conversation is like those that so often bring detective stories to an end: the astute detective, after capturing the criminal, tells his friend "over a bottle of wine" how he found out everything. Otherwise, the reader wouldn't understand. But if you told it earlier the whole effect would be lost.

"I don't know whether it will work, but I should like to live the rest of my life simply as a *rentier*. It's probably a pleasant life. The French bourgeois are intelligent people."

"You're going to do nothing until the end of your life?"

"But why not? Have I got so much left? A month of my life has to be counted as a year. I shall have time to prepare myself. To my mind, one needn't die overhastily; one should think about death properly."

"A matter of taste. And easy to say at forty," said the colonel discontentedly, and drank his wine. Schell looked at his watch again.

"I'm afraid I must leave you now; my wife is waiting for me."

"Then I won't venture to keep you. Once again I congratulate you. . . . But if you change your mind, we shall always be at your service," said the colonel, shaking him firmly by the hand, this time without any squeamishness. One of the most interesting specimens in my collection, a cello player! he thought. I remember Jim's quoting someone who said about someone, "He was an original, even though he tried to be one."

20

"WAIT a bit, I'll treat you to some champagne," said the colonel. If even champagne doesn't calm Jim down it's obvious that things are really in a bad way, he thought. His Dostoevski mood, absolutely catastrophic. Jim went on with his monologue.

"... Fundamentally, your work isn't even of much use. During wartime the greatest armada in history crossed the Atlantic Ocean and made a landing, and Hitler knew nothing about it. In 1939 France and England didn't have the slightest notion of Germany's military power. In 1941 Germany didn't have the slightest comprehension of Russia's power, while Stalin didn't know that the Germans were preparing to attack him. Meanwhile, all of them had spent hundreds of millions on espionage! That's how it is now, too. What can your agents on the other side of the Iron Curtain tell you? Their reports are

244

either true and have no significance, or else they are significant but false. . . ."

"Don't talk about something you don't understand," the colonel interrupted him angrily. "The most important thing now is to understand, to understand with certainty, what is going on over there. And that's why the activity I'm engaged in, though it sounds immodest, is the most useful in the world now."

"You have gotten for Washington, of course, a quantity of reports about the Soviet atom bombs. But not so long ago President Truman said he didn't know whether Russia had atom bombs or not. Now you've succeeded in one project, you've sent a piece of important misinformation where it was necessary, and you're happy. But ten other projects don't succeed, and the money of us taxpayers is simply thrown out for nothing. And even those things that come off are made up for immediately by *their* projects, so that almost everything cancels out. That's the least of it; they will always have the bulge on you since they stop at nothing, while you have moral limits you don't overstep. Everything done by their intelligence service is most likely an out-and-out crime, which doesn't upset them in the slightest. And of everything done by our own intelligence about a fourth only, let's say, is criminal, and there are things which you don't do at all and have no intention of doing. That is to say, a priori all the advantages are on their side. . . . You're getting angry, Uncle; that's a bad sign. And for that matter is the 'truth' which your agents are supposed to be getting for you necessary? Secrecy would amount to a certain, of course very flimsy, guarantee against war. Fear of the unknown would be the restraining factor."

"Criminals also carry on a struggle against the police and also, in contrast to them, stop at nothing; nevertheless, the work of the police is very useful and generally successful. With the help of their agents the Bolsheviks got hold of some reports that were of great value to them about our atomic arms. We would be absolute fools if we didn't do the same

245

thing they're doing. That would simply be a crime against the country. Just suggest to the Kremlin that *it* cut down on its espionage."

"I know that that's a powerful, in fact irrefutable, conclusion," said Jim sadly. "Suggesting anything the least bit decent to the Bolsheviks would be useless if only because they would make promises and not keep them anyhow. But you, too, can scarcely sincerely desire an agreement here; if they were to arrive at an agreement you would have absolutely nothing to do and your entire life would prove to have been a mistake."

"Please don't get upset about that."

"The usefulness of your work is very small and the harm it does is great. If a third war were to begin some time it would most likely spring out of some incident or other contrived by the intelligence. The fate of the world is dependent on some five or six colonels in the world! Perhaps one of them may inform his government that its opponent is very weak, and his government will start an offensive war. Or he may inform it that the opponent will soon become too powerful, and his government will begin a preventive war. As far as I'm concerned espionage is now the symbol of the evil in the world, and it crystallizes this whole god-damned cold war!" said Jim, and calmed down. He had unburdened his heart.

"Thank you. I've been occupied with this business all my life, which is what, by the way, has enabled me to give you an education."

"I'm not forgetting that, Uncle," answered Jim, embarrassed. He looked around at his uncle's modest room, and it made him ashamed that his uncle, who had given him money so often, was living in a cheaper hotel than he was. But that's how it must be: older people knew what real life was like before the first war, while our own unfortunate generation hasn't much of anything good, he thought, suddenly overwhelmed with self-pity. "My dear uncle, I think you've forgotten about the champagne."

246

"Quite so! I'll order it at once. But what nonsense you talk. It's enough to choke a mule!"

"That's the only thing you can say. What a proud look and tone intelligence officers have, as though they were dealing with something extraordinarily important and useful!"

"You're simply making things up! I don't look proud, act proud, and never have!"

"I'm not speaking about you personally, Uncle. You know perfectly well how attached I am to you and what I think of you. You're a most remarkable man and I owe you everything. But—please don't get angry with me—for the first time in your life you gave me some bad advice. I did something vile."

"Simply say that you've fallen in love with that scatterbrain!"

"And you still think you can see through people! Not only did I not fall in love with her, I find her repellent. I understood that in the real sense when I came here from Paris, I understood both her and myself. Travel sharpens feelings, a man in a railway car or on a steamer is not exactly the same as he always is, he understands everything more clearly. And then I found myself repellent."

"But what have you done? What misfortune has there been? She just took to her heels and she's no longer in any danger. Judging by what you told me about her, she's a depraved tart. They were trying to do us great harm. We broke it up, thank God, and turned their own weapon against them; we did them some damage, I hope more than a little. You played your role excellently. What is wrong? What do you expect of me?"

"If you had a personal enemy, would you give me an assignment to get acquainted with some woman of *his* in order to do him harm?"

"There's not the slightest similarity. States are constantly doing what individuals don't have the right to. It's always been that way and always will. You can read about it in the Old Testament. Joshua also sent out spies into the Promised Land in advance of the expedition: 'Joshua the son of Nun sent out two men to spy secretly, saying, Go view the land,

and they went, and came into an harlot's house, named Rahab, and lodged there.' I won't quote any more, it's in the Book of Joshua."

"Probably every intelligence agent remembers and repeats this one quotation from the Bible."

"Well, all right, you can have the last word, I have nothing against it.... I can tell you that in my youth, when I began my career, I had doubts, too, though they were much weaker. I swiftly overcame them in myself. You don't wish to overcome them—that's your affair. I didn't think you were so sentimental. Well, I see you're not suitable for my department. Consequently ..."

"Whether I'm suitable or not, I don't want to work in it. I repeat, your department is becoming an enormous social problem, or rather, more exactly, an enormous political danger! But I know very well I can't suggest any way out. For an individual perhaps there may be, but it's also a bad one: it consists in avoiding everything evil that's going on in the world."

"A fine way out for a government! And that's enough of all this!"

"You did with me as you pleased, now you say 'enough of all this.' I've lost my self-respect. I told myself that if they arrested her I would commit suicide," said Jim, although actually this had just come into his head.

"But you've gone completely out of your mind! That's what comes of being steeped in Dostoevski!"

"Dostoevski has nothing to do with it."

"No one's holding you back by force. *Bon voyage* and be happy. You can go back to your former job any day you like. You probably haven't forgotten all those names?"

"Alidius Warmoldus Lambertus Tjarda Van Starkenborgh Stachouwer?" asked Jim, laughing. "No, I haven't forgotten. But I'm not going back there."

"Do whatever you like. It would be best if you went back to the regular army. Two of your ancestors were soldiers. Cavalry officers," added the colonel with a sigh. "I won't put any

248

obstacles in the way, I'll even help you. . . . What is the problem now? How to separate from her, from Rahab? I know she's leaving for Berlin tomorrow."

"How do you know that?"

"As you see, the intelligence knows something after all."

"You've spoken with her, Uncle!"

"No. But of course I'm having her followed," the colonel added, satisfied with the impression he was making on his nephew.

"By the way, you might congratulate me: I didn't indicate by even so much as a look that I knew you at the café, did I? I do so like being congratulated! You probably do, too. But did you like Edda?"

"I went into a frenzy when I first clapped eyes on her. And of course I adore your traveling about with her."

"In the first place, don't forget that I took up with her on your instructions, and secondly, you can't deny she's beautiful. At some time you must have known something about women. They say you had a great success with them in your youth," said Jim.

"That's no concern of yours."

"So you already know about this idiotic festival?"

"As you see, I do."

"A fine spectacle the West is confronting the Communists with!"

"Don't tell me you're becoming a fellow traveler!"

"You know perfectly well I detest the Communists, the fellow travelers even more so. But that's just why I'm infuriated. It's just such festivals and just such characters as that Filipino that are made to order for Bolshevik propaganda!"

"There I agree with you. It's amusing that he's arranging this as propaganda against the Bolsheviks! The humor is heightened by the fact that the chief part in the show is going to be played by a Soviet agent. . . . Well, she's leaving for Berlin. I don't advise you to go with her, very much the contrary. Actually, she probably won't even ask you to. In addi-

249

tion you say you find her repellent. So much the better. Is the question simply one of money? To purge your conscience, please give her some."

"I have none."

"You should have said so! Well, here, I want to make you a present of a thousand dollars. You've been longing for a good car. According to your rank and age a Ford or a Chevrolet is entirely adequate for you. In three years you will have matured enough for a Buick. I hope you're not aspiring to a Cadillac or a Packard? But I think that with a thousand dollars in cash you might be able to get a Packard, too, by paying something down, if your impudence is sufficient. The rest, of course, you can pay off from your own salary. . . . But I don't even have anything against your giving part of the money to your charming mistress. You can even give it all to her, if you're a complete jackass."

"I'm terribly grateful to you," said Jim, embarrassed. "A present, and such a big one! For what?"

"For no reason. You absolutely don't deserve it. . . . Probably even without this you've spent a great deal on her?"

"Yes, of course, but . . ."

"In my opinion you don't have to give her any more. She's going to get a good deal of money from the Filipino."

"Do you know that, too?"

"I know all."

"Then you're an astounding exception in the profession! So you think I needn't give her any more?"

"I'm not going to decide that complicated conflict in your complicated soul—Rahab or a Packard."

"You're a cruel man, Uncle. You know I yearn for a Packard."

"Struggle against this temptation. Make this sweet, good-hearted, lovely woman happy."

"I'm going to give her a present anyhow."

"How much, if I may make so bold as to ask?"

"What d'you think? Five hundred?"

"No, that's too little," said the colonel, enjoying himself. "Five hundred is too little for such a lovely woman." He laughed. "Here's what we'll do. I'll give you eight hundred dollars after she leaves. But take two hundred now and do what you like with it. And stop sulking. You had more than a good time with her, she really is very pretty. Is she a terrific idiot or only medium?"

"Extraordinary! Disarming!" said Jim, reviving. His uncle was always able to calm him.

"With anyone else things wouldn't have gone off so smoothly. And has she unstrung your nervous system?"

"Yes. And her own still more. I don't know what came over her! She's completely safe here, but ever since yesterday she keeps looking around her every minute and turning pale at the sight of every passer-by. Just imagine, she looks under the bed, to see whether there isn't an assassin there!"

"And of course you have pangs of conscience for having destroyed the soul of this divine creature! No, you'll have to give her the whole thousand dollars."

"I'll give her your two hundred," replied Jim. The habitual teasing of his uncle evoked his habitual reaction, and he passed over to the offensive. "Then we'll be able to make sure that you gave a Soviet agent a present."

"You are a fool," said the colonel, taking out his wallet.

21

NATASHA read a German newspaper every day; she couldn't find any *émigré* Russian ones in Venice. She ignored the economic articles, serials, sports section, and parliamentary debates, and read with interest about books, the theater, movie stars, and now, for the first time in her life, even about fashion; with horror she glanced at the reports of the various murders, about women found strangled in bathtubs and cellars; out of a feeling of duty she followed the major political news—that printed on the first page with big headlines. If only there's no war! Otherwise, everything is exactly the same: Dulles said, Eden said, Molotov said, and they never say anything the least bit interesting. How can they stand it? . . .

It was, however, essential to read about Dulles, Eden, and Molotov; Schell sometimes spoke of them, invariably adding, "Rot and blast 'em." She would very much have liked him to drop this remark, though he made it now without malice, simply by force of habit. He was much more cheerful here than in Berlin. He hardly ever looked at women, although there were a number of beauties at the hotel.

It was annoying that he still spent so much time with the Filipino. There was, to be sure, an explanation, but it was one that didn't satisfy her particularly. All right, so he bought something from him, did him a favor or two; well, let him just thank him with a little advice and work with him two or three days. But isn't it altogether too much this way? Once she even mentioned this to him cautiously (she kept daring more and more every day, to her own joy).

"But it's extremely entertaining, this Festival of Beauty of his. And our house is still being fixed up and painted. By the way, Ramón asked me today whether you wouldn't like a part in the procession?"

"Me! In the procession?" cried out Natasha, with such horror that Schell burst out laughing.

"I told him beforehand you wouldn't agree."

"I don't even understand how he could suggest it seriously. I should look just fine as some Venetian noblewoman or other. After the underground factory!"

"You would be better than any of them. And once and for all stop thinking about that underground factory. . . . But you're right, there would be no point to it," said Schell. Actually the Filipino had asked him again whether Natasha didn't wish to participate in the festival, and even added: "Her conditions are mine." All Schell could think of was Natasha and Edda appearing in the same procession.

When Schell was not at home, Natasha worked at her dissertation or read Turgeniev. She went to the Lido almost every day and somehow or other made herself understood to the painters working on their house. They liked her very much; all ordinary people liked Natasha and felt that she was almost as "simple" as they. The work was going well and rapidly. The walls in two rooms had already been painted, and it would have been possible to arrange the furniture. One of these rooms

253

was supposed to be Natasha's bedroom. Schell called the other the boudoir. She decided to turn it into a nursery. She passionately wanted to have a son and a daughter.

Schell reluctantly consented to have her buy the furniture. He bought a book in German about the various periods. Natasha read everything attentively, learned their distinguishing points, and bought a bed, two plush easy chairs, two similar ordinary chairs, a large mirrored cupboard, curtains, carpets, lamps, a night table—she had no idea what the period was but it was all very cheap. The furniture was brought in the morning; the painters arranged it, though this wasn't part of their work; she gave them a bottle of wine, for which they thanked her and asked her to drink with them; they drank straight from the mouth of the bottle, since there were no glasses, giving her the bottle first.

During the day, at her request, Schell came over. He said nothing about what she had bought. Natasha saw that he was not very pleased: he's angry at my spending so little of his money!

"For the time being don't buy any more. We can bring down my own furniture quickly enough. Immediately after the festival we'll go to Berlin and get it. I'll buy the chandeliers myself. That metal pole with the little lamp wasn't even worth hanging from the ceiling," said Schell, and seeing that she was hurt, he added, "But buy the linen, and for heaven's sake don't skimp on money. These things are to last a lifetime." The villa looks petty bourgeois already, he thought with irritation.

"But what's wrong with the lamp? Very well, you buy it, although it'll cost you twice as much. And can the books be brought down here now?"

"Why not? But of course don't carry them yourself, have the hotel send them by boat."

They had accumulated a few dozen books. Schell bought some practically every day. Natasha was astonished at how quickly he read. There were a good many expensive editions

254

of the history of Venice, which had been bought at Ramón's expense.

Natasha put the books temporarily in the linen cupboard, covering the shelves with white paper. She painstakingly wiped off every book with a cloth. A sheet of paper fell out of a heavy lexicon. It had some figures in Schell's handwriting: "320.28 . . . 56.25." For some reason the slip gave her an unpleasant sensation. Money? Bills? They seem to be uneven figures, she thought uneasily.

In the evening, when they got back to the hotel, she handed Schell the slip of paper. He glanced at it and, to her surprise, blushed, something which he never did. I forgot to destroy it! I've lapsed right back into childhood, he thought. I left the profession just in time!

"It fell out of the dictionary. Did you need it? Probably something about some—*stocks?*" she pronounced the unfamiliar word carefully.

"Yes, I suppose so. I jotted down the quotations from the newspapers." And did I have to say "I suppose so"?

22

EDDA was nearly always discontented with everything—both by character and by her own principle: anyone who was satisfied with everything was given nothing. But on the way from Venice to Berlin she emerged from her usual state. Like Schell, she had never been so well taken care of.

In spite of the danger that, in his words, was threatening them, Schell took her to the station: "For you I'm ready to risk being shadowed." They said good-by—as he said, tentatively—while still in her hotel, and rather nicely at that, even though it had been in their usual manner: with "boor," and with "sweetie pie." Edda was no longer in love with Schell (if she ever had been), but she was afraid of him and at heart appreciated him. He's gotten me so much money! He hardly ever lies about money. They'll pay up!

She had a single first-class compartment. He was sitting there with her, repeating his instructions and interrogating her like a schoolteacher; that was why he had come to the station: Edda never understood anything the first time. Finally, not long before the train left (she was already getting alarmed), he gave her a check on a bank in Berlin.

"Three thousand dollars," said Schell, having prepared an effect here, too.

"Three!"

"Three. You're going to be the dogaressa."

"Dogaressa!?"

"Yes. The doge's lady. Ramón is the doge. I hope you understand to whom you're indebted until the end of your life for this unheard-of success? The greatest actresses in the world have been fighting for this part. You might say they were groveling at his feet. I told him that you are a movie star, the new Greta Garbo! And I talked him into giving you five thousand dollars! To you! And for what?"

"Nevertheless, Greta Garbo wouldn't have become a dogaressa for only five thousand dollars."

"Fool. Who d'you think you are? I won't say what you are. As it is, you're being given an advance of two thousand five hundred. And here in this envelope is a color sketch of the costume of the dogaressa. I'll arrange for you to have unlimited credit for it."

"What does unlimited credit mean? I adore precision."

"That means, my beloved, that you may buy the most expensive materials, silk, velvet, and brocade, without being bothered by prices. Keep an account, which, of course, you'll pad. I have nothing against that, but don't fly off the handle, you have to have a conscience: not more than 10 per cent."

Edda took the drawing out of the envelope. "Oh, what bliss! I'll be stunning!"

"You're stunning in any costume. Even in Eve's. Now listen, my little blossom, you must come back two days before the show: neither earlier nor later."

"Why such precision? I'll come back whenever I feel like it!" said Edda, who felt far more reassured now that she had the check. Schell took her by the hand, squeezed it so that she cried out with pain, and took the check away.

"Fool! B-boor! You very nearly broke my fingers! I was joking, and you . . ."

"I was also joking. You'll come back two days before, d'you hear? By the way, remember, this is an advance. If you're late or arrive earlier, then I give you my word, you won't get a single penny more! And we'll find another _____," he said, using a coarse word rather unlike the "new" Schell. But Edda liked words like that. "Now here's the check, take it, and don't forget."

"Please don't frighten me so! Oh, very well, very well, I'll come back two days before."

"In the drawing there are a great many jewels. Of course they're fakes. We'll give you the crown here. But you'll be able to buy real lace. If you don't find anything in Berlin go to Vienna or Brussels, not, of course, to Paris; that's out of the question for you."

When they said good-by, he kissed her.

Edda was feeling tender. "In my memory you'll always be Eugene the Beautiful."

"In your memory I'll always be Eugene the Beautiful," he agreed. "Aside from which I'll soon turn up in your memory again, we're going to see each other in the near future. Both Ramón the Beautiful and myself."

"You're a boor, but I adore you!"

"At another time I would have said: *fais voir*. But the train's leaving immediately. . . . Remember, you have to make a thorough accounting," said Schell, more in order to cut short the sentimentality.

From the platform he waved to her, turned away, and went out while she was still blowing him kisses. Nevertheless, in spite of his coarseness, Edda was pleased with him. She also appreciated his not having deducted his own five hundred dollars from the advance.

She walked through the corridor of the railway car, didn't

258

notice anyone suspicious, and felt reassured. She returned to her compartment, took the check out of her handbag, and read it all, from the figure to the signature. It's all right! Thank God! Both the money and then such a part! She was delighted with the word "dogaressa." In her tiny mirror Edda put on a look like a dogaressa. I'll do it! I'll be a celebrity! There's no doubt he's much better than that youngster Jim. She divided men up very clearly into categories; but she loved all the categories. Jim isn't serious, he's a flibbertigibbet. Poor thing, he's got practically nothing left, he spent everything on me. Of course I would have given him some, but he would never have accepted. . . . Jim had been told he oughtn't to go to the station, for reasons of conspiracy. He had nothing at all against this.

In the dining car Edda asked for half a bottle of champagne. Her neighbors glanced at her in some astonishment. She responded with a proudly challenging look: yes, I'm drinking champagne alone, I'm so used to it! Schell hadn't told her whether her expenses were being reimbursed individually or being deducted from the five thousand; she had forgotten to ask. But she had decided to live "well" anyhow, she had never been sparing, even when paying for herself. Then she tried to write an elegy in her compartment: "Farewell." But the car rattled a great deal. She put away the notebook and opened a novel by Sartre.

There was, however, one fly in the ointment: the passage across the Iron Curtain, the conversation with the Soviet colonel.

Edda went to see him three days later in a state of painful excitement—going over the border she had the feeling that some curtain was actually going to manifest itself then and there. On a signpost there was inscribed in black letters like an epitaph: "*Achtung! Sie verlassen nach 80 m. West Berlin.*" Farther on there was another one in English: "You are now leaving the British Sector." She had lived in Berlin for a long time and had seen these signs quite often before, always with a feeling of slight alarm.

Her reception was cordial.

The papers gotten by Edda had turned out to be extremely important. The colonel had sent them off to Moscow at once and, after a preliminary examination, his superiors had expressed their gratitude to him. As usual, they expressed it not too warmly, saying that the papers would be carefully studied, but he saw that they were enraptured by the treasure that had fallen into their laps. Now he could count on some reward, even a promotion. The very idea of pilfering papers from the Rocquencourt furnace could not help but make an impression by virtue of its showiness.

Edda had done the cause a great service, but once again the colonel was astonished by her manifest stupidity. Although the question wasn't one of brains, he thought; as a matter of fact, she is very beautiful. He interrogated her in detail.

"... You have executed the assignment rapidly. Let me thank you," he said. He seldom said this to agents; in his mouth it sounded effusive.

"I had to do a great deal of work," said Edda, managing to calm down a little. Just as at their first meeting there was something about the colonel's looks that frightened her. "I'm simply worn out! You cannot imagine, Comrade Colonel, how this work exhausts one!"

"You don't say!" said the colonel. "Perhaps you can rest now. That bast—that American got a furlough for a whole month?"

"Yes. For two years he hasn't had one."

"But mightn't he go back to his old post immediately?"

"I'm afraid that would attract the attention of his superiors, Comrade Colonel. People seldom turn down a furlough," said Edda. Schell knows everything! she thought.

"Yes, that may be so. Then it's not necessary. Of course you must maintain—a close contact with him. The closest of contacts. That's not hard for you, you have a great deal of sex appeal," he said with a sneer. "And for us that's very important with respect to future conjunctures. Is his position there sound?"

"I don't know," said Edda. Schell had not foreseen this question. "For some time now he's been expecting a promotion," she added, hoping to gladden the colonel.

"For the time being I'm not going to give you any further directives. Throughout the present conjuncture you'll carry on with him. . . . Might you be getting some dough from him, too? On a purely personal basis, of course, purely personal. . . . He's probably a joker with jack on the hip. I guess you got yours, eh?" he asked. Edda looked at him perplexed. This mixture of bureaucratic jargon and his own brand of American slang, which gave the colonel pleasure, had already startled his professional colleagues.

"Go off to Italy with him," continued the colonel, "and lap up some champagne. Or is he just a water guzzler? They have ones like that, too, for little birds to know. Instructions remain as before. Watch him like a bloodhound and behave yourself properly, eyes forward and belly pulled in. Are you still writing verses?"

"You know that, too!" said Edda, shyly casting down her eyes.

"I do."

"Do you like poetry, Comrade Colonel?"

"Nothing of the sort," he said, shrugging his left shoulder. "And how is that what's-his-name of yours? Schell? He hasn't deigned to see me any more. . . . But to hell with him!"

"I'll make a thoroughgoing report, Comrade Colonel," said Edda, attempting to speak in a peculiar way; she said Comrade Colonel with a purely martial intonation.

The colonel gave Edda a thousand marks altogether, saying the final remuneration would be decided on afterward. The skinflint might even pay more, she thought; the sum no longer meant so much to her, however, and she decided not to haggle. The main thing is for me to have some peace of mind now.

"And there's something else," said the colonel impressively. "I know that bast—that lieutenant may have given you a lot of money; that doesn't concern me. But—don't think of retiring!

261

Our people never—retire. I'll tell you myself as soon as you stop being of any use to me. Until then you're obliged to work. You have the lexicon; if anything happens write it to me in abracadabra."

Edda was disconcerted. It took her a moment to understand that he meant code.

He pretended to be raising himself a little in his chair. . . .

Edda ordered a dress. She had been about to go to Brussels and pick out some lace there: Flemish lace? Brussels? Valenciennes? It could also be gotten in Berlin, but she had long since gotten sick of Berlin; she still felt a need for frequent changes, especially now with sleeping cars, champagne, and such. But as it came out she didn't go to Brussels. A letter arrived from Schell—brief, and with no code. "I want to tell you something," he wrote. "Brush up your Spanish. I know your ability at languages. You'll easily find some girl in Berlin to make you perfect. All it needs is some practice. Your good fortune depends on it. A word to the wise!" It was signed—"with genuine esteem and thoroughgoing devotion, your B-b-b-boor."

She immediately hired not a girl but a man teacher—she was very bored without men. The teacher, who was, however, aged and uninteresting, came every day for two hours. Now it was impossible to leave. The lace was also bought in Berlin. The grand total, plus expenses, came to one thousand six hundred and twenty-seven dollars; precise, not round figures always made the best impression.

Out of boredom she began writing a story in which the heroine, a celebrated actress, did not "say," but "quoth," and instead of walking "glided."

23

EDDA returned to Venice two days before the festival. Schell met her at the station and respectfully kissed her hand. A camera clicked, a photographer was waiting on the platform. There was also one dejected reporter. Edda gave an interview. Schell had been awaiting it apprehensively, but it went off very well. She spoke of the beauties of Venice: "... I've been in your divine city a great many times. What can be more beautiful than St. Mark's Square? And the Doges' Palace! And the Grand Canal! I've carefully studied all the material for the festival. ..."

"Please, madame, don't say anything about the festival," interrupted Schell. "The day after tomorrow everyone will see everything, but just for the time being it's a little secret."

"I submit," said Edda with a charming smile.

"A downright Sarah Bernhardt," Schell praised her when they were alone. "And what you said about Venice was unusually interesting, original, and valuable. A suite with two rooms has been reserved for you." He named one of the best hotels. "At our expense."

"I should think it would be! But why not at your hotel?"

"What's the point of meeting his mistress? I'll introduce you to him tonight. We'll arrange it so that she's not there. He's fed up with her already. . . . Your old hotel isn't bad either, but after all your American is still there, isn't he?"

"Yes, and I have to keep contact with him; the colonel insists on it."

"Keep contact with him," he said, just as the colonel did. "You can also dine with him today. Preferably in his suite. And how is our dear colonel, rot and blast him? Has he lost his mind definitely yet?"

"Why should he have lost his mind?"

"Well, he does have abnormal eyes, surely you noticed it?"

"But what sort of man is he altogether?"

"He's a mixture. Five per cent Lenin, ten Suvorov, twenty the Gogol madman, while the rest is vodka, *aqua distillata.*"

That evening Schell introduced Edda to Ramón. Her success exceeded his expectations. What especially enraptured the Filipino was that Edda spoke Spanish. Schell approvingly nodded his head: Atta girl! But he looked outstandingly reserved, almost neutral, like an observer at a diplomatic conference who represents a friendly but uninvolved power. Ramón wanted to see Edda in the dogaressa's costume immediately. The festival was going on without any rehearsals. "Rehearsals would kill the spirit of the show!" Schell explained to Ramón.

"But why didn't you come to my hotel?" Ramón asked Edda.

"Because there are no adequate suites here," answered Schell.

"For me they would have gotten one!" Ramón exclaimed. He was about to fly into a temper, but didn't. "When shall I see you?"

"But where should I change?" asked Edda coyly. "I can't

264

go out of my hotel over to yours in the costume of a dogaressa. Could you come over to see me?"

"With delight."

"Of course you can't trot about in the costume of the dogaressa," said Schell. "The journalists would start hunting you down in gondolas. As it is, they besieged Señora Edda at the station with their photographers," he explained to his employer. "But for the same reason wouldn't it be better, Señora Edda, if you came here? You could change here, there are four rooms in this suite."

"As a matter of fact that's still better!"

"Then talk it over between you. Now, unfortunately, I must leave," said Schell, getting up. "Till tomorrow, my friend, till tomorrow, Señora Edda. Although I might be unable to see you tomorrow either, there are so many things to do. Ramón, why don't you show Señora Edda the surroundings of Venice? You might go on a little excursion. But try to slip away from the reporters."

"Wait a bit, I want you to see me in the crown. You can tell me whether everything is as it should be. I'll bring it in right away," said Ramón, and went into the next room.

"Light of my life, your fate is in your own hands now: he's even stupider than you," said Schell in Russian. "This is a genuine *coup de foudre,* everything in Ramón is genuine. In Venice there are, to be sure, no women who can speak Spanish. It's terribly awkward making love through an interpreter. And how did the contact with the American youngster come off?"

"Brilliantly," answered Edda radiantly.

At first Jim was depressed, not at all as he had been in Paris. His uncle had left for Berlin some time before, Jim knew no one in Venice, and disliked admitting to himself that he was rather bored in this city of joy and happiness. But when Edda told him in a tragic tone that they had to part—Fate is stronger than man!—he rather rudely cheered up at once. This irritated Edda.

265

"In any case we must keep up our professional relations. Further assignments are going to be given you."

"I'm afraid that's impossible," he answered, embarrassed. "Uncle writes that I'm being transferred to the United States."

Now it was her turn to cheer up rather rudely. Then what will they be asking me to do? she thought.

"We'll talk about that later, we'll be seeing each other here."

"Of course!" said Jim. "You're looking wonderful. Now you look still more like that portrait by Gabriel Joshua Trevelyan."

"Thank you. . . . How are the circles under my eyes now? Bigger or smaller?"

"Much smaller."

"Were you very bored?" asked Edda, swallowing a pill. She was always taking various pills and powders. "What did you do the whole time?"

"You'll never guess. I've turned into a writer!"

"What? You, too!"

"I'm not going to write verse, don't worry. . . . D'you know the name of Monteverdi?"

"I don't and I'm proud of it."

"He was a composer in the seventeenth century. He lived most of his life in Venice and died here, too. I accidentally ran into some material about him and I've decided to write a book about him."

"But surely you're a musician?"

"I love music passionately but I play the piano only mediocrely and I don't think I have any talent for composition at all."

"I'm *sure* you have talent! I'm terribly happy for you."

"My aunt Mildred Russell is also terribly happy for me," said Jim. He had the same feeling people have when leaving a steamer after a long crossing: I knew these people for a while, but I'll never see them again and thank God, too!

Everything really had happened accidentally. When Jim was left alone in Venice he visited palaces, churches, museums, and looked at the Titians, Veroneses, Tintorettos, and Giorgiones with a guidebook. He was sincerely and quite honestly enthu-

266

siastic, but he was not terribly attracted to painting. Once, when he intended to go to Murano, where there was an important Bellini in the old church of San Pietro Martire, after asking himself whether he could live out the rest of his life without seeing this Bellini, he answered that he could, and didn't go. Yes, I think I'm going to turn into a happy failure. Uncle may be wrong in the most important thing, in his work and in his understanding of life, but as far as I'm concerned he's completely right about a lot of things. I really am primarily an arguer; I like to contradict both in words and deeds. And I don't know myself what I want. I want an interesting life, but nothing interests me especially.

That was the day he wandered into a concert of old Italian music. The *Missa Papae Marcelli* was being played. It did not make a strong impression on him. For some reason he had thought Palestrina's music extremely melodious; actually it had almost no melody at all or else he couldn't detect it. Vexed, he thought he had no real gift for music at all. In that case what do I have any for? And what if I wrote the biography of this composer? Wasn't he a singer who had no voice, then was exiled, then lived in poverty, and it was not until late that he was recognized?

In the intermission he bought a program and learned that the composer of the mass, Pierluigi, was called Palestrina after the village where he was born. Then to study the materials I might have to go to that village. There I'd collapse from boredom altogether, if I'm bored in Venice. And there are probably other biographies of Palestrina.

After the intermission excerpts from the opera *Orpheus* of Monteverdi were played. Now this charmed him. He scarcely knew the myth about Orpheus, he vaguely recalled that the hero had descended after some woman or other into hell and dragged her out, and that he charmed people either by singing or by eloquence and died a tragic death, he thought, torn limb from limb. Jim listened to the music and, like most people who are musical but not musicians, made an effort to interpret it in

267

terms of life. Partly seriously and partly ironically, he began to substitute himself for Orpheus. *I did descend after Edda into her own hell, though to be sure I still haven't died a tragic death, and neither has she.*

In Paris he had actually had pangs of conscience, although he exaggerated them when talking to his uncle. The same day Jim handed the packet over to Edda it crossed his mind that she might be sent off to forced labor. While upset, he thought he had to disclose the whole truth and implore her to leave this frightful profession. But he didn't think about this very seriously and called himself a fool, and a base fool at that. *If I told her the whole truth, that would be a betrayal of my side! Of course I could never do that! Why did I ever agree to Uncle's proposition? Just because of my perpetual light-mindedness!* His pangs of conscience ended when Edda left France safely, not only without having done any harm to the United States but after involuntarily doing it a great service. But Jim was left with a very disagreeable feeling. His conversation with his uncle soothed him, but he definitely made up his mind that he wouldn't stay on in the intelligence service.

Orpheus was evidently also a light-minded and inconstant being. Jim sometimes would repent of his shortcomings, and sometimes flaunt them a little in front of himself. *Yes, there's an element of Orpheus in me. . . . Doubtless he left hell, as I am doing, to these sounds. Only I'm leaving without any Eurydice, indeed my Eurydice turned out to be very nasty. Strange that on the first day I didn't feel like this at all. How wonderful that she's gotten some sort of work!*

In the program he also read about Monteverdi, about whom he had known even less. The latter was evidently, by contrast with Palestrina, a success. Jim sympathized with people who had suffered from life, but had no desire whatever to be a failure himself. *Why shouldn't I write his biography? It seems both that he is less known and his music is much better.* Monteverdi's dates were indicated in the program. Jim rummaged about in his head, collecting his stock of historical information.

The epoch seems to have been very interesting. The Thirty Years' War? Wallenstein's hordes? But could he have seen Wallenstein with his own eyes? It doesn't matter, it must have been reflected in his music. The struggle between two worlds, just as now. Not entirely as it is now, but that doesn't matter. And Cardinal Richelieu was then ... ? But what was going on in Italy then? Damned if I know. There's no doubt the epoch was colorful. That will be the canvas, the background of the book.

He was so excited that he left the moment *Orpheus* was over; No more Monteverdi was being played. It was not more than five o'clock, the shops were still open. At a secondhand shop he found an old edition, a score on parchment with little squares instead of little circles. Monteverdi! He bought the parchment at once, and didn't even get as far as Florian's. He sat down at a table at the very first shabby little café, ordered not wine, but coffee, and started reading; he could read notes quite freely. Charming! His decision became firmer. In front of him he clearly saw a thick—though not very thick, some 300 pages—bound book. On top of the title page was his name, and underneath, in large letters, "Claudio Monteverdi."

A few days later he received a letter from his uncle telling him that his wish had been fulfilled: he was going to be transferred to the United States. "You can look around there and pick out whatever you like. My advice to you is to stay in the army." This time his uncle did not write in the jocularly mocking tone they both liked.

Jim started going to the library, bought a few expensive books and scores. The work, vaguely called a collection of materials, went forward. Now the only thing left was to separate from Edda. This was why he had been so happy at what she had told him; it was her initiative, the break was not hostile, and Eurydice, too, was leaving hell.

24

THE masquerade didn't go very well with the election of a doge, but for greater picturesqueness it was decided to arrange one as well, though the guests were free to appear in masks and old-fashioned costumes or not.

The newspapers published notices of the Festival of Beauty. There were far fewer of them than Ramón had expected. The newspapers that did not fawn on wealth also published sneers. The "secretariat," that by now consisted of several people, did not translate these for their employer. Anonymous well-wishers energetically sent excerpts by air mail—everything was thrown into the trash basket. Ramón was hurt that nothing was said in the notices about the *idea* of the festival. He himself now said less about rich people's duty to society, but whenever he was annoyed he declared with defiance that he spent millions on his own pleasures and didn't have the slightest interest in anyone's opinion. His interest in the election of the doge was falling off somewhat; Edda happened to arrive just in time.

Three days before the festival Schell's costume was brought to the hotel. Natasha saw something black and gold and didn't ask to have the costume taken out of the box. Schell was unpleasantly surprised. She herself resolutely refused to wear a masquerade dress. "No, really, spare me! To tell you the truth I'm not particularly pleased about your being in costume either."

"But I can't represent a bodyguard in a dress suit."

"But why should you represent a bodyguard?" Natasha wanted to ask, but didn't.

"I think diversions are essential. Especially for you, you married a man so much older than yourself. How does Lermontov put it? 'And what is the use for passion, pray, of a man whose hair is turning gray?' "

He's the one who needs diversions, Natasha thought sadly. Nevertheless, an evening dress for her was indispensable. Schell, stung by Edda's remarks at Florian's, insisted that the dress be expensive. It took him some doing to get Natasha to agree.

"It's simply absurd to squander so much money on a single evening! And where else could I wear it? There are not going to be any friends staying at our little house on the Lido, to say nothing of balls and soirees! We're going to have a modest life of work," she said. He heard this about the modest hardworking life morosely.

The dress turned out to be even more "evening" than Natasha had thought. She refused to have a train. That would really make a cat laugh! she thought. At the first fitting she was embarrassed at the sight of herself in the mirror with a naked bosom and without sleeves. Oh dear, she thought, they'll all say she's not even able to wear such a dress! Most of all, of course, she was afraid of what Schell would think, but he praised it, just a trifle more coldly than before.

After introducing Edda to Ramón, Schell considered his role in the festival finished. The entire matter passed to the secretar-

271

iat. The principal secretary worked all day, without forgetting to watch out for her own interests. Schell knew this, while she knew that he was also taking care of himself. They got along excellently. In the evenings she gave him brief reports, chiefly about the misunderstandings between the guests, the insults, and the scrambling for places.

"Let him go to hell . . . let her go to hell," Schell answered indifferently. "Just remember that only one thing is important: they must all get drunk. Has the champagne been bought already?"

"The icehouses can't hold it all!" she said with a smile. She didn't quite understand why his mood had changed; the festival, of course, was supremely silly, but it had been so from the very beginning. Before, however, Schell had looked into everything. He scarcely understood this himself and explained it all as nerves.

"It doesn't matter; they can drink it warm. And if they don't like it, they can go hang!"

An hour before the show began Schell went to see Natasha in his gilded crimson velvet robe. With his height the costume suited him very well, and he wore it as though he had always dressed that way. Natasha gasped. "But you're magnificent! Simply magnificent! As usual you'll be the handsomest one there! I didn't sympathize before, but it's absolutely beautiful!"

"If you're going to play the fool you might as well do it properly."

"What a pity people don't dress that way nowadays!"

"Your dress is very pretty, very," he said, kissing her.

"Are you telling the truth? I'm simply ashamed of going to the lobby!"

"Today that won't surprise anyone. The whole hotel is going to the festival. Even the servants and the maids. I had tickets given them. The plebs will get drunk downstairs, while the elite, headed by Ramón, will do it on the mezzanine."

"Please don't say plebs. I myself am a pleb."

"The amusing thing is that most likely half the plebs, if not

272

three quarters, will consist of Communists, or at least will vote for them in the elections. By the way, simply out of curiosity I asked Ramón whether champagne should be passed out down below or whether Asti would be adequate for the masses," said Schell. Again a pang went through Natasha: just like a salesman! "He answered, 'Champagne for everyone, and the best!'"

"Yes, he's a goodhearted man, I know."

"In any case, one of the most generous people I've ever seen. However enormous his fortune is, with time he's going to squander everything. Luckily he's given up talking about his democratic idea, but by nature he actually is something like a 'democrat.' Not long ago he invited all the extras to dinner; they all felt extremely shy."

"What language did they all talk in?"

"They were probably silent the whole time. A hundred and fifty years ago in England it was considered impolite to converse at large parties. Everything went on in deep silence; it was an excellent custom. The other day he told the secretary that at the festival, 'They are all equal. There are no princes or counts around me!' It must be said à propos that rather few princes and counts came at all, that's to the credit of the aristocracy. In my reports to Ramón I've even been obliged to bestow titles on many of the guests."

In his reports! Oh, if all this would only end right away! thought Natasha. Schell noticed a shadow on her face, guessed what it was, and with irritation said to himself that there, too, he had begun making superfluous remarks.

25

THE dogaressa was brought to the Festival of Beauty in a magnificently decked-out gondola with a huge brocaded pavilion.

Edda's dress was ravishing. The ladies of the entourage observed it with envious acknowledgment. They were not stars —not very many stars had come either—the company consisted of second-rate actresses who were perplexed: "Who is she? Why has no one ever heard of her? How did she get the role of dogaressa?" Schell set rumors going to the effect that Edda had only just escaped from Rumania, where she had been celebrated. Rumanian stars might not, after all, be known in western Europe. The ladies of the cinema were obliged to admit that the Rumanian star was extremely beautiful and that she was superlatively dressed and made up. Her crown made a powerful impression on the company. "Ten thousand dollars, if it's not fake!" one woman said with decision. "No, seven or eight!" protested another.

274

Only the evening before the diamonds and rubies of the crown were artificial. The secretary had brought them to Ramón that morning. He glanced at them and exploded. "At my festival the dogaressa's crown cannot be adorned with glass rattles!"

The secretary understood what he said, all the more so since it was accompanied by violent gestures. She had managed to accustom herself to his explosions. She had adopted not Schell's tactic, but her own, which was far better. Each time she entered Ramón's suite she assumed the coyly rapturous air a young girl might have when asking Frank Sinatra for his autograph; but when an explosion took place, the secretary put a look of dreadful fright on her face. He liked both one and the other. This time, too, she made it clear to him that she was going to fall in a dead faint from horror at once. She mumbled something inarticulate, which in any case he could not make out.

"You would put false stones even on my own crown!" he said more gently. His crown had cost an enormous sum of money. Although Ramón was already known in Venice by now, and although the newspapers wrote about his fabulous wealth, when the jeweler received the check, before sending the crown to the hotel, he telephoned the bank to inquire whether there were funds to cover such a sum. "There is enough for ten times more," answered the director, a friend.

"Put this rubbish back in the case; I'll take it with me," said Ramón. The secretary was about to carry the case after him, but he wouldn't let her and, with the case in his hand, went to the gondola—he now had his own, the finest in Venice. People precipitated themselves to besiege him. He set out for Edda's hotel, as arranged with her.

"Before going on the excursion we'll go to see the jeweler," he declared. Edda modestly cast down her eyes. He liked this a lot, too, even though he also liked "women of prey." "Those numskulls put false jewels on your crown! *Your* crown!"

A ring or a brooch would no doubt be a present, but about the crown it was impossible to say with certainty. Perhaps I'll have to return the crown, Edda thought. But if it turns out to be a present, why, that's an enormous amount of money! Edda got extremely excited. In the shop she translated what he said; she could scarcely breathe. She made an attempt to bargain for him, but he stopped her: it was needless! Should I thank him? But if he's not making it a present? For his attentiveness? But you can hardly thank someone for being attentive the same way as for a present! flashed through her mind. She thanked him as though for his attention, but "threw him a heavenly glance," as though he might expect more.

The dogaressa was followed in twenty gondolas by the frenzied populace: all the "trades" were there. The people sang, music played. At the entrance to the palace Edda met the doge, in a long gilded cloak, wearing a crown and carrying a sword. A gold umbrella was held over him. Edda glanced at the doge's crown and sighed: Millions! Now he'll be a boor if he doesn't give me mine! With a gesture of Dandolo or Marino Faglieri, Ramón extended his hand to her and kissed her, though with two crowns it wasn't easy. Stormy applause and enthusiastic cries burst out of every window in the palace. Someone, however, yelled, *"Evviva Lenin!"* The orchestra broke into the march from *Aïda*. The procession drew up and strung out upward along the staircase. The people kept on hurrahing more and more enthusiastically. For half an hour now a torrent of champagne had been flowing. The doge and dogaressa were now supposed to throw coins to the populace from the balcony of the mezzanine. Edda disliked this very much.

"It's quite unnecessary ... really, quite unnecessary.... It's bound to fall into the water anyhow," she said to the doge. But the orchestra and the applause drowned out her words.

Edda had given a ticket to Jim, too.

He knew no one in the crowd, and strolled about through the rooms and drank champagne. In the Tiepolo room he noticed a young woman, or girl, shyly leaning against the trelliswork. Very pretty indeed, sweet. How did she get in here? he thought.

A moment later a giant bodyguard went over to her and talked to her, smiling cheerfully, shook his head affectionately, and returned to his post. When he appeared she looked radiant; as soon as he left the smile vanished.

Because of his duties as a bodyguard Schell scarcely saw Natasha at the festival. From a distance she saw him walking through the ballroom, actually saw only his head raised above the trellises. Just like the movies, where they sometimes show you not the whole person but just his legs, for instance. It's always terrifying, it makes him look like a criminal. . . . Could that mean I'm less in love with him? Of course not! Much good I'd be without him! But he might come over to see me; after all, I'm here alone and don't know anyone. . . . Oh Lord, what's the point of this festival, where half the people are drunk and the rest are just pretending to be so gay? If only this farce would come to an end quickly! He said, "We're leaving the day after." High time, too! thought Natasha.

Probably her husband, Jim said to himself, irritated. It would be a very good idea to get acquainted with her, but who's going to introduce me?

The loud-speaker explained in three languages that a marionette show was going to begin at once upstairs on the third floor. Part of the public rushed back from the buffet tables. The girl sighed and also went upstairs. Jim followed her indecisively. Music was heard from all sides. *"Di te Venezia, E il simbol vero,"* sang a tenor. What a voice, thought Jim. He should properly have had a feeling of revulsion for everything taking place in the palace, but actually the only thing he found repellent was Edda, who had manifestly sold herself to this billionaire. He saw her sitting on the throne and from a distance bowed to her. The dogaressa majestically nodded her head at him and, with a tender smile, started talking to the doge. Even if she weren't a spy she's simply incredibly poisonous! And for three days I almost liked her!

The long, crowded room of the puppet theater, with numerous rows of seats, was brilliantly lit. The elite were seated in

277

front, with the ordinary people in the back rows—the seating took place instinctively. The curtain was not yet raised. In front of it on the stage stood the puppet master, an aging typical Italian in a dress suit and white cloak. He told the history of the marionettes in a somewhat incorrect French that nevertheless reproduced all the intonations of French speech to perfection. . . . Jim glanced around the room and sat down at the edge near the door. Where has she slipped off to? he asked himself, and suddenly saw her where at first he hadn't even looked; she was sitting among the ordinary people in the last row, all ears. Jim also listened attentively. Suddenly the man on the stage began speaking in English, just as well, and in a woman's voice. At first the audience did not grasp it, then it roared with laughter. The puppet master explained the content of the play. It was about the royalist conspirators and spies at the time of the French Revolution. According to him, among the puppets of that time there were royalists, plotters, and spies, and a great many of them were executed.

Now if only I had a wife like that! There'd be something for me to do in life! thought Jim, recalling his book on Monteverdi with renewed pleasure. Love and work, interesting work, nothing else is necessary. I would stay on in the army; anyhow, it's impossible to live on Uncle's money at the age of twenty-six. Poor Uncle! He thinks he's led a sensible life! Well, I can no more convince him than he can me. That doesn't stop his being a wonderful fellow. And whatever the misanthropes say the good people are in the majority, there's something good in everyone, perhaps even in Edda. . . . I won't become a composer, I'll be a historian of music. And I'll get married—to someone just like her—he thought, gazing at Natasha in the last row, almost enamored. I don't know who she is, but I want to fall in love with someone just like that.

The puppet master finished, bowed to the audience, and hurried along his little ramp to the hidden watchtower from which he controlled the network of wires. The light in the room went out. . . . An invisible orchestra started playing something

278

old-fashioned, unknown to Jim but now as though it were familiar. Yes, just like a Monteverdi ballet! The curtain rose.

Toward ten o'clock the discipline in the palace slackened.
Down below a gay hubbub could be heard. The mezzanine was
also very animated. The doge and the dogaressa left their
thrones. Ramón passed from one ballroom to another, politely
responding by gestures to the enthusiastic greetings, and ordered the servants to keep uncorking more and more bottles.
Alone, and with the regal look of a chatelaine, holding her train
over her left arm, the dogaressa sauntered to and fro. Shouts
were also addressed to her. She blew kisses to the crowd,
stopped at every table, and drank a full glass. Her head was
swimming. She also stopped before the mirrors; each told her
that she was the fairest of them all.

Schell came across her in one of the rooms. In spite of being
in such a happy state Edda's face very nearly twitched with
fury. With the peremptory gesture of a dogaressa she indicated
her desire to speak with him. She can't do a thing, we're leaving
tomorrow no matter what.... Natasha's upstairs, he thought.
One of the salons had not been used for the festival, and he
respectfully led the dogaressa into it. They sat down in the
easy chairs.

"You are magnificent, my sweet," he said. "I have never seen
a better dogaressa in my life!"

"You're also magnificent, a magnificent scoundrel!" she replied. Schell raised his eyebrows.

"And wherefore this unkindness, O woman of splendid
rages?"

"A scoundrel of scoundrels! You said I was a fool, didn't you?
'F' as in fat-headed, 'o' as in obstreperous, and all that, what?
But I sensed the truth, with my heart and my mind! Your boss
has told me the truth! You tried to pass off that bedraggled wife
of yours to me as his mistress! But there's a limit even to shame-
lessness and lies! I almost fainted when he asked me whether I
knew your wife!"

279

"Almost doesn't count," said Schell. "It would have done you no good at all if you'd fainted."

"And if I didn't faint it was only because you became loathsome to me a long time ago! But I'm going to tell him everything!"

"And will you also tell him, my little cherry blossom, that you're a Soviet agent?"

She was speechless for a moment. "I see you're a blackmailer, in addition to your other virtues.... I'll drown her in vitriol!"

"I don't advise it," he said, and his eyes became malevolent and cruel. Edda was alarmed. "I have reason to think that afterward the vitriol would fall back on to your own little face. Let's talk seriously. Yes, I did get married, but what about it? I had a right to; even in Berlin I noticed that I had become loathsome to you. That subjected me to severe spiritual torments. And even more when you went off with that young American. You're allowed to do everything, is that it?"

"Who is she? He called her Natalia. Were you already married to her in Berlin?"

"No. You know perfectly well that I loved you and you only. As long as you didn't throw me over.... You are sublime, like Ho Chi-minh. The name Ho Chi-minh means 'He who shines.' "

"I'm so fed up with your stupid jokes!... No one's ever thrown me over! It was I who threw over my two husbands. One, as you know, was my real husband, while the other was almost real."

"I thought there were more 'almost real' ones."

"B-boor!... But what did you do after I threw you over?"

"I tore my hair out. But when I had restored my equilibrium after the upheaval I decided that love can't be forced. Also, I would like to part from you amiably. Agree that I made you happy. Without me you'd never have clapped eyes on a doge any more than you could fly. Is he already your lover, or is he only going to be in the next hour or two?"

"My private life is absolutely no concern of yours.... He has unfeeling black eyes. I don't like that. Eyes should be fiery, or steely, like yours."

"He has kind eyes. The left pupil is lighter than the right."

"I haven't noticed it. He doesn't understand what real love is! For him it's probably the same as a good dinner. I myself love fine dishes and choice wines, but it's hardly the same thing! Can you make a tragedy out of fine dishes and choice wines? Even Jim was better! Though for me he was too pure."

"And myself?"

"There's a great deal you don't understand either, but you're something else again. . . . Is she Russian, your dear little wife?"

"My private life is absolutely no concern of yours. Wait a moment! What's this? Have the artificial diamonds on your crown been replaced by real ones? I'm cut to the quick!"

"D'you think he's going to give it to me?" asked Edda uneasily.

"Possibly. If you behave yourself I'll advise him to. Generally speaking, he intends to gold-plate you. And you're going to be wholly indebted to me for it."

"I know he has a high regard for you; I simply can't understand it. But I'm going to open his eyes about you."

"Then I'll open his eyes about you, too. And what sort of a complex have you now? Cleopatra or Messalina? Have you written any new poems?"

"Now I'm writing simple, classical ones. Like Victor Hugo. But I've also been very strongly influenced by T. S. Eliot. He's amazing!"

"But isn't he very Right-wing, a royalist, I think?"

"Poetry is above all that! And I've always detested everything halfway, that's absolutely not my style. I never even bought dresses from middle-of-the-road dressmakers. That is, I got my dresses from them, but with contempt. If you're going to buy dresses, they must be by Christian Dior. And how annoying that just now, when the money is there, it's impossible to go to Paris! That's your fault, too. . . . And your monolithic characters, that's so *vieux jeu!* I'm beginning to think that even

281

royalism has its charm. Have you ever heard *O Richard, O mon roi?*"

"No. And the Soviet colonel probably hasn't either. So better not say it to him."

"I'm on very good terms with him now. He's a boor, but I think he liked me," said Edda with a coy smile. Basically, she regarded her role in espionage as a charming lark; she did not even understand quite clearly whom she was actually working for.

"That's splendid, and for that matter quite essential. I repeat, we must part on good terms. We know and are fond of each other. Let's make a gentleman's agreement. I urge you strongly to babble less. Then I'll say nothing but the nicest things about you. In general, take it easy with Ramón. Don't go in for hysteria, hold yourself down to a few simple little scenes. Though you're not hysterical, I mean you rarely lapse into hysteria. But keep in mind that he's primitive and hot-tempered, he might even beat you up. You probably won't have anything against that, but his generosity will be cut down by it. Whatever he says to you say: 'That's just what I was going to say!' or 'I was just going to suggest that!' Go into raptures about his ideas. And now, radiant Dogaressa, you must return to your subjects. Go out first, by yourself. But why are you without a mask?"

"Are you afraid your dear little wife might see us together? It doesn't matter. I can always get you away from her the moment I feel like it. I'd give half my life if she ran away from you!"

"I'm afraid the doge might see us together. Then he would throw me from the balcony into the Grand Canal. Aside from which you wouldn't get the crown then."

"Well, all right, then, I agree to the gentleman's agreement. You always had an influence over me. Only you! The explanation I give is that it's because I was careless enough to surrender to you the very first day I met you. That's dreadfully important!"

282

"On what day of your acquaintance did you surrender to Jim?"

"The first day, too, but that was because of duty."

"And Ramón?"

"Ramón on the second."

"Hang on to him, light of my life."

"I'm trying to. The men I throw over don't forget me. And you won't forget me, either. *Tu ne quitteras plus les hontes triomphales/Qu'inventa, une nuit, mon vieux démon charnel!*" she declaimed menacingly.

"Are those your verses?"

"How are the circles under my eyes now? Smaller or bigger?"

"Much smaller. No circles at all. There's just one more thing, my little lotus flower. Everything in your life so far has always ended up with a fiasco. This time strain every cell in your tiny little brain. Devour everything that comes your way with the avidity of a barracuda. Take as much money from Ramón as you can, it's a work pleasing to the Lord. Castle immediately, as though you were playing chess. Make yourself secure. Squeeze out of him thirty-six million gold francs, as the Marquise de Pompadour did from Louis XIV."

"I've already heard about Pompadour twice from you. You're repeating yourself . . . now tell me *merde* thirty times."

"What for?"

"Surely you know that's the old-fashioned custom in all French theaters? Before the actress goes on someone has to tell her *merde*."

"I can't pronounce such a word at the coronation of a doge."

"In my ear," she suggested, offering him her cheek.

"In your ear, perhaps, I should do so with pleasure."

When he was alone he started smoking another cigarette; he smoked incessantly now. I simply haven't the strength, he thought. What an idiotic festival! During the past few years there have been three or four of them like this. A Left-wing sociologist would regard it as the symbol of doomed bourgeois culture. That may be, but even that is better than what might

283

succeed it. And even this is far from the worst thing in my life. . . . How horrible the world is in which I've spent nearly my whole life! If it's come to the point when I myself am stifling, a magnificent scoundrel, as she said. It's simply hard to believe. . . . After all, there's light in the world, there are so many good people, why have I been so unlucky? But now I'm going to crawl out of the muck once and for all. Tomorrow we'll be off. . . .

In one of the drawing rooms he collided with Ramón.

"Well, what d'you think? Is everything all right?"

"Stunning. Your festival will go down in history."

"Now even you can see what a private person can do who's aware of his duty to society! . . . Let me extend my thanks for your help and advice."

"I've given the final accounts and what's left of the money to your secretary," said Schell. "As you know, we're leaving tomorrow evening. Tomorrow I, and doubtless you, too, will be taken up the whole day. Let me say good-by to you now."

"I'll come to the station."

"That's awfully kind, but why should you disturb yourself? But as you like, then we'll say good-by at the station."

"Are you going home right now? Surely you're staying to the end of the festival?"

"No, I have a terrible headache."

He actually had. And never before had he had such feelings of self-disgust. He was not afraid Edda was going to drench Natasha in "vitriol," but as was always the case with him, a vague presentiment of great misfortunes had suddenly begun tormenting him. There's not the slightest reason for it; on the contrary, everything is going very well indeed. . . . Where's Natasha? We must go home at once, instantly.

He went up the staircase and into the puppet show, paying no attention either to the puppets or to the audience that glanced around at him in annoyance. He scanned the semidarkness for Natasha. She's most likely in the last row. Yes, she has an inferiority complex, and I have acute neurasthenia, one

284

is just as good as the other. He went up to Natasha from behind, and leaning over her seat said:

"You're probably very bored. Let's go home, eh?"

"Wonderful, let's leave," she replied in a whisper, looking at him astonished. "But you said at three. . . . Do you want to go right now? It's not so convenient to leave just now, people are looking at us askance. . . ."

"Let them look askance as much as they like, rot and blast 'em!" he said angrily. "We're going to the Lido this morning, we have to get a good night's sleep. But I still have to say good-by to the secretary. I'll go down and call our gondola. In a quarter of an hour I'll be waiting for you down below, at the door. All right?" he said and, without waiting for an answer and without even looking at the stage, he left. Natasha looked after him in alarm. What can be the matter with him?

The large, opulently costumed puppets, with bedaubed faces and carefully plaited hair, hurtled about the stage chattering and turning their eyes around in their motionless faces. Jim could scarcely believe that behind them and bringing them into movement there was one invisible man in a little box. There was also a carousel; Robespierre was chasing after Marie Antoinette. The elite in the first rows appreciated the symbol and nodded approvingly. I suppose that's also the last word in art, thought Jim, perplexed, remembering the play he had seen with Edda in Paris. A female spy with a foxlike face was finally captured, and a paper with some numbers was found on her.

Suddenly Natasha felt a pain in her heart. What is it? What's happened? For a moment she couldn't remember: it was the sheet of paper that had fallen out of the dictionary: "320. . . ." Well, and what of it? What nonsense again!

Suddenly her eyes filled with tears. And even later she still couldn't understand what was happening to her. The strangest, most unexpected thoughts suddenly took possession of her. Could the whole thing have been a mistake? It can't be! I'll simply go out of my mind. . . . And if it's a mistake, what can I

285

do now? Go to a convent! But there are no Russian Orthodox convents here.... And I love him.... What can I do? I mustn't cry, people might notice.... It's dark, they can't see. Surely I can't leave him! No, I'm just dreaming everything, like that night on Capri. Hide everything from him.... Of course, of course, hide everything.... But he says I'm incapable of lying.... It's all nonsense, all of it! she cried out to herself. Her tears kept flowing all the more copiously.

Jim saw that at the end of the show the girl once again was approached by the gigantic bodyguard. Her husband, of course, thought Jim, sighing. I'd like to have a wife like that, but she could only be American, you have to marry your own people....

The puppets were dancing around a guillotine on the stage and shrieking out terribly in shrill voices. The orchestra played at a frenzied tempo. The puppets sang just as frenziedly: *"Ah, ça ira, ça ira, ça ira! Les aristocrates à la lanterne!"* The people in the back of the hall applauded tempestuously. The elite also applauded. Jim was not in a revolutionary mood. It's all disgusting, revolutions, guillotines, wars, espionage! My job in life is clear and simple: love, art, work. I don't need anything else. And let others do as they please!

26

THEY left Venice the following day. Ramón really did arrive to escort them to the station, bringing Natasha a huge box of sweets. He was extremely affable. Schell chatted with him cheerfully. His premonitions had somehow evaporated even during the night in the hotel and especially that morning in their little house on the Lido.

"The main thing is one's health," said Ramón to Natasha, as though he were expressing a remarkable thought. "Today you look wornout."

Schell did not translate this for Natasha.

Ramón did not wait for the train to leave; he had to hurry home. He thanked Schell warmly, and it was not quite clear whether he was thanking him for the festival or for Edda.

"We may see you again in Berlin. She told me she's going to have to go there to settle her apartment and get her things. Of course I'll be going with her," he said, a little embarrassed,

287

although he didn't hide his liaison with Edda. Schell nodded approvingly and asked to be remembered to her. "What a charming woman," he said, "and so unselfish! Just imagine, she wanted to give you back that crown! She thought you would take it back! I could scarcely persuade her that that was your present to her. Knowing your character of *grand seigneur* as I do, I don't think I made a mistake, did I?"

"Of course not. What a question! Now I understand why she didn't thank me for it. . . . She has great regard for you. She told me what an extraordinary man you are." Quite so, thought Schell, although he had not had any doubt that even Edda would keep this gentleman's agreement. "Though I knew it without her. And how was the festival?"

"Beyond all praise," said Schell. "I'm convinced the world press is going to be trumpeting about the Festival of Beauty for another whole month. You've done society an enormous service. And everything was just exactly as it was with the doges. But they could hardly have spent so much money on festivals as you did. The secretary told me that four thousand bottles of champagne alone were drunk."

"Let's assume that only half was drunk, while the rest got into the hands of the secretariat and the servants," said Ramón cheerfully. "That's in the nature of things. A rich man must understand that poor people have to live off him, too."

"Naturally. But where are you staying in Berlin? I would like to offer you my own house. I have a house of my own there," Schell put in carelessly, vaguely hoping that Ramón somehow still believed in his being rich. "But my own flat in it is not large enough."

"What an idea! Are there no hotels there? We'll probably go there in three or four weeks." Then everything is all right, thought Schell, we'll have long since left. "We're going to make another short trip. I suggested that we go to Paris, but for some reason she doesn't want to. We'll probably fly to Seville. At last I'll be understood without any interpreters."

As was proper he said he would stay at the station till the

288

train left; as was proper Schell replied that that was quite un-necessary—why waste his time, and it was so nice of him to have come to the station. One hand won't be enough, thought Schell, I'll stretch out both. We're plainly passing from the stage of friendly acquaintances to that of old friends; if he were Russian we'd have to embrace, too. Ramón kissed Natasha's hand; concealing her impatience, she was waiting for him to leave; once again he wished her good health and left for his gondola.

"He's told me a hundred times he's very busy. I've always felt like saying, 'I suppose you're solving a crossword puzzle.' But he really is nice. And not so 'obvious' as I had thought. I shouldn't be surprised if he doesn't commit suicide someday."

"Don't talk such nonsense. He's very nice, very nice, but thank God he's finally left! Though it's bad to say things like that."

"You always put in 'It's bad to say things like that,' then you say them."

"Not in the least. You're just making it all up, Eugenio. Tell me, what's my name?"

"Have you taken leave of your senses?"

"My name is Natalia Ilyinishna *Schell*. Say it!"

"Natasha Schell, Natasha Schell, very stupid, but unusually sweet. In this world, in this 'all-hating world,' decent people hardly make up a substantial majority, but some manage very successfully to pass themselves off as decent. Some of them don't even notice this, with others it gets to be a habit, but you . . . "

She was looking at him, hardly hearing what he was saying, but thinking her own thoughts. Then she burst out laughing. "Always the same nonsense! I've heard that quotation from you before. What fool does it come from?"

"Shakespeare. . . . So you're satisfied with being Natasha Schell?"

"Not especially," she said. In some incomprehensible way her depression had also somehow evaporated.

The trip was unusual. It was actually their first trip together; from Naples to Venice they had traveled by day with other people in the same compartment. Now they were alone; no one was going to disturb them. The conductor respectfully asked them to give him their tickets, in order not to trouble them any further. Everything in the railway car was of leather and velvet plush, all polished; everything was bright and cozily lighted. The luxury seemed astonishing to Natasha but had already stopped provoking any pangs of conscience. They had only their brand-new expensive overnight cases on the racks— in Venice Schell had made her a present of an overnight case, too—the rest had been put into the baggage car.

At the border an official came into the coupé and said, *"Pässe, meine Herrschaften."* With Schell there she wasn't even afraid of Germans. They had dinner in the dining car—Natasha for the first time in her life—which gave her great pleasure, even though in her opinion one *had* to live poor. As usual Schell drank a great deal and joked along very gaily; he teased Natasha by telling her he might very well marry a rich woman and was seriously thinking of a divorce. Again she burst out laughing.

" 'An attack of unprovoked merriment?' " asked Schell. With an unpleasant feeling he noticed that these attacks, which he liked so much, had begun to take place with her far more rarely since their marriage.

"No, not 'unprovoked,' provoked!" she replied.

In the coupé they raced each other through the sweets, and ate up very nearly half the box.

Natasha praised Ramón. "You mustn't think I don't like him. In the first place, I like everyone. . . ."

"That is, no one."

"You least of all! And secondly he's a kindhearted man, although he has his faults like all of us."

"His misfortune is that his faults are a little absurd and are reinforced by his enormous wealth. But actually he's not a bad fellow. In a thousand people he would be in the first hundred

... or rather in the second. His virtues are partly due to there being nothing for him to desire for himself."

Schell got up, looked at himself in the mirror, and was reassured as usual. Natasha watched him with tender curiosity. "Yes, yes, very good-looking," she said mockingly; before she would never have talked *that* way. He smiled and got one of Turgeniev's novels out of the overnight case. Monsieur is fed up talking to me, she thought good-naturedly. She opened a book, but didn't start reading. They scarcely conversed any more, they simply sat next to each other side by side, occasionally taking each other by the hand, though they were both wearing gloves—Natasha by now no longer in her old cheap ones. With an abrupt, terrifying noise, exactly as though an accident had taken place, an oncoming train hurtled past at such devilish speed its lights barely had time to flash by. Natasha cried out in fright; Schell laughed and kissed her. She had not had such a feeling of complete happiness since the night of the tarantella on Capri.

They stayed in Schell's Berlin apartment. Natasha liked the furniture very much. The study and bedroom reminded her of rooms in movies showing the lives of advanced people with a great deal of incomprehensibly acquired money.

"This is German 'sophisticated,' that is, something rather worse than simple sophisticated. I cannot understand why I bought anything like it."

"But, on the contrary, I like it terribly," protested Natasha, and began elaborating on how she could arrange this furniture in their little house on the Lido (she never said "villa").

"There's only one bedroom," she said irresolutely, and blushed. "It's a large bed, but if you like I'll sleep in the study on the divan; it's very comfortable."

"What nonsense! . . . D'you know you've gotten even prettier? Now you look like the queen of diamonds."

His cello made her wildly enthusiastic. She begged him to play, but he refused, his face twitching.

"I'll never play again. I've given it up."

"Why have you 'given it up'?"

"For no reason. I'll have to sell it. I once paid a great deal of money for it. They say it belonged to Romberg himself."

"You probably bought it after winning a lot?" asked Natasha. She didn't know who Romberg was. And in order not to pretend that she did, she asked at once, "Who was Romberg? Some famous cellist?"

"Yes, I bought it after winning," said Schell unwillingly. He had bought the cello after one of his most difficult assignments.

"And you have so much music! Paganini, *Streghe* . . . but wasn't he a violinist, not a cellist?"

"He was a great violinist, but also played the cello. He was a strange man, and a terrible one, an adventurer and they say a murderer, too."

"And what's this? The notes are written in your handwriting! *Presto. . . . Animato. . . .*" Natasha read. "Don't tell me you write music! And you've never, not once, said a word!"

"But I didn't, I just transcribed it. It's Chopin's 'Tarantella.'"

"'Tarantella'!"

"Not the one we heard on Capri. The rhythm, of course, is the same, but it's a different one. That one was probably homemade. I think there are three famous tarantellas: Chopin's, Mendelssohn's, and Tchaikovsky's. All three are excellent. I transcribed Chopin's for the cello, the one Schumann called mad."

"Won't you play even that for me?"

"Not for anything!"

"As you like. It's a very great pity," said Natasha, astonished by what he said and by the altered expression on his face.

He soon recovered; he had to go to the post office and get a cleaning woman through an agency, an *Aufwartefrau*.

Natasha protested: "I can do everything very well myself, there are only two rooms, it's just an hour's work or two a day."

Alone she scrutinized everything again, this time far more attentively, with the eye of a housekeeper. Odd that there's not a single photograph on the walls. Surely he must have some

292

people who are close to him? . . . What an enormous bathtub! She tried the water from the hot tap; in half a minute it came out boiling. How wonderful! I'm going to take a bath immediately. There was a medicine chest in the large wall cupboard containing dozens of little vials and boxes. All that for my Hercules! And I have nothing but aspirin. To Natasha's astonishment there were five or six sleeping pills in the medicine chest.

She also found several decks of cards; she looked for the queen of diamonds.

They went to plays and movies and dined in the best restaurants; Schell threw money about even more than before. He was in a good mood. Berlin aroused painful memories in him, but that was in the past—there would be no more colonels from now on. Nevertheless, he went over to spend some time in the eastern part of the city, without any special need to. The atmosphere there seemed to him not quite what it had been before. Perhaps some more "incidents" are being readied up. In that case we'll have to leave sooner. I detest "incidents" more than anything in the world. I've had enough of them! He went home with relief and was puzzled at how he could have gone over there. There's very little risk, but with Natasha I didn't have the right to assume even a small risk.

He was now living just like a *rentier,* with nothing to do. Every day he bought the *Figaro,* the *Manchester Guardian,* and German newspapers, but didn't spend much time reading them. He stopped thinking of his reminiscences. I could hardly tell the whole truth about my life. Autobiography is the falsest and most shameless genre of literature. But there's a desire "to pass on to posterity." In a winning position, naturally. It would be possible to find the position, he thought idly. And thank God we're not seeing anyone, we don't have to discuss the war, the Kremlin's intentions, or Senator McCarthy.

He was not in the least bored with Natasha. She had to go to the library. The work didn't take very much time. There was nothing else she had to do in Berlin. She went to her pension,

293

and with bashful pride announced that she had gotten married; the landlady congratulated her very amiably. Natasha moved her things to their flat and arranged them with a smile, they were so conspicuous there. She arranged her books on the same shelves as Schell's, which she had examined with curiosity the very first day. On a shelf in the middle she noticed a large medical reference book, about a thousand pages. When she was alone she examined this at length; she didn't know in just what months the signs of pregnancy made their appearance. She felt awkward going to a physician or midwife. But she couldn't find anything.

Schell had more books than there was room for, some of them to his annoyance lay flat on top of the equal-sized volumes. When Natasha pushed the tight-fitting reference book back in, a capacious folder fell out and some engravings were scattered about on the floor. Never mind, I'll pick them up again at once, she thought. The engravings were old-fashioned and very fine. The first was the *"Embarquement pour Cythère."* That's one picture I know, that's Watteau, he's famous. Natasha began looking through the other engravings. Most of them had a signature that was new to her: Baudouin. She put them all back in the folder upside down. She had a disagreeable feeling that kept growing. All the engravings had very frivolous themes; someone with austere tastes might even have called them pornographic. How surprising! He must have collected them a long time ago, when he was very young. . . . He's simply fond of art. Odd that it was just these he collected. This Baudouin is prob ably also famous, I know so little. . . . For some reason, though there was no connection at all, Natasha recalled once again the sheet of paper with the numerals on it. She hastened to put the folder back in its former position.

They went together to the movers' office; the movers undertook to transport everything to Venice very quickly.

"But how are we going to live here, when our things are taken away and still haven't arrived there?" she asked on the way home. "Will we have to go to a hotel?"

"There's no point moving in Berlin. It would be better if we waited for them in Italy."

"In Venice?"

"What's all this about Venice over and over again? And I'm not so eager to see Ramón again," answered Schell. Natasha sighed more freely. "After all, you've never seen Rome. Let's go to Rome. And when the things arrive we'll be off for the Lido at once."

"A splendid idea! Splendid. I like being with you everywhere, but it'll be best of all in our little house after it's thoroughly fixed up. I'm just afraid we'll have to buy something else. We have very little bed linen. Is it all right if I buy some?"

"Fine."

"We're going to live wonderfully! Don't you think that?"

"I think so, and for that matter I'm sure of it," answered Schell.

Still, when they got home he sighed. What a pity to leave this apartment, he thought. It's seen a great deal of living. A big chunk of one's life will leave with it. Disgusting, but big. Although there were no disasters, since I'm still alive and kicking. But I've never applied myself to anything. The main thing for a man is to have something to apply himself to, to a family, a job, a career. Now I'm finally applying myself to something, thank God. . . . My whole life has been one delirium; with or without *ololiukvi*, it was all delirium. And what's happening in the world today is also delirium. How is it they don't see that? And such boring delirium.

Suddenly Prince Metternich, Johannisberg wine, and Chesterfield cigarettes flashed through his mind. For a while he didn't grasp the meaning of this, then it became clear. Ah yes, that first conversation with the colonel, he was sitting over there. An important conversation, too; as a result of it I very nearly went back to that world. A cigarette holder with fingerprints . . . *T-short!* Yes, it's a good thing all that is over with for

295

good. Now I have a peaceful haven, and no disaster is going to come within even an inch of it. He knocked on wood.

At Natasha's request they went off to Grunewald that evening for dinner, to *that same restaurant*. Natasha, very excited, wanted to sit at *that same table*, too—she remembered it well—but it was taken; she was vexed: *their* table, being sat at by strangers! They dined on the terrace, ordered the same dishes, the same wine—she remembered everything. They sat around until ten. The little lamps with colored shades on the tables had long since been turned down, and the terrace had turned cozy as a result; but the evening was rather chilly, with a wind blowing.

"Won't you catch cold?" Schell kept asking.

"Never again!" she answered too fervently for the question, as though under his protection even catching cold was impossible. On the way back she started to sneeze. She was dreadfully ashamed of this: a head cold!

That night she began coughing. She suppressed her coughs in order not to disturb Schell, but he woke up. Natasha overflowed with apologies. "I've stopped your sleeping! D'you want me to go into the study right away? And for three months now I haven't coughed once! It had to happen just now!"

"But isn't this how it used to be with you before, too?" he asked in alarm.

"Oh no, it's not *that* way. . . . Yes, it used to be . . . of course, it used to be," she said, coughing and trying to wipe away her tears imperceptibly.

Neither slept any more that night. Toward morning she had a temperature. Schell rang up the same specialist he had forced her to see in the autumn. Natasha begged him not to call a physician, but if one had to be called at least it should be an inexpensive one from the neighborhood.

"It would be best simply to buy something at the drugstore. It's all nonsense, anyhow. It's just the simplest little cold."

The specialist thought it advisable to give her an injection of penicillin. He calmed Natasha, who was taking great pains to

296

look as though she were not in the least upset. But in the study, talking to Schell in a low tone, the specialist did not hide the fact that the patient's left lung was not in very good condition.

"It will pass off, of course. Nevertheless, the patient should not remain in Berlin. Is it possible for you to leave?"

"Whenever I please for wherever I please."

"Then get ready to leave in a week."

As ill luck would have it Natasha unfortunately turned out to be allergic to penicillin, and that evening she got worse. The specialist came again, canceled the previous treatment, prescribed a new one, and once again advised Schell to leave, this time even more insistently.

"We have a villa near Venice, on the Lido. Would that be all right?"

The specialist frowned. "The sea, canals . . ." he said reluctantly. "No, for the time being I'd advise you to begin by staying in the mountains. In a good sanatorium."

"In Davos?" asked Schell, changing countenance.

"Why Davos especially? There's no tuberculosis yet."

"Really not, Professor?"

"Really. There's only the danger that it might appear. An analysis will show everything. I don't deny that the patient has gotten worse since autumn. But I don't foresee any danger. She has a very tired organism. Probably her life hasn't been easy?"

"No, not easy! At the age of sixteen she was a prisoner of war!" said Schell. He recalled the underground factory and suddenly his eyes blazed in frenzy. The specialist glanced at him, and in embarrassment, without asking any further questions, took his leave.

27

THEY took two rooms in the Swiss mountains, in a sanatorium
that gallantly called itself a rest home. A physician examined
Natasha, made all the tests, and confirmed the diagnosis of the
Berlin specialist: there was no tuberculosis, there was only a
tendency toward it, the organism was very feeble, the left lung
was slightly touched. No terrifying words, such as pus, were
mentioned. The treatment consisted of rest and pure mountain
air reinforced by nourishment. Natasha was instructed to pass
the greater part of the day lying down, either in the large garden of the house or on the intricately constructed sun terrace.
Well, that's not so difficult, part of the day he'll sit with me,
too, we'll read side by side, thought Natasha. While still in
Berlin it had occurred to her that she was probably not long-
lived. Perhaps I love life so much just because of my illness; all
consumptives are that way, that's why they have such high
color. Of course it would be better, incomparably better in our

298

little house on the Lido, but what can be done about it, life is possible here too.

Natasha had arranged her things on the very first day, began knitting, and the work, as it always did, flew through her hands. On the terrace, when there was no one near by, she sang "Bublichki" to herself in a low voice, or "Begone, torments of Passion"; she sang better because he had praised her. Schell wanted to tell her that it was harmful for her to sing, but he couldn't make up his mind to. She soon acquired the general sympathy of the rest home.

"You like people, that's a rare quality even among kind people," Schell told her.

"Not rare in the least. I'm terribly sorry for everyone; after all we're all going to fall ill and die. I also like books and knitting. Your pullover—is that the word, pullover?—will soon be ready."

"Really? It'll come in very handy. I'm so grateful to you. We're going to have a wonderful summer here together, Natalia Ilyinishna!"

"Wonderful!"

"But there's one English expression 'to put all your eggs into one basket': that's what both of us have done very carelessly. What will you do if I suddenly die? Yes, death. . . . Usually an incurable grief for one of the survivors and a superfluous chore for all the others: 'Well, now I have to express condolences, go to the service, go to the funeral. . . .' Forgive my talking about such things in general, but I'm so much older than you. I think someone said that before forty a man lives on the interest on the capital of his health, but after forty on the capital."

"For heaven's sake, don't say such things!" In spite of herself Natasha thought that an athlete like himself might have foregone saying that, especially to her. "In any case you won't be ahead of me. . . . I don't intend to die either, but if my illness were to become dangerous then nevertheless I'd feel like moving into our little house. Gogol says Italy's where one must die: in Rome you're a whole mile nearer God. In any case not here."

"What nonsense you're talking!" he said. His face twitched. "We're not moving to Italy so that you can die there!"

"But I only said that just in case. Forgive me, I won't any more. I know I'm going to get better. Oh, if only he would say clearly just how much time I'm going to have to live in the sanatorium!"

"In the rest home. He has told me. It's true that there our interests diverge from theirs," said Schell gaily. Now he usually spoke to her in a very cheerful tone, which was just what frightened her a little. "After all, we're their best clients here, they would like us to stay on longer."

"But what d'you think? How much longer must we stay here?"

"June, July, and August," he said with assurance. "That's when life in the mountains is very pleasant, and in Italy it's too hot. But in autumn we'll go home."

"May God grant it! But how I've complicated your life! I've absolutely ruined it!"

"Probably just the opposite! You're my salvation!" said Schell sincerely. Natasha looked at him questioningly. "Without you I simply shouldn't have known what to do with myself. And would probably have gambled away everything I have at cards. I've told you, didn't I, that gambling used to be my passion?"

"You told me, but I didn't realize you gambled so heavily."

"Alas, I did. But from now on I'll probably never take another card in my hand. With Ramón I was just amusing myself, and even then rarely. If I had played a real game with him we would be much richer now!"

That's true! thought Natasha with relief. He did tell me that Ramón didn't know how to play at all. . . . But now, *no matter what*, I think I would forgive him everything! she said to herself, recalling with horror all her own obscure feelings at the puppet show. And I'm never even going to think of that again, never!

"This rest home is going to cost you so much! And I'm not earning anything. . . ."

300

"I've already told you more than once that it would annoy me if you earned money. It would be unnatural. It would be just as though the man didn't lift the woman dancer on his out-stretched hand over his head in a ballet but she lifted him."

"I couldn't lift you on one hand," said Natasha, bursting into laughter. "But in our little house we could live quite cheaply. Of course I'll cook myself. Even at home in Russia they said that no one could cook Ukrainian borsch like me. D'you like Ukrainian borsch?"

"I adore it."

"I'll make some for you. But when will that be? I thought that by June we would be settled in at home completely, once and for all."

"Well, so it's turned out to be September. Not such a catastrophe. And you'll be through with this little infection in your lung for good."

"D'you really and truly think so?"

"It's not I who 'think' so, the doctors have confirmed it categorically."

"God willing! But I think so myself. I'll soon be strong as a dancing bear. And meanwhile you go on paying these doctors all that money every week! They must count everything up separately, each and every examination!"

" 'A rich man who's aware of his duty to society should not begrudge his money.' That was Ramón's favorite remark. In Spanish it sounds even more stupid . . . but don't worry about that either, we have enough money."

Schell was especially happy now at having some money. A fine fellow I should be now without any! He had taken the two best rooms, sent to Zurich for a radio and gramophone for Natasha, and ordered a great many Russian records and books in Paris. There was not a bad library at the rest home, but he forbade Natasha to use it:

"This rest home doesn't accept any tubercular patients; you saw that no one on the terrace has one of those paper bags. But there may be some sick people here anyhow, and we might

301

still get infected: the books are not dishes and aren't washed. Heaps of books will soon be arriving, I've gotten a whole lot of Soviet novels for you. About milkmaids, managers of hydroelectric stations, and factory directors."

"And why not write about milkmaids?"

"I have nothing at all against milkmaids. It's just that everything they say about them there is a lie, too. And especially for some reason or other about the factory directors. About these particular comrades there's not a single syllable of truth."

"Don't say 'comrades.' There are just the same kind of people there as anywhere else."

"I'm afraid they're not quite 'just the same.'"

"But don't you love me? And I'm just the same as they are."

"No, you're a white crow, and I've told you a hundred times that you're a mysterious wonder of unknown origin, a flying saucer. Well, all right, I'll take my words back. And I'll do nothing to stop you from reading about Comrade Fedya, read as much as you please. . . . And we're bound to run into someone we know on the Lido, there are some Russians in Venice. You're very sweet in company."

"A real lady of the manor. And what kind of people will we know there? I don't need them at all, I'm going to be working. You see, I've already arranged everything on the desk. But what are you going to be doing the whole day?"

"I won't be bored in the least. I've bought a great many novels for myself, too, English, American, and French. Practically the whole of Simenon."

"Those detective stories? I must say in that case it's better to read the Soviet ones. And have you also ordered novels by some *émigrés?*"

"I think I ordered everything there is. For that matter actually there's not very much; after all, they're all dead, those Chiang Kai-sheks without a Formosa."

"Nowhere near all of them! I very much like to read them, too. As long as it's in Russian! My French is very bad and I

302

just can't imagine how I could even begin reading a German novel! Scholarly books are something else again."

Sometimes he would read aloud to her in the evenings. He firmly refused to read any Turgeniev; it was one of Natasha's sorrows that he didn't like him. But among her books a little volume of Chekhov's plays turned up. Schell read them gladly.

"To my mind the best play in Russian literature is Tolstoy's *Fruits of the Enlightenment,* especially the first two acts," he said. "Then comes *The Inspector General,* by Gogol. It's only after these that Chekhov's plays come in. They're very good, especially *Uncle Vanya.* Chekhov may have created a 'new genre,' but actually all his effects are cheap, all those sweet old nannies, the same sweet old nannies and the same guitars and little bells as in the old plays, the same elemental people who say the same clichés over and over. And all those sensitive, tender Sonyas, Anyas, Irinas, and Sashas! And what lapses! 'The former Ivanov has woken up in me!' Or Irina, speaking of herself, 'My soul is like an expensive grand piano to which the key is lost!' And immediately after her husband's murder she begins to babble something or other about people's sufferings, about some secrets, about the winter, the autumn, about toil. In prerevolutionary Russia they got more and more enraptured by this nonsense, dreaming of what was going to happen 'in two or three hundred years.' It was also given some 'social significance.' In *A Boring Story* the professor thinks his greatest misfortune is that he has no general ideas—and if those don't exist then nothing does. That is, if he were a Liberal, a Marxist or a Populist, then everything would be perfectly all right and there would be no 'boring' story! And the critics naturally ate this up with an excellent appetite. Oh well, now those scoundrels in the Kremlin have a general idea, may they choke on it! Chekhov was a great, great writer, of course the most truthful writer after Tolstoy, but his ideas! ... And everything has turned out exactly the opposite. My God! That he should have lived off the capital of these cheap, boring ideas!"

"You mean they weren't original? But just why is originality so absolutely indispensable? The main thing is for an idea to be good, kind. . . . Then we have to make allowances for his era."

"Allowances for his era! It was a wonderful era! Chekhov's heroes 'silently grieved' because life was dull. And I don't know what I wouldn't give to be able to have lived in *their* time."

"Yes, it was quiet, peaceful. I would have liked it. But . . . but *you* could hardly have lived that way. Have you never dreamed of tempests?" He frowned. "I meant, have you never dreamed of fame?"

"No, I never dreamed very much," he said morosely, almost angrily, a way he never spoke to Natasha. "I don't like neon light, it probably even interferes with living. May God let you become famous; after all, you've started writing even here."

"Please don't joke! You may not like Turgeniev, but he did say, 'Who knows how much every living thing on earth leaves seeds behind which are destined to sprout only after its death?' Yes, and how many such seeds did *he* not leave! I—am nobody, but it may be that even I shall leave one. In you. If I die, remember me. . . ."

He was about to make a joke, but he felt that he might also burst into tears.

And in fact Natasha did begin work again on her dissertation, and was very content. She was coughing less already. She had been advised not to take walks, and Schell walked about by himself. He said he had been a mountain climber when young and had often walked along precipices over paths a couple of feet wide where there were signs posted saying, "Only for those not subject to dizziness." She could not even imagine this without horror. She made him promise that he wouldn't walk along such paths. Nor did he specially want to; he felt tired, heavy, and no longer fit for mountain climbing. He spent the greater part of the day indoors. He abandoned his drugs once and for all; they were unsuited to his new life and useless. He read novels or listened to music. The gramophone had an automatic record changer, and he listened especially often to the *Symphonie Pathétique,* although Natasha was afraid of it and did not like it.

Her "baseless happiness" came on her in the sanatorium, too. Then she was especially engaging. Schell loved her wit, which was simple, without any *mots,* and full of benign humor. He would laugh, which made her still happier.

Nevertheless, the thought that he was bored with her pursued Natasha. About two weeks later she thought up a diversion for him: "Now look, our things are in Venice already, and we have to have them moved to our little house," she said to him. "Go down there for a few days and do all that. Or else the authorities will sell them right at the station!"

"They won't sell anything. We'll find everything in complete security."

"Yes, but even if they don't sell them, if you moved everything over, arranged it, and put some order into it, then in September I would have much less work to do. And at the same time you'd have a little change, too. Where is he now, your Ramón and his dogaressa?" said Natasha, through some train of thought that was not clear to her or agreeable. "And you can leave me alone now perfectly well for as much as a whole week. I feel very well. I won't even be too bored; my work is going ahead."

The first time Schell did not agree. She mentioned it a second and a third time. He bet himself: heads I go.

"That's always the way! Women do just as they please with us. Probably they did it with Napoleon himself. I think it was he who said that in love there was only one victory—flight."

"And you'll be able to take advantage of the opportunity: you can go and not come back, eh?"

"That's very possible. But have no fear, I would settle up the bill for the rest home from Venice. I'm a gentleman."

"We would have to arrange things so, by the way, that we don't have to pay for your room while you're away. D'you think they'll agree to that?"

305

"Yes, they will," he said more coldly. Now that they had some money, Natasha's thriftiness annoyed him even more.

"You might speak about it with the director."

He did not speak to the director about the room, but to make up for it got his word as well as the doctor's that they would give special heed to Natasha. He even asked one of his new dining-room acquaintances to do that, too. They all joyfully gave him their word.

In Venice he called up Edda's hotel while still in the station, without giving his name, and when he heard she had left for Berlin he sighed with relief; Edda had become just as repellent to him as to Jim. Sometimes he was even irritated at the thought that it was thanks to him that she was now rich.

He stopped at the same hotel, where he was greeted deferentially. The manager, laughing, spoke about Ramón: the guests at the Festival of Beauty had been well satisfied. He had spent a lot of money on presents, too.

"I think there's an Eastern saying that 'A man carries with him into the grave only what he has given away in his lifetime,'" said the manager, who often chatted with writers in his hotel. "In that case your friend will carry quite a good deal with him into the grave."

"I'm delighted, though he's not my friend," answered Schell, and automatically filed it away "for his memoirs." He himself had acquired part of his dubious erudition in just the same way as the manager. And nevertheless he's not a vulgar fellow, Ramón, and almost not ridiculous, actually tragic, though not very, he thought.

The work in the little house did not turn out to be much. For three days he arranged his things and books together with the workmen, hammered in nails, mended and repaired things; he was fond of tinkering and was a very good handyman. He himself was surprised at the amount of rubbish he had accumulated. He threw out a great deal, he didn't even hang up all the pictures—some of them either bored him or had ceased to

306

please him. How could I ever have bought such trash? And the statuettes are trash, even if they're "genuine." To hell with them. Even more books turned up which were completely useless for him. There was an edition in many volumes of *Reminiscences and Correspondence of Prince Metternich*—Metternich again! Not one volume was cut. But when did I buy them, and what for? I'll have to give them to a binder, I can't cut the pages myself. Perhaps I'll even look into them then. He placed them on the right shelf for their size. He didn't impose any order on the library—that would be later; till then let it stay this way. It would be a week's work. He came across a huge envelope with photographs of the women who had loved him. He glanced through them and thought, not without satisfaction, that these women were now completely indifferent to him. I practically never even think of them. And a very good thing Natasha hasn't come across the envelope. It's also surprising that a lot of kind people still haven't told her about Edda.

Now the villa, drenched in the June sun, was extremely cozy. He sat in each room and in each smoked a cigarette through, in order not to offend any room and not to attract bad luck. Yes, if only she gets well! Surely we won't have to move into the sanatorium for good? And sell this little house, *our* house! Natasha, to his satisfaction, said *our* house, *our* books, *we* got hungry; it was only about money that she always said *your* money. No, that's impossible! That would be a terrible blow to her. And to me an even worse one. He felt that, even if it was sometimes a little dull with Natasha, without her it would be boring and oppressive. The doctors had not calmed him very much about her health, even though they hadn't frightened him very much either. Yes, I was telling her the truth, without her I'd be completely done for. I couldn't endure this solitude in which my life has passed! And with her, perhaps, I'd even live to a ripe old age. Stranger things have happened! And people would be in raptures when they speak to me, as they often are when talking to old men: he's so old and still has all his faculties! Do I want that or not? Not in the least. It would be a strange finale for Count Saint-Germain. It's turned out oddly even as it is. I've had a lot of different complexes in my life; I'm evidently ending up now with the Philemon complex.

He also thought about Edda—nearly always with repugnance, but now even more with shame. I treated her shamelessly. To be sure I fixed things up a little. Under Natasha's influence Schell was trying to find good qualities in everyone. It was particularly difficult to find them in Edda. Natasha herself is an angel. Colonel Number One is simply a goodhearted man, the Soviet colonel also is not a bad chap although only semi-intelligent, and there are a number of attractive traits in Ramón; there may even be some in a scoundrel like myself. But in Edda, at best, aside from her stupidity, there are "extenuating circumstances." Such as bad luck, lack of roots, the terrible milieu she's been living in almost since childhood, complete pennilessness. Yes, substantial extenuating circumstances. What's rather more astonishing if anything is that she has any sort of talent at all; not very much, it's true, and purely derivative at that. It would be a good thing if I never saw her again in my life. . . . Yes, this is how I'll live to the end of my days. . . . Avoid evil, is that all? Not very much.

Without any reason he decided to stay overnight in the little house, although it was extremely inconvenient; he hadn't taken anything with him, either pajamas, soap, or toothbrush. Once again he assigned all the rooms and the furniture in them. He thought that instead of a pointless "guestroom for friends" he would arrange a living room, although that was also pointless. How should it be furnished? There's something "modern" here that's repulsive. I could hardly hang upon the walls old pistols, old-fashioned rifles, daggers, as in the old novels about country squires' lives? he thought with a smile. Or this thing in the study? And shouldn't I put in a workbench, too? I'll start a lathing business. I'll kill time, somehow. . . . Nevertheless, there's never been any other worldly wisdom, and there never will be.

He felt hungry, recalled that in this little hole everything doubtless closed very early, and went out, carefully turning the key in the lock—the instinct of a new proprietor. The café was already in fact shut, but they let him in and gave him some cold meat and wine. He was also trying out the café. I'll probably be in and out of it a thousand times. He was also trying himself out on these deserted streets, on the skies gilded over with stars, on the trees bathed in the vague moonlight. Now this is *mine*, it's *my* sneezewort.... How unspeakably beautiful the world is, and what a pity it is all the more that we still don't know why anything is or what for!

"At home" he vacillated between the easy chair and Natasha's bed. He took off his slippers, and as painstakingly as ever hung his jacket on the back of a chair, unbuttoned his collar, and lay down, putting a leather cushion from the study under his head. He had a feeling he was not going to fall asleep. The moon was reflected in a white spot on the floor of the bedroom. The silence was as though there were no Venice, no Italy, nothing: the stratosphere. He recalled the most terrifying and shameful things in his terrifying and shameful life. Has my spirit changed? That happens no more often than a change of sex! he thought, and had the feeling he used to have before, that his soul was empty, empty, absolutely empty. He went out into the garden—now it was not *his* garden, not *his* land. Everything is strange, and the strangest of all may turn out to be Russia today. Schell remembered that he and Natasha intended to plant some fruit trees. We're not going to plant them, flashed through his mind. He went back into the house with a feeling close to horror. Not the whole thing all over again! No, now I have a life line.

He opened a newspaper. He read it in a peculiar way: he would understand a few lines, then the thought would flicker off as though for a moment he had lost consciousness; this went on for quite a long time. I think all those drugs have made me a little shaky, even though I haven't taken them for so long. He woke up at dawn. People often lie about nights like that: "I didn't close my eyes." I slept three or four hours, I'll go back by the very first motorboat, there'll be a telegram from Natasha at the hotel. They had agreed not to write each other letters. I've never been able to produce any love letters. "I love you *passionately*." That's the plain truth, but if I write it down it will seem to me myself that I'm lying. . . . How odd that there are so many words that simply affect my nerves, especially random expressions, to say nothing of the hundreds of clichés in Soviet novels.

Only a single telegram had come from Natasha as yet: "Hardly coughing stay as long as necessary kisses love." It made him happy; it even moved him, though the telegram, in Russian and written with Latin characters somewhat garbled in spots, looked peculiarly unnatural.

There was no new telegram at the hotel. It's true they had forgotten to agree on how many times they were going to wire each other. Nevertheless, it might mean that Natasha was worse. When he didn't receive a telegram the following day he left for Switzerland.

At the very entrance to the rest home he asked the hall porter whether everything was all right. "*Mais oui, Monsieur, Madame va très bien!*" Thank God! he thought, and almost ran to their rooms. Natasha cried out for joy and threw her arms around his neck. And Schell, despite his happiness, thought to himself, "they melted together in one long kiss," like a long movie fade-out.

". . . I've gained two pounds, or more nearly two and a half! And I'm not coughing! I'll ask for your coffee right away. . . . Your pullover's ready. . . . My Eugenio, my own Eugenio! . . . And how is our little house? . . . Poor darling, you're probably exhausted! . . ."

That evening Natasha sat at her desk with a pen in hand reading Nil Sorsky's *Sixth Meditation of Melancholy*. She usually read in a chair by the window and made notes in pencil; but now on the table there was arranged the magnificent set of instruments Schell had brought her as a present. "With

310

your pen, on your blotting pad, I'll write better!" she said. Schell, without his jacket, in his pullover, was lying on the couch, having propped up his long legs, which couldn't fit on the couch, on the back of a chair he had pulled up. Once again —this time somehow aggressively—he was listening to the *Symphonie Pathétique* and thinking about his own thoughts, about "It's never too late," and about Natasha.

Natasha was reading about Melancholy, and was deeply impressed by Nil Sorsky's insight, how the "evil hour" could be avoided and the "good life" secured by maintaining firmness of will and elevation of mind, by determination and good cheer.

How true! she thought, how good! That's how I'll live, and I won't give in, and there won't be an evil hour. She shuddered, remembering her own illness, the underground factory, the engravings, the sheet of paper with the numerals on it, and then expelling these memories from her mind. What was I thinking about? Yes, that I can't have anything more to wish for myself and I don't: only for everything to stay as it is now, only to get completely well, and nothing more. And I wish everyone, everyone, the same thing: for no one to know need, for there to be no incurably sick people, for no one to work under the lash, in underground factories, for gardens to be everywhere and rest homes like this, books, good work, and the main thing is for everyone to have a tenderly loved husband as I do. And that would be the good life.

"... Of course we all have streaks of madness. I know what yours is: you have a pathological but not malignant honesty," said Schell. Natasha wrenched herself away from her books and looked at him; she thoughtfully went over his words in her mind. His usual nonsense! "The main thing is to 'apply oneself to something.' You applied yourself to the Recallists."

"I know what I'm applying myself to. Oh, if only you didn't have to speak in that tone! But I love you terribly, terribly! And your face is so unusual!"

"Yes, a 'fine figure of a man,' a 'fine-feathered fellow,'" said Schell, and reflected that she was right: he himself was fed up

311

with this tone, which it was difficult for him to discard now. He went on listening to the music.

And we'll live together for the rest of our lives, if not on the Lido then here, even here it's not so bad, he thought. No, not everything is that way, Peter Ilyich, he answered Tchaikovsky in his thoughts. Count Saint-Germain passed through all his adventures and landed in a peaceful haven. . . . You're mistaken, Peter Ilyich, there are joys in life, big and little ones. It may even be that there is happiness.

28

IN Berlin Edda, like Natasha, had had only one room in a pension. She had taken nearly all her things along to Venice. Now she moved everything she had left into a huge suite taken by Ramón in the best hotel. She came across a photograph of Schell in a dressing gown, with a not very decorous inscription. Usually whenever she provided herself with a new lover she burned the photographs of his predecessor; she ascribed some mystical significance to this. But she didn't feel like burning this one. What if everything still isn't finished with him? In addition there's no fireplace, I can't ask for a spirit lamp! She hid the photograph in a box and put the key in her bag.

Ramón had been somewhat startled by her proposal to go to Berlin. What for? A boring town. It had not been easy for Edda to persuade him. She didn't very much want to go back there herself, but she thought it imperative to see the Soviet colonel

313

and get his release, final and permanent, on friendly terms; she was frightened by what Schell had said to her.

She particularly did not like to go over to the eastern section of the city now, although tens of thousands of people passed back and forth daily and came back unhindered. This time she, too, had far less time than before; she bought and ordered everything it was possible to buy and order. The bills were sent to Ramón, who paid them unprotestingly. How can he be so unconcerned about someone's forging his signature! thought Edda, who was not used to checks. But his signature is very ingenious; those flourishes wouldn't be easy to forge. As for money, he didn't offer her any. If I ask, he'll probably give it to me, she thought, but in the long run I'll get more.

She herself did not understand very clearly what "in the long run" meant. Sometimes she thought irresolutely about marrying him. It's true he said he would never marry anyone. Well, they all say that! But is it worth it after all? There's a *contra* as well as a *pro*. The *pro* was obvious enough, but the *contras* were varied. She didn't like him in the least, he bored her, she wanted to keep her freedom. And what if he wants to carry me off to the Philippine Islands? I wouldn't go so far away for anything, to such a wilderness! But we can live both here and in his palace in Seville, and there he'll have to fork over a sum of money. Edda also didn't know just what sum of money to ask for. Should I rely on his generosity or would I be letting him off too cheap?

In Berlin she had an attack of hysterical lying. She told Ramón about her fabulous successes and adventures. When she was fourteen years old none other than John Barrymore had predicted a tremendous future on the stage for her. Later, in Rome, Mussolini had taken an unusual interest in her. "But I wouldn't even hear of him. I wasn't going to be one of those Petaccis of his! I fled with my mother from Italy immediately; he was simply in despair!" Ramón listened inattentively and sourly.

Ramón was really bored. In Venice he had been busy with

the festival, in Berlin the twenty-fours of the day were free. He knew no one. No reporters or photographers appeared; the newspapers had not even mentioned his arrival. He had no great interest in publicity, but a complete absence of it was not quite agreeable to him. In addition Ramón did not understand why they were hanging around there; it was boring wherever you were, but in Paris, and especially in Seville, it would be gayer. Edda tried to humor him by thinking up diversions and by telling anecdotes over dinner. They lost still further in being translated into mediocre Spanish. Once she also tried to tell him an off-color story, even though she didn't happen to know the key words in Spanish. It turned out badly: Ramón exploded and said that he didn't like stories like that in general and that for *ladies* they were quite inadmissible.

". . . Poetesses are allowed to do a great many things that other ladies of course shouldn't," said Edda, embarrassed. This idea and her embarrassment mollified him. He calmed down and even asked her to forgive his fieriness.

". . . You shouldn't prostitute your personality with words like that!" he said portentously. Edda's face at once took on the expression members of Parliament must assume as they shout, "Hear, hear!" when the heads of their party speak. "Now listen to this! Write a play on the theme of the Soviet Revolution! I'll hire the most famous artists and take it throughout the world! We'll show an unprecedented historical tragedy."

"I've never written a play," replied Edda. His suggestion appeared to her interesting. They say playwrights get 12 per cent of the gross sales, she thought.

"I haven't a very clear idea of just what you write. Read me something of yours."

"I'd love to," answered Edda with pleasure. She loved to read her verses aloud and read them to all her lovers. She took out a notebook at once.

"But these verses are not entirely my own. On the quays in Paris I bought a little book written by an old poetess. I was

315

interested in an epigraph of Goethe's: *'Liebe sey von allen Dingen, Unser Thema, wenn wir singen.'* 'Let Love be the theme of all our songs.' The poetess was not very good. I kept having to correct everything, so that you might actually say they're my own now. I'll translate them for you later, but now when you read you'll be able to appreciate the music, the rhythm, the melody." She read in the manner of poor actors: carefully concealing the rhythm and applying all her efforts toward making the verses sound like prose, but then sometimes abruptly raising her voice to an enthusiastic shout and just as abruptly and without reason returning to an ordinary tone:

> *"La trompette a sonné. Des tombes entr'ouvertes*
> *Les pâles habitants ont tout à coup frémi,*
> *Ils se lèvent, laissant ces demeures désertes*
> *Où dans l'ombre et la paix leur poussière a dormi.*

> *"Quelques morts cependant sont restés immobiles;*
> *Ils ont tout entendu, mais le divin clairon*
> *Ni l'ange qui les presse à ces derniers asiles*
> *Ne les arracheront."*

He listened carefully, thinking that what was being spoken of in the verses was love. But when Edda had translated them he strongly disliked the sense of the verses. Ramón hated talk about death. It's enough that people die, why speak about it, too! But here there was nothing but tombs and corpses. He particularly disliked the explanation of the corpses, just why they did not wish to leave their tombs. These explanations were thoroughly unsatisfactory; what the corpses were complaining about had never happened to him. And if she detests life so much why does she keep on buying so much rubbish of all sorts! He thought he was about fed up with Edda. One harpy was the same as another.

It would be a good thing if he only began even to read, then
316

I'd be freer myself, Edda decided. In a bookshop near their hotel she came across two books in Spanish: *Don Quixote* and the *Four Horsemen of the Apocalypse*. She bought the Blasco-Ibáñez novel, which she liked very much. She discovered in herself a resemblance to Marguerite Laugier, a woman who was both chic and intellectual. She made a small introductory remark to Ramón: "Pay special attention to the vision of that Russian Socialist Chernov! It could be considered prophetic!"

Ramón read the novel with pleasure. He particularly liked Chichi, who was also a magnificent woman. Compared with her Edda lost out—she never could have thought that the book she was making a present of would be a disaster for herself. The thought came to him that he, too, might be able to do something for the struggle against the horsemen of the Apocalypse. But just what? Buy a yacht and go to starving countries, to be at the head of the Aid to the Hungry?

A new idea preoccupied him. Sell the palaces in Venice and Seville and buy up bread with all the money? No, even the starving have *some* bread, what's necessary is somewhat better things. The poor and unhappy people must be given joy, too. Preserves! All kinds of preserves, especially pineapple! That's also necessary in the fight against Communism. If the money from the sale of the palaces isn't enough I'll supplement it, no matter how much is needed! Ramón was just as inspired as the day the thought of the Festival of Beauty first occurred to him.

One evening he got a letter. It had been addressed to Venice and marked "Please forward" on the envelope. A kindhearted fellow who failed to sign his name had sent him a newspaper clipping about his festival. Since the secretariat was no longer in existence the clipping had not been censored. Edda translated it with constantly increasing embarrassment. Without mincing matters Ramón was called a fool, and much was made of the ignorant and shameless plutocrats who evidently thought everything was permitted them and who made a mockery— and at such times!—of the needs and woes of nine tenths of

317

humanity: "These gentry are manifestly even incapable of understanding that their preposterous schemes render an enormous service to the enemies of culture and liberty, the Communists."

Ramón flew into a rage. He was not used to a jeering tone; for twenty years he had been drowned in praise. Aside from which it was clear that the idea behind the Festival of Beauty had remained completely incomprehensible. "Is it worth while paying any attention to fools and good-for-nothings!" said Edda indignantly. But for some strange reason his vexation transferred itself to her, as though it were she who had written the article.

"Probably the scoundrel wanted to steal something from me! Like *everyone else*," he said.

"Of course! Naturally! Blackmailers!" said Edda.

He was still angry at dinner and contrary to his custom drank a whole bottle of wine. Then he said it was time to go to Seville. "I've had more than enough of Berlin! I very much regret having come here. I've never been so bored anywhere."

"I, too.... I was just going to suggest it myself; let's leave," Edda hastened to agree. "Is there a direct flight to Seville from here?"

"There must be. And if not, we'll change in Paris."

"No, in that case Madrid would be better. I've never seen Madrid. I'll go to the agency and ask."

"What for? The hall porter will do it. Just name the day."

"But perhaps there won't be any tickets that day."

"For me there are always tickets any day I like!"

"Then let's say Thursday or Friday.... How fantastic it was, our meeting! You're simply my destiny!" She tried to soothe him by repeating what she told all her lovers.

"I don't know why I'm your destiny," replied Ramón glumly. He had decided to leave her once they were in Spain. It won't be too difficult to buy myself out. In Seville I'll say I'm going on a trip around the world; maybe I will at that. It's futile working for people, they don't understand anything or don't want to! Of course there's no point paying attention to those blackmailers! he said to himself. But he thought Edda's corpses were not, perhaps, so wrong after all.

29

CATASTROPHE struck Colonel Number Two quite unexpectedly.

After the answer he got from Moscow he had every reason to expect a reward. Promotion to general was practically assured, and they might give him a medal as well as a financial bonus. While extremely agreeable, it would not settle the question of his job. He no longer felt like staying in the West; everything there was alien to him and almost all of it distasteful. He couldn't obtain front-line duty, indeed he was probably no longer fit for it. There wasn't much chance of staff duty. In his present department a still higher post meant still nastier work. In spite of everything I'm still a combat officer, I'm not cut out for the police, he repeated to himself for the hundredth time. He himself felt that this was becoming one of his fixed ideas: not to get mixed up with the secret police! It was very easy to get involved. People of the secret-police type were crowding into his department more and more, and with every day that passed he felt more and more clearly that he was a white crow. He thought it might be best, after all, to retire.

He was confronted by the same question, the same wretched question of aging people: what should one do with the remaining years of one's life? The colonel was meditating on everything. He scarcely paused at all over the usual, banal idea of writing his memoirs. No one in Russia writes his memoirs, except perhaps someone who has a safe-deposit box abroad, and even for him it's dangerous. And besides, in the war I never saw anything particularly important, I just saw what everyone else did. And as for the job I now have it's best to think about it as little as possible, to say nothing of writing. In his time he had wanted to start on a biography of Suvorov, but he had stopped that, too; it would have been a paraphrase of the old books, with a bow in the direction of the High Command and of economic materialism. Added to that he felt that in spite of the Order of Suvorov Medal the government was not so well disposed toward the tsarist field marshal; consequently, it won't be so easy to publish an honest book: Suvorov was not an economic materialist. Could I write a history of some major operation from the time of the great war? Now that Stalin is dead there's no point going into raptures on every page over his military genius, but it would be imperative to extol all our commanding officers, that is, once again lie unscrupulously, say there were no blunders, and that everything happened in accordance with a predetermined plan. The colonel had a definite opinion about this: the plan was bad, and at the beginning of the war there hadn't even been one; it was as though there had never been any plan of any kind. A multitude of grave blunders had been made, complete confusion on the part of the High Command had been displayed, and everything had been saved by the bravery of the Russian troops and the self-sacrificing endurance of the Russian people.

In his free time the colonel would sometimes go to a bookshop. He bought primarily books about war, sometimes about

321

history. This June, too, he went into a shop. There were no new war books. He came across an old book of Serge Aksakov. His attention was attracted by its binding, which was very good and wonderfully preserved. The binding was yellow, with a very broad leather back and corners made the same. The colonel opened the book; his eye fell on a sentence: "Aside from the three species I have described, Orenburg Province is occasionally visited by black hares, of usual shape and size; I have never succeeded in killing any of them." These words struck the colonel; he *had* to kill a black hare!

He could not consider himself a real hunter. He didn't shoot very well in the air, and didn't like swift hunting dogs (although Aksakov didn't either). In his youth he had hunted in his free time, which even then he had never had very much of. But this book was a revelation to him: that was what was left in life! But at once he made the objection that with a lame foot he couldn't walk through the fields, swamps, or woods. Practically, therefore, the book was not of much use to him, but he felt he had to buy it without fail at whatever price. He saw a chapter heading about hunting with snares and traps. He was still fit for this kind of hunting, which wouldn't be too tiring. He also came across an exhortation from some old-fashioned hunting manual: "Be a hunter, have fun, enjoy your good amusement; for it is a lovely occupation and a becoming one; so that no sorrows and troubles may overcome you—oh my good counselors, and true ones, and ye wise hunters! Be happy and of good cheer, be contented and delighted in your hearts through the remembrance of all these joys of former years." Made to order for me! he thought, and bought the book, even though it was printed in the old Russian orthography that hurt his eyes.

When he went home that evening he put the coffee on, sat down at his desk, and turned over the pages of the whole book. There were two volumes bound as one: *Notes on Angling*, and *A Hunter's Tales and Reminiscences*. He did not pause very long over the first volume. In his youth he had tried angling, but it had seemed rather tedious and dirty; he had to put live muckworms on the hook, he never caught anything with bread pellets. Now he simply glanced a little at these *Notes*. He liked Aksakov's wonderfully simple, unaffected style. Yes, we don't know how to write that way now! He liked the technical and at the same time purely Russian words, without any "isms." He liked the writer's astounding powers of observation and his extraordinary visual memory—he wrote about the manners and customs of fish as though he had spent his whole life under water.

The colonel quickly passed over to the traps and snares. He was struck by the similarity of this kind of hunting to what he had been dealing with himself during the past few years. Wolves and foxes were caught in just the same way as he captured spies. The choice of the bait, the verisimilitude, the unobtrusiveness, all just what we do! With the handle of a spade the hunter would skillfully imitate a wolf's tracks on the snow in order to deceive the wolves and to cover up his own. He even had to walk in unworn bark sandals, since the smell of leather or boot polish might frighten the wolves. All this had to be done so skillfully that the animal's sharp eyes didn't notice it and his keen sense of smell and hearing didn't detect anything, Aksakov advised. Perhaps a real intelligence agent actually ought to be a hunter. I think Schell said that that American hunts, thought the colonel, happily recalling the documents from the Rocquencourt furnace. A full-grown wolf might fall into the trap, or even better a black hare. Yes, it's described perfectly, no doubt of it. It's true Aksakov had an easy time of it, he'd been fishing and hunting since youth, while I was a pauper, he said to himself, struggling against Aksakov's influence. But he felt more and more that he would always be enchanted by this squire, who had perceived things that for most people were invisible.

The book determined his plans. Even if they suggest another post, would it be worth taking? To be sure our people don't suggest posts, they appoint us to them. Nevertheless, it's possible to get out of it, on the grounds of my lameness and disability. I'll say I've become unfit for work. They won't insist. And then a retired general could settle in the provinces. Then I could really be at home. I'll buy a horse, I can still ride. Could I build a little house? . . . I'll get up at five in the morning, take along a thermos bottle with coffee, a bottle of Crimean wine. . . . He writes that old and tired hunters in bad health lie in ambush for the animal not far off in a cabin where they sit smoking in easy chairs. Well, I can get along without easy chairs, but I suppose I might take along a pocket chess set. Aksakov liked hunting alone; that's what I'll do, too. The only people I'll get to know will be the peasants, that's what I came from and that's what I'll go back to, too. They're our best people. I wonder whether they'll accept me? Who can understand their souls? It may be that what they want above all is for foreigners not to mingle in Russian affairs, but it may be, too, that the one thing they're longing for is for someone, anyone, the devil himself, to wring the Bolsheviks' necks! They're Russia's chief hope, them and then the officers, even more so. . . .

He read until late in the night and grew more and more enthusiastic. That fellow, he thought, knew all the different hedge sparrows, jacksnipes, woodcocks, skylarks, shovelers, wood pigeons, and sandpipers even better than he did the tenches, perches, catfishes, and turbots! The colonel was enraptured to learn that dogs can be polite and impolite; that wolves are ordinary and troublemakers; that shooting wild geese has nothing to do with hunting; that a hunter of noble marsh game can only be disdainful of such shooting; that a duck who wants to lull her drake to sleep lovingly tickles his neck at great length; that north of the Orenburg Province mercury will freeze over in winter, while at its southernmost borders the most delicate wine grapes grow. All that in just one province! Truly, Russia is boundless! He didn't finish the book until dawn.

Thanks to his satisfying decision and to his great professional coup he had become far more cheerful than he had been. He also became more condescending to people; his colleagues and

324

subordinates noticed a certain change in him and didn't know what to ascribe it to. They were very familiar with his difficult character. Before very nearly half his time and labor had been spent on undoing the intrigues, plots, and snares of his colleagues. Now this took up somewhat less time.

And then the misfortune exploded.

In a new memorandum he got from headquarters he was menacingly informed that he had received misinformation, which had already led to pernicious and wasteful measures on the part of the military authorities!

The misinformation had been composed so skillfully that at first Moscow headquarters had believed it, too. One circumstance that had gone unnoticed by the colonel had also not been noticed immediately there either. It had left no doubts—all the documents had been fabricated for the purpose of misleading the Soviet military department; the chief document sent them, containing alleged information on atom bombs, was dated March 18. However, the female agent who had so successfully procured these documents directly from the American furnace at Rocquencourt had transmitted them on the seventeenth. The evidence was irrefutable. The colonel was stupefied.

Instead of a brilliant affair it had turned out to be scandalous and damaging. Instead of a decoration, promotion, bonus, he now had to wait for a major catastrophe. At best he could only count now on retirement pure and simple, together with all the consequences of disgrace. As to what the worst might be only gloomy guesses were admissible. You can't avoid your fate, the colonel said to himself. This fatalistic saying, which has often ruined Russians, helped him. The road to the concentration camp is broad, the road back narrow. . . . And to think I'll be judged on the basis of one mistake! All my work, all my achievements, all my services will be forgotten in a flash, they'll just recall this one single blunder! And the ignorant will say: he made a foolish mistake there, so everything he's done must be foolish! . . .

He had only been ten when the October Revolution took

place. Thirty-five years of Soviet propaganda had not gone by in vain for him. The colonel considered all foreign governments Fascist and imperialist, although without putting any especially offensive sense in these accepted tags. As before, he did not understand why any other parties were necessary when nothing but trouble came even from the one there was. As before, everything harmful to his cause, i.e., Russia, was immoral. As before, he irresolutely considered Stalin a genius—or else thought that calling him a genius was very useful to the cause. Before he had said to himself: Stalin will die, but Russia will go on. He regretted his death, all the more so since he expected the power to go to Beria: if we have to have another Georgian Stalin might just as well have remained.

Now he thought all these people were going to destroy the world. Their aim might be to benefit mankind, but because of them—and who is responsible but them, of course?—mankind is spending hundreds of billions a year unproductively. For that kind of money it would be possible to transform all life on earth without any revolutions and put an end to everything in two shakes of a lamb's tail, and that's what they're stopping. The colonel could not honestly wish for the complete disarmament of the world, but he would have liked things to be as they had been in the old days; he would have liked armies, guards, flags, ranks, distinctions, and decorations with other, more agreeable names. The Order of Lenin or of the Red Flag was very highly esteemed, but their names did not caress his ears. What sounded far more pleasing was St. George, St. Vladimir, St. Alexander Nevsky, with their age-old traditions. So it was with a lot of other things, too. For instance, he had been very happy at the abolition of "Highness," but in his heart he sometimes regretted that there was no longer any "Excellency," or "Most Noble Excellency." And the main thing was that before there had been no atomic bombs and no cold war. When there had been wars, they were hot and didn't last very long; the rest of the time there was peace. Although the colonel disliked foreigners, it would have been pleasant for him to maintain good

326

and comradely relations with the Allied officers. He gave their High Command its due and had particular regard for Eisenhower, who from lieutenant colonel had become a commander in chief with such unusual rapidity.

Once, toward the end of the war, over supper, a friend of his who was a captain, after drinking a lot, had said that without the revolution he would have been a "servant to the tsar, father to his soldiers." At supper this aroused an embarrassed laugh, although it had no consequences of any kind for the captain; in the regiment people didn't bear tales against each other. Now the colonel thought that this little line might also refer to himself. He told himself that it would be a very good thing if the only Party still left in Russia also went to the devil. And while it's there, what else is going to happen to us? No one knows where Russia is going or how everything is going to end up. . . .

30

"I'M going to be busy this morning," said Edda. "If we're flying the day after tomorrow I'll have to pack."

"That's what there are servants and maids for."

"They may pilfer something. If we notice it in Seville you'll have a fine time writing a complaint from there to the Berlin police!"

Ramón shrugged his shoulders. "As you please," he said. He was getting more and more bored with her. There was nothing to talk about; in contrast to Schell she didn't appreciate his ideas and in spite of everything didn't quite understand him, although she had been improving her Spanish very quickly. Now the conversations between them were identical: "Tonight we're going to the theater." "Very well, which one?" "What a pity you don't know German! You won't get very far with nothing but Spanish." "As you see, I've been living with nothing but Spanish and not badly at that." "You would be living far better if you knew, for instance, even French. I speak French like a Parisian. . . ." "So there's no point going to see any of the plays." "You might go alone." "I don't want to go alone. Opera is also on the way out, I like only Anton Weber's music, but he didn't write any operas. So should we go to see a musical comedy?" "Very well, let's go to an operetta." "What's the weather like today?" "Hideous." "It was you who picked Berlin." "Yesterday the weather was lovely. And where d'you want to dine?" "It's all the same to me. Perhaps here in the hotel? I'm a little tired." "Why should you be tired? I, on the contrary, am bubbling over with life. I'll order a *salmi* of some kind of rare game. And tonight I'll drink a lot of champagne. I feel like forgetting myself a little. Nothing in life matters a damn," Edda would have added, but she couldn't think of a Spanish expression.

They began to bicker more and more often. Once he bought her a bracelet. She was delighted, but exchanged it for some earrings—on pendants, enormous, ruby-colored, almost terrifying. "They suit my style, there's something fateful about them. They're a little more expensive than your bracelet, you can send them a check, won't you?" He sent a check, but got angry, not about the extra money but because she ought to have kept the present *he* had sent. But even the tiffs seemed noble to Edda; with penniless lovers they degenerated into a money quarrel and turned into abuse.

"I'm going out tomorrow morning. I have to do my last shopping, you remember I told you."

"Buy whatever you like."

She thanked him, not very warmly, also according to her own rule: the more grateful you are the less he'll give.

"I'll probably be back for lunch, but if I'm not have lunch alone. Will you be bored? To make up for it we'll go anywhere you like tonight! I'm ready for anything."

The things were packed, however, by the maid under her supervision. The maid put herself out a great deal for rich people. Edda was going to give her a cheap old dress but she reconsidered: tomorrow she might need it. She gave the maid some of her old underclothes.

Alarming rumors were already spreading throughout Berlin about the expected riots in the eastern sector of the city, but she knew nothing about them; they didn't know anyone, she didn't talk to the servants, while with tailors and milliners she talked only about far more interesting things. Edda did not read any newspapers; twice a week Ramón looked through the Spanish newspapers that got to Berlin after a slight delay.

Edda went out the next morning very early, having put on an old dress and sealed her visiting card in a little envelope. Schell in his time had showed her this. She instructed her chauffeur to stop quite far away from the boundary. Once again she saw the gloomy warning: *Achtung! Sie verlassen nach 80 m. West Berlin,* and again thought it might be better not to cross over; again she crossed over and continued on foot. She deliberately generated the gloomiest premonitions—she thought it would help: if you expect the worst the best will come out.

She gave the little envelope to the officer on duty, and was received immediately, which reassured her. But going into the colonel's office she had a feeling—something was wrong! The expression of his eyes, which had frightened her even at their first meeting, was now simply terrifying. He didn't pretend to get up, did not shake hands, did not respond to her ingratiating smile; he merely nodded, and didn't even nod as people did, but quickly and sharply lowered and immediately raised his head, the corner of his mouth twitching the while.

"What day did you get the papers from the American lieutenant?" he asked in an icy tone without allowing her to say a word. Edda was extremely frightened. For a moment she couldn't recall, then she did and answered with precision.

"What day did you hand them over where you were told to?"

"The same evening," she replied, and trembled; she remembered that Jim had instructed her to hand over the packet on

330

the eighteenth, but she had done it earlier, because of her fittings.

The colonel looked at her viperishly. Edda's look left no doubt that the last thing she herself was thinking of was any kind of "misinformation." Arrest her and ship her off to Moscow! he had thought in the very first moment. But in that case his unwitting fault would be even more serious: headquarters would see to what a fool he had entrusted a most important assignment.

"Did this lieutenant tell you *when* you were supposed to hand over the packet?"

"No. . . . Yes, he said . . . I think he said on the day after, the eighteenth," Edda stammered, trembling more and more. "But I thought . . . I decided the sooner I did it the greater would be my zeal."

Now the matter was completely plain. Idiot! thought the colonel. His face had become almost rabid. This time the silliness of what they were doing appeared to him with particular clarity. The whole thing is futile, he thought, mean, base, and vile. We involve people in a bloody swamp, even jackasses like this one. . . . This time I really did kill a black hare! I set out a snare, put on fresh bark sandals! . . . With some relief he thought that to make up for it the American hadn't killed a black hare either. He also fell into it like a fool! I made a fool of myself, but so did he, although I daresay less so. Of course, this was *his* doing, *his* style. The blasted son of a bitch concocted a crafty scheme and still doesn't know it fell through! Never mind, he soon will! . . . But he's not going to catch hell for it, and I damned well am. . . .

The colonel shot a glance at Edda. And unexpectedly he said to himself that if *his* agent hadn't been an idiot the American would have succeeded in his scheme of misinformation. . . . Of course, that's it! It was only because of her stupidity that we succeeded in detecting the fraud. Suddenly he thought there was no point in destroying this woman. I'm through, but she can make off. No one can know she's seen me again. Her card was

331

in an envelope. I'll destroy it right now. Arresting her would be no use at all, more likely to do me harm. Let her go to the devil. . . .

"I'm kicking you out of the service! Get out of here at once! Don't dare show yourself to me again!" he shouted.

31

THAT seventeenth of June, in both parts of Berlin, the signs "Ami, go home" with which the Berliners had tried, rather unsuccessfully, to annoy the Americans, began to disappear. The "Amis" were accustomed to this in various European capitals and paid almost no attention: they understood that people never liked benefactors and that there was nothing to be done about it. To make up for this in the eastern sector of the city from the morning on little boys, and not only boys, had been shouting, "*Uhri! Uhri!*" That was what the Russian looters in 1945 had cried out to the Berliners as they snatched their watches.

The border between the two worlds passed through the Brandenburg Gate, along the Ebertstrasse and the Potsdamerplatz. This was where people assembled from the various sections of western Berlin. It was said that in the eastern sector of the city demonstrations were going on which were being fired upon, that Soviet tanks had been brought into action, that houses were being burned everywhere, and that thousands of people had been killed. Somewhere in the distance smoke was rising. At the border a number of inhabitants of the western quarters had also been wounded. The young people ran through the Brandenburg Gate and flung stones at the "Vopo"— the *Volkspolizei,* who responded with shots. The crowd was shouting and arguing: "But it's all senseless! What's the good of stones!" some said. "So you think you shouldn't do anything but look through your field glasses!" the others answered indignantly. "The Allies can't allow things to go on this way! They'll be bringing up troops today!" "What troops? They haven't even got any!" "If they haven't got any here they've got some elsewhere!" No one in West Berlin wanted war; on the contrary, they were all mortally afraid of it. But that day nearly everyone shared a vague desire for the events to take on the "grandiose character" which the newspapers were writing about in an obscurely ominous way.

Soviet tanks and trucks were standing on the other side of the Brandenburg Gate, symmetrically and evenly spaced from each other. The Soviet soldiers looked very glum. Some daredevil clambered to the top of the Gate, holding something in his hand. He was watched with excitement. "They're going to kill him now!" "They'll start shooting at once!" The red flag was flung down and its place was taken by a black, red, and gold one. The crowd expressed itself by clapping.

Edda was sitting in a café and trembling as she had never trembled before in her life.

When she left the colonel she very nearly ran to the underground station, though this wasn't sensible. She was clutching her heart with both hands, and pressing her bag against it. What's happened? Oh, my God, what have I done? It's simply incomprehensible! Why was he so furious? ... Arrest! They'll arrest me! Carry me off! But wouldn't he have arrested me on the spot? But he'll think it over! He'll have me hunted down!

The station was closed. "A strike!" someone said happily.

334

That was all I needed! A taxi? Dangerous! And there aren't even any! What should I do? Oh, my God, if I could only get home!

Someone ran past her, quickly set up against a fence a gigantic photograph of Karl Marx without his beard, and rushed on farther. With her last strength Edda began to run. There was a café not far from the square. No, that's dangerous, this is where his people will be looking for me! I have to get rid of my traces. She ran into another café farther on, where there were a lot of people. She collapsed onto a chair at the first free table, in an obscure corner far from any windows. They won't find me here, they can't have any way of knowing where I went. . . .

For a long time no one came over to her. She began to breathe more calmly. Without turning her head she eavesdropped on the conversations at neighboring tables. She overheard snatches: "*Schluss! Schlimm!*" What's happening? she thought. They're talking about an uprising! An uprising here? My God! Why did I ever come! She tried to understand why the colonel had lost his temper, but she could not. Well, what if I did give them in a day ahead of time? If Jim had gotten angry about it, I'd understand it, but why should that accursed colonel?

A waiter came over and glumly asked what she wanted. Edda thought she'd have to ask for beer or coffee, that would look poorer, more socialistic. No, I must have something very strong. She swallowed a pill without water. The gloomy waiter brought her a double glass of Weinbrandt's. Give him a mark tip, or else he'll denounce me! No, a mark's impossible, it would look suspicious! And the others'll see! She eavesdropped again. Yes, that's what it is, an uprising! Damn them! They couldn't postpone it for two days! We'd be in Spain by them. . . . Franco's got law and order, he's a tough egg, he knows them!

The café was old, built at some time in imitation of something else, with an enormous hearth, beer steins, and porcelain plates on the walls and shelves, one of those countless cafés scattered throughout Germany. Edda, breathing heavily, thought of what would happen if she were held up at the Iron

Curtain. In a day Ramón would alert the western police, they'll take steps; with his money it's possible to do everything everywhere! But then the police are sure to open the box in the drawer of the desk and find that photograph! My God, then Ramón won't do anything for me! He'll simply leave by himself! And he won't leave me a sou! And he'll take away all his presents. . . . I'm done for!

She decided to make her way home on foot. In the streets it didn't seem as though anything so terrible were happening, it was simply that the people looked unusually gloomy and mean. Suddenly shots were heard in the distance. Edda cried out; she started to run back to the café. But you can get killed there, too! And I think that's just the side they're shooting from! So she kept on running in the first direction she had taken. It's not so far now. . . . If only I can get through! And then I'll insist that we leave today, today without fail, for Spain by air, or somewhere else! We'll take off to wherever there's an airplane for! What a mistake it was to come here! she thought. And suddenly it crossed her mind that her whole life had been a mistake, that everywhere, in the safest place, with or without money, her existence would be what it had always been, squalid and shameful.

A mob was surging out of a side alley into the square. The demonstrators were moving in step, marching with flags aloft and singing. Edda listened to them and could make out some of the words: *Ulbricht, Pieck und Grotewohl—Wir haben von euch die Schnauze voll!* Does that mean they're not Communists? Surely I can't go after them. In a frenzy the crowd on the sidewalks applauded the demonstrators. They were being slowly followed by trucks full of German police carrying machine guns in their hands. The police also looked very morose, as well as somehow extremely embarrassed. Suddenly there was a stillness.

"Pigs!" a woman with a broom standing near Edda suddenly screamed out in a hysterical voice. And as though this were just the cry they had all been waiting for, a frenzy swept over the crowd.

"Scoundrels! Killing your own brothers! Hang them on the lampposts!"

With a screech of desperation the woman hurled herself from the sidewalk and raising her broom on high flung herself toward the last truck. The policeman, turning pale, pointed his tommy gun at her. "A-a-a-a!" the woman screamed, beside herself. "Shoot, you son of a bitch, shoot!" The roaring grew wilder and wilder. A young man in a short jacket rushed out from the doorway, leaned over low, bent himself to one side, and hurled a stone into the truck. That same second shots rang out. The woman dropped the broom and clutching her stomach went on screaming on her feet. Behind her, on the sidewalk, with scarcely a moan, Edda collapsed. She had been killed outright.

32

THAT day from early morning on Colonel Number One received one report after another in his office. He was considerably better informed than other people, but he didn't know much either. In any case, it was clear to him that in and for themselves the events could not be considered "grandiose"; the moment Soviet tanks entered the city no successful uprising was possible. Armed uprising can only just barely be successful now in Asia or South America, the colonel thought, and on top of that this uprising isn't even armed. Various considerations came into his mind—such as, for instance, what effect would the events have on the situation of the Adenauer regime? Would the Social Democrats get stronger, or the Christian Democrats? He preferred the latter, but had nothing against the former either. To his mind it wasn't very important. The administration is going to be blamed for everything anyhow, for not having

338

foreseen anything. When a patient dies, people always say he was badly treated, that he might have been cured....

There was something else that was more important. The Communists are naturally going to claim we arranged the riots. By itself that doesn't matter, but suppose they're looking for a pretext for war? In spite of his knowledgeableness the colonel wasn't sure in his own mind whether the Soviet government wanted a war in the near future or not. There was a lot to be said in favor of both propositions. It's true they don't need a pretext very much, they can seize on anything. But what if they seize on this? They still have a huge preponderance of forces which are going to diminish gradually whatever happens, and they'll be risking the loss of the occasion. It may be that right now, today, at this very moment, there's a stormy argument taking place in the Kremlin: Should we exploit this pretext? If Stalin were alive, they probably would. The ones there now would sooner not decide; they still haven't established themselves, they still haven't settled accounts among themselves. Nevertheless, it's perfectly possible; the temptation's enormous, fifty-fifty. And that's what the fate of the human race depends on! What a nightmare this cold war is! The only thing worse would be a real war.

Toward noon he learned that the dead were numbered in the dozens and the wounded in the hundreds. He felt sorry for the people who had been killed; he considered the cause hopeless, but the whole time even he was unable to detach himself from the same confused, terrifying, and joyful feeling: Things were moving! An uprising! The first uprising they've had! This reconciled him to the Germans. He didn't understand how a people which had shown such bravery in two wars had surrendered to Hitler without a shot. There might be a war, at that. What's happening now is just an episode—a bloody episode—in the cold war. We weren't the ones who began the cold war, and we're ready to cut it short at any moment, if only they would. And even if this uprising turns out to be some sort of prologue to a world war, it's not our responsibility.

339

He no longer had very much to do. He was receiving reports, comparing and grouping data, forwarding his summaries to headquarters. For all this it was best not to leave his office. "On the spot" no one ever sees anything, or hardly anything, he thought; here the picture is much clearer. But he felt restless. Now they wouldn't even let me through. A trip to the eastern sector of the city, and in an American car at that, was tied up with considerable risk. This was not a factor either for or against it; like Schell, the colonel knew there was no fear of *his* being reproached with cowardice. But even if they let me through, he thought, it might only be with some provocateur's trick in mind: in order to compromise our government, myself, and the insurgents.

But it was possible to go as far as the Iron Curtain, to the Brandenburg Gate or the Potsdamerplatz. The colonel ordered a car. He usually drove himself, but this time he took a chauffeur along. While still some distance away he saw the smoke rising in various places over East Berlin. The shooting was not very heavy; nevertheless, it was shooting of a kind he hadn't heard for a long time, and which in the past had always stimulated him. People were streaming toward the Brandenburg Gate. They had a very somber look, apprehensive and happy at the same time.

He had to leave the car some distance from the Gate; a mob of many thousands made a dense wall. Another man would not have squeezed through, but the colonel was in uniform, in front they all made room for him, and he passed through fairly quickly. He saw that everyone was looking at him, as though he were doing something very important. Do they want me to declare war on Russia? He also felt clearly that the expectation of something "grandiose" was falling off gradually, and that nothing would be left of it by evening.

The colonel reflected on the world situation not merely from time to time, in his free moments, or while reading the newspapers, like the great majority of people; he had thought about it uninterruptedly, over the course of many long years; his pro-